# Hinchinbrook's Hunted

## The Frank Mattituck Series
## Book Three

by

P. Wesley Lundburg

Gaslamp Scriveners Press
New York

## Dedication

This book is dedicated to Alec Lundburg, a fantastic and fun son . . . An emerging young man with keen intelligence and a compassionate heart. Thank you for all you mean to me, and for the great times we share together.

## Acknowledgements

Special thanks to Tania Gavino, Brandon Lundburg, Michael Hood, and Jean Coldwell for their beta reading and expert editing skills. Without your help, there would still be a lot of sentence errors and more than a couple of inconsistencies in the story. Thank you all for your keen eyes, helpful input, and the time you put into reading and editing.

The cover was designed and produced by:
SelfPubBookCovers.com/LaLimaDesign

*Keep in Touch....*

Get regular updates on all of P. Wesley Lundburg's books at his website:

pwesleylundburg.com

Go to the "Contact" page and sign up for the email list and keep up with the progress on the next book in the series, connect with other fans of the series, and get announcements on promotions and sales. Or just drop him a line and strike up a conversation about his books or the writing process.

Like Wes' Facebook page at The P. Wesley Lundburg Author Page

Email him at pwesleylundburg@gmail.com

Follow him on Twitter @pwesleylundburg

*You may be interested in these.....*

If you missed the other books in The Frank Mattituck Series, you can continue enjoying the ongoing adventures of Mattituck and Todd Benson by ordering your copy of Books 1 and 2 at:

pwesleylundburg.com/page/

Or start the hard-boiled private eye series, the Clayton Chronicles, set in sunny San Diego. Pick up a copy of The Stateroom Tryst and watch for The Desert Throwdown, due in January 2017:

Prince William Sound, Alaska

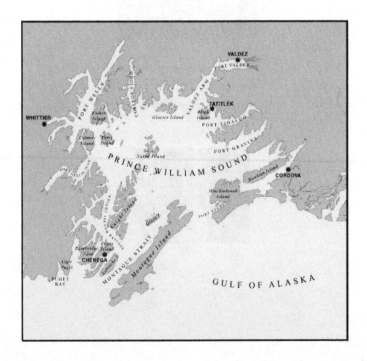

# Prologue

## The New Arrival

Izzy Giovanni sat in seat 4F, a window seat in first class, on one of the many mid-morning flights out of Seattle bound for Anchorage. The seat had been intentionally selected by the man in Valdez pretending to be her uncle, a man they called Pappy Amatucci. The old man had wanted to make sure she had the best view of the glaciers and mountains along the southcentral coast of Alaska as she came to the state for the first time. The scenery below was indeed breathtaking, she thought as she gazed at the tall snow-blanketed peaks and jagged ridges. Between them there were frequent rivers of ice, the glaciers that were front-and-center in the so-called debate about climate change.

"Mt. St. Elias," the man in 4D said.

He was a complete stranger in his early 40's, and Izzy didn't take warmly to strangers unless it was within the scope of her job to do so.

Izzy turned and looked at him.

"There," he said, pointing to a peak towering over those around it in the distance. "Tallest peak in Alaska, except Denali."

Izzy smiled politely and nodded, then turned her attention out the window.

"Denali, of course, used to be known as Mt. McKinley. Tallest mountain in North America."

She held her gaze out the window, hoping he would pick up on the social cues of disinterest. Not just disinterest in the conversation, but in the man himself. Several times on the flight, he had made varying attempts at talking to her in that way that every beautiful woman was accustomed to. The way that says he wants more than just casual conversation on a long flight.

"Denali means 'The Great One,'" the man went on. "The name comes from the Athabascan tribe of Alaska Natives . . ."

Izzy nodded vacantly. "That's interesting," she said with an intentionally flat tone.

She tuned him out as his voice droned on. Her thoughts focused on the job ahead. To be sure, it was no more difficult than any other job—at least on the surface. But something about the way the target had been described was eluding her. There was an importance to this particular job that carried special weight with The Ühing. She had studied the target, a man they called the Takistus—a word meaning 'obstacle' in Estonian—about as extensively as possible from the records The Ühing had provided. But as was

7

the case with every assignment she'd been given, she was told very little about why The Ühing was taking the action it was. All she knew was that he had apparently been some kind of obstacle, and they wanted her to get close to him. Once she accomplished this, they would provide further instructions.

She also knew that whatever role she might play in this world, one of the last she would want would be something worthy of a name like 'Takistus' from The Ühing.

One of the many things Izzy loved about flying first class was that those seats de-planed first. Within three minutes of the cabin door being opened, she was walking the jet-way toward the Anchorage airport terminal. Unfortunately, the man from 4D held back and waited for her.

She felt his eyes moving up and down her body as she struck a fast pace up the jet-way.

"I'm hungry," he said.

Izzy suppressed the urge to roll her eyes.

"Want to grab a bite to eat?" he asked, falling into stride beside her.

"I have a plane to catch."

"Yeah? Where you headed?"

"Fairbanks," she lied.

"Have time for a drink at least? On me?"

She looked over at him, deliberately making eye contact.

"Look," she said, "I'm sure you're a very nice guy. But I'm one of those people who are completely focused on my career—"

"Which is what, by the way?" he interrupted cheerfully, reluctant to accept a no answer.

"Doesn't matter," Izzy returned, complete dismissal in her tone.

Finally, the man bore the full brunt of the repeated rebuffing, and gave up on decorum.

"You're one fine-looking woman," he said, the lust nearly oozing. "Trust me, you're going to get hit on a lot up here. Alaska's the land of five-men-to-every-girl, and very few of those women look a quarter as good as you do."

"Thanks for the tip," Izzy said, emerging from the jet-way and cutting an immediate right to escape around a family trying to arrange their carry-ons.

"If you—" the man started.

"I won't," she interrupted with a wave as she increased the number of people between them.

She wanted to pause to figure out how to get to the plane for Valdez, but she dared not stop and invite the man to rejoin her. She decided to keep on toward the main concourse, following the signs for baggage claim. Her best guess was that the smaller planes would be someplace away from the large plane gates.

# Chapter One

## Tragedy in the Wilderness

Hinchinbrook Lighthouse was located on the southwestern end of the island. It sat tall and proud over Hinchinbrook Entrance, the main entrance to Prince William Sound for cruise ships bound for Whittier and oil tankers bound for the Valdez oil terminal. The Entrance was narrow, and relatively shallow with rocky outcroppings that presented dangerous passage for unwary mariners. Hinchinbrook Entrance was one of only two openings between the expanse of Prince William Sound and the Gulf of Alaska. With a tide change of as much as 18 feet, the currents flowing through the Entrance were treacherous and unforgiving.

Chief Petty Officer Sammy Johnston stood on the helicopter pad next to the lighthouse, watching his crew assemble their equipment for departure. They had been there three days maintaining all the machinery, the electrical circuits, and swapping out a faulty electrical box. The solar panels were in good shape, thank god, he thought, but the generator was nearing the end of its life and would need to be replaced on the next trip.

"Just about ready, Chief," Simmons said.

Simmons was his machinist mate, 2nd class, and about the best he'd ever had serve under him. Chief Johnston hardly had to do anything when Simmons was along.

"Very well," the Chief said. "Helo should be here around 1600." He looked at his watch. "It's 1100 hours now."

Simmons nodded, then crossed the pad and strode over the walkway, then ducked into the base structure of the tall square lighthouse. It wasn't the prettiest of lighthouses, but very functional. In its own, reliable way, the building was beautiful.

A noise on the other side of the lighthouse drew both men's attention. Something was pushing through the undergrowth toward them, and bears were something always to be alert for. The Chief unclipped his sidearm and pulled it out of its holster.

Simmons glanced back at the Chief, his own .45 in hand and ready. He stepped to the corner of the building to peer at whatever was approaching the lighthouse.

"H—hell—lo...?" The voice was almost faint, out of breath. "Help. Help!"

Simmons straightened and stepped away from the building.

"You okay?" he hollered to the approaching figure.

Chief Johnston holstered his issue-.45 and started at a fast clip across the helo pad toward the approaching voice.

"My—my friend . . ." The man's voice was labored and heavy as he came into view.

He was wearing an orange vest over a camouflaged hunting jacket and jeans. He had a hunting rifle—it looked to the Chief like a Winchester 70 with a scope—but nothing else except a hunting outfitter ball cap.

"Easy, easy," Simmons said as he met the man at the edge of the compound.

The man nearly fell into Simmons' arms, stumbling as his legs reached the level concrete pad. Chief Johnston could now see the man's face was glistening with sweat, the color flushed with over-exertion and exhaustion.

"My friend, I think he's dying," the man stammered.

"Where is your friend?" the Chief asked, reaching Simmons' side as he supported the man's collapsing body.

"I—I don't know exactly. About two miles back that way," he gestured in the direction he'd come from, "over that ridge." The man's throat wheezed as he tried to draw in air.

"You just came over that ridge?" Simmons asked, incredulous.

The man merely nodded vigorously.

"What happened," Chief Johnston asked. "Why do you think your friend is dying?"

The man turned a scruffy unshaved face up in panic.

"He wasn't wearing his vest," he blurted with desperation. "He wasn't. Goddammit, he wasn't wearing his vest!"

"Okay, okay," the Chief said calmly, patting the man on the chest. "Let's take it one step at a time. You were hunting?"

It was almost a rhetorical question. Very few ventured onto Hinchinbrook Island, except hunters.

"Yeah," the man nodded. "Yes. We've been here three days. Justin has a bad habit of not wearing his vest—he believes deer can see them, so he takes it off a lot while he's out there."

"Justin," the Chief said. "That's the guy you think might be dying?"

The man nodded.

"You said he wasn't wearing his vest," the Chief went on, pretty sure of where this was going. "Tell us what happened."

"We had split up," the man started, "and he had gone north and me south. So he wasn't even where I thought he was—"

"Okay," the Chief interrupted. "Hunting accidents happen. We need to get to your friend. So just tell us what happened and where to go to get to him."

"I couldn't see very well with all the trees and undergrowth, and I thought Justin was a mile north, so when I saw the movement—I saw the body, I swear to God it was a deer. I swear it!"

The man's pain and desperation were apparent, but Johnston was feeling the minutes ticking by.

"And then?"

"I fired two shots. And the deer went down. Only when I got to it, it wasn't a deer. It was Justin . . . Jesus! Please God, let it be a bad dream!"

13

Johnston looked up at Simmons.

"Go get Baker and Phipps. Tell Phipps he's on gunnery alert, so bring his piece—the rifle as well as the sidearm."

"Aye, Chief," Simmons shot as he rose.

"Tell Baker to bring all his gear. Throw it in the back pack."

"Aye, Chief."

"And everybody muster up here. NOW!"

With a quick nod, Simmons sprinted for the main building adjacent to the lighthouse, leaving Johnston alone with the man.

"What's your name?" he asked.

"Garrett. Wilson Garrett. I live in Cordova."

Johnston was scribbling on a small notepad he carried in his breast pocket.

"And your friend's name is Justin?"

"Yeah, Justin Harris. We've been buddies since we were kids."

"He lives in Cordova, too?"

"Yeah."

"Okay, Wilson. Are you good enough to lead us back to your friend?"

"Yeah, I think so."

"Good. You can tell me more on the way, but I don't want you talking too much. The Alaska State Troopers will get all the info. This will be their jurisdiction."

Wilson Garrett fell silent. Chief Johnston could imagine what the man was thinking: the jurisdiction comment probably wasn't all that wise, Johnston thought in retrospect, but he couldn't take it back now. Johnston had never killed another person, let alone a friend. Whatever Wilson Garrett was feeling in that moment, Johnston knew it had to be pretty hellish.

"Look," he said, wanting to reassure the poor guy, "Maybe your friend's okay. We'll get there as quick as possible. We got an EMT—helluva good one, too—and we're pretty set up with the medic kit."

Wilson merely nodded, his eyes vacant.

"You just catch your breath. Here, drink some water," he said, offering the water bottle he always carried as part of his promise to his wife to lose weight.

Wilson Garrett took the bottle and put it to his mouth, emptying it as Baker, Phipps, and Simmons emerged from the lighthouse buildings. Baker, the EMT, was slinging a large medic pack onto his back as they approached. Phipps, a hard-featured man in his upper 20s, lurched forward with his rifle at ready in case any bears tried to stymie the group.

Johnston stood and placed his hands on his hips.

"All right, men," he said. Petty Officer Simmons is in charge. This man's friend is down a couple of miles over that ridge." He pointed as he said this. "I'll call for a helo. Depending on where this man is down, maybe it can pick you up there. You got your radio and GPS, Simmons?"

"Yes, Chief," Simmons replied, tapping the breast pocket of his Coast Guard jacket, then indicating the VHF radio on his hip. "I also have the flare gun."

"Good thinking," Chief Johnston returned. "All right, men. Stay in touch. I want frequent reports."

"Aye, Chief," Simmons said.

Phipps helped Wilson Garrett to his feet.

"You'll have to lead us," he said. "But I'm right behind you with this baby." He patted the M4.

Chief Johnston watched as the four men headed into the foliage. It was tough going, this territory, particularly from this end of the island. Which was why they rarely saw hunters on Cape Hinchinbrook. The flatter, more hunter-friendly grounds were more toward the middle of the island, more than four miles away. Vaguely, the Chief thought how lucky this hunter had been that the Coast Guard was here doing major maintenance on the lighthouse. 355 days out of the year, the site was unmanned.

Frank Mattituck's charter boat, the DeeVee8, rose and dropped over the swells from the Gulf as the occupants worked the sandy shelf along Cape Hinchinbrook for halibut. Lines in the water were manned by Frank, Monica Castle, Todd Benson, and Todd's wife, Keri. As Frank and Todd had worked together more frequently, their personal lives had begun to follow the same pattern. On this day, the Fourth of July, they had decided to celebrate the day on a double-date fishing trip.

"So," Todd said, banter in his voice, "we've been here for almost an hour and no fish. What's up, Frank? I thought you were the hot-shot, best-ass charter boat captain in Valdez."

Monica poked Frank in the ribs with her elbow, grinning.

Frank Mattituck glanced halfway in Todd's direction, giving the off-duty State Trooper shade before his eyes fell on Keri.

"Tell your husband that for a fisheries cop, he knows jack shit about fishing."

Keri smiled.

"Hey, husband," she said, "the hot shot charter boat captain says you know diddly about fishing."

"Tell him he's not only a charlatan fisherman, but he's cowardly in his communication lines."

"Hey, Frank," Keri began.

"I heard him," Frank cut her off. "Just belt him, would you?"

"Hey, husband," she began, rising and drawing back her hand, ready to strike.

"Damn!" Todd complained. "If I want this abuse, I could stay home!"

"Well," Frank said, watching Todd work his line. "You do jig the bottom pretty well. Who showed you that little one-two-pull move, there?"

Todd shot him a silencing look.

"Don't you have beer on this rust bucket?"

It was Frank's turn to give the silencing look.

"I'll get you a beer," Monica said. "Here, Frank, hold my rod."

"I've got a rod you can—"

"Cut it, Mattituck," she interrupted with a sultry grin.

"A Guinness for me," he said in reply.

"As if I didn't know," she said as she disappeared into the cabin.

Mattituck was relieved at the light bantering. On the three-hour run from Valdez to the Gulf, Todd and Keri had bickered at least half the time and sulked in angry silence the rest of the time. He and Monica had exchanged concerned looks several times. Mattituck had only been with Todd and his wife once before over a dinner they had invited him to at their house near the elementary school, and he had noted the tension then as well. This morning had been worse, so the apparent easing of that was more than welcome.

Monica appeared again clasping four beers by their bottled necks, two Longboards for Keri and for her, an Alaskan Amber for Todd, and a Guinness for Frank.

Just then, Todd's cell rang.

"Trooper Benson," he answered, then listened silently for several minutes.

Keri looked impatiently at her watch.

"Well," she said, undisguised annoyance in her tone. "10:25, and they're calling him in."

Todd dropped his brows at her, still listening.

Frank looked up at Monica, who returned a blank gaze. She bent down and kissed his forehead.

"All right," Todd said into his phone. "I'll see what I can do."

"Great," Keri said as she began reeling in her line.

"What are you doing?" Frank asked.

Todd slid the phone into his pocket.

"There's a hunting accident," he said.

"See?" Keri said to Frank and Monica.

"I'm sorry," Todd said to Frank and Monica. "Frank, any way we can get to the Hinchinbrook Lighthouse?"

Frank grinned and pointed.

"Right there," he said, pointing at the structure visible on the point.

"I know where it is," Todd said. "Can we get on shore there?"

"There's the old loading dock. It isn't used any more, but it's pretty calm. We could try it. What's going on?"

Frank had been deputized when he and Todd chased a killer through Prince William Sound, and that official status had never been rescinded, which came in handy for Todd when he needed a partner. Todd was the sole Alaska State Trooper in the region, and Frank Mattituck not only filled a much-needed support role, but did it very well.

"Hunting accident," Todd said. "Meaning probably one guy shot another. Happens more than any of us would care to know."

"Is the hunter dead?" Monica asked.

"Probably," Todd answered. "Won't know until we're there. The hunting buddy showed up at the lighthouse—lucky there was a crew there maintaining it. They put together a team and are hiking their way to the downed hunter right now."

"All right," Frank said. "Let's pull up the lines and get underway."

Keri started reeling a little too fast. She stood at the gunwale watching the water at her line, her back to her husband.

Frank looked at Monica, who shrugged and stepped forward. She raised her lips to his and kissed him.

# Chapter Two

## An Entry and an Exit

The approach to the abandoned dock below the Hinchinbrook Lighthouse was uneventful, thanks to a mostly-protected cove and relatively calm seas and wind. Nonetheless, as they pulled up to the slightly dilapidated dock Mattituck noted he would never want to attempt such a mooring without GPS and a good chart.

"How they did this back in the day. . ." he said, then merely shook his head rather than finish the sentence.

Todd was securing the mooring lines as Mattituck said this. Monica was at Mattituck's side, as he stood ready to run the throttles back in the event of trouble.

"It is amazing," she said, "what those guys used to do. Demands a lot of respect."

"Spot on," Mattituck said, cutting the engines as Todd signaled that the mooring lines were secure.

A uniformed Coast Guardsman was making his way down the wood walkway to the dock as Monica and Mattituck emerged on the bow of the DeeVee8. Keri was stepping onto the dock aft from the fish deck.

"Hallo!" hollered the Coast Guardsman.

Even though the man was thirty yards away, Mattituck could see the emblem on the man's dark blue color. He was a Chief Petty Officer. Probably the man in charge of whatever unit was here—most likely a lighthouse maintenance crew.

Todd waved and walked up the dock toward the man, careful not to step on a rotted board that might break through.

"I'm Trooper Benson," he said. "Todd Benson."

"They said you'd be here pretty quickly," the Chief said. "I'm Chief Sammy Johnston. I'm the crew chief and was there when the hunter came in."

"Where is he now?"

"Probably gettin' close to the hunter's friend. I sent a team with him, including an EMT."

Todd nodded. "What do you know about the friend's condition?"

"Nothing yet, but the hunter thought he might be dead."

"Why'd he think that?" Todd prodded.

"It was a hunting accident. He thought his friend was a deer and took two shots. When he went down to check on his kill, it was his buddy."

Todd was staring blankly at the chief as Mattituck came alongside him.

"Two shots?" Todd asked. "Why two shots?"

The Chief looked surprised, his head drawing back. He scratched his head.

"Well, I don't know. I guess maybe he thought it would take two shots."

"All right," Todd replied, deciding to let it go for the moment. "I can ask him about it when I see him. Anything else I need to know?"

"Yeah. Helo's due in ten to twenty minutes. Hopefully my team will be on scene then and will give their position. I'm hoping the helo can get in close enough to medevac the man."

Todd pictured a helicopter hovering over the dense woods along the foot of most of the mountains on Hinchinbrook. Although there were some open areas, most anything on the Cape Hinchinbrook area where the lighthouse was located was forested with tall spruce. Unless the accident happened higher on a mountain, above the tree line, it would be very difficult for a pickup by helicopter. Todd said as much to the Chief.

"Well," Chief Johnston replied, "you'd know better than I would. I've been on this island plenty of times, but I never venture into that wilderness. I grew up in Chicago, for Pete's sake."

Mattituck chuckled.

"Better have a backup plan for getting that man out of there," Todd concluded.

The Coast Guard helicopter arrived on scene sooner than the team reached the site of the accident, so the pilot decided to put down on the helo pad at the lighthouse. This worked well, as it turned out. When the pilot found out Todd Benson knew this island well, it was decided that he should fly with them to help guide the effort, particularly if they needed to deploy the basket to lift the injured man to the helicopter. Among first responders, there was a reluctance to refer to people as dead until it was sure they were.

The group went into the main building adjacent to the lighthouse to have coffee in the makeshift galley. There were two old metal-framed tables with Formica tops lined up next to each other, with metal folding chairs. The pilots and crewmen took seats opposite Todd as the Chief went to the counter and poured coffee. Fortunately, the Chief was a coffee fiend and always had a pot going.

Mattituck watched, not taking a seat.

"Take a load off and stay awhile," the Chief said to him as he returned with the first round of coffee.

"I'd probably better get back to the boat and get underway," Mattituck returned. "I'm not too sure about that dock or the currents, to say nothing of the tide."

"There's a reason the Guard stopped using it," the Chief joked.

"Let me know what you want to do," Mattituck said to Todd.

Todd nodded. "Will do. I'll probably fly to wherever they're taking him, so I doubt you'll need to pick me up."

"Maybe I'd better stay close by just in case," Mattituck said.

"Probably a good idea."

"I'll duck around to Port Etches. We can fish the cove or something until you know."

Todd nodded as Mattituck turned for the door and disappeared into the midday sun.

Chief Johnston filled in the pilots, giving a more detailed version of Wilson Garrett's story to Todd as he recounted the story. Todd listened carefully, jotting notes on a borrowed pad of paper. The pilots listened less attentively. For them, the only details that mattered much were those that might affect the medevac effort – and with a nice day like this one, those were sparse.

Finally, the VHF radio crackled with the voice of Petty Officer Simmons.

"Chief, Simmons on channel 22-alpha. Do you read?"

Johnston picked up the hand held radio.

"Roger, I hear you."

"We're here. Doesn't look like the guy's alive. There are a lot of trees, but spread out enough that I think the helo could drop the basket."

The pilots were sitting forward now.

"Ask him how tall the trees are."

Todd knew the answer, but let the Coasties have their own reports.

"I'd say 40 to 60 feet. Low enough for the helo to stay above them and still drop the basket."

The Chief was looking at the pilots. The lead nodded and stood up.

"Get the coordinates. You can pass them to us when we're in the air." He turned to Todd. "You coming?"

Todd was already on his feet, poised for the door.

Mattituck followed the trail down to the dock, thinking about the turn of events on such a nice fishing day. A part of him missed the days of only running fishing charters, never being interrupted or distracted. It had been a tranquil, controlled life. Until he'd become better acquainted with Trooper Todd Benson, and then caught up in chasing Jim Milner's crazy killer all over Prince William Sound. Todd Benson, as the only Trooper assigned to the Sound, had deputized Mattituck to help him with the case, and then conveniently never un-deputized him.

It had changed Mattituck's lifestyle drastically, returning him to a former self that he had thought he'd put away forever. The old adage that you can't shirk what you were meant to be sprang to mind, and Mattituck suppressed a tinge of irritation. He'd never asked for that, so why couldn't he just live peacefully and be left alone?

Monica and Keri were sitting on the bow of the DeeVee8, watching him approach along the old wooden dock.

"Where's Todd?" Keri asked.

"He's going with the helo to pick up the hunter." Then he remembered they knew nothing of the story, so he filled them in.

"Figures he'd have to go," Keri said, annoyed. "Always happens. And of course he always goes."

Monica looked at Frank.

"Well," Mattituck said, "he doesn't really have a choice."

Keri's lips pursed and she shrugged.

"Of course," she said, the irritation clear. "Why couldn't he just be a patrolman, driving a cruiser up and down the highway around Anchorage?"

Mattituck and Monica both knew she was talking more to herself.

"We're getting underway," Mattituck announced. "Todd is likely to fly with the hunter's body to wherever they take it—probably Anchorage. But until we know, we'll pull around into Port Etches—the inlet on the other side of the cape—and wait to hear from him." He paused a moment. "We can drop our lines in the water – we'll pick up some chickens, anyway," he said, using the affectionate Alaskan name for small halibut.

Monica nodded, stepping onto the dock to handle the lines. Keri went to the aft line to help as Mattituck rounded the cabin and manned the pilot's station. A moment later, the twin Volvo Penta turbo-diesel engines rumbled to life, then settled into a smooth purr. Within minutes, they were up to speed and rounding the Cape.

Todd leaned forward in the rear seat of the HH-60 Jayhawk helicopter, the workhorse of the U.S. Coast Guard. They were approaching the coordinates the ground team had provided, hoping to lower the basket and get the hunter out of the Hinchinbrook wilderness. If they were not able to do this, it would be a long, arduous hike for the team, carrying the body more than two miles back to the helo pad in the folding gurney they had packed in, just in case.

The massive helicopter slowed to a hover, and Todd could see the Coast Guardsmen below with the hunter who had come to them, and what appeared to be a man lying on the ground.

"Trooper Benson, what's your assessment?" came the pilot's voice on Todd's headset.

Todd surveyed the black spruce jutting upward from the muskeg and gravel ground below, noting the way they swept up what must be a slope leading up to the mountain to the right. From the air, it was always hard to judge changes in the topography.

"Probably a 10 percent grade, going upward to the right. I'd keep a 20 foot clearance above the tree tops. It looks to me like there's enough spacing between the trees, but that's your call," he said.

The co-pilot was doing his own assessment.

"I concur with the Trooper," his voice cackled in the headset. "I think it's safe to lift."

With that, the right rear door slid open and the crewman motioned for Todd to slide to the seat farthest to the left. Todd complied, watching the operation with measured fascination. He had watched many times from the ground—or sea—as this procedure took place, so it was particularly interesting for him to watch from inside the helo.

Within three minutes, the downed hunter was aboard the helicopter, lying in the basket across the Jayhawk's deck. Todd slid forward and knelt next to the man. First he checked the pulse, although he knew what he would find there: the man was dead. He then did a quick scan of the clothing, noting two bullet entries—one just below the left collarbone, and the second several inches lower, around the area the heart would be.

It was too difficult to come to any conclusive observations with the man fully clothed and in a Coast Guard lift basket. But the two bullet holes in the hunter jacket were different. The upper hole was frayed, with most of the threads protruding outward. It had all the appearance of an exit point, meaning the man had been shot in the back and the bullet exited here. The other wound, however, was interesting more because it was the opposite. The threads were singed and short, the few that had any length to them curved inward. These details were consistent with an entry point, not an exit.

Todd paused, staring at the two holes.

Why would one shot be in the back, and the other from the front?

It was possible that the collarbone shot had spun the man around before the second shot hit him square in the chest, but it didn't seem likely. The wound was too close to the man's center, making it less likely to throw his body into a spin.

Todd pulled his notepad out and jotted notes. Usually, his notes in these situations were comprised of statements and observations. This time, however, they were mostly questions.

Already, Todd was suspicious.

# Chapter Three

## The Big Fish

Frank Mattituck sat astride the gunwale on the port quarter—the left rear side—of the DeeVee8, staring at the point where his line entered the water. He was watching for the tell-tale tugs that would tell him he had a halibut nibbling. Or any kind of nibbling.

Behind him, Keri and Monica sat inside the starboard gunwale, jigging their lines. Mattituck had anchored them over the edge of a tried-and-true shelf for chicken halibut. He loved targeting the chickens, as they were the best eating. Anything over 80 pounds was fun to catch, but the meat started getting more stringy and tough with the older, larger fish. The 35-60 pound range of the chickens suited Mattituck—and most Alaskans—very well, and were the preferred target on the halibut charters with Alaskan clients.

"I'm sorry," Keri suddenly said from across the fish deck.

Mattituck kept staring at his line, giving it a three-inch pull up from the bottom as he jigged. When neither he nor Monica responded, Keri continued.

"That wasn't cool, bashing Todd. It's just that—" she paused.

"There's nothing to be sorry for," Monica said.

Mattituck remained silent. He wasn't feeling keen on hearing a different side of his friend than he already knew. Or maybe it was that he and Todd didn't really venture into their personal lives much, despite the fair amount of time they'd spent together working cases.

He glanced up to catch Monica's gaze. She gestured to him with her eyes.

"Yeah," he said, picking up on the signal. "No worries here, Keri. Things can be frustrating."

He hoped his voice didn't give away his lack of spirit in the comment. Monica was looking at him. He couldn't read what the look was supposed to mean, but he definitely sensed something was being communicated to him. He gave her a subtle shrug, shifting his eyes to Keri. Keri's eyes were on her line.

"It's just that he's always gone," Keri said finally. She looked up at Monica, then at Mattituck. "You know what I mean?"

Monica nodded. "I can only imagine," she said, her voice empathetic.

Keri was looking at Mattituck.

"I'm going to guess it's tough on him, too," he said. "I mean, not defending him or anything, but I'm sure he loves you and would rather be home. He's just very dedicated to what he does."

He paused, looking back at his line before continuing.

"And your husband is very, very good at what he does. It has meaning," he said meeting Keri's eyes again. "It matters. He figures shit out that a lot of cops never would, and he does it right. No fucking it up." He was silent a moment as Keri absorbed it. "I get what you're saying, and it's real. It really is. But I'd guess that anybody who's really good at that job has to be away a lot more than they'd like to be."

Keri's eyes were hanging on his words.

"Do you really think so?" she asked, her voice quiet and uncertain.

Mattituck nodded.

"Absolutely."

"I mean, you've been out there with him . . ." Keri's voiced trailed off.

Mattituck nodded again. "I have no doubt he's torn, but I have to be honest, too. We never talk about our personal lives. Don't know why . . . we just don't."

Keri smiled and nodded.

"Guys," she said.

Mattituck smiled back at her. "And as guys go, I think Todd and I are pretty much the stereotype."

Keri chuckled and Monica smiled.

Whatever edge had been in Monica's eyes a few minutes ago was gone.

The VHF radio pulled his attention. It was his hired skipper for the other boat in Mattituck's charter business hailing him. He put the butt of his rod in a holder and pulled in the line a few inches so it wouldn't drag on the bottom as the boat swung around on her anchor.

"Knot Skunked, the DeeVee8 on channel 16. Switch six-eight, skipper?"

"Roger, 68," came Hank Porter's voice in return.

Mattituck had hired the seasoned fisherman to captain the first boat Frank had bought when he started Sound Experience Charters. Now with two boats operating in the business, Mattituck was able to book as many as 10-12 full-boat halibut charter runs per week—Hank running the Knot Skunked five days, and Mattituck frequently running the DeeVee8 seven days a week. For a charter boat fishing company that had only been in business for six years, business was booming. He was already booking charters for the next season, a year ahead.

Lately, he'd been considering adding a third fishing charter boat. In addition to the Kimberly Marie—the boat he and Earl Darrick had inherited from Jim Milner after the elder man's murder—this would technically make Sound Experience Charters a four-boat operation. The Kimberly Marie, a 72-foot cabin cruiser, was more of a small overnight sightseeing charter and had attracted a celebrity clientele. Earl was now captain of the Kimberly Marie, and Mattituck's partner for that part of the business.

Now he stood next to the captain's chair of the DeeVee8 as he listened for Hank Porter to call him on channel 68.

"Pick me up, Frank?" came his employee's voice over the VHF.

Mattituck keyed the mic.

"Yep, got you loud and clear, Hank. What's up?"

"Well, I saw you haul up lines pretty early, and knowing you were out with Todd and friends, I figured he'd been called in to something. If you need me to cover for you tomorrow, let me know."

State Trooper Todd Benson had deputized Mattituck when the two had found themselves chasing down a ruthless killer—Jim Milner's killer. Since then, Mattituck had assisted Todd on several cases, and when he did, Hank usually worked extra days to cover Mattituck's charters. It was extra money for Hank, a man who enjoyed taking his kids to Disneyland during the off-season and considered the extra days his vacation fund.

"I don't know what he's working on," Mattituck replied, "but that's good to know if he needs me. I'll get back to you, okay?"

"Yep," Hank said cheerfully. "No prob. Happy to do it if you need me."

"Thanks – how's it looking out there? Where are you, by the way, that you saw us?"

"Seal Rocks. Got a boat load of Derby chasers," he said, referring to the Valdez Halibut Derby. The Derby was an annual competition for the largest halibut caught in the season, with each entrant purchasing a ticket.

"Ah, very good. Go get 'em, Hank," Mattituck said with a grin.

Hank loved chasing the big fish, and had clients who placed two of the past three years—all aboard the Knot Skunked.

Mattituck hung the mic in the clip on the side of the radio and went back out to the fish deck just in time to see Keri's rod in a sporadic dance.

"Oh—Oh!" she cried out, jumping to her feet to work the line.

"Not yet," Mattituck said. "Don't set the hook yet. Remember, that's a circle hook. It'll work its own way into his jaw. Let him nibble it some more, then when you feel a dead weight, we'll start working him up."

Keri was nodding, holding the rod steady as directed.

"Just keep it up off the bottom, and you're good," Mattituck continued. "As you work him up in a few minutes, he'll struggle and that circle hook will work its way in deeper. You won't lose him, don't worry."

Keri listened attentively, her eyes riveted to the spot where the 100-pound test line disappeared into the water.

"Should I pull mine up?" Monica asked.

"Naw, it'll be fine. We're steady on the anchor, so the boat won't swing around and tangle the lines."

Monica nodded. It was what she'd hoped he would say. She had a feverish addiction to halibut fishing, and was always reluctant to pull her line in unless she had a fish on.

Keri's rod bounced four times in rapid succession, then stopped.

"Ah, shit!" she blurted. "Did I lose him?"

Mattituck shook his head. "No . . . pull very lightly up, and you'll feel he has it in his mouth. He's not hooked yet, so don't pull hard."

Keri nodded and pulled very lightly on her line.

"No shit!" she whispered loudly. "Fucking heavy!"

Mattituck smiled. He'd never heard her swear before. It was funny how even a church pianist could swear with the excitement of fishing. Witnessing that contagious excitement was one of his favorite parts of the job.

He waited a moment, then watched as the end of the stout rod began to dance again, this time punctuated with hard pulls downward.

"Jesus!" Keri blurted.

"He's on now," Mattituck said at her side. "Remember, reel down, pull up . . . then reel down, and stop while you pull up. Reel down, pull up . . . reel down, pull up."

Keri nodded vigorously, her excitement having erased whatever dark thoughts she'd had earlier. Mattituck reached out with two fingers and lifted the bottom of her rod, half way to the tip. He was gauging the pull of the fish below.

"How sure are you it's a halibut?" Keri asked.

He looked back into her eyes, the corners smiling.

"Very sure," he said simply.

"How do you know?"

"Halibut are the only ones who dance your rod that way. It's how they go after their prey—voracious and aggressive as hell."

Keri nodded as she began the alternating action of pulling up on the rod, then reeling it back down for another pull.

"That's it," Mattituck said, "keep working it just like that. Slow and even . . . we're in no rush here."

Keri nodded again, following his lead.

"Let me know if you want me to spell you," he offered, just as he did with all his clients. Under Alaska law, it was the person who hooked the fish who was the owner of the fish. Charter boat captains were allowed to help reel halibut in after the fish was hooked, in recognition of the long, draining fight. A hundred-pound halibut could take up to an hour to bring on board, and often the angler was almost as exhausted as the fish before it was time to land it.

This fish was no exception. Monica had hooked and landed a ling cod and two Pacific cod while Keri continued working her halibut to the surface. Periodically, the halibut on the other end would pull the line out, then dead weight it back toward the bottom. Halibut did not fight like most fish, with violent jerks and dramatic breaching. Instead, they used their size and ability to dive.

"Let the drag out," Mattituck said.

Keri shot a glance over her shoulder, questioning him.

"He's got too much fight in him. Trust me, the more tired we get him, the easier it'll be to bring him aboard."

Keri reached to the reel with her left hand and turned the drag wheel. The line began to pay out as the fish dove back toward the bottom.

"Jeez, Frank," Keri complained. "Now I have to reel him back up all that way."

"Yes you do," Mattituck returned with a wry grin. "Again, trust me. It'll be easier in the end, and you won't risk him snapping the line."

"That's a hundred pound test line, isn't it?"

"Very good – yes it is."

"Shouldn't it be enough? Unless you think it's bigger than a hundred pounds," she added, suddenly excited.

"Could be, but even if he isn't, a halibut is a powerful fish. When he jerks his head to the side, it's a lot more than a hundred pounds of force."

Keri nodded her understanding, and went back to working the fish to the surface.

Forty minutes later, they saw the telltale flash of white appear 25 feet down as the halibut rolled and showed its belly, attempting to dive again. Clearly, the fish was spent.

"Time to bring him up," Mattituck announced as he pulled the .22 caliber sidearm from its holster on his thigh. "Bring him up alongside and I'll finish him."

"Do we need that?" Monica asked, excitement rising.

She was experienced enough to know that the .22 meant it was a good-sized fish. Usually, Mattituck liked to harpoon them. The bigger fish, however, were more safely shot in the head.

"I'm guessing over 100 pounds. Might be pushing 150."

"No shit?!" Keri blurted.

Mattituck was leaning over the side, trying to get a better look as the fish came slowly to the surface.

"Looks bigger, actually."

Keri worked the fish to the surface very well, carefully following Mattituck's guidance. The white underbelly of the great flat fish rolled as the exhausted behemoth tried to muster strength for another dive. But the halibut was spent and following the line to the side of the DeeVee8.

"You were right," Keri said. "That thing has no fight left in it."

Two minutes later, blood was pooling alongside the DeeVee8 from Mattituck's shot to the head. The fish was dead in the water, and once sure, Mattituck leaned over the side, pulling on Keri's line as he worked a small mooring line through the fish's huge mouth and through the gills. This line, once he looped it back onto itself, would safely hold the fish until he was ready to haul the beast aboard.

As he worked the line through, he was thinking this fish was better than 180 pounds. A respectable fish, to be sure.

Mattituck nodded. "But if we tried to bring it on board and it found one more spurt of energy, one of us could end up with a broken arm or leg." He gyrated his hand with the .22 and said, "That's the beauty of this thing. One shot and the only fight left is we three trying to get the thing on board."

"We have to haul that thing aboard?" Keri's face was aghast.

Mattituck chuckled.

"Nope," he said, gesturing to the boom just aft of the cabin. "We'll do it the modern way. With machinery."

"Thank god," she breathed, relieved.

Twenty minutes later they had the huge fish aboard, lying on its belly with the dark green dappled back shining in the sun. Mattituck was relieved that he'd ordered the largest fish hold the boat builders had to offer, 7 feet long and 5-1/2 feet wide. It was capable of holding a 320-pound halibut, far more than most of the bigger catches and enough for the larger of halibut. On the earliest charter runs, the chicken halibut or salmon caught had sloshed around in the large hold, like a small child's toys in a large bath tub. It had bruised some of the fish, so Mattituck had recruited a welder friend to install four flip-up braces that would hold two 4x8 planks. This enabled Mattituck to split the hold into essentially two separate holds that he could easily convert into one large hold.

Before shooting the massive halibut in the head, Mattituck had removed the planks and readied the deck. Then he'd put the fish out of its misery and looped a line around its tail—the most secure place to lift a halibut. He then swung the boom around and over the gunwale, and lifted the fish aboard. The sheer size of it was humbling, even for a charter boat captain who had seen plenty of large fish.

He took a tape measure and had Monica hold it at the center of the tail while he ran the tape out to the nose of the fish.

He whistled.

"How long is it?" Monica asked.

"Just a smidgeon over 72-1/2 inches."

"How much is that in weight?" Keri asked.

Mattituck was already pulling out his conversion chart.

"Could vary a little, of course, but according to the chart, it'll be right around 200 pounds. My money's on it being a bit over that, judging by the girth of this one."

"Holy crap!" Keri exclaimed.

"Forgot about Todd's diversion?" Monica chided.

The three laughed as Keri nodded a generous smile.

"Damned straight!" she said. "This thing'll feed us for a year."

"Only if you have halibut about every night," Mattituck said.

"You guys have to have some of this fish," she said seriously.

"Gladly," Monica said quickly.

Just then, Keri's cell rang. She pulled it out.

"It's Todd," she said. "Wait'll he hears what he missed!"

She stepped into the cabin for privacy while Monica helped Mattituck pump in cold sea water to help preserve the fish. Her ling and cod were dwarfed next to the big halibut.

A moment later, Keri stepped back onto the fish deck.

"He's in Anchorage, at the hospital. He said he's going to be the rest of the day, most likely, and will fly back to Valdez tonight."

"All right," Mattituck said. "What's the vote? Back onto the Gulf, home, or something else?"

Monica chimed in before anybody had a chance to say anything.

"I'd like to pick up some chickens, if we can, and then see the sea lions."

Keri nodded agreement.

"Okay," Mattituck said. "We'll scoot over to a nice chicken shelf over between Zaikof and Rocky Bay, then head up to Bull Point to see the sea lions."

Monica finished closing the fish hold and securing the boom as Mattituck fired up the engines and winched the anchor aboard, then cranked the helm on a course for one of his favorite chicken halibut spots.

# Chapter Four

## Fishing Isn't Catching

Earl Darrick was sitting on his usual stool in the Crow's Nest, talking to Seamus O'Brien the bartender. Vaguely, Mattituck wondered as he entered The Crow's Nest if Seamus ever took a day off. The Irishman had started a few months ago at the bar and restaurant, and seemed to be always working ever since he'd arrived. Mattituck had taken a quick liking to the man when he'd single-handedly broken up a brewing brawl just before the murder of Ned Simmons, the halibut poacher.

Mattituck made his way to Earl and slid onto the stool next to him. Seamus nodded and without asking, pulled a glass and tipped it under the Guinness tap. Mattituck smiled and nodded a greeting to the bartender.

"What's up?" Earl asked, turning toward Mattituck.

"Just put Monica on a plane for Cordova."

"Ah," Earl returned. "So you thought you'd pop in an' drown your sorrows?"

"Something like that."

"How was fishin'? You took Todd and his wife out, too, didn'tja?"

"Did well," Mattituck said, grinning broadly. "Keri pulled in a 207 pound halibut."

"Damn!" Earl exclaimed.

Seamus placed the Guinness in front of Mattituck.

"There's a good-sized fish," he said in his Irish accent.

"Indeed," Mattituck said, raising the glass.

"She have a derby ticket?" Earl asked.

"Nope. I know," he added. "She'd be in second place right now if she had."

Earl nodded.

"You hungry?" Mattituck asked.

"I could be in for a bite, if'n your buyin'," Earl returned.

Mattituck laughed. "Yep. On me. I'm in the mood for Italian."

"Bella Luna?" Earl asked, referring to the pride-and-joy restaurant of Pappy Amatucci, the owner of both that restaurant and The Crow's Nest. "Sounds great. Let's go!"

"Seamus just poured me a stout," Mattituck complained, only half joking. "Sit your ass back down and have another whatever you're drinking."

"Twist my arm," Earl returned delightedly. "My next set of clients on the Kimberly Marie are next day after t'morrow." He gestured to Seamus, who gave him another shot of Jim Beam and Coke.

Fifteen minutes later, they were at the crowded entrance to the Bella Luna.

"Damned tourist season," Earl griped.

Mattituck didn't respond.

"Franky Mattituck!" came Pappy Amatucci's voice from behind the hostess. "Come! Come this way!"

Although the man had immigrated right after the Vietnam War, his accent remained heavy. The older man pulled at Mattituck's arm, guiding him into the dining room. Earl followed.

"How things are, eh?" Pappy shot back at him as he navigated them through the tables.

"Good, good," Mattituck said.

"You did well with the Ned Simmons murder, yes?"

Mattituck nodded, embarrassed. "Yeah, we got it solved."

"What happens now with the young man, Toby Burns?"

"It's looking okay for him. He has a solid self-defense case going."

Pappy stopped at a two-person table near the bar.

"Here, you sit here, you and your friend. I feed you. What you want? I have a nice tortellini in white sauce tonight. A nice bottle of Pinot Grigio to go with it, yes?"

Mattituck yielded, despite Earl's resistant expression.

"That sounds great, Pappy."

The old man seated them, then signaled for a server. A beautiful dark-haired woman in her early thirties approached, in the signature black skirt and white blouse of the Bella Luna.

"This one, I want to introduce to you," Pappy said, placing his arm around the small of the woman's well-tended waist.

Earl's eyes took her in, then looked at Mattituck.

"This," Pappy said, "is my niece, Izzy Giovanni. She is just in from home. My home in Italy, I mean. She is here to work for me this summer."

Mattituck started to rise. Earl remained seated, his eyes fixed on the woman's face.

"Nice to meet you," Mattituck said, offering his hand. "Your uncle is quite the man. He seems to have taken a liking to me and feeds me full every chance he gets."

"This," Pappy said to Izzy, "is Frank Mattituck. He is good friend. And he is hot-shot crime solver now, working with the local State Trooper."

Izzy looked meaningfully at Mattituck, nodding and shaking his hand.

"It is a pleasure to meet you," she said. "My uncle has told me of the story of you solving this murder mystery with the fisherman."

Izzy's voice was alto and smooth, giving it together with the accent a sultry, seductive lilt.

"I'm Earl. Frank's business partner."

Izzy turned and shook his hand. Pappy suppressed a look of impatience.

"Yes, yes," he said. "Earl is in the charter boat business with Frank. Yes."

"I'm very happy to meet you as well," Izzy said politely.

"Izzy will be your server," Pappy announced, then clapped his hands once as if to signal the finality of his decision, and disappeared in the throng as he made his way back to the hostess' station.

"I will be happy to serve you," Izzy said, her brown eyes steady on Mattituck's.

"Thank you," Mattituck said, impervious to the suggestion her eyes were communicating. "It sounds like Pappy's decided what we're having," he finished, looking with a grin at Earl.

"Yeah, that's right," Earl confirmed. "Tortellini and white wine."

"Pinot Grigio, Pappy said," Mattituck said in answer to Izzy's quizzical look.

Her face relaxed and she nodded, then turned for the kitchen.

"You're a married man," Earl said when she was out of earshot.

Mattituck looked up at him.

"What?"

"You're taken."

"I'm taken?"

"This chick is hot on you."

Every now and then, Earl really irritated Mattituck. He shook his head impatiently.

"Shut it."

"No, really—"

"I said shut it. I have no interest, so cut the nonsense."

Earl fell silent and fumbled with the menu. The mood went somber. Several minutes passed.

"Look, I just thought—"

"Don't worry about it," Mattituck said, not looking up. "I'm just not into all that."

"All what?"

"Games and shit. Monica's amazing. That's all I care about."

"Of course," Earl said. "I didn't mean anything. Just that she looked at you like . . . You know."

"Okay," Mattituck said flatly.

"Like she might have a bead on you."

"Yeah, I get it. Can we talk about the charters now?"

"Sure, yeah. Okay." Earl felt uncomfortable.

Izzy approached the table with the bottle of Pinot Grigio and two wine glasses. Mattituck looked up and found her warm brown eyes watching him. Instantly, he recognized that what Earl had observed was spot on. This woman was attracted to him.

"The wine my uncle wanted for you . . ." she said, proffering the bottle.

Mattituck nodded.

"Looks good," he said.

"You don't want to look at it?" she said with an inviting smile.

She had full lips, curled at the corners in a manner that would have tugged at most men's hearts. And loins.

"No. If Pappy sent it, it's the right one."

Izzy nodded as she smiled again.

Earl was shifting his gaze between them.

*Damn the luck*, he thought. *I'm available, sweet thang!* Knowing Frank was reading the menu and Izzy was focused on Frank, he let his eyes take in her form. She obviously kept in shape, and filled the Bella Luna uniform very well, modest but showing enough in the right places to reveal everything Earl needed to know.

How Mattituck was able to ignore this was beyond him. Although, he had to admit, he'd never truly been in love with anybody. So maybe that was the difference.

He looked at Mattituck. He supposed his friend was a good-looking guy. Hell, if he had Monica, one of the most beautiful women in the area, he must have something going that turned on the womenfolk. And Earl . . . well, he knew he'd been little more than the town drunk until very recently. Specifically, until Jim Milner's will and Frank Mattituck's trust had transformed him into something more.

He looked back up at Izzy. Her long straight brown hair hung just over the small of her back, and below that was the firm roundness of her buttocks. It made him think raw male thoughts.

Izzy looked at Earl and smiled, but it was nothing more than one of those polite smiles. The kind a hot chick makes to the friend of the guy she wants. A pang of sadness washed through the core of Earl's spirit, and he suddenly felt dejected. Worse than when he'd been drunk all the time. At least when he'd been drunk, he wasn't aware of all these kinds of feelings. Or he hadn't cared. Either way, it hadn't touched him.

Mattituck looked up from the menu to Izzy, still watching him.

He smiled kindly.

She seemed encouraged.

"Your order?" She paused momentarily, then added, "What would you like? You can have anything," she said demurely.

Earl wasn't used to hearing women come on to men that strongly.

Mattituck hesitated.

"Just the tortellini," he said. "Unless Earl would like something more," he added as he shifted his eyes to his friend.

Izzy looked at Earl, taken aback. Earl read it for what it was.

"Naw," he said. "I'm good."

Izzy almost looked relieved, then turned to Mattituck.

"Well, if you change your mind . . ."

"I won't," he said, smiling politely.

The smile on Izzy's face faded, followed by the hint of a pout on her lips, then she turned away without saying anything further.

"You're an idiot," Earl said, more at himself than Mattituck.

"How so? You said yourself I'm taken." He gave Earl a wry smile.

"Some guys have all the luck," Earl said irritably.

"Trust me," Mattituck shot back. "I'm no lady's man. I probably remind her of her first love or something."

Earl stopped another server.

"Gimme a bourbon—a double—with a splash of tonic."

Mattituck made a face at him.

"What?" Earl said. "I been good."

"I know you have," Mattituck said. "But bourbon and tonic? Really? And you give me a hard time about the Guinness."

The jest caught Earl off guard, and he found his mood lightening. The girl all but faded away as gratitude returned to him, filling him better than any wine and bourbon could.

They finished their meals and relaxed with the wine and light discussion of the charters they had run lately. Earl was feeling pretty happy, after a repeat of the bourbon and tonic, doubled up, plus the wine. Even two platefuls of tortellini wasn't enough to dilute the effects of the alcohol, particularly for a thin man who had in recent months cut back from complete alcoholism to a normal intake.

Pappy seemed to appear out of nowhere.

"The meal is good, yes? And the wine?"

"Outstanding as always, Pappy," Mattituck said. "Thank you. But seriously, I can't keep taking free meals--"

"Tsk, tsk!" Pappy interrupted. "But the young lady, my niece . . . she is something, yes?"

Mattituck's mouth closed, his eyes narrowing.

"Boy, is she!" Earl interjected. "She is one beautiful young lady."

"From the homeland," Pappy said. "She is smart, too. She finished university well, but her parents decide she needs a change. She needs something to, um, give her new perspective."

Mattituck nodded. "Well, Alaska will do that."

Pappy nodded, and leaned in to him meaningfully.

"She is good girl. Passionate and loyal. She was studying art in university. Very passionate thing, agreed?"

Mattituck nodded. "I'm sure it is."

Earl chimed in, "I studied art in college."

Mattituck looked at him, surprised.

"I thought you studied culinary arts—being a chef."

"Yeah, yeah, that too. But art was my passion!" he said too enthusiastically.

Pappy looked at Mattituck.

"Maybe I'd better get him home," Mattituck said.

Pappy nodded.

"Wha--?" Earl started to protest, but then realized Frank was probably right. He recognized that old feeling of crossing the boundary between feeling good and being drunk.

It was time to stop. He looked up at Pappy.

"Mind calling me a cab?" he asked, suddenly serious and ready to crash for the night.

"Of course, my friend," Pappy returned.

Izzy was suddenly behind Pappy.

"My shift is over, I think, Uncle."

Pappy turned to face her.

"Yes, yes . . . You did good work today. Now you go enjoy the outdoors of Alaska." He glanced at Mattituck. "Perhaps my old friend can introduce you to some of the sights?"

Mattituck knew a set-up when he saw one. As a single man, he would have jumped at the opportunity to pursue a woman like Izzy. But he did not consider himself single.

"I have an early charter," he lied. The next day was an off day for him. "Maybe another time. Monica will be in town next week. Maybe she and I can take you and Izzy out on the boat."

Pappy's face fell slightly.

"Yes, this would be nice. Yes, Izzy?"

Her eyes were on Mattituck.

"Yes, of course, Uncle."

Mattituck helped Earl into the cab Pappy had called, then walked down to the marina to check on the boats. Not that they needed checking; he just wanted to walk and be with the boats.

As he came alongside the Harbormaster's Office, his cell rang.

*Must be Monica this late,* he thought as he pulled his phone out of his pocket.

It wasn't. It was Todd Benson.

"Did I wake you?" Todd asked.

"No. I'm just checking on the boats."

"Good. Listen, I want to check out some things back at the scene where these hunters were. Do you have a charter tomorrow?"

"No," Mattituck said. He'd been looking forward to a leisurely day, but these opportunities of working with Todd always piqued his interest. "I'm available."

"Want to take a ride out to Hinchinbrook with me? Do a little hiking?"

"Sure."

"Can you be ready by 7:00?"

"Of course. Just one day?"

"Probably. But you know how it goes. May be best to be prepared."

"Got it," Mattituck replied. "Your boat or mine?"

"Can we take yours? Less conspicuous. I can get you reimbursed for gas and wear-and-tear."

"Meet you at the DeeVee8 at 7:00," was Mattituck's response.

# Chapter Five

## Deceptive Appearances

The DeeVee8 had cleared the jetty at 6:48 a.m., with Todd and Mattituck equipped for what appeared to be a week-long trip. While Todd had said it would just be a routine hike into Hinchinbrook to the site of the hunter's death, both were well-versed enough to know that being prepared was wise. Add to that Todd had to pack in the forensics kit in case he found anything of interest.

Just in case they needed a place to stay, Mattituck had called Monica to see if they could overnight at her place, should they need to. Cordova, where she lived and maintained her law practice, was very close to Hinchinbrook Island.

"Of course," she had said cheerfully. "You know I'd love another chance to see you."

Mattituck had smiled into the phone.

"Well, truth be told, saying yes to Todd meant being close to Cordova. I'm thinking we'll be late on the island," he had added, coming up with excuses.

"Listen, my client just came in. Can I call you later?" she had asked.

"Definitely. Talk to you later."

Monica had ended the call regretting her client was sitting right there. It meant no displays of affection, and she liked displays of affection with Frank.

"Thanks," she'd said to her client, Tara Garrett.

Tara had been working toward divorcing her husband, Wilson Garrett, for nearly a year. It was a complicated case, with a co-ownership of one of the largest outdoor outfitter store chains, AK Outfitters, in Alaska. Although Tara had fronted the money with backing from her family, it had been Wilson Garrett's idea and his business and outdoors savvy that had made the stores so successful. They now had stores not only in Cordova, but also in Valdez, Fairbanks, Anchorage, Seward, and Homer. Lately, they had been talking about expanding to the Lower 48 by installing a store in Seattle.

But Tara knew the marriage was doomed. Wilson was all ego, and too inattentive to Tara's needs. She had become increasingly dissatisfied. But when she had suggested counseling, he'd been repeatedly dismissive, insisting that they would be fine. As soon as they launched the store in Fairbanks, they could focus on each other. Then it was the store in Seward. Then in Homer.

His plans to expand to Seattle had been the last straw for Tara, and she had retained Monica Castle to represent her as she built her case for divorce.

At least this was the story Monica's client had given. Monica was too seasoned to think that any story from a client was 100% true.

This night, however, Tara had been visibly shaken. She paced while Monica ended the call, then when she finally sat, she pulled several tissues from the box on Monica's desk and buried her face in them.

Monica had waited respectfully for Tara to gather herself.

"What's wrong, Tara?" she finally asked.

This only triggered more distress, and Monica had again waited, before nudging her again.

Finally Tara sat up, composed, and dried her eyes.

"One of our closest friends is dead," she said bluntly.

"Oh my god, I'm so sorry," Monica said, instantly compassionate.

Tara nodded and dabbed her eyes again.

"A hunting accident. Wilson's best friend, Justin. They were hunting on Hinchinbrook, and Wilson mistook Justin for a deer and—" she stopped as her body shook. "He shot him. Wilson shot Justin."

Monica instantly put it together with the incident that interrupted the fishing trip the day before.

"It sounds like it was an accident," she offered.

Tara nodded.

"I'm sure they'll figure it out. The Troopers are heading out there now to investigate. I'm sure they'll close the case quickly and Wilson will be fine."

"I'm sure you're right," Tara said, her voice becoming calmer as she tried to maintain composure. Then she looked up.

"We have client confidentiality, right?" Tara asked unexpectedly.

55

"Yes, of course," Monica said.

Tara was staring at her feet. Monica saw tears moistening the woman's cheek.

"What is it?" Monica asked.

Still, Tara hesitated.

"He was my lover," she finally said, not looking up.

As an experienced attorney, Monica was used to handling cases where her clients were on one side or another of an affair, and she'd suspected for some time that Tara was having an affair.

"Well," she said, attentive to how she sounded. "That will complicate things. Does anybody know?"

She asked knowing that affairs were nearly always known by somebody. Such things were hard to keep completely secret. Especially in a town of less than 3,000 like Cordova.

"No, no!" Tara said quickly. "Nobody knows. There's no way they could know."

"What about Wilson? Husbands often at least suspect something."

Tara shook her head. "No. I'm very sure of it. Justin and I were very careful. Even if it meant going weeks without seeing each other."

Monica was silent as she absorbed this new information. It would certainly complicate the divorce proceedings, unless Justin's death changed Tara's plans.

"It may be a little early for you to decide, but you should take some time to think about this. Do you want to continue with the divorce proceedings? We're ready to file any time you want, but I know you've been waiting and wanting to handle the business issues carefully." She looked into Tara's eyes as the woman looked up at her. "But you need to be honest with yourself. Were you wanting to divorce Wilson because of Justin?"

Tara's eyes dropped, and she started crying again.

"Again," Monica said. "Nothing to decide right now. But you'll want to start sorting out how this changes things."

"I—I don't know," Tara said. "Justin was a part of it, but not all of it. Not at all. I was planning on leaving him long before things started with Justin."

Monica nodded.

"Okay. Well, if you do decide to proceed, we'll need to at least prepare for the possibility that Justin's accidental death might not have been an accident."

"What?" Tara asked, "But how can—"

"I'm not saying it is. Or that it's what happened. But it could raise some suspicion, and any good DA would be interested enough to at least give it a look."

"I don't know how Wilson could have ever known anything." Tara's face was insistent.

Monica's gaze held steady.

"Whether it's a wife or a husband, Tara, they often do know."

Tara's face turned ashen, and her eyes became unfocused as the tissue she'd been holding drifted down to her lap.


Todd and Mattituck had taken the DeeVee8 for two reasons: it was ten feet longer and two feet wider than Todd's trooper boat, and the DeeVee8 had a head. Todd made use of the latter of these comforts as they entered Valdez Arm, heading south for Hinchinbrook Island.

"I cleared docking at that little dock under the lighthouse with the Coast Guard, as long as you're okay tying up there," Todd said when he returned from the head.

"My only worry," Mattituck said, "would be if a storm picked up."

"That little cove is pretty protected," Todd countered. "I imagine that's why they built the dock there."

"Oh, yeah. I know. I'm thinking more if we needed to get back out. I'm not so sure it'd be all that safe to head out from that dock if the weather's bad."

Todd hadn't thought of that.

"There's a little beach inside a notch in Port Etches," Mattituck continued, "just north of where the accident site was. I thought we'd put in there. Shouldn't be a problem at high tide. Low tide might be a problem, but I like our chances better there."

He looked up at Todd.

"That sound okay to you? Might even be closer than the Coast Guard dock."

"Yeah, sounds good," Todd said, peering out the front windshield as Mattituck guided the DeeVee8 onto a course straight down the Arm. There was only a low swell, and Mattituck was able to get the aluminum charter boat up to her high cruising speed of 34 knots. She was among the faster of the boats in the Valdez charter fishing fleet.

Todd seemed distracted as he settled onto the passenger seat with a fresh cup of coffee.

"Everything okay?" Mattituck asked.

Todd didn't answer right away. Instead, he gazed through his Trooper-style sunglasses at the water ahead. Mattituck decided not to press. He wondered if he'd probed too far, as he was sure there had been some words exchanged between Todd and Keri after Todd returned from Anchorage.

"Two things," Todd finally said. "One is whether or not I should pack in the full forensics gear. Don't normally need it for a routine investigation. I usually only bring it if there looks like something isn't adding up right."

"I can help pack something in," Mattituck said. "Isn't that why you drag me along on these expeditions?"

Todd grinned at the jibe.

"Yeah," he said. "My mule. No, I just don't want to haul a bunch of shit we don't have to. How far is that beach from the accident scene, do you think? Show me on the chart."

Mattituck stood and looked at the rolls of charts in the overhead chart storage, and pulled down NOAA Chart 16700.

"Here you go."

Todd took the chart and unrolled it on the large dash of the DeeVee8, designed to double as a chart table. Mattituck leaned over and found the beach, then took the compass rose and pointed.

Todd looked it over, his finger on a land point southwest of the beach.

"This is where the scene is. Looks like it's actually a pretty straight shot in. Around this little ridge, then straight up this ravine. A couple of miles and bam, we're there."

"Perfect."

"We can leave the bulk of the stuff here. Come back for it if we need it."

"Okay. So what about the second thing?"

"Second thing?"

"You said a moment ago there were a couple of things on your mind," Mattituck prompted, expecting him to bring up the tension with Keri.

"Oh, yeah. Well, when I was looking at the body on the helo ride to Anchorage, the exit wounds for the two shots were opposite each other."

"What do you mean? I don't know what that means."

"One shot entered in the shoulder, from the back, and exited the front just under the left collar bone. The other entered from the front, at the heart."

Mattituck waited. When Todd didn't elaborate, Mattituck pressed further.

"And that means what?"

Todd looked at him.

"It could be that the first shot was in the back, spun him around. Then the second shot caught him in the heart. Bam, bam. One second apart."

"One second?"

Todd nodded.

"Who puts two shots in a deer that quickly? Most guys'll wait to see if they hit it, and if they did, if it's going down."

"Exactly. That's why I'm curious what the autopsy will show," Todd finished.

"What are you looking for with that?"

"It looked to me like the exit wound on the heart shot was higher on the guy's torso than the entry."

"You mean like it was shot from below? But they were at the bottom of the ravine," Mattituck said, confused.

"Unless the guy were lying down on his back when he was shot in the heart. Maybe a minute or more after the first shot in the back."

He was looked at Mattituck meaningfully.

"You think this was intentional?"

"Can't rule it out."

"And you're thinking there might be some clues at the scene," Mattituck added.

"Yep. No idea what. But more times than not, when something's afoul, there are things lying around that don't fit the lie."

Mattituck nodded. He really admired Todd. The man knew his stuff. But he didn't give any indication of his admiration. Instead he opted for humor.

"How about you be my mule and grab me some more of that coffee?"

# Chapter Six

## Inward Trek

Todd and Mattituck had enjoyed a smooth ride south as the DeeVee8 carried them to Hinchinbrook Island. They had been silent for most of the more than two-hour trip, taking in the scenery around the Sound and spotting sea lions and other marine life along the way. It was a sunny morning, and both men were absorbing it before the weather turned in the afternoon, as forecasted.

As they traversed the mid-point of Hinchinbrook Entrance, the wide mouth of a large inlet opened up on the left, and Mattituck steered the DeeVee8 in closer to the shoreline, keeping a closer eye on the GPS as he navigated toward the deep water channel into the inlet.

"Port Etches always blows me away," Mattituck said of the inlet. "Those rocks jutting up to the left . . . it's stunning."

Todd nodded.

"They must come up at least 300 feet," he said.

"And when the sun is to the west," Mattituck added, "the bright white of the sandstone really stands out. It's like something out of a movie."

"Well," Todd returned with a smile. "It is Alaska, after all."

Mattituck's eyes turned toward him with a grin.

"True that."

He slowed the DeeVee8 as they ran up the inlet toward their destination.

"I'll start staging the gear on the fish deck," Todd said.

Five minutes later, they turned right into a small lagoon with what appeared to be a sandy beach straight ahead. Todd stepped up to the chart table and compared the chart laid out to the GPS and their heading. He could see where they were coming ashore then, and began studying the best route to the accident scene. He quickly marked in pencil where the accident had occurred, then followed back on the topographic map to the beach.

"This won't be too bad, actually," he said.

"I thought it might be a better spot to land than that lighthouse dock."

"It may even be easier hiking," Todd said, scrutinizing the route inland. "It follows right up the same ravine the hunters were in."

"Even better than that we're not putting in at the lighthouse dock," Mattituck returned as he steered the DeeVee8 in a wide turn toward their destination.

They nosed the DeeVee8 up to the beach a few minutes later. Since they came in on high tide, there was no need to try to run the boat further aground.

Mattituck hit the release on the anchor and went around to the bow while Todd readied the equipment and the Colt AR-15 patrol rifle. He also checked Mattituck's Ruger .375, a powerful bear-hunting rifle called the "Hawkeye Alaskan," and set it aside.

Mattituck hopped over the bow to the soft sand and pulled the anchor and its line up the beachhead. They had come in on high tide, which would help a great deal, but it was essential to run the anchor as far up the beach as possible and secure it. This time he found a nice rock edge that protruded toward high ground, so he flipped the forks of the anchor down and forced them into the sand under the rock outcrop. He stood and looked around. The little lagoon was circular and well protected. Like most beaches in the region, it was headed with dense grasses and brush, with spruce and various deciduous trees further up.

He turned and looked at the DeeVee8, sitting proud and large on the sand, her stern still in the water. He allowed a tinge of pride to surge through him. It was a beautiful boat, and perfect for his needs.

Todd was hauling the last of their gear to the bow.

"Ready? Or are you going to admire your boat for the rest of the afternoon?"

Mattituck smiled and strode toward the bow to help offload. First were their packs, complete with sleeping bags and a small amount of provisions should they need to overnight for any reason. Hiking around remote Alaska underprepared was widely considered to be plain stupid. Most of the provisions had been loaded into Mattituck's pack to make room for the crime scene kit Todd was to carry in his backpack. Next, Todd handed down the belts and holsters for their sidearms, a pair of Glocks. Last were Todd's AR-15 rifle and Mattituck's .375 Ruger bear hunting rifle.

*I need to invest in something a bit more apt for this work, if I keep it up,* Mattituck thought as he lay the Ruger next to the AR-15. He decided to shop around next time he was in Anchorage. Sooner rather than later, preferably. He needed to see his sister and nephew anyhow. It had been several weeks since he'd last seen them.

Todd jumped from the DeeVee8 over the bow and his boots kicked sand as he thudded down.

"All set?" Mattituck asked.

Todd looked at him and nodded gravely.

"So serious," Mattituck ribbed.

"You know what can happen out here," Todd returned.

Mattituck nodded, his mind returning to what Todd had told him about the bullet wounds.

Without another word, they each swung their packs over their shoulders and bounced the packs into place, buckling the hip belts first so that the pack's weight was born mostly there. They then snapped the shoulder and chest belts into place. Todd checked his hand held VHF with a double click of the mic button. Mattituck's own hand held picked it up, and he returned the check. Todd then held up a pair of two-way radios, a beefed up version of a walkie-talkie, and handed one to Mattituck.

"In case we're out of VHF range but in line with each other."

"Right-o," Mattituck said. Although there was no plan to split up, it was crucial to always be prepared.

They started up the beach toward the tall grasses.

"Have you landed here before?" Todd asked. He liked that Mattituck did a lot of hunter drop-offs and knew a lot of the terrain.

"A couple of times, but I never left the beach. I have no idea what's up there," he said, nodding ahead.

"Other than the trek the other day, I've never been on this part of the island," Todd said.

"Always a first, I suppose."

Todd couldn't shake a feeling of misgiving. Something didn't seem right, though he couldn't put his finger on it. He'd had this feeling many times before, and as unnerving as it could be, he had long learned that they stemmed from the hints of an unsolved crime. Usually with a suspect yet to be caught or identified. To his mind, this was preferable to the overtones of Hopi beliefs from his lineage, of a spiritual world where ancestors might offer guidance and warning. All hooey, as far as he was concerned. Mattituck here had stronger beliefs in the spiritual than Todd did.

Which was why he had quickly learned not to share these misgivings with the charter boat captain.

Mattituck led the way to the grassy beachhead, alert to any activity as they approached. There was a decent bear population on the island, and while there was plenty of food for them this time of year, it was always wise to be cautious. Todd followed, his boots slipping in the soft dry sand below the grass. He too kept a wary eye out as they made their way up.

At the edge of the grass, they stood and took stock of the flatter ground ahead. To the right a small ridge rose out of the water, then rounded and sloped down toward the middle of the island. There was a wide canyon there that rose back up to the mountains that were the spine of Cape Hinchinbrook. The canyon led up to the right between the ridge and the spine, narrowing in a slow grade upward until it leveled a couple of miles away and then sloped back down the other side.

"Up that way should be where the site is," Todd said. He pulled a topographic map out of a Ziploc bag and found their location, then nodded. "Yep. Up that way, over that knoll."

Mattituck nodded as he stretched and took in the scenery around them. In front of them and to the left, the canyon gave way to a moraine with low scrub and muskeg, like a patchwork carpet in a large family room with no furniture. Spanning from the right to the left, the spine of mountains stretched through the center of the island itself and as far as he could see. It pointed almost directly toward the town of Cordova, another island over.

He thought of Monica, probably at work in her office right at that moment. In addition to being beautiful, she was smart, well educated, and patient. She balanced him, he felt, in nearly every way. He could feel the impact she was having on him, filing down his sharp edges and rounding out his serrated personality. He imagined her long black hair hanging past her cheeks as she studied some document or other on her computer screen, her dark brown eyes fixed on the screen and veiling the scrutinizing mind behind them.

A stirring in the tall grass ahead pulled his thoughts back to the present.

In an instant, Mattituck's deer rifle was at ready, pointing in the general direction of the sound. He chanced a glance back and saw the AR-15 ready at Todd's shoulder. Mattituck quickly set the safety on the rifle and slung it over his shoulder, preferring the maneuverability of the Glock. He took the safety off and held the handgun steady with both hands.

"Too much noise for a duck," Todd whispered behind him in a lame attempt at humor.

This was when Mattituck hated the tall grass. Anything smaller than an adult moose could easily hide in there.

The stirring again, about twenty feet ahead. A clump of grass moving opposite the soft breeze confirmed it. Something was definitely there. Mattituck felt vulnerable, ahead of Todd and sure to be the target if whatever it was wanted to attack. He stood stock still, waiting.

The rustling definitely was moving toward them, although in an erratic pattern. The grass moved 90 degrees to the left of them, then back toward them, stopped, then moved several feet to the right, stopped, then away from them. It stopped again, then moved directly toward Mattituck. His forearms and fingers increased their tension, ready.

The creature kept coming in a slow slalom toward Mattituck. Instinctively, he wanted to step back, but he fought the urge knowing that it would put him off balance against whatever attack might occur. Behind him, he heard Todd step to the right, probably to make sure he had a clear shot at whatever it might be.

Without further warning, something sprang from the grass in front of him, hitting Mattituck in the belly and knocking him backward. He hadn't gotten a clear sight of the thing, but it was smaller than a bear and furry—and a hell of a lot quicker. It hit him hard, and he fell back with the thing on top of him, snarling like a devil.

"I can't get a—" Todd started.

The thing was tearing at Mattituck's vest jacket. He tried to get his hands on it well enough to push it off, but he was reluctant to let go of the Glock.

"Try to hold still!" Todd shouted. "I'm trying to get a shot at it!"

Mattituck realized he was rolling back and forth with the thing, instinctively trying to throw it off. He was glad for the thick rugged material of Carhartt's, as the thing—was it a rabid dog or what?—tried to dig through the thick vest.

*The Glock*, he thought. *If I can* . . .

He forced his left hand under the critter, hoping to pry it, but it was moving too fast. All he needed was a couple of inches and he'd have the Glock pointed at it.

Suddenly, the thing flew off him as Todd kicked it hard, sending it flipping through the air.

*Pop! Pop!* went the Glock, jumping in Mattituck's hand.

But the creature kept at him. Todd descended on them, rifle at the ready, but instead of firing he went at it with the barrel. He pulled the gun butt back and drilled the point of the barrel into the animal's back.

Without warning, it turned on Todd and leaped at him as he scurried back from the snarled teeth. It was high enough to fire without risking hitting Mattituck, so he took the safety off and fired. The dirt kicked up several feet behind the furry mass as it came toward him.

The sound of the AR-15 must have startled it as it suddenly turned and scrambled quickly through the grass.

Mattituck sat up, breathing heavily.

"Jesus!" Mattituck blurted. "What the fuck--?"

"Wolverine," Todd answered. "And something wrong with it, too. Did it get you?"

"Get me?" Mattituck snapped. "What the fuck do you mean 'did it get me?' Fucking thing was all over me!"

Todd laughed.

"What the hell's so damned funny?!" Mattituck demanded, anger rising.

"Chill," Todd said. "Are you okay? That fucker was really digging at you—did it claw you or bite?"

"I don't know," Mattituck said, turning his attention to his torso.

The vest was shredded in the front, but it looked like the fabric had kept the claws away from his body. He unzipped it and checked his stomach and chest. Not a scratch, nor a tear in the shirt. He then looked at his arms as Todd stepped forward to inspect him.

"You're lucky he stayed focused on your belly. He might've torn your arms up." Todd looked into his friend's face. "Not a scratch on you."

"Mother fucker destroyed my new vest," Mattituck complained.

They both looked off in the parted grass where the wolverine had disappeared. They listened, but heard nothing of it.

"Vicious little shits," Todd said.

Mattituck looked at him.

"You think?"

"Are you sure neither of us hit it?" Mattituck asked. "I'm pretty sure I didn't get him with the Glock," he added, "but it looked like you might have had a clean shot."

Todd shook his head. "I thought so too, but I saw the shot hit the ground behind him."

Mattituck scooped a white-ish frothy substance from the shredded vest.

"See that?"

Todd leaned in. "Yeah. I noticed it when it was after you."

"It's frothy, like rabies."

Todd nodded. "Yep. Never heard of a rabid wolverine, though."

Mattituck walked to a large driftwood log and sat down, and drew a deep breath. He closed and rubbed his eyes, then opened them and stretched, taking in the scenery across the lagoon. Ironically, whatever was wrong with the wolverine might have saved him serious injury—or worse. Normally a wolverine will go after the neck or at least move around in its attack. The fact this one had been fixated on the vest may well have saved Mattituck's life.

His mind drifted through the many incidents that could have taken his life. The special operations . . . his time as a U.S. Park Ranger in the investigations unit . . . it seemed he had the luck of a cat, with their nine lives. Times like this tended to make him reflective, introspective. What was it all supposed to mean? Why should he be spared, while so many others hadn't been?

Monica drifted into his mind again as he heard Todd securing the cooler. Like the scene before him, the thought of her seemed to offer an answer. An answer that could never be captured in words.

"All set?" Todd hollered as he stretched and picked up the AR-15.

"Yep," Mattituck replied, standing and checking his backpack straps. He decided to keep the Ruger handy and ready. He kept the safety on, but his index finger was close to the trigger as he followed Todd back up the beachhead.

# Chapter Seven

## Divergent Trails

Monica Castle stood at the window of her office, taking in the tall conifers along the mountains behind Cordova. It was such a familiar scene. This office had once been her father's, and it had been his habit to have his little girl bring lunch and eat with him. He had been a good father to her, not only after she was an adult with a J.D. and bar certification, but as a child as well. He had always made time for her. Always.

Another part of her mind was working through some of the details of Tara Garrett's case. The death of Tara and Wilson's friend, Justin Harris, was unfortunate. Certainly, it was not the best timing. Tara had been close to deciding to file the divorce papers, and this seemed to complicate things for her. Especially given the news that Tara and Justin had been carrying on an affair. She hadn't asked Tara how long it had been going on—not yet. But she got the impression it had been going on for some time.

Which raised the question for Monica of whether Wilson might have suspected something. From Monica's experience both in working cases and consulting with colleagues, affairs were eventually discovered by the spouse. Without exception. Tara said she was sure Wilson suspected nothing, but Monica wasn't convinced. Tara felt sure she had gone to great lengths to hide the affair, even setting up a separate email account through which she communicated with Justin, but it was a small town, and very few secrets stay hidden for long in a small town like Cordova. Sure, people believed in "live and let live," but that didn't mean they didn't talk.

The trick was how to find out what Wilson might know. And if he did know something, what would that mean regarding the hunting accident? Was it an accident at all?

Her cell rang. She stepped away from the window to see who it was.

Tara Garrett.

"Hello, Tara. What's up?"

"He's gone—Wilson's gone!"

"What do you mean, gone? Gone where?"

"I—I don't know. Gone. We had a fight, and he stormed out, and now he's gone."

"Okay, take a breath," Monica said, trying to express calm for the panicked woman to grasp onto. "One thing at a time. What was the fight about?"

She could hear Tara breathing, trying to follow Monica's guidance.

"He got all jealous."

"Of what?"

"He said I was too upset about Justin dying. But Monica, we've all been friends for so long—why wouldn't I be upset?"

Monica thought of how distraught Tara had been the day before. If Tara had been that way around Wilson, then Monica could see how the man might read into things.

Except Monica knew he wasn't reading into things.

"Well," Monica started, "you were very upset yesterday. Almost too much so . . . more than just a friend would be."

"Whose fucking side are you on?!" Tara screamed.

"Look, I know you're upset. Why don't I come pick you up and bring you back here?"

"I'm not a fucking invalid!" Tara snapped. "I can drive myself."

Monica took a deep breath.

"Okay, drive on over, then."

"I can't. The police are coming."

"The police?"

"Yeah," Tara said. "I called and reported Wilson missing."

"Missing? When did this fight happen?"

"Last night. Well, early this morning, I guess. Around 1:00 a.m."

Monica tried to absorb this. It was past 2:00 p.m. now. It wasn't so much that this much time had gone by that Monica was trying to understand, but why Tara was so upset. Monica had never heard the woman swear, and already she'd dropped the F-bomb twice.

"Okay. Well, if the police are coming, I should probably be there."

"Why?"

"Because I'm your attorney."

"So?"

"I'm your attorney in a divorce suit about to be filed, with a family friend with whom you were having an affair—a friend who happened to be your husband's best friend. A friend who just died in a hunting accident where your husband was the only other person present."

She paused to let this sink in.

"Oh," Tara finally said slowly. There was no longer any trace of her being distraught. "Okay."

"I'll be there in less than 10 minutes. Don't answer any questions until I'm there."

Howie Long had been the Chief of Police for as long as Monica could remember. Certainly since she had been in high school. She knew the man well, and was not surprised to find him at Tara and Wilson Garrett's home when she pulled up in front of the house. It didn't necessarily mean anything, but Monica knew he only investigated directly when something big might be happening. That didn't bode well for Tara.

"Hi, Howie," she said as she approached him. The older man was leaning on the front fender of his Cordova Police SUV, apparently waiting.

"Took you long enough, Monica. Your Dad was always a faster driver," he said with a wry grin.

"He had a lot more tickets, too," she quipped back.

"She wouldn't talk to me without you here," he said, eyeing her closely as she approached.

"Yeah, well . . . you know how we attorneys are."

"I suppose I do, yeah. But why the attorney thing in this incident?"

"Not really at liberty to say anything at the moment, Howie, except that I'm on retainer for Tara."

"Can I ask why?" he asked, watching her evenly.

He was a sharp lawman, she thought. Which was part of why he had held the office so long.

"You can ask," she said with a smile.

He waited a moment, but she didn't say anything more.

"Okay, we can play it that way," he said, his smile drifting. "But I have to tell you all this makes a guy start feelin' a bit suspicious."

"Nothing to be suspicious about, Howie."

He held his gaze on her long enough to make a person start shifting. It was a strategy he'd developed, and had probably seen success with. Not this time, Monica thought.

"What do you know about Wilson's disappearing like that?" he asked.

Monica looked at him.

"I know, I know," he said. "You can't say anything. But I gotta say, you being here makes a guy really suspicious."

"You're getting to repeat yourself a lot, Howie."

"I'm getting old," he said with a smile, then started for the door into the house, where Tara Garrett had appeared.

Monica followed.

Mattituck and Todd Benson had made good progress up the ravine by mid-afternoon. They had picked up the trail of boots some distance back, presumably a hunter and very likely one of the two from the accident. The tracks were sporadic on the alternating soft and hard ground. Since they led in the direction they were headed anyhow, they followed them up the ravine.

At a flat clearing with a slight depression, halfway up the sloped canyon, they paused at the inviting scene to rest a moment and drink some water. They were at the edge of a large pond that covered the expanse of the depression in the flat area, stretching maybe a quarter mile across. They stood silent, Todd slightly ahead of Mattituck. Both were clearly still wary of wildlife, as Todd carried the AR-15 at ready and Mattituck's bear-hunting Ruger .375 was also poised in his hands. Despite the weight of the weapons, neither thought of having the rifles slung over their shoulders. Not after the incident with the wolverine.

Todd crouched to consult the map, looking between it and the upward slope of the ravine ahead.

Mattituck walked to the edge of the pond, careful to stay back from the mud that ringed the water. The mud created a band of soft sticky ground at least five or ten feet wide all the way around the pond. Something seemed unnatural several feet ahead, and he stepped forward to get a closer look. At the edge where the hard ground gave way to the mud, there was a boot print, a different pattern than the one they had been following. He turned toward Todd.

"Hey, Todd, check this out. I think we found the other set of boot prints."

"Yeah?" Todd said, standing upright with interest.

He quickly came up alongside Mattituck and peered down at the boot prints. He looked up where the prints led, parallel to the ones they had been following. He strode ahead, following them and stooping here and there to get a closer look. He broke away to the trail they had been following and examined the boot prints there, then returned.

"Interesting."

Mattituck was intrigued.

"What?" he asked.

"Why wouldn't they be walking together?" Todd asked the open terrain, almost vacantly.

"Who?"

Todd peered ahead, predicting the parallel trails.

"The hunters," Todd replied. "These two. This Wilson Garrett and his friend. Justin Harris."

"Maybe they were just spread out."

Todd turned and looked at him.

"What for?"

Mattituck shrugged.

"The trail is easy walking," Todd said. "Over here by this pond . . . it's not so easy going. You see?" he asked, pointing ahead.

Mattituck could see the uneven ground, interrupted by low scrub brush periodically. It would certainly be tougher hiking than the trail they'd been following, ten to twenty feet to the right.

"Okay," Mattituck said. "I'll bite. What are you thinking?"

"They weren't walking together."

"Again, maybe they were just spread out," Mattituck returned. "You know, to . . ." his voice trailed.

He was going to say *to spread out and see if they could spot a bear covering more ground*, but he realized that ten to twenty feet wouldn't increase their coverage at all.

Todd was looking at him meaningfully.

"Something's up with this," he said. "It's really hard to tell after a couple of days, but I'm pretty sure these tracks by the pond are a bit of time after the ones on the trail."

Mattituck's brow pulled together.

"How can you tell that? One's on hard ground, and the other on mud."

Todd's lips pulled into an unhappy smile.

"It's not just the tracks themselves, but the pattern. If they'd been walking together, this would be more straight. But look over here, by this taller shrub." He paused to let Mattituck study the ground he indicated. "Balls of the feet, as if this one were crouching behind the brush."

Mattituck nodded.

Todd pointed to where the tracks came back out and around the low brush. He pulled out his phone and took pictures, then measured the length of the footprint.

"We need to check boot sizes, I think," Todd said. "These seem a bit small."

Mattituck watched Todd, wondering what was going through the Trooper's mind. The man knew his stuff, there was no doubt about that. Mattituck had worked alongside him enough now to see when Todd's detective mind was working.

"You get to read these things," Todd continued. "Remember, my Dad was a damned good tracker."

Mattituck did remember. While Todd was half Hopi Indian on his mother's side, he'd learned his outdoors savvy from his hunting guide father.

"What are you thinking?" Mattituck asked, not countering the Trooper's conclusions.

"I'm not. Not yet, anyway. But it's interesting to note. I can't think of a reason they would be walking so separately."

"I can," Mattituck offered.

"Yeah?" Todd asked, genuinely interested.

Just then, his cell phone rang.

"Trooper Benson," he said. There was a moment's pause as he listened.

"Okay," he finally said. "I'm on my way. It'll probably be a couple of hours, though. I'm on Cape Hinchinbrook."

He nodded as if the person on the other end could see him.

"Yep. Got it. Tell Chief Long I'll be there in a couple of hours."

He ended the call and slipped the cell back into his pocket.

"We need to turn around," he announced. "That hunter's gone missing."

"What? Which hunter? This guy?" Mattituck gestured around them.

Todd nodded.

"Yep," he said. "The guy who accidentally shot his friend. Twice."

Mattituck fell into pace behind the Trooper, thinking. Todd Benson's tone had not been lost on him. *Accidentally . . . Twice.* Todd's suspicious mind was again at work. Mattituck suspected things were going to get interesting.

"Where we headed?" he asked Todd.

"Cordova. Apparently he had a falling out with his wife and stormed off. Nobody knows where he is. Been gone more than 12 hours."

"A falling out with his wife?"

They were moving at a good clip back toward the DeeVee8 now. Todd shot a glance back over his shoulder.

"Yeah, a falling out. As in an argument."

Mattituck thought about this. Could the argument have been related to the accident? Or was it unrelated? He asked as much of Todd.

"No way to tell just yet," Todd responded. "But we'll find out."

They had covered a dozen yards more before Todd stopped unexpectedly. He was peering at the ground, stepping to the side. Mattituck looked down to see what he was interested in.

"What's up?" he asked.

Todd shook his head, then turned to where the sporadic line of scrub brush continued. He strode over and inspected the ground around the low brush.

"That's odd," he said.

"What?"

"There's two sets of tracks down where you are, and we still have that set up here."

"Really?" Mattituck said, walking quickly to see what Todd was studying.

The boot prints were clearly defined. Todd went farther up the ravine on that side of the scrub line, then broke through to check the game trail with the two sets of prints. He then went back up to this side of the brush and followed the single prints up further, then back to the game trail. He rejoined Mattituck after being sure of what he was seeing.

"What are you finding?"

"Definitely three sets. And I still say the set up here was following the other two."

"So our two hunters weren't alone?"

"Nope," Todd said, his brow drawn together. "They weren't alone."

"Well," Mattituck said, "that might complicate things a bit."

Todd looked at him out of the corner of his eye as he shot water from his bottle into his mouth.

"Or simplifies it."

Mattituck's puzzled expression made him smile.

"I have a feeling we're going to find things that don't quite make sense up there. Things that this third set of prints might explain."

"Are we still going to Cordova?"

"Have to. We have a missing person report with a person we're interested in being the person that's missing." He looked back up the ravine. "Whatever's up there will wait. We'll be back tomorrow, most likely."

He started back down the ravine toward the DeeVee8, moving at an even faster pace than he had been.

Mattituck slung his Ruger rifle over his shoulder and started down the game trail behind him, picking up his pace to keep up with Todd's high clip down the ravine.

# Chapter Eight

## Debt Collection

The DeeVee8 entered the Cordova harbor a few minutes past 5:15 p.m. among a number of pleasure boats. They had made good time, arriving more than a half hour sooner than they had told Howie Long. Mattituck had only met the Cordova Police Chief once, when he and Todd were tracking down that killer making the drug drops.

"Remember the last time we were here together?" he asked Todd.

"Oh, yeah. I remember, all right."

"Wonder what Eddie Etano's up to, the hotel manager."

Todd looked at him.

"You know," he said. "I'm glad you bring that name up. He owes me, as I recall. I wonder what he knows about Wilson Garrett."

Mattituck hadn't thought of that. Todd had worked the hotel manager in that earlier case in a way that left the man in a reluctant informant's role. It appeared now that Todd intended to collect.

"What do you want me to do?" he asked Todd.

"Let's talk to Howie, then see what we're going to do here. I'd like to have you here and ready, but I know you have a business to run."

"I'm free and clear until Saturday," Mattituck returned.

"And you have a hot girlfriend here, as I recall," Todd ribbed.

"Indeed I do," Mattituck smiled back.

"I'd like to do a little poking around, now that you mention Eddie Etano. Maybe just keep an eye on your cell. If anything turns up, I'll probably need you."

"Sounds good," Mattituck said, thinking of Monica.

An hour later, Mattituck was sitting with Monica on the porch of her house. When he'd called to let her know he was coming in to port with Todd, she had taken Tara home. From there, she went to the Harbor Grocery and picked up the items for a good salad and readied two filets of silver salmon that she had in the fridge.

It rained often in Cordova, but this particular evening gave the couple clear skies and the promise of a fantastic sunset. The only problem might be that they would have to stay up past 11:30 p.m. to see that sunset. The sun would dip down, then reappear a couple of hours later a little further along the horizon.

"I don't know," Mattituck started, a grin appearing, "as good as that was, I don't think anybody can top my way of cooking up silvers."

Monica turned an incredulous expression on him.

"What the—how *dare* you insult your host! Frank Mattituck, I am truly ashamed of you!"

He could tell by her eyes she was teasing him back.

"Yeah, of course. You're right. I'll just keep that info to myself, then." He winked at her.

She raised an eyebrow.

"Well, maybe you can make it up somehow," she said, getting to her feet.

He merely watched her as she stepped over to the wicker armchair he was in. She stepped over him, straddling her legs over him, never once taking her eyes from his. He reached up for her hands. She clasped his as she lowered onto his lap and leaned in to kiss him. Her long black hair seemed to envelope them in a private cocoon.

Mattituck moaned approval, feeling her slide back and forth on him.

"I'd be willing to do anything, Ma'am, to win back your favor."

"Anything?"

He nodded.

She kissed him slowly and gently, then rose to her feet, still holding his left hand in her right. She pulled his hand, guiding him into the house.

The Alaska State Troopers had recently placed a cruiser in Cordova, which was parked at the Police headquarters. Todd Benson called in to the Glennallen office to let them know he was in Cordova and would be using the ground unit to continue his investigation. Then he caught a ride with Howie Long to the station, where the police chief got the keys for him and had him sign for them.

"Really? I have to sign for my own agency's vehicle?"

Howie chuckled.

"You know how bureaucratic things've become, Todd."

Todd nodded. "That I do, I have to admit."

He signed the form and took the keys.

"Is the radio tuned into your network?" he asked.

Howie nodded. "For the local, yes. It has the HF as well, which should be tuned to your Glennallen office. But there's marine VHF as well. It's a pretty well equipped unit, actually."

Todd gave a quick nod in acknowledgement.

"Thanks," he said, putting on his Kevlar vest, then his uniform shirt.

"Need somebody to tag along?" Howie asked.

"Nope. I'm good."

Howie nodded.

"Well, you know how to contact us if you need us."

Outside, Todd was surprised to see that the unit the state had sent was a new unit. He'd expected something close to retirement. They had also recently retrieved the 41-foot Trooper boat that was kept in Cordova. It was being upgraded in electronics and new motors installed. Probably the result of a revenue boost in the state, and the Cordova representative had some longevity. The Coast Guard helicopter station, used only in summer, probably helped with the funding bump as well.

He secured the shotgun to its rack to the right of the steering wheel, noting the computer tray jutting from the dash. He shook his head. He didn't even have a laptop. He started the motor and put the cruiser in gear, nosing it toward the Copper River Inn.

Eddie Etano.

He hadn't thought of the guy since he and Mattituck had stumbled onto the Copper River Inn as a dropoff point for drug deliveries. The big Samoan had nearly lost his life when the killer Todd and Mattituck had been chasing thought Eddie had double-crossed the organization and opened fire. Later, Todd had persuaded Eddie that sharing what he knew would help keep Eddie out of jail.

Of course, there was a catch. Todd had impressed on Eddie that he would be expected to be an informant in the future as well. Now Todd intended to collect.

He followed the highway through town and past the high school, then out of town toward the stretch where the highway wound along Eyak Lake. The name alone forced his thoughts back to the Hopi Reservation of his childhood. He had mixed feelings about his heritage, feeling connected and disconnected at the same time. An apple, they used to call his type on the rez: red on the outside, but all white inside. All because he'd always wanted to be a cop. Join the Navajo Nation Tribal Police, everybody told him. But they had limitations, and Todd wanted to break away from the Rez anyhow. He wanted to experience life a long way away. And a long way away was where he eventually landed.

He wasn't an apple. The accusation angered him, when he thought about it. Which was why he tried not to think about it.

His grip tightened on the wheel, and he had to force himself to hold back on the gas pedal. He was fully Hopi and fully white at the same time.

"It's complicated," he said under his breath, submerging these thoughts beneath the work at hand. He turned his thoughts to what he hoped to find out from Eddie Etano.

The distance to the Copper River Inn was shorter than he'd remembered. He steered the cruiser into the familiar gravel parking lot and parked in front of the manager's office. He imagined Eddie Etano inside, watching the monitors and seeing him pull in. Then groaning.

Todd suppressed a grin.

When he entered the lobby area, he was surprised at the renovation that had occurred. The entire room had been nearly destroyed by the shooting when Todd had last seen it, but now it looked like it was probably the nicest room in the motel. He stopped in the middle of the room and looked around, then whistled. His eyes came to rest on the wide face of Eddie Etano sitting on a raised chair behind the desk. The 62-inch screen on the wall showed a Mariners game.

"Looking really good here, Eddie."

Eddie didn't respond, his eyes watching Todd.

Todd stepped to the high counter and leaned on it with his elbows.

"How's business?" he asked.

"Oh, you know. 'S been good, I guess. Boss is happy, so I'm happy."

"I meant the other business," Todd said.

"So did I," Eddie said.

"Don't be a wise ass," Todd said, his tone going flat. "We have an arrangement."

"I remember. Don't mean I have to smile about it."

Todd grinned, but it came out more of a grimace.

"Well, nonetheless . . ."

"What do you need? Sooner you're out of here the better."

Todd looked him over, his face showing annoyance.

"All right," he said. "I'm fine with things that way. There are always other ways of getting information."

He turned and started for the door.

Eddie's face contorted a moment in confusion, then registered understanding.

"Hey," he blurted. "Wait a sec."

Todd paused, only half turning.

"I'm good, man. I'm good. Sorry for that. I just—"

"No need to explain. I get it. I just need cooperation."

"Okay, yeah. You got it. Like I said, I'm good."

Todd turned back.

"Things have been smooth since last time," Eddie said, his voice streaming like a mountain brook now. "I mean, shit, I used to hafta deal with cops dropping in all the time, you know? Not no more, man. You're cool. You keep your end, I should keep mine. Like I said, I'm good."

Todd stepped back to the counter, remaining straight this time.

"You know about this hunting accident?"

Eddie looked surprised.

"Sure, man. Who doesn't? Shame, man . . . dude was pretty cool."

"You knew him?"

"Justin? Yeah. 'Bout everybody did, I guess."

"You ever do business with him?"

"Which side?" Eddie asked, smiling nervously.

"Either."

"For a while there, more one side than the other."

"Which?"

"The legit one. He useta come in with this same chick. Quite a bit. He used a fake name when he was here with her. I figured it was a girlfriend or something. But the weird thing was, he has his own place. Why use the motel, you know?"

Todd nodded. That was odd.

"So what happened?"

"With those two?" Eddie asked, then shrugged. "I dunno. Just stopped."

"When?"

"'Bout three weeks ago, I guess. Maybe two." He shrugged. "I don't know."

"What about the other business?"

Eddie nodded with a smile.

"Yeah," he said. "Justin was fairly regular. Mostly just pot, you know? Nothing heavy. He wasn't that type."

Todd nodded.

"Are you investigatin' this thing?" Eddie asked, leaning forward with increased interest. "They said it was an accident. It warn't, eh?"

"No indications of foul play," Todd returned. "This is routine poking around, just to be sure."

"Ah, yeah sure. I gotcha," Eddie said with a knowing nod.

"What else do you know about Justin Harris?"

"Just that he's real tight with Wilson Garrett, guy who owns AK Outfitters. That's the guy who shot him, right?"

Todd nodded. "It is."

"I wonder about them hunting accidents, you know?" Eddie said thoughtfully. "I mean, if you wanted to knock a guy off . . ." he let his voice trail off. He jerked back upright. "I mean, I ain't sayin' that's what happened or nothing."

Todd smiled. "Of course. If we thought that were the case, we'd be at this a whole different way."

"I bet," Eddie said. "I bet you would."

"The woman Justin brought around here a lot, do you know who she was?"

"Nope. No clue. I could check the books, but guaranteed it ain't her real name."

Todd nodded. "Makes sense."

Several seconds hung in the air, interrupted only by the drone of the TV.

"What about Wilson? Know much about him? Where he hung out, what he liked to do?"

"Naw, I don't know much about him. He warn't a customer, you know?"

"Any idea where he might go if he got pissed off or wanted to be alone or anything?"

Eddie shook his head slowly. "Naw, I don't really."

After another moment had passed, Eddie asked, "Do I get to ask any questions?"

Todd looked at him, amused.

"Sure. Shoot."

"Why you care where the guy is? He just lost his best friend, bro."

"It's my job to care," Todd countered. "He's been reported missing. Any ideas?"

"You asking me? I ain't the fucking detective—you are."

Todd grinned a threatening expression.

"Don't get all mouthy and shit with me, Eddie."

"He runs an outfitter store, man," Eddie said. "He's always out camping and shit. Wander around out there and see what you find."

Todd looked around again.

"Looks really great, Eddie. Things are good for you. I'm glad."

"Thanks, man," Eddie said, his tone changing. "You should see the rooms. Owner re-did the whole place. Every last room. Wants to draw in more of the tourists. Next summer he's going to re-do the whole outside. Parking lot, too."

Todd noted the excitement in the big Samoan's voice.

"That's great. Well, Eddie, thanks. I'll come back by if I need anything else."

Eddie nodded, still puffed with pride in the new appearance of the Copper River Inn.

# Chapter Nine

## Drinking Secrets

Todd sat in the cruiser for several minutes, his head resting on the seat headrest. He hadn't really noticed the new car smell before, but now it filled his nostrils as he looked over the front of the Copper River Inn before turning the ignition. The outside could indeed use a facelift, so if the owner really did want to draw in more of the tourist trade, the planned upgrade would do the place some good. And with the view of Eyak Lake behind it and the mountains looming on three sides, Todd could imagine the place might just do well.

He wondered what that might mean for Eddie Etano's side business with the drugs.

The engine roared to life with that big-cruiser motor sound, although he wasn't sure where to go next. He decided to continue down the highway toward the airport and the Coast Guard helicopter station. He drove three miles east before a sudden sense of emptiness took hold of him. He was at the point in the highway where the mountains surrounding Cordova gave way to the flat expanse of the Copper River delta. All around, tall grasses swayed in the breeze, broken only by the grey asphalt highway and the occasional stream cutting through.

At a turnout, he pulled off and cut the motor. He got out and leaned against the hood, watching the lowered sun as it crossed behind the mountains to the west. It would be a couple of hours before it actually set below the horizon. He gazed back toward the flowing grasses and fixed his eyes on a wide creek that cut beneath the highway under a bridge. It was probably why there was a turnout here—so that tourists could stop and look at the salmon as they ran upstream to spawn. No doubt local anglers took advantage of the spot for easy catching as well. Spawning salmon in a stream were not difficult to catch, especially if one worked the line in a way that snagged the crowded fish. Not legal, but also not an uncommon method, particularly when the local State Trooper Fish and Wildlife officer was stationed out of Valdez.

He and Keri had stopped at one of these turnouts two or three years before. Maybe it was this very one. Impossible to tell. They had been headed out on a rare vacation for the Million Dollar Bridge, so named for its price tag some decades earlier. The bridge had been built as a means of accessing the vast Copper River Valley to the northeast, but had been abandoned when the mining operation it was intended to access had been abandoned. Now the bridge stood as a sample of exorbitant governmental waste of tax dollars, except for the tourist draw it now carried. Todd and Keri had camped for a week beyond the bridge, enjoying the Alaska wilderness they both so deeply loved.

It had been some time since they had taken a week off together. Both their jobs were demanding, and scheduling during the busy summer months was difficult. Almost impossible, in fact. Not just for him, with the busy fishing and tourist season, but for Keri as a nurse, with the increase in patients that came with the influx of fishermen and tourists.

It had been an amazing week of just the two of them. Hiking, relaxing, outdoor cooking, romping on top of the sleeping bags in the tent. . . .

He exhaled heavily and looked again toward the sunset. He was in the shadows now. In the past, such a moment would have had his cell phone in his hand, dialing Keri.

With a sudden motion, he stood and rounded the cruiser and got in. He started the motor and turned the cruiser back toward town.

Mattituck rolled over, finding Monica sleeping on her side. His hand found its way along the curves of her side as he moved closer to her. As if awake, she shifted and moved closer in to him, making it easy to hold her close. The smell of her hair around his nose made him smile, and he nuzzled in and kissed the nape of her neck.

It wasn't late. They had gone to bed early, well before the sun was ready to dip below the horizon. He had an urge to glance at the clock on Monica's nightstand to see what time it was, but he was too comfortable. And very tired. He closed his eyes and let the warmth of her against him carry him toward sleep.

Before he could drift completely into a slumber, his phone sounded an incoming text. He tried to ignore it, but two minutes later, the second alert for the message sounded, and he rolled over to see who it was. Sometimes Derek, his fatherless nephew, texted him when he was struggling with some adolescent issue. Mattituck, normally a bit gruff and aloof, was very responsive. He remembered well those painful years, and he loved his nephew.

The message was from Todd Benson, however.

*You up? Feel like working?*

Jesus, he thought.

*Up now. Thanks. What's up?*

*Got a lead. Could use ur help,* came the response.

Mattituck lay on his back, debating.

"Everything okay?" Monica's sleepy voice asked.

"Yeah, I guess. Except Todd needs me and I have this amazing woman up against me, naked and sexy."

"Oh, poor you," she said, humor at the edge of her tone. "Tough decision."

"That helps a lot. Thanks for the guilt trip," he teased back.

"Do what you need to do, baby," she said. "I'll be here when you get back."

Mattituck smiled, then leaned over and kissed her cheek. He could feel her cheek muscles smiling in response.

He moved to the edge of the bed, swung his legs to the floor, and picked up the cell.

*Where are you?*

*Outside*, came the reply.

The mother effer was outside waiting for him.

*Asshole*, he texted. *I'll be out in a few.*

*Piss ant*, came the reply. *And good. Hurry.*

Mattituck put on his clothes, thinking where he left his Glock and holster through the fog of waking. Less than three minutes later, he was pulling Monica's front door closed and turning to the State Trooper cruiser waiting in the street.

Todd was carrying them in the cruiser at a high rate of speed as he filled Mattituck in. A lead police chief Howie Long had received told them that Wilson Garrett had been seen driving his Hummer out of town, toward the airport. The tip had come from a friend of Wilson's, his assistant manager at AK Outfitters, who was concerned that he might not be dealing with the death of Justin very well.

Mattituck watched as the Copper River Inn slid past the left side of the cruiser.

"How'd it go with Eddie Etano?"

Todd shot a glance at him.

"Okay," he said. "Didn't get much from him. He doesn't really know Wilson Garrett, but Justin was a regular customer. He usually had the same woman with him, though we have no way of knowing who she was. I got a description, but she always signed in with a fake name."

"Of course she did," Mattituck said. "Nothing can be that easy."

"Especially if she was hiding something," Todd said.

Mattituck eyed the seasoned Trooper.

"What are you thinking?" he asked.

Todd shrugged.

"Nothing yet," he answered. "But let's see how things pan out. I'd love to find out who that woman was."

Mattituck's again eyes drifted out the left side windows at the buildings sliding past. The Klondike Roadhouse was a mile or so down from the Copper River Inn, and from what Todd had told him, was a source of customers for Eddie Etano. Both the drug and hotel business.

"Hey, didn't you say Wilson Garrett drives a Hummer?"

"Yeah, a yellow one. Why?"

"There's one in front of the Klondike there."

Todd's head spun around as they had just passed it. He hit the brakes hard and pulled into the far inlet to the parking lot, barely making the turn with their speed. Mattituck gripped the armrest and pressed his feet into the floor. The cruiser lost traction as the tires hit the gravel, and the vehicle started sliding until Todd spun the wheel to the right and straightened it.

"Really?" Mattituck said, irritated. "Was that necessary?"

Todd ignored him and began driving back through the parking lot toward the other end, looking for the yellow Hummer. The parking lot was full, and it wasn't even a weekend night.

"This place does a good business, it looks like," Mattituck said absently, trying to cover his now-waned annoyance.

"Yeah, in a lot of ways that would keep any police vice squad busy." He shot a sardonic look at Mattituck. "But this is Alaska."

Mattituck nodded.

"There it is," he pointed.

Todd nodded and pulled in behind it, then checked his notes.

"Yep, that's him," he announced, pulling the cruiser around to the side of the building. "Times like this I hate being a uniformed cop."

"How about I go in?" Mattituck offered.

Todd looked at him. It wasn't a bad idea.

"You know what he looks like?"

"Do you have a picture?"

Todd nodded, pulling out his cell. He showed it to Mattituck. Wilson Garrett was a good-looking guy in that outdoorsman way, with a closely trimmed beard and slightly weathered skin. He had a squint to his eyes that drew his cheeks up slightly, a characteristic that was distinctive because it wasn't due to a bright sun when the picture was taken, but was a natural countenance for the man. His sandy brown hair was curled at the ends, hanging above his shoulders with a well-groomed appearance.

"Got it," he told Todd.

"I'll send it to your cell in case you need it."

Mattituck nodded.

"And I'll be right here if you need me."

"Right. But I have this little buddy that'll be a hell of a lot quicker," Mattituck returned, patting the Glock holster.

Todd shook his head. "Don't you even—"

"Fuck, I'm just kidding," Mattituck said, annoyance returning. He opened the door and stepped out before Todd could reply.

That was the one thing that worried Todd about Mattituck being deputized. His temper. The man had an underlying, seething anger that festered at times. Todd's training in profiling had given him a keen eye for reading people, and this was an observation that had been there from the beginning. And it fit with Mattituck's reputation for having a short fuse.

He watched his friend's back recede under the awning as he turned the corner of the building toward the front door.

Inside, Mattituck surveyed the scene. The roadhouse was one large, open area with a long bar that ran along the left wall, then curved along the back wall. In the front right corner was a stage area for live music, and a dance floor in front of it. The tables were a mix of high tables along the far side and lower tables in the middle and closest to the front. There had to be nearly a hundred people in the bar, but it was not even half full.

Mattituck began walking through the tables, keeping close enough to the bar to see who was sitting there. The size and darkness of the room made it likely he would have to pass through a couple of times to get a read on everybody there. In an effort not to draw notice, he acted as though he were watching for friends. There were mostly groups around the tables, some mixed, some gender-based. A thirty-something woman perked when she saw him and hit her friend's forearm, causing the woman to turn. The others at the table turned to see what they were looking at. Mattituck could see she was attractive and fit enough to pull-off wearing the tight sleeveless blouse she was wearing, showing off tan, shoulders and cleavage in a way that would draw most men in right away, and probably did.

Mattituck wasn't most men, though, and kept scanning the faces.

"Hey there, handsome!" she blurted, clearly on better than her second drink. "We're what you're lookin' for, right here. More spefically—more spefic—mostly me!" she slurred.

Her friends broke into laughter, watching to see how Mattituck would react.

"I'm good," he said, giving them no more than a glance.

The woman got up, reaching for his arm. Mattituck stopped, took in her hand gripping his forearm, then looked into her face.

"I'm not interested, sweetheart. I got things to do."

"Oooo!" she chortled. "Busy man! Too busy for a good time, are ya?"

Her friends joined the teasing, none of them catching that Mattituck really wasn't interested.

"C'mon, handsome," the woman continued, leaning forward. She stepped into his chest and wrapped her arms around him.

He took hold of her upper arms and nearly lifted her out of his way.

"I'm serious. Not interested," he said, his annoyance from outside returning.

"Hey! I'm not useta being man-handled like that!"

"No, I'm sure you're used to plenty of man-handling, though," he shot back, trying to step around her.

"Hey," came a gravely voice from behind him. "No need to insult the little lady, now."

Mattituck turned to face a rugged looking man about his own age, wearing a leather biker vest.

"I have about as much interest in trouble as I have in her," he snapped.

The man placed his right hand on Mattituck's chest.

"You ain't from around here, are you?" he sneered. "And you come in here insultin' our wimmen?"

His friends sitting at the table he'd been at laughed and jeered, one lifting his beer in salute to his tough friend.

"I said I want no trouble. I'm just minding my business," Mattituck said, his eyes hard into the man's. Behind him, the woman was pulling at his shoulder.

"C'mon, handsome! Give a girl a chance atcha!"

"I have things to do," Mattituck said to both of them.

He took a step forward in attempt to leave, but the man stepped in.

"You'll 'pologize to the lady."

"No. Don't think I will," Mattituck returned, his voice going deep.

Again, he tried to step around, but the man took a step to the side. Mattituck saw a flash at the man's left side and knew a left jab was on its way, the spiked bracelet giving it away in the darkness.

Without his giving it conscious thought, Mattituck's right arm shot downward in an expert block. The man's fist connected with his forearm and glanced off. Mattituck gripped the man's collar with his left hand and lifted as he pushed the man back onto the table.

"You sum bitch!" the man blurted, gaining his footing and springing forward.

Mattituck wanted none of this, and decided to end it quickly. He stepped aside easily from the drunken man and sliced down on the man's neck at the muscle and jugular as he passed. The man dropped instantly, belly flat on the floor.

Everything seemed to go silent, but the man didn't move. Mattituck knew he'd hit his spot and the man was momentarily unconscious. He turned to the friends.

"I came in here with no interest in trouble, and I still want it that way." He pulled a twenty dollar bill out of his pocket and placed it on the table. "Appeasement. Beers for you boys and your buddy when he comes to. In exchange for no more bullshit."

The men looked at him, then each other. They were still taking in what had just happened. They'd never seen a man dropped that quickly, and immediately nodded.

Mattituck turned to the women.

"Trust me, there are better men than me all over in here."

They stared blankly at him.

He turned and continued looking for Wilson Garrett, picking his way through the now silent tables nearest the incident. Three tables out and beyond, nobody had taken notice, and Mattituck was relieved to escape the zone of attention.

Half way down the bar, he spotted Wilson Garrett atop a barstool, nursing what looked like a straight Scotch. He took a stool one removed and signaled to the bartender. He looked over the tap handles and spotted his favorite.

"Guinness," he said as the bartender approached, wiping his hands on a towel."

"You got it," he acknowledged. "There wasn't any damage over there, was there?"

"How's that?" Mattituck asked, surprised.

"You were in a scuffle over there," the bartender indicated the table with the women. "I saw you put that guy up on the table. No damage?"

Mattituck shook his head in answer. It wasn't so much that the bartender was that observant that was striking, but rather that he took the incident in stride as if it were normal.

"No damage," Mattituck said.

The man nodded as he drew Mattituck's stout from the tap.

"You don't seem alarmed by a fight in your place," Mattituck said, watching Wilson Garrett in his peripheral vision.

"As long as there's no damage. Happens now and again, so why bother?"

"Good point," Mattituck said, noting Wilson watching him.

He turned to him.

"How's it going?" he asked.

Wilson grunted and nodded.

"You must've handled yourself pretty good," the bartender said. "Gildy's a tough guy. He's the one you laid out."

"He should learn to mind his own business," Mattituck said, less interested now that Wilson was paying attention.

"Got in a fight?" Wilson Garrett asked.

"Just a little scuffle."

The bartender placed a square napkin on the counter in front of Mattituck and set the tall dark Guinness on top of it. He slid a small bowl of bar nuts next to the beer.

"This place can be rough sometimes," Wilson said. "Fishing town."

Mattituck nodded.

"I haven't seen you around here," Wilson said.

"I'm from Valdez."

"Ah . . . Great town. Been thinking of opening a store there. I own AK Outfitters."

Mattituck looked at him and again nodded.

"Heard of it?"

"Yeah, I think so."

"We have stores in Fairbanks and Anchorage, too. Seward, Kenai, and Homer, too."

"Wow," Mattituck's tone was politely impressed. "That's quite an operation."

"What do you do?" Wilson asked.

*What an ass*, Mattituck thought.

"Charter boat captain," was all he said.

"You have any sponsors?"

Everything about this guy was beginning to annoy Mattituck. First the positioning of himself as a major business owner, and now hinting at the practice of charter boats being sponsored. The arrangement was usually the company would promo the charter in their advertising. Usually it was done indirectly by using the boat in an ad. But in the case of an outfitter store, they might also offer customers a booking service. A direct funnel to the charter boat, while enhancing the business of the store.

In this case, however, Wilson Garrett seemed to be using this powerful tool to dangle something in front of Mattituck. And that kind of person rubbed him the wrong way.

"Nope, no sponsors."

"Which charter are you?"

If he wasn't helping Todd with this case, Mattituck would have shut this conversation down. Then again, he probably wouldn't have come into the place in the first place. He decided he'd better get his head in the game.

"Sound Experience Charters. Two boats, the DeeVee8 and the Knot Skunked." He shifted on the stool to face more toward Wilson. "It's a growing operation. I added the DeeVee8 last season after realizing the Knot Skunked wasn't enough to keep up with a growing business."

"I've heard of you. Yeah, you're the one that's supposed to be good with kids, right?"

Mattituck was genuinely surprised. The guy wasn't just bull-shitting.

"Yeah, that's one of our business niches."

"What'd you do, hire a skipper for the second boat?"

He grinned. "Nope. The second boat's the better boat. Hired a guy to run the first boat."

Wilson laughed. "My kinda business man! That's what I would've done! Nice!"

Mattituck laughed harder than he felt like, shrugging as if to say 'what's a guy to do?'

"Lemme buy your next one," Wilson said.

It was clear he had a good head start in drinking.

"Sure. Thanks."

"No problem. But I should disclose that I may have an ulterior motive. I've been looking for the right charter company to partner up with."

He gestured with this thumb back toward the tables.

"Maybe that fight was serendipitous," Wilson said.

Words like that indicated a good education, Mattituck thought. Not exactly the norm in a rural Alaskan town.

"I'd be interested." Mattituck put his hand out. "Frank Mattituck."

"Wilson Garrett," the store owner returned with his hand.

Within a half hour, Wilson Garrett was well within the realm of drunkenness where people lost their filters.

"Can I tell you shomethin'?" Wilson said as he emptied his tumbler and held it up for the bartender.

"What's that?"

"I feel like I can trusht you."

"I appreciate that," Mattituck said.

The bartended looked askance at Wilson, then at Mattituck. Mattituck shrugged.

"Maybe you've had enough for tonight, Wilson," the bartender said.

"I can hold my own," Wilson said.

"Give me your keys, then," the bartender said.

"I'm awright." Wilson's eyes were taking on a vacant look.

"Maybe just one more," Mattituck suggested, then felt guilty for taking advantage. "But give him your keys," he added to Wilson. "He can call a cab for you."

Wilson wobbled a moment as he leaned to pull his keys out of his pocket. He half placed, half slammed them on the table. It was a gesture more from the drinking than anger.

"What were you going to tell me?"

"Can you keep a secret?"

"I'm pretty tight-lipped with other people's business," Mattituck said.

"I hadda big fight with my wife lash night." His eyes wavered in keeping with the sway of his head.

Mattituck waited.

Wilson took a sip off the fresh Scotch, then turned his unsteady face back to Mattituck.

"My besht friend jus' died," Wilson continued.

"Man," Mattituck said. "Sorry to hear that. You do need a few drinks, don't you?"

"Nobody understands, you know?"

Mattituck nodded.

Wilson sat several minutes in silence. Mattituck waited.

Suddenly, Wilson leaned toward Mattituck. "And I'm pretty sure my wife's fucking around on me," he said.

Mattituck paused.

"Wait . . . what?"

Wilson nodded meaningfully.

"That's right," he said. "pretty sure she's—that she's having an affair—" he broke off as his voice cracked. "She was—she's fucking some dude." He stopped with a choked sob.

"Dude," Mattituck said. "That's pretty heavy stuff. I mean, that's a serious accusation. Sometimes we think we see stuff. Something we see or overhear. You know, sometimes we think we see more in very innocent things. You know what I mean?"

Wilson nodded. "Yeah, I know. But no. I'm really, really sure of this."

He stopped and sat up straight.

"Fuck, man. I shouldn' be tellin' you all thish."

Mattituck shook his head.

"No sweat, man. I don't know many people around here. And like I said, I keep people's business quiet. I won't say anything."

"Thanks, man." Wilson half slid on the stool, then downed the rest of his drink. "I gotta go, man."

"You want the bartender to call a cab?"

"No . . . I mean I gotta go piss."

Mattituck had to suppress a laugh.

"Okay. You go ahead," he said.

He looked at the bartender, who was watching now. The man raised an eyebrow as Wilson stumbled, his hands moving from stool to stool to steady himself as he made his way to the restroom.

"Maybe I'll call a cab anyway," the bartender said.

Mattituck nodded.

"Think I'll be on my way," he said, putting a hundred dollar bill on the counter. "A tip should be in there. Enough to keep secrets."

"I didn't hear anything," the man replied.

"Not his secrets," Mattituck said with an even gaze. "Mine. He probably won't remember me being here. I'd appreciate you holding to that story."

"Sure, mister. You got it."

# Chapter Ten

## Patterns and Details

It was past 2:00 a.m. when Mattituck slipped quietly back into Monica's bedroom, trying not to wake her. He pulled off his shirt and jeans, leaving just his boxer briefs, and slid under the covers, scooting stealthily back into a spooning position.

"Everything okay?" Monica asked. There was no trace of sleep in her voice.

He pulled her close.

"Yeah, I think so."

"What's going on?"

"Trying to find that hunter—the guy who shot his friend."

"Wilson Garrett?"

"Yeah."

"Any luck?"

"Yep. I spent close to an hour with him at some roadhouse past the Copper River Inn."

"The Klondike?" she asked.

"That's the one. You know about it?"

She shifted so she could look at him in the faint light coming through the window.

"Frank," she said. "I grew up here."

His white teeth appeared in a smile.

"What'd you find out?" she asked.

"Not much," he said. "Just a little bit for Todd to run down."

"Such as?"

"You seem very interested in this," he replied.

"It's all a buzz around town. And it's a small town."

"All the more reason not to share," Mattituck said.

Monica chuckled.

"True. I was just curious what pulls my man out of my bed."

"Ah!" he said, raising up and leaning over her to kiss her. "Jealousy!"

"Guilty as charged," she returned, her hands up as if caught at something sinister. She lowered her arms around his neck and pulled him down to her.

Todd lay on the hotel bed, unable to sleep. The information Frank had been able to get from Wilson Garrett was eating at him, and he couldn't put his finger on why exactly. Sure, there were things out of the ordinary that should be looked into, and he would. But all them by themselves didn't mean much: a different entry and exit wound direction on the dead man's body, the possible tension between Wilson

Garrett and his wife, and the news that Wilson believed his wife was having an affair, Eddie Etano's info that Justin Harris was a regular and with the same woman . . . Lots of little tidbits that might be suspicious, but they didn't add up to anything in particular.

But this was when Todd tended to really buckle down in order to be sure there were no connecting dots. Sometimes there were. And if an investigator wasn't meticulous in turning over every stone, then cases could go unsolved. Guilty people could walk free. That was bad enough in itself, but Todd knew that very often guilty people with freedom tended to do guilty things again.

It was his job to prevent that, and he took his job very seriously.

He rolled over and looked at the glowing red time on the clock on the nightstand. 3:23 a.m. He sighed heavily and rolled back onto his back, staring at the popcorn ceiling. Ever since he was a kid, he loved those ceilings. He would lie for hours in his grandparents trailer—mobile home his grandmother insisted—staring and looking for patterns in the sprayed popcorn bumps. If he looked long enough or hard enough, he almost always found them. Sometimes a person or an animal, or a tree, or a close up of an eye or snarling mouth. But he nearly always found patterns.

And he'd learned over the years that there were almost always patterns to be found. Sometimes someone was behind them, sometimes not. But when there was, he found deep satisfaction in finding the pattern and nailing the person behind it.

His mind wandered to Keri. What was she doing right then? She had the night-shift tonight, so she was on the floor at the Valdez Hospital. Earlier in their relationship, and well into their marriage, she would eagerly call him on her breaks. And he couldn't go to bed without hearing her voice, even when he worked late. And she had always loved him calling, even if it woke her.

But tonight he hadn't even bothered calling her, and she was obviously doing other things on her breaks. Not even a text had passed between them since he'd left Valdez, in fact. She hadn't even stirred when he got up for the early morning departure with Frank.

He threw the hotel sheets aside and got up, walking tiredly to the bathroom area. He turned the sink faucet on cold water and let it run for a full minute before bending over and splashing it over his face. He scrubbed at it as if hoping the cold water would shock some sense into him.

He straightened and toweled his face, folded the towel neatly and lay it on the counter, then turned back to the empty bed.

Mattituck was out of bed before Monica, banging around in the kitchen looking for the skillets and implements he needed to work up one of his famous (in the family anyhow) homemade breakfasts. Monica lay listening to his sporadic humming of unidentifiable tunes, punctuated periodically by the metallic sound of pots being moved around in the drawers. She moved her head so she could see the time: 5:51 a.m.

He must have found the skillet for the bacon. She could smell it wafting through the house. She smiled. She loved his making breakfast for her.

She got up and took a quick shower, then pulled the robe behind the bathroom door around her and joined Mattituck.

He stopped to watch her.

"Now, that's what I've been waiting to see," he said, grinning. "My muse has arrived. Now be prepared to be dazzled by the most amazing breakfast ever."

He paused and looked around with a baffled expression.

"That is, if I can find any decent food in here . . ."

He began rummaging through the refrigerator.

Monica's amusement came out in her voice.

"What are you looking for, exactly? There's plenty of Mini-Wheats."

He spun and feigned a stunned look.

"Mini—? Are you kidding me? I said *decent* food."

She stepped around him and pulled eggs out of the refrigerator, then a variety of vegetables, and shredded cheddar.

"There."

"What's this?"

"I want an omelet," she said simply. "Whatever you want to mix together from those ingredients will be just fine, thank you." She stepped up to him and kissed his chin, then took a seat on a stool behind the island to watch him.

"The interesting thing from last night," Mattituck said unexpectedly, "is that Wilson Garrett thinks his wife is having an affair."

This hit Monica hard.

"What—why does he think that?"

"He wouldn't say. But he seemed very sure of it."

"Does he know who?"

"If he does, he didn't say."

Monica tried to absorb this. Tara had been so sure that Wilson suspected nothing, but clearly he did. She was almost afraid to ask any questions, for fear of giving something away.

"What do you and Todd make of it?"

Mattituck paused from scooping coffee into the coffee maker, then turned to face her.

"I'll let you know as soon as Todd tells me," he said with a grin.

"You must be thinking something," she prodded.

"Well, Todd talked to that hotel informant before we found Wilson Garrett at the roadhouse. You remember the guy? Eddie Etano?"

"I never met him, but you guys told me about him. The guy who was shot, from the hotel?"

"That's him. He told Todd that Justin Harris was a regular there, and that for months he came with a woman Eddie didn't know. And they used fake names, of course."

"Married woman, maybe?" Monica ventured.

"Could be."

"And you're thinking it might be Tara Garrett?"

Mattituck was still watching her.

"That's what I was thinking," he said. "I didn't say it to Todd, though."

"Why not?"

"It'd be a pretty far-fetched coincidence," he said. "And I'm still trying to impress the new boss."

Monica laughed. "You don't really work for him. Deputized doesn't mean you get paid, so he's not your boss."

Mattituck was smiling back. "I still don't want to look like an idiot."

"I hear you," she said, feeling uncomfortable. To her thinking, he might not be far from the truth.

And she couldn't say anything about it.

Todd woke up with a headache. He looked at the red lettering on the clock. 7:24 a.m. He closed his eyes for a moment, wishing he could sleep in. But with Wilson Garrett located, and a little more information gathered, he was anxious to get back out to Hinchinbrook and see if there were anything useful at the scene of Justin Harris' death.

He picked his cell off the nightstand. He opened a text window to Mattituck.

*You up?*

It took a moment for a reply.

*Yep*

*When can you be ready to get back to Hinch?*

*I am ready. Just refueled the DV8.*

Todd grimaced, feeling embarrassed.

*On my way.*

*I'll be at the slip.*

Todd took a very fast shower and donned the blue coverall uniform, zipping it over the Kevlar vest, then buckled the belt. He scooped his cell and two-way radio and headed out the door, his backpack slung over his right shoulder.

He parked the cruiser in its spot near the Alaska State Trooper dock. The DeeVee8 was lightly tied up, her engines running. He left the keys to the cruiser under the driver's seat and sent Howie Long a text asking him to have an officer pick up the keys right away. The text acknowledging was immediate. He strode down the dock and tossed his backpack onto the fish deck of the DeeVee8, then got to work releasing the lines keeping the DeeVee8 tethered to shore. He hopped over the gunwale and made his way inside to where Mattituck was working the big charter boat away from the dock.

"You look kinda rough this morning," Mattituck teased.

"Didn't sleep well. Any coffee made?"

"What the hell kind of question is that?" Mattituck shot back with a grin.

Todd got himself a cup as they cleared the jetty and moved into the channel. Mattituck pushed the twin throttles forward, and the boat lurched forward. Then Todd felt the DeeVee8's hull lift up out of the water as she got up on step.

"Same place?" Mattituck asked.

"What?"

"On Hinchinbrook. Same place we landed before?"

Todd nodded.

"Damn, you did have a rough night," Mattituck said, concern rising.

"Just thinking about this case."

"What about it?"

"Something's not adding up. There's a pattern here we're missing."

Mattituck waited, but the seasoned lawman didn't elaborate.

"Maybe we just don't have enough pulled together yet."

Todd looked at him. Mattituck was right. He nodded.

"You're right. I always get this way when there are pieces that aren't falling into neat little places. And god knows this world ain't made up of things in neat little places."

That was all they said for the rest of the two-hour journey to Hinchinbrook. The waters were calm and there were few boats on the water. The skies were clear and the temperature was a perfect 73. Even Hinchinbrook Entrance, which they had to traverse to get to the bay called Port Etches, was relatively calm.

They eased into the lagoon and beached the DeeVee8 in the same spot they had been the day before and readied their gear.

Within ten minutes, they were well on their way back up the ravine toward the site where Justin Harris had died, with Todd leading the way and as quiet as Mattituck had ever seen him.

For the rest of the morning, Monica tried focusing on the more mundane tasks she had on the docket for clients: the will of an aging couple that needed to be updated, the contract for a hair salon she represented that wanted to expand into doing nails and massages as well, but were having problems with a landlord who objected to what he considered a shady business.

"You don't know what them ladies are *really* doing in them massage rooms," the conservative old man had complained.

But none of this kept her mind completely distracted from the Tara Garrett case. She kept thinking about the potentially complicated mess Justin Harris' death might bring with the divorce, but worse yet the apparent fighting Tara was having with her husband. Monica's work with the divorce preparation recently had been more focused on the business side, trying to sift through what steps in the expansion had been solely Wilson's work and what had been in clear partnership with Tara. The man did have a tendency at times to work on his own, with no documents showing that Tara had any knowledge of his wheeling and dealing.

That was one leg in the basis for the divorce, according to Tara. She wanted to build a case that would support Tara's claims that Wilson frequently worked without her knowledge, putting the company at risk. One of the key pieces to this was Wilson's planned expansion into the Seattle area. He had wanted to break into the Lower 48 market, and Seattle was the place to do it. He had a business plan that branded AK Outfitters as the premier outdoor clothing and supply retailer.

But Tara opposed it, almost vehemently. And her Dad, who had been the source of nearly all the money Tara had, was behind her one hundred percent. And Tara's money had been the entire bankroll for the stores from the first day opening the first store in Cordova. While Wilson argued it was his business savvy that had built the company to its now five stores, there were enough documents and emails showing that she had played a significant role in most of the expansion. Significant enough to position her—along with the original bankrolling—to retain full ownership, although it meant buying out his share.

But two key expansion moves had almost no evidence of Tara's involvement: Anchorage, which was now generating nearly 47% of the company revenues, and Seattle, which was still in the planning phase.

Monica had been staring out the big window of her office at the ravine leading up toward Eyak Lake. The low grey overcast featured wisps of mist that ran slowly along the tree tops on the mountains on either side, giving Monica the sensation of floating in a dream.

She turned and pulled the Garrett files from a file drawer, thumbing through documents until she came to the Anchorage and Seattle proposals. Everything seemed pretty normal. Emails negotiating some aspects of deals, others arranging business meetings. And a few signed agreements, non-binding in terms of closing deals, but to clarify how they would proceed.

She shuffled the emails to the side and focused on the agreements. For the Anchorage deals, every signature was Wilson's, without an exception. She turned to the Seattle documents and found the same.

One document's signature stopped her for a moment.

Was that Wilson's signature? It looked different. Monica leaned in, peering intently. The loop on the

"L" and those at the tops of the "t's" in Garrett swooped wider than on the other documents.

She pulled documents from the Anchorage file as well. On every document, the loops on the "L" in Wilson and the "t's" in Garrett were so narrow there was barely white space in the middle. All except that one document.

The anomaly document was a formal letter. She read through it closely. It delineated the terms that had been discussed, then added a "deal breaker" clause involving the building under consideration, located in a prominent spot off I-5 and the major boulevard leading to Safeco Field, where the Mariners played baseball, and CenturyLink Field, where the Seahawks football team played. The clause required that the building be brought beyond code requirements to "like new" conditions, and included the parking lot.

Monica shook her head. What building lessor would agree to such terms?

And why the anomaly in the signatures?

# Chapter Eleven

## Boots and Vests

Todd and Mattituck paused half way up the ravine and took stock of where they were. Todd consulted the topographical map while Mattituck took a long drink out of his water bottle.

"I think this is the area where we stopped," Todd said, scrutinizing the map.

Mattituck looked around at the ridges on either side. He nodded.

"Yeah, just about." He walked off the game trail past a low line of scrub brush. "It's either really close, or this other set of tracks runs all the way up."

Todd's head jerked up.

"Those other boot tracks?"

"Yeah," Mattituck said, pointing at the ground.

Todd stood and joined him.

"I'm not sure what to make of these," he said, crouching for a better look.

"Hard to make out?"

"No," Todd said. "I mean I'm not sure what to make of their being here. If there were two sets, that would be one thing, but it's clear that there are two sets down there, and one up here."

"Three people," Mattituck said.

Todd squinted up at him. "Exactly. And we both know this is no territory to be out in alone."

"So either there was a third member in the party—"

"Or they had company they didn't know about."

"Well," Mattituck sighed looking up the ravine toward the accident scene, "you said yesterday that you thought we'd find something up there. Let's go find out what."

Todd grimaced and nodded. He turned and led the way up the game trail.


It only took a little over two hours to reach the scene, in large part due to the fast pace they kept all the way up the ravine. Mattituck had never been there, and Todd had only seen it from the helicopter, so they almost passed it before the orange triangle marker the Coast Guardsmen left behind caught their attention. Todd changed direction toward a mish-mash of foliage comprised of the standard scrub brush and tall spruce.

Followed by Mattituck, Todd stepped through a break in the scrub and trees and paused, looking down. Mattituck stopped beside him.

The gravel and dirt ground was stained black by Justin Harris' blood where the man had been shot. It was always a sobering moment, staring down at blood-soaked earth, knowing a person had suffered their last few moments of life there. Mattituck wondered what it was like, those last few moments. A slow, cold slipping into foggy thoughts and physical fatigue, he imagined. Nobody knew, of course. And he knew from experience that watching it happen shed absolutely no light on the subject.

He stepped back a moment and looked back down the ravine, more to break his thoughts than to see anything.

"You okay?" Todd asked.

Mattituck nodded. "Yeah, I'm fine."

Todd watched him for a moment. His head jerked down in a quick nod.

"Here's what I'm wondering," he said. He gestured around the area, indicating a fair distance out from where they were. "One of the bullets went in the victim's shoulder, back here," he indicated a spot over his left shoulder, outside the shoulder blade. "And it came out the front, here," he pointed to a spot just under the collar bone.

He looked meaningfully at Mattituck before going on. Mattituck stood patiently waiting.

"But the second wound, the one that apparently killed him, entered in the front and exited the back. It entered here," he said, pointing to a spot left-of-center at his heart, "and went straight through and exited the back."

Mattituck's brow furrowed.

"How's that happen?" he asked. "From the back and then the front? How's that possible?"

Todd shrugged. "You tell me."

Mattituck thought for a moment.

"Two different shooters? I mean, two different people firing from different directions?"

Todd shook his head. "Probably not, although you see that with some gang shootings. I don't think this was a gang execution, though."

"The one in the back was the first shot," Mattituck said, thinking, "then the one to the heart." He was quiet a moment, then said, "would that shot to the back be enough to spin a guy around?"

Todd grinned.

"You are one astute civic cop," he said. "Spot on. And notice it's out from the body's center of gravity. So you get shot this far out your shoulder with a high powered rifle, and it could spin you around."

Mattituck listened, watching the Trooper. But Todd said nothing more.

"Okay, and then what?"

Todd looked around, then back at Mattituck.

"Well, that's the mystery."

Mattituck looked around, listening to the breeze as it drew through the needles of the spruce over them.

"How about a wild idea?" he finally asked.

"Shoot," Todd returned.

"What if the first shot wasn't an accident?"

"Okay," Todd said. "What if it wasn't?"

Mattituck was emboldened.

"So for whatever reason, maybe Wilson wants to take Justin out. Takes him out on this hunting trip, and then shoots him. But he's off center with the shot."

"But the first one downed Justin," Todd proffered. "Maybe Wilson shot him in the back, and the shot spun him and dropped him."

Mattituck picked this up and continued. "Justin isn't moving, so Wilson's not sure. He comes down to check on Justin. Sees he's still alive."

"What do you do in a case like that?" Todd added. "You have to finish him."

"Yes, you do. So you step in close and take a sure shot where you know it will finish him."

"Exactly," Todd said. "And at close range. But you said 'he comes down,' meaning Wilson comes down after the first shot. Comes down from where?"

Mattituck hadn't been thinking anything in particular, but Todd was right. He must have had something in mind.

"Well," he started, "I guess I just assumed he'd be on higher ground."

"I agree."

They both looked across the ravine. There was plenty of cover about a hundred feet up the opposite slope.

"And," Todd continued, "the close range would be right about . . ." he pointed to a spot down from the scrub brush cover a hundred feet up the opposite side, "right about there."

Mattituck stepped to where he indicated.

"There's quite a few boot prints here," he said.

Todd joined him. "All those Coasties stomping around during the medevac. Too many boot prints around here," he said, turning around and around to survey the area.

He stopped and thought.

"But," he said finally, "if we're right, then there would be boot prints coming down from up there."

They both walked around the boot-printed area and rejoined where they ended. Todd crouched, then moved up the hillside. He stopped and took a series of pictures with his cell phone.

"Boot prints?" Mattituck asked.

"Yep."

"Pointed downward?"

Todd looked up at him. "Say. . . . you are getting good."

Mattituck smiled.

"Yes," Todd said, "and plenty of good ones for a cast."

He stepped to the side and lowered the pack with his crime scene kit to the ground. He rummaged through and pulled out a plaster cast kit, then went to work mixing the powder with water from his water bottle. He then poured it over one of the boot prints and stood up.

"Takes a few minutes for that to harden."

"That's like out of an old Kojak episode or something," Mattituck teased. "What good's that do?"

"Kojak wouldn't do this. Maybe Cannon or Columbo."

Mattituck shook his head.

"Cannon was too fat to bend over for that," he said.

They both burst into laughter. It was familiar to Mattituck, the act of making light of a serious situation. He'd seen it many times in combat. 'Psychological dissonance,' the psychoanalysts had called it. The mirth left him and he turned and stretched, his back to Todd.

Behind him, Todd was still chuckling.

"Seriously, though," Todd said. "It may not help at all. But if we find a boot from a suspect, we can use this cast to match it up."

Mattituck turned to him.

"Are you thinking this really was an intentional killing?"

"It's my job to think every possibility," Todd said.

Mattituck nodded, then started up the hill to the clearing they'd spotted, careful not to defile the boot prints already there. When he reached the scrub brush and circled around it, he nodded to himself.

"We're right!" he shouted back down to Todd, who was now removing the cast from the ground. "Boot prints all over here."

"Okay!" Todd hollered back. "I'll come up and take some pictures in a few minutes."

Mattituck wandered the area, noting that the boot prints came from the trail below, down the ravine. He also noted that they didn't deviate at all, as though the walker knew exactly where he was going. This in itself didn't mean anything. Many hunters picked a spot to hide and wait well in advance and went straight to it. But it also fit the scenario of a killer taking position to take out his victim.

He stopped fifty feet across the hill, surveying the ravine. He raised his hand to his brow to shade his eyes, peering to a spot across the ravine, but a distance up from where Justin Harris had been shot. He checked his footing then strode at a good clip down the slope, to the bottom and up the other side. When he reached the point he'd spotted, he stopped and leaned to the low brush in front of him.

He rose and turned toward Todd, down the slope.

"Hey, Todd! I think you should see this!"

Todd straightened from packing away the fresh cast.

"What's up?"

"Were Justin and Wilson wearing hunting vests?"

Todd peered up at him.

"Only Wilson. Justin wasn't wearing one. Supposedly, he preferred not to wear one."

Todd was now marching up the slope toward him.

"Well, quite a coincidence that one is tucked into this brush, then."

Todd reached his side.

"Well, I'll be damned. You'll make one helluva fucking great detective yet," he said, smiling sideways at his deputized partner.

He pulled latex gloves from his pocket and snapped them on, then reached into the branches. He pulled out the orange vest. Once it was free of the branches and leaves, Todd spread the cloth out to inspect it.

Both Todd and Mattituck froze. On the left front, there were two bullet holes, matching the area Justin had sustained the shots that had taken his life.

Todd and Mattituck had spent two more hours scouring the area for additional evidence and clues, but nothing more had emerged. Todd had placed the orange vest in a large evidence bag, and secured the casts of boot tracks in his pack, and they headed back down the ravine.

After they had returned to the DeeVee8 and nosed the charter boat out to open water, their conversation turned to what they had discovered.

"So," Mattituck began, "how does a dying man take off his hunting vest, run it seventy-five to a hundred yards away, and then shove it into the bushes?"

"Well," Todd returned, sarcastic humor in his tone, "if a guy's desperate to disguise his own murder . . . you know . . ."

Mattituck grinned as he steered the DeeVee8 left toward Hinchinbrook Entrance, where they would turn back right, to the north, to round the north side of the island back to Cordova.

"What are you making of all this?" Mattituck asked in conclusion.

"That we don't have a mere hunting accident on our hands."

"And Wilson Garrett is looking pretty guilty?"

"Yep," Todd said. "Leaving us with the question of why." He was silent a moment as he watched the towering sandstone pillars—a well-known landmark in Port Etches—slip along the starboard side. "And, of course, cautioning ourselves that very often things aren't what they seem."

Mattituck shot a quick glance toward Todd.

"Meaning?"

"Meaning that while it's clear Justin Harris couldn't have been shot to near-death, then walked his vest up the hillside . . . it isn't clear that Wilson Garrett did or didn't do."

Mattituck turned to look at Todd, annoyed.

"Well, who the hell did walk that vest up there, then? It was only two of them on that hunting trip."

Todd shook his head.

"Nope. You're forgetting about that third set of boot prints down the ravine."

Mattituck straightened with a jerk.

"Right," he said, his ire quickly gone. "I'd forgotten about those. So . . . they weren't alone?"

"I don't know. Maybe. But now it's our job to find out."

Mattituck's eyes were fixed on the water ahead, sliding under the bow of the DeeVee8 at about 32 knots. His mind wandered over the facts of the case as they understood it so far.

"I'm guessing," he said to Todd, "that we can't really count on being done with the evidence. I mean, maybe new things are going to turn up."

Todd nodded acknowledgement, his eyes set on the waters ahead.

"That's the nature of the business," he said. "We have to stay open to new facts as they emerge."

"But right now," Mattituck asked, "your best guess is maybe foul play on Wilson's part?"

"As one possibility," Todd answered. "And another that somebody else was up there with them."

Mattituck mulled all this over.

"But one thing's for sure," he said with finality.

"What's that?" Todd asked after waiting for him to continue.

"That this wasn't an accident."

Todd grimaced and nodded.

"Yep. That and we keep our mouths shut about this until we can piece more together."

Mattituck nodded agreement.

"Where to now?" he asked.

"Valdez," Todd said. "I need to check in all this evidence and catch up the logs."

"Not back to Cordova?"

"Nope." He glanced at his friend. "Not to worry, though. We'll need to get back down here pretty quickly. Most of our investigation is in Cordova." He eyed the weathered charter boat skipper. "You'll get to see your woman soon enough."

Mattituck turned the trooper a scolding but guilty look.

"Need me in Valdez?" Mattituck asked.

"Yes, actually. You're making yourself too damned useful," the Trooper said.

"Good," Mattituck replied. "I kinda like helping out."

"Got any charters coming up?"

"Always, but I'll have Hank and Earl cover them. Earl's quiet on the Kimberly Marie for another 10 days."

Todd was looking at him.

"You really trust him, don't you?"

"Earl? He's a good man, Todd. And he's keeping clean, especially on the job." He steered the DeeVee8 around a deadhead bobbing in the water. "But I am going to move Hank to the DeeVee8 and put Earl on the Knot Skunked. Best to give him the easier to handle boat."

Todd watched him, knowing it had a lot more to do with Hank's proven ability to handle a boat, and that the DeeVee8 was Mattituck's baby.

"I'm surprised you're letting anybody run the DeeVee8," Todd said.

"You should be feeling privileged," Mattituck returned without looking. "It's more about how much I'm enjoying this sleuthing around."

Todd grinned and peered out at the water moving under the bow.

# Chapter Twelve

## Fresh Waters

Monica Castle sat at the Cove's Café under a clear vinyl roof covering the deck where her table was. She picked at her salad, listening to the rain pelt the corrugated vinyl, her thoughts lingering over the contradictory documents she'd found in Tara Garrett's files. She wanted to ask her about them, but something held her back. There was something about the woman that wasn't quite sitting well with Monica.

Of course, she was a seasoned enough attorney to be skeptical of most of her clients whenever something didn't seem to add up in their stories. Any good attorney had that reaction. It didn't change how a good lawyer represented her client, of course, but you also couldn't ignore the facts.

Especially when they might put you in a dilemma.

The possible dilemma for Monica was that if Tara had forged that document, then she was committing fraud. And if that fraud drove the case, in particular Monica's representation of Tara, then Monica had an obligation under the bar ethics code to decline further representation.

"Hey, Monica Castle!"

She turned to see Betty Ingram smiling broadly at her. The older woman was third generation Cordova, and the town gossip, in Monica's opinion. But like so many others, she loved the woman anyhow.

"Hi, Betty," she said, inviting her to sit.

"Monica," Betty started with her knowing tone, "word is that you've been seen with a new man."

"New man? He's the first and only in a long time, Betty."

"Oh, now . . . no need to get prudish with me, Monica. I knew your Mom and Dad, you know."

"Yes, I know."

"I knew you when you were in preschool, for Jiminey's sake!"

"Frank is a good man, Betty. And it doesn't much matter if people are talking about it."

"Well, you know how people are!" Betty declared loudly, gesturing to everybody seated on the deck as though implicating them.

"More than I care to, yes, I do," Monica returned with a sardonic grin.

"People sleeping around," Betty continued, not hearing her, "cheating on their husbands, even. Like that store owner's wife, what's his name? The one who owns that outfitter store. . . ."

Monica suppressed any reaction. Wilson and Tara Garrett, Betty was referring to. Was the affair known?

"AK Outfitter?"

"That's the one!" Betty blurted. "AK Outfitters. Yep, that's the one. The wife of that poor man, running around with that boyfriend of hers behind his back—"

"Running around? Betty, really," Monica's voice took on a lecturing tone. "If that were the case, there'd be a divorce underway." Never mind that there actually was, Monica thought to herself.

"Well, not always. There was the Campbell divorce a few years back, for example, where . . ."

Betty's voice droned on and on, and Monica tuned her out. She hoped this rumor wasn't widespread, although there was little doubt that it had to be, if Betty had picked it up. Or, more accurately, if Betty was on it then the rumor was no doubt already widespread.

"Listen, Betty. Great to see you, but I need to run."

"Oh . . . well, all righty then. You take care, dear!"

Monica returned the nicety and ran through the heavy rain to her car.

Mattituck and Todd Benson made it to Valdez in less than three hours, pulling into the boat harbor just before 6:00pm.

"Hungry?" Todd asked.

"We haven't eaten since breakfast," Mattituck replied. "Crow's Nest?"

"I was thinking more along the lines of Bella Luna."

Mattituck didn't respond for a moment as he turned the DeeVee8 tightly into the channel between the breakwater walls leading into the marina.

"What's Keri up to?" he asked absently.

Todd didn't look at him. He shifted his weight to his left foot and continued gazing out the starboard window.

"Not sure," he said finally. "I think she's on shift."

Mattituck didn't look at Todd, but kept his eyes on the narrow passage into the boat harbor. He wanted to say 'not sure?' but he didn't dare. His thoughts drifted back to the previous days and the tension between Todd Benson and his wife. But Todd said nothing further.

"Sure," Mattituck said. "Bella Luna sounds good. I'm sure Pappy's got something good on."

"I'll get these items checked in at the station and meet you there," Todd said.

"Sounds good."

Mattituck worked the DeeVee8 into her slip, and Todd exited the cabin to hop on the dock, moving quickly to secure the lines. Mattituck cut the engines and helped offload their gear and the evidence.

"I'm going to do a quick wash down here while you do your thing," Mattituck said. "I'll meet you there in about a half hour?"

Todd nodded, shouldering his packs and turning toward the ramp up to shore.

Mattituck had thought about running home to take a quick shower before going into Pappy's restaurant, but it would have taken too long. Instead, he walked across from the harbor and entered the Bella Luna, noting that once again, it was packed with several people waiting at the hostess station. He stepped over to put in his name, looking down to make sure he didn't step on any feet.

When he looked up to put his name in, he was met with Izzy Giovanni's warm brown eyes. He shifted uncomfortably and wished that Todd were with him.

"Hello, Mr. Mattituck." Her alto voice made him think of the myth of the sirens. She was in the hostess role tonight, apparently, as she wasn't in the wait staff's white shirt and black skirts or trousers. She was in a dress that showed off her smoothly clear olive-skinned shoulders and accentuated her form.

"Hi, um, Izzy?"

Her red lipsticked mouth curled at the edges and her eyes narrowed in a warm smile.

"Yes, it's Izzy," she said. "Are you . . . alone?" she asked, looking around behind him, eyebrows raised.

"No," he nearly stammered, "I mean, yes, for the moment, but a friend will be joining me quickly."

"A female friend?" she asked.

Mattituck's brow drew together. "How's that?"

She laughed lightly, the smooth sound of her voice coming through the sound.

"I only mean to ask so that I can give you the best table for a date." Her head turned downward toward the table graph, but her eyes remained on his face, achieving a demure effect.

"No, no date," he said tightly.

Her face turned back fully to his.

"I see," she said, holding her eyes on his. "So a table for just you and a . . . friend."

Mattituck was visibly confused.

Izzy laughed lightly, and Mattituck tried to chuckle along.

"I do not mean to make you uncomfortable, Mr. Mattituck."

Mattituck's mouth opened to reply, then closed.

"No, no," he said awkwardly. "I'm not uncomfortable."

"This way," she said grabbing two menus and turning to lead him through the tables. "I assume Pappy doesn't know you were coming tonight?" she said over her bare shoulder, her head tilted again in a suggestive manner.

"No, I just came in from the Sound," he said, skirting through the tables less gracefully than Izzy.

"I'll let him know you're here. Would you like some wine? I know an excellent malbec."

"Um, sure," he said. "That'd be great."

"Here we are."

She pulled the chair at a two-person table back for him, then set the menus over each place setting. Mattituck moved to step around behind her, but she moved back into him. It was an awkward moment that again caught Mattituck off guard. She looked back at him and smiled. He placed his hands on her shoulders to move her forward so he could continue around to his seat. She didn't move for a full two seconds, then stepped to the side. Time seemed to stand still a moment, and all Mattituck could think was about how to get away from her. Quickly, he lurched to get past her, taking his hands off her shoulders and sliding past her in the narrow space. Finally, he lowered himself into the chair with relief.

Izzy remained standing in front of him, her breasts protruding firmly at his eye level. He looked up at her, only to find her lips pursed at him in a feigned pout.

"Mr. Mattituck—"

"That malbec would be great," he interrupted, regaining his composure.

"I—"

"Yes, bring another glass for my friend, although he'll probably opt for an Alaskan Amber instead," he said, turning his attention to the menu.

He was relieved when he sensed her turn and move away toward the front of the restaurant. There had been a time when he would have enjoyed this kind of attention, particularly from a woman like Izzy. But now it only made him uncomfortable. He wished he hadn't come to the Bella Luna, or that Monica had been with him.

He was scanning the list of stuffed pasta when the table moved under his hands. He lowered the menu expecting to see Todd on the other side of the table, but the soft brown eyes and full-lipped Izzy was gazing at him instead, a smile again at the corners of her mouth.

"I'm on break," she announced, "but I thought I'd deliver the wine nonetheless."

It was like a game of chess, this back-and-forth with her. And Mattituck didn't like games. He suppressed a rising irritation, thinking of his friend Pappy Amatucci.

Izzy reached out with her hand, slipping it into his on the table. He felt the other hand on the inside of his forearm. At the same moment, she leaned forward, allowing her breasts to rest on the edge of the table in a way that forced the tops of the mounds to swell up into the low cut of her dress. The gesture simultaneously highlighted her breasts, smooth complexion, and the line of her collarbone.

Mattituck pulled his hand out of hers, his head moving back and forth in a negative gesture.

"I'm not interested," he said.

"You can be if you like," she returned before he went on.

"No," he said, his voice firmer. "I can't."

"You mean you won't," she said, allowing the Italian female irritation to show.

He paused a moment.

"Yes," he said. "That's right. I won't. Like I said, I'm not interested."

The finality in his voice made her rise abruptly and stride away in one smooth movement, swaying the back of the dress in a way that made several watch her.

A woman at a table across the aisle had her cell phone poised in his direction, her eyes watching Izzy retreat toward the hostess station. When she looked back, her eyes met Mattituck's and she immediately blushed, putting the phone away.

Mattituck's gaze moved back to the front of the restaurant, where he saw Todd picking his way through the tables.

*About damn time*, he thought.

"Sorry it took so long," Todd said as he sat across from Mattituck.

"It's okay. Just left me to the fucking sharks is all."

Todd's eyes jumped up to him.

"What's that mean?"

Mattituck shifted in his seat.

"Nothing. I ordered a bottle of malbec," he said.

"I see that. I prefer—"

"Alaskan Amber. Yeah, I alerted the hostess."

"You okay?"

Mattituck looked up from the menu. He realized then that irritability had shone through.

"Yeah. I guess. Sorry. I'm just annoyed."

"With what?" Todd said, perusing the menu. "I said I'm sorry for being late."

"No," Mattituck returned. "You're fine. You need to get shit done. It's nothing. Forget about it."

Todd watched him a moment, then returned to the menu. A moment later, Izzy was at the table, much cooler in her demeanor than she had been a few minutes earlier. Mattituck took a breath, relieved of the awkwardness. Coldness was familiar ground.

"Something to drink?" she said to Todd.

Todd was already staring at her. He watched her face before a quick downward glance took in her form. He drew deep air.

Mattituck hadn't missed this, also taking in the shift in Izzy as she noticed Todd appreciating her. She glanced at Mattituck with a hint of satisfaction, as if to say 'see what you missed?'

He only turned his attention back to the menu, leaving Izzy to whatever pleased her, so long as it had nothing to do with him.

"What would you like, sir?" she asked Todd.

There was a pause.

"What are you offering?"

Mattituck inwardly rolled his eyes.

"For the moment, the menu," she said, the alto seduction back in her voice. Mattituck could feel her eyes on him. He turned his attention to the dessert menu.

"That makes me look forward to post-menu," Todd said to Izzy.

Again, a pause, which Mattituck imagined from behind the menu as being filled with meaningful gazes back and forth. He wanted to excuse himself.

"First things first," Izzy returned. "Would you like an appetizer?"

Mattituck braced himself.

"Well . . ." Todd started.

"Cut it, for fuck's sake," Mattituck snapped, lowering his menu.

Izzy's and Todd's heads both turned in surprise.

"Just order your food," Mattituck said with a growl.

Izzy smiled. Mattituck knew she was thinking she'd made him jealous. Another indicator of how far off she was with him.

"Look," he said suddenly, "how about you two get on with it. I have things to do." He looked at Izzy. "I'll have the tortellini to go."

Izzy was taken aback. Mattituck's irritation and rebuffs, she was realizing, were genuine. He really wasn't interested. That woman he'd been with must really be something, she thought. This man was obviously well within the clutch of that woman's talons.

"All right, Mr. Mattituck," she said, her tone placating. "I'm sorry if I—"

"Don't worry about it," he interrupted.

Todd sat looking at him in a curious silence.

"My uncle wanted to see you," she added.

"He'll see me another time," Mattituck said, his voice firm and even.

Izzy turned for the kitchen and disappeared.

"What's eating you?" Todd asked.

"Your bullshit."

"What?"

"Fuck, Todd. You're married, and this fucking floozy is sucking you right in."

Todd tensed.

"You don't know how it is," he said.

"Maybe not," Mattituck said. "But that's not—"

"She wants to leave me."

That stopped Mattituck.

"She what? Who?"

"Keri," Todd answered. "She wants a divorce."

Mattituck was silent. He wasn't easily surprised, but this surprised him.

"Keri?" he finally managed.

Todd nodded, his head low. He glanced around to see if anybody had overheard him. It was a small town, with small town gossip.

"Fuck. I'm sorry. I had no idea."

Todd shook his head.

"It's okay," he said. "It's been a long time coming."

"When did this happen?"

"I went home for a quick shower. We got into it. Me not being like I used to be. Me not calling when away. Me being cool and stand-offish. Me, me, me. You know. The usual. Everything's all my fault."

He was quiet for several moments. Mattituck waited, not knowing what to say. Everything that came to mind seemed hollow and shallow.

Todd's eyes met his. "Only this time," he said, "she says it's over. She says it's all an indication that we're done."

Mattituck thought about all this. "She seemed fine the other day on the boat," he said.

"Yeah, well, apparently she wasn't. She hasn't been for a long time." He looked at Mattituck. "Honestly, neither have I."

He let that sink in.

"So," he went on, "you see why maybe a hot lady like that . . ."

"Yeah," Mattituck said sullenly. "I get it. Listen, I don't judge. Do whatever you do. Just give me a heads up on when you want to head back south."

Todd watched his friend for several minutes before responding.

"Okay. Will do. I'm thinking in the morning we head back down."

Mattituck nodded.

"Franky Mattituck!" came Pappy's voice as he approached their table. "How things are?"

"Good, good, Pappy," Mattituck returned. "Only I need to run. I ordered—"

"Yes, yes, I know, I know," the older man said. "My niece, she tells me. I have right here," he said, holding out a square Styrofoam take-out box. "Your tortellini. With a little something for you on the side— your favorite, the meatballs," he said with satisfaction, referring to his popular specialty. The meatballs had been the start of Pappy's success at the Bella Luna.

Pappy held the box to Mattituck.

"Thank you, Pappy. And the check?"

"Check?!" Pappy's voice rose. "There is no check! You go. Enjoy!"

Mattituck nodded.

"Thank you, Pappy."

"I walk you to door, yes?"

Mattituck nodded, turning back to Todd. "7:00 departure?"

Todd nodded. "Sure. You have charters on your boat, so we'll take AST 32067. Meet me there."

"Okay," Mattituck confirmed.

Pappy waited until they were clear of the table before speaking.

"My niece," he started. "You don't like her?"

Mattituck watched him as he followed the older man through the dining room.

"Why do you ask?"

"Because," Pappy said. "She is a nice girl. Very sweet. And beautiful, yes?" he glanced back at Mattituck.

"Yes, she is. But Pappy, I'm very happy with Monica. You know that."

Pappy continued several steps, then stopped at the front door, handing Mattituck the box.

"But I am saying, she is very nice girl. And beautiful. A dream by most men's thinking, yes?"

"Maybe so, Pappy. But I'm not most men."

He took the box and pushed the door open, not looking to see how Pappy responded to that.

Outside, the light was fading as the sun dropped below the mountains to the west. He closed his eyes a moment and breathed in the salt air, intermingled with a tinge of post-spawned salmon. He drew several crisp breaths, slowly, imagining the air passing through the tubes to his lungs. He stood still, imagining the lungs themselves filling and expanding with the cool Alaska air. He opened his eyes and let his eyes take in the beauty of the scene before him.

The heat of the tortellini through the box pulled him back into the moment, and he turned toward his truck.

# Chapter Thirteen

## False Appearances

When Todd and Mattituck headed out of Valdez in the State Trooper boat, AST 32067, there was an awkward silence. They exchanged enough words to cast off and get the boat underway, but nothing else had passed between them other than the cup of coffee Mattituck had brought for Todd in a gesture of goodwill.

Todd was in his uniform, but he looked a bit rough, as though he hadn't slept much. Mattituck didn't ask; he didn't really want to know. Whether it was a night with Izzy Giovanni, or a night of fighting with Keri, Mattituck didn't want to know. He sat in the passenger seat and watched the oil terminal across the bay from Valdez as it slid behind them.

It wasn't until they had reached Tatitlek Narrows, nearly an hour out of Valdez, that the silence was broken.

"Nothing happened," Todd said.

Mattituck looked at him. Todd met his gaze.

"Nothing happened with the hostess," he said again.

Mattituck shrugged. "Why would that matter to me?"

Todd's eyes returned to the water ahead.

"Just making sure."

"Well," Mattituck said. "Be sure. I would never do that to Monica."

Todd glanced at him.

"Any good guy will say that," he said, "but a lot of guys might be thinking different inside."

Mattituck sipped down the last of his coffee and continued looking at the town of Tatitlek as they passed by.

"Well, I'm not 'a lot of guys'." He looked at Todd. "It's disturbing how often I have to say that."

A moment of silence passed.

"Well, you woke up in a good mood," Todd said.

"It's the weather," Mattituck quipped back.

Todd looked at the clear skies and noted the warm breeze coming through the side window, and decided to drop it. Whatever was eating Mattituck wasn't going to come out, apparently.

"I have a warrant to get into Justin Harris' place and search some things, including his computer," Todd said, changing the subject.

"You got that last night?"

Todd nodded.

"I called the judge after dinner, then spent the night in the station. It's adjacent to the firehouse, remember."

Mattituck did know this. It would have had a bed, shower, kitchen—probably even breakfast with the fire crew.

"Why are you telling me this?" he asked Todd.

Todd waited a moment before answering.

"I guess I want you to know. You should know who your partner is."

He looked over at Mattituck. The rugged charter boat captain was watching him, a hint of a smile in the corners of his eyes.

"Okay," Mattituck said.

Nothing else needed to be said.

Monica met them at the dock when they arrived in Cordova. Mattituck hopped off the boat with the bow line in hand, but postponed tying up the boat long enough to pull Monica in to him and hold her a moment, breathing in the scent of her hair. Then he broke away, Monica smiling broadly, and tied off the line to a cleat before running aft to secure the stern line. With the boat moored, he turned and gave Monica a proper greeting.

Todd stepped past them, greeting Monica as he headed up the dock toward shore.

"Guess he's anxious to get to work," Mattituck said.

"What do you have going? Must be pretty big if he had you come along. As his deputy, I take it?"

Mattituck nodded. "Guess so. He called me his partner on the way down."

Monica made an exaggerated face of being impressed.

"Look at you!" she said. "Moving up!"

He laughed.

"It actually feels good to be working on this stuff. Like I'm part of something bigger than . . ." his voice trailed off.

Monica waited, but didn't press when he didn't finish the sentence.

"Do you have time for breakfast?" she asked.

Mattituck looked at Todd's receding back.

"I'm going to guess no on that," he said.

"Lunch?"

"Don't know about lunch, but something for sure. Let me call you when I find out how things are going."

"Okay, what are you working on?"

"He has a warrant to search Justin Harris' place."

Monica was taken aback.

"Justin Harris' place?"

"You know—the guy who was shot the other day."

"Yeah, I know. But why a warrant to search his place?"

"Maybe I shouldn't be telling you this stuff, but it's you. We're thinking it wasn't an accident."

Monica was ashen.

"Not an accident?"

"Some things out on Hinchinbrook point to there being more to the story than a hunting accident."

Monica tried to take all this in. Immediately, her thoughts turned to Wilson and Tara's failing marriage and the growing animosity between them.

"You mean Wilson might have shot him?"

Mattituck was looking at her, trying to read her, but she couldn't tell what he might be thinking.

"You know Wilson's name but not Justin's?" he asked.

"What?" Monica was confused. "What are you talking about?"

"You didn't know who Justin Harris was, but you know Wilson Garrett's name."

"Oh . . . no, I didn't say I didn't know Justin Harris' name. I was just surprised." Her eyes were on his face, but her mind was racing over the implications of all this. "I wonder what Tara knows about all this."

"Tara?" Mattituck said, surprised. "Wilson's wife? What does she have to do with anything? I mean, besides that she's Wilson's wife."

Monica's focus came back to him.

"Oh, I'm sorry," she said. "Tara's a client of mine."

"She is?" The surprise jolted Mattituck. "Why didn't you tell me?"

"Attorneys aren't in the habit of giving out lists of who they represent," she teased. "No, really, it just didn't cross my mind."

"Well, what are you representing her for?"

"Now that I can't tell you," she said with a smile.

"Client privilege?"

"Something like that."

"But you'd tell me if there was something related to what we're doing."

She shook her head. "Not likely. Even if it were pretty serious, I couldn't. Bar ethics," she added.

Mattituck nodded vaguely.

"Okay," he said. "Fair enough."

"Good," she said, then kissed him. "Todd can have you during the day, but you're mine tonight," she announced.

"Now that sets the day in the right direction," he returned.

After Todd and Mattituck drove away in the new State Trooper cruiser, Monica stood watching the car depart. She hoped she'd concealed the unease she'd been feeling since the warrant had been mentioned. She had been dying to ask what they'd found on Hinchinbrook that made them think that Justin Harris' death wasn't an accident, but she dared not probe too far. In fact, she was now feeling that she and Frank shouldn't talk about anything touching on the incident—at all. Doing so could put her at risk of revealing something about her client, or might contribute to what already was feeling a bit like a professional dilemma.

There was too much coincidence here for Monica's liking. The discovery of the potentially forged letter that ended the establishment of a new branch of AK Outfitters in Seattle had already launched Monica on thinking that something was amiss with Tara's stories, but the addition of this news was particularly disturbing. She told herself to be cool-minded about this, and not to jump onto threads of thought without any solid evidence for doing so. But she couldn't stop her mind lingering on it.

She turned to her car as her thoughts rambled, and headed for her office for the day's work. When she got there, she went straight to Tara's files to see if she had overlooked anything.

Of course she couldn't tell Frank anything about the case, but she wished she could. Not only might what he knew shed some light on her misgivings, but she had come to trust his judgment. And his intuition. For an outdoorsman who had dedicated his life to taking people fishing, he had an intellect and wisdom mixed with gut-instinct that she'd never seen before. And more times than not, it seemed, he was right on with whatever he pieced together.

But discussing the case with him was absolutely outside the ethical boundaries. She simply had to figure all this out on her own.

She went back to the letter with the possibly forged signature. The only way to know for sure would be to send it to a forensics lab for analysis. She thought it over, then made an electronic copy and wrote her contact at Seattle Forensics Lab to see if it was something they could analyze for her. Then she set to work looking through the rest of the documents she had in the file to see if anything else seemed odd.

As she did, she found herself wondering where Wilson Garrett was, and how he and Tara were faring. The last Tara had told her, Wilson had decided to stay at a hotel until things between them settled down.

Before she knew it, it was almost 1:00 p.m. and she hadn't heard from Frank. She decided to go to Latitude Six-Oh, named for the latitude of Cordova, and grab some lunch. She replaced all the files and locked the drawers—a precaution she had learned from her father. *You never know when somebody might wander into your office and see what's on your desk,* he used to say. And he was right. Anything was possible.

God knew she had learned that much in the decade she'd been practicing law.

It only took a few minutes to get to Latitude Six-Oh, and Monica found a front line parking spot right away. Her heart sank when she entered the restaurant's door, however. Standing right there, waiting to be seated was Betty Ingram. What were the odds of seeing her twice within three days?

"Oh, Monica Castle!" the woman blurted. "I've been dying to talk to you! Ever since I was in Valdez last night, I've been thinking about you."

The woman's face took on a concerned look.

"You poor dear," she said sadly.

"Poor dear?" Monica asked. "Why poor me?"

"Well," Betty started, glancing around her. "I really shouldn't say. I mean, what's not my business simply isn't my business."

*Like that's ever stopped you before,* Monica thought. Instead, though, she said, "What's going on, Betty? You can tell me."

The older woman pulled out her cell phone and went to work on the screen.

"Well," she started, "I was in Valdez visiting my sister yesterday, and she took me to dinner at this nice Italian place. You know the one, probably, right across from the marina? With the funny little Italian owner."

"Bella Luna?" Monica asked, thinking of the times she'd been there with Frank.

"That's it! That's the one! Well, I'm sitting there minding my own business, when I see your man come in."

"My man?"

"Frank what's-his-name? With the charter boat business. That is your man, isn't it?"

"Frank Mattituck? Yes, I guess you could say that."

"Monica, I'm so sorry, but you really should know." And with that, Betty opened the photos app on her phone and turned it to Monica. There was Frank, sitting at a table in Bella Luna, his hands entwined with a woman across the table from him. She was leaning in toward Frank with an inviting, engrossed expression.

Monica felt her breath catch.

Betty continued scrolling through a series of pictures, two or three of them, all showing Frank with this woman at the table. The woman was gorgeous, and in a dress that would knock any man over. And she filled it well. There was even a photo of the woman standing almost against Frank, her buttocks close to his crotch as she looked back at him, their eyes locked.

Monica closed her eyes.

"You took these last night?"

"I'm so sorry, dear," Betty said, almost regretfully.

When Monica merely stood still, her eyes focused on the floor, Betty gracefully stepped away without saying goodbye.

Monica was numb. She had lost her appetite. The day had been too much. She turned and made her way slowly to the car, then home. With no particular thoughts, she decided the day was finished. She didn't go back to the office, but instead went straight into the house, locked the door, and to her bedroom.

She didn't bother to undress. She simply crawled into bed and pulled the covers over, seeking a barrier between everything and herself.

Only a few times in her life had she felt utterly overwhelmed, but when she had, she found herself exhausted. And usually, after a good long sleep, things came into perspective.

That perspective, at least in the past, had always involved shedding the complications from her life.

Todd and Mattituck had spent the morning in Justin Harris' apartment, focused on the specific items listed on the warrant. Todd had warned Mattituck that they could not go looking for anything else. If they happened to come across something while investigating the items on the warrant, that was another matter. But they couldn't just go rummaging through the dead man's home.

During the search, they found credit card receipts for the Copper River Inn, but these revealed nothing they didn't already know—namely that he had spent a number of nights in that hotel rather than at home. But there was nothing that indicated who the woman was.

"I did a search of his cell phone calls and contacts," Todd had shared as they went about the search, "but there weren't that many contacts. It did look like there were a lot of calls to Wilson and Tara, but that's understandable given their friendships and the business."

Mattituck nodded.

"How many calls to Wilson compared to Tara?" he asked.

Todd answered without looking up from the mess of a filing system Justin kept.

"Close to the same number, maybe," he said. "I didn't count, but I'd guess maybe more to Wilson. Although one interesting thing. The calls to Tara were longer."

Mattituck stopped searching Justin's desk drawers and looked at him.

"Might not be odd," Todd said. "Women talk more than men do, so it makes sense those calls would be longer."

Mattituck shook his head.

"You don't agree?" Todd asked.

"Nope. And it should be noted," Mattituck said, mirth in his tone, "that the objective State Trooper just dropped a major sexism bomb."

"Fuck you," came Todd's reply.

"Seriously, though," Mattituck said. "I don't buy it."

"What don't you buy?"

"There's no reason Justin would need to talk to Tara a lot more than he did his best friend."

"Maybe he and Tara were close."

Mattituck looked up thoughtfully.

"Yeah," he said, grinning. "I kinda think they were close. Like, really close."

"You think they were having an affair?" Todd asked.

"Why not?"

*Why not indeed*? Todd thought. Then his thoughts turned to what it might mean if Tara Garrett and Justin Harris had been having an affair. What would happen if Wilson Garrett had found out? That would introduce an entirely new scenario to the death of Justin Harris.

He stood and stretched, then went to the window.

It might also explain why Justin had been shot in the back first, then the front. It would especially explain how the second shot to the heart had been at closer range and from a lower angle, as though Justin had been shot while lying down. Todd let these thoughts sink in.

But it would do nothing to explain the third set of boot prints they'd found on Hinchinbrook. The orange vest, perhaps, as Wilson might have ditched it to cover his story that Justin never wore a vest. But it wouldn't explain the third set of boots.

What if Tara were the third set of boots, though?

Todd mulled this over, mixing in the possibility of an affair. What if she and Justin had been planning to kill Wilson, and make it look like an accident? He quickly shoved this to the side of his thoughts; it seemed like a bit of a stretch to build an investigation on, but it was certainly worth keeping in mind.

"Let's get some lunch, shall we?" he asked Mattituck.

Mattituck quickly agreed, and they began wrapping up the scene. The computer would need to go to the Anchorage lab for searching, so they would confiscate that. Everything else had been searched and anything that was even remotely having a bearing on the case had been seized and sealed.

Todd's thoughts returned to the third set of boot prints. Was it possible those boots belonged to Tara Garrett?

He again dismissed the theory. It just didn't make sense. Why would Tara be out there tailing them? And why would she kill her lover? Even if she and Justin had been plotting to take Wilson out of the scene, it would be one hell of a coincidence that Wilson shot Justin just then. And if they had been in a scuffle, as in a botched murder attempt by Tara and Justin, wouldn't that be the first thing Wilson would say? Sure as hell, he wouldn't have hiked all the way to the lighthouse and claimed he accidentally shot Justin.

The only scenario left was even more remote, and that by a long way: Tara accidentally shot Justin thinking it was Wilson just at the same moment that Wilson fired his shot. Not very likely at all. And that's not even thinking through how the second shot could have happened.

Most importantly, what evidence was there that Tara and Justin had been having an affair? Little to none. In fact, it amounted to nothing more than a possible gut-instinct on Mattituck's part.

No, Todd thought, it had to be somebody else hiking behind Justin Harris and Wilson Garrett.

# Chapter Fourteen

## Departures

Mattituck had been sending texts to Monica all afternoon, but she hadn't replied. It was not at all like her. Well, that wasn't completely true. It was how she'd been the previous times they'd stopped seeing each other. But that wasn't the case here. Mattituck knew they were on a much better path than in those previous runs with their relationship. A lot of the garbage that had gotten in the way before was his own, and he since he'd put that aside—or most of it anyhow—they had found themselves in a much better place as a growing couple.

But then why was she not responding to his texts?

Sometimes she was busy with clients and it took a while to reply, but she always did. The afternoon was slipping away, and still not a word. This was not like her.

After wrapping up at Justin Harris' place just before 4:00 p.m., they loaded all the evidence being seized into the State Trooper cruiser and headed to the Cordova Police station to package it all for shipment. It was tedious work, this search and seizure stuff, but Mattituck understood it was all part of the job. Particularly in today's world, where every "T" needed to be crossed and every "I" dotted, they had to be meticulous about how items were handled, packaged, and sealed.

"I'll be flying to Anchorage with all this stuff," Todd announced as they sealed the last box. "I have to be there to check it all in. It's not always necessary, but I really want to be there when they dig into his computer."

"Should be interesting," Mattituck agreed.

Todd gave an impressed look. "Those computer forensics guys really know what they're doing," he said. "I've seen them dig stuff out that people thought they'd killed and buried, let alone deleted."

Mattituck nodded.

"Would you mind running the boat back up to Valdez?" Todd asked.

"I can fly back. Or see if Earl's down this way with the Kimberly Marie."

"Your choice," Todd said, lifting the last box over to the top of a stack ready to go.

"Do all those go in the cargo space?" Mattituck asked vaguely.

"Yeah, but I have to watch them load and then see the cargo door closed. Then on the other side, they can't open it until I'm there to observe."

"Really?"

Todd nodded.

"No wonder the luggage is sometimes late to baggage claim."

Todd chuckled.

"Best part of it," he said, "is that I get to fly first class. They want me off the plane quick so they can open the cargo hold."

"How about I escort the evidence sometime?" Mattituck asked with a smile.

"We'll see. Maybe if you're a good boy. Let's get this stuff loaded up. The plane leaves in a little over an hour."

After Mattituck saw Todd off at the airport, he drove the State Trooper vehicle back to town, trying again to contact Monica. He was getting worried now. This was not at all like her. He decided to try calling her on the way back into town, sure that she had been busy all day and perhaps had forgotten to reply to his texts.

When she didn't reply, he decided to swing by her house and make sure she was okay. The Roadhouse brought a smile to his face as he cruised past, thinking of the little scuffle a few days before. Then the Copper River Inn came into view, and he thought of the previous year when he and Todd had been chasing that crazy killer with the drug ring.

The thought of that guy sobered Mattituck's thoughts. He was as ruthless as they came. Mattituck had learned about all the killings the man had committed in those few short weeks, including the brutal murder of two sets of older folks. There was still some mystery about that guy, but he and Todd had come across what they were sure was the same guy while working the Ned Simmons murder. There was really no question in Mattituck's mind about who they had been chasing to Glennallen on that case, and even Todd admitted it had to be that same guy.

What they didn't know was why. Why had the guy re-appeared out of nowhere? And why was he targeting them? Well, more accurately, targeting Todd. Todd had assumed it was because he was the Trooper of record who had chased and nearly caught him. But Mattituck had never shaken the feeling that there was more to it than that.

He turned from the highway onto the road that led to Monica's home and office. A nervous pang wrenched his abdomen as he caught sight of her house coming into view, the lights on inside even though it was nowhere near dark.

He pulled the cruiser in and parked in front of the house. He shut the motor, but remained seated behind the steering wheel.

It was as though something besides a seatbelt were holding him in the seat.

He picked up his cell and checked for text messages. Nothing. Same with missed phone calls. Nothing. He looked at the house and knew she was in there, and that she was safe.

Normally he would have simply walked up to the front door and knocked. Maybe, given their closeness now, he would have tried the door knob. But he remained in the seat of the cruiser as if he were Velcroed to the seat.

He opened a text and tried her again.

*Hey you! I've been trying you all afternoon!* ☺ <3

He waited several minutes. Nothing.

*Sexy babe . . . where ARE you?*

At least a minute passed before a reply finally came.

*I'm fine. I need some time.*

It was more the lack of affection than the message itself that gave him pause.

*Clients?*

*No. I just need some time.*

He thought about this, a sinking feeling permeating his mid-section.

*I'm confused. I thought you wanted to see me tonight.*

*I did.*

He waited for more, but it didn't come. The past tense stood out for him, adding to the building anxiety. In the past, he would have sent an 'okay' and left it at that. Then he would have set his mind on other things and put the woman out of his thoughts. Usually, he would have put whatever woman it was out of his life. It just wasn't worth it, all the drama. But this time, with this woman, he didn't want to do that.

*Monica, what's wrong?*

Silence.

*Did I do something?* he tried.

Again, silence.

He sighed, the sinking feeling in his gut solidifying into a full knot. Nonetheless, he pushed it down. He didn't want to react from his emotions. If something was bothering her, it was worth dealing with.

*Monica, I love you. Whatever it is, please talk to me.*

Silence.

*I'm sitting out front of your house. Can we talk?*

Another full minute passed before she replied.

*No. Just go, please.*

He felt his balance go for a second, and was relieved he was sitting. Just go? What the hell was going on?

His thoughts raced. He thought about several approaches he could take, all in hopes of getting her to tell him whatever was on her mind so he could put her at ease. Whatever it was, he knew he loved her, and although he had no idea what was bothering her, he knew he wanted to work through it with her.

The thought of losing her gripped him, filled him with fear. He almost dialed her, then stopped. Maybe it would be better to try knocking on the door. Maybe that's what she really wanted. Maybe she wanted him to hold her and reassure her of his love. Or reassure her that whatever thoughts had taken root in her, they were nothing to worry about. He loved her, he wanted to say . . . and that's all that mattered.

But he stopped himself. "Just go, please," she had texted.

What the fuck? he thought. What the hell could possibly turn her suddenly cold like this? He hadn't done anything to deserve this kind of treatment. Whatever fucking demons she was fighting with, she should either give him a chance or . . . Or what?

He thought about this. He thought about Janelle, his fiancée from several years ago. The woman who had cheated on him after swearing up and down that he was absolutely the man she'd always dreamed of. Just like Monica had done, or might as well have done.

Fuck it, he thought. He had done nothing to deserve this.

He started the car and put it into reverse, backing carefully into the street. He imagined her watching the car preparing to leave. And then driving away.

Or maybe she wasn't.

Who cares? Maybe there's an explanation for all this, but even if there was, why would she treat him so coldly?

No . . . even if there was something to explain it all, there was no explaining that cold treatment. Nothing.

He had been able to get hold of Earl Darick right away on his cell. He was in fact out on a charter, so Mattituck had remembered right. It bothered him, suddenly, that he hadn't been tracking the details of the charter trips for the Kimberly Marie, and he decided to get himself back to more involved with his business. He couldn't even remember the detail of this trip with the Kimberly Marie, nor when exactly the next charter for the DeeVee8 was. He had made arrangements for Earl to captain the Knot Skunked, and for Hank Porter to shift from the Knot Skunked to the DeeVee8 so that Mattituck would be free to work with Todd on the case, but he had to admit to himself that it had also been about seeing Monica.

Fat lotta good that was, he thought bitterly.

He forced his mind back to the Kimberly Marie, his business, and the case with Todd. Whatever was going on with Monica, he was better off without it.

"I need to just stay the fuck away from relationships," he muttered at the windshield as he pulled the cruiser into a parking spot to the side of the Cordova Police station. Todd had arranged for the Chief, Howie Long, to move the car back to its spot adjacent to the dock where the Trooper boat was tied up.

Luckily, Earl and the Kimberly Marie were not far away. They were anchored in Sheep Bay, not far from Cordova. By now, Earl had pulled anchor and was piloting the big yacht with its cruise clients to pick Mattituck up. The normal routine was to cruise Prince William Sound by day and anchor at night. The clients wouldn't complain about an evening cruise into Cordova.

Mattituck turned in the keys to the cruiser at the dispatcher's desk and walked to the harbor. No surprise to Mattituck, Tom Graffinino, the rugged harbormaster, was working the desk.

"Hey, Tom," Mattituck said as the big man looked up from under his desk lamp.

"Frank Mattituck!" he said, rising to his feet. "I didn't hear you call on the VHF as you came in."

"Because I didn't. I was in town with Todd Benson."

"Are you still working with the Troopers?" the former logger asked. Tom was as Alaskan as they came, having spent years in the wilderness during a long logging career before the industry had slowed. He had decided to settle in Cordova, and landed the harbormaster's job to make it his permanent home.

"Yes, when he needs me."

"I thought that deputy thing was just a once-in-desperation thing."

Mattituck chuckled.

"So did I. Guess he likes having me around to give shit to."

Graffinino laughed a deep grumble.

"Where is Trooper Benson? You guys working that Justin Harris case?"

"Yeah. Todd's headed to Anchorage to work on some things. Earl Darick's coming in with our big charter yacht to pick me up. You have a place for the Kimberly Marie to tie up?"

"Overnight? She's a 75-footer, right?"

"72. But good memory."

"Goddamn tragedy, what happened to old Jim Milner. Glad you and Todd nailed that motherfucker."

Mattituck's memory went back to the drug/murder case, and Tom's attempt to stop the murderer from skipping out without paying his slip fees. The killer had handed Tom his ass in a sling. Tom Graffinino was big, and despite his age still muscular and foreboding. But this killer, Norm Peck, and laid Tom out on the dock, dizzy and wondering what had hit him.

"Almost nailed him."

Tom's attention was back to the Kimberly Marie. He was studying the harbor docks, tapping at slips on the scheme with his pencil.

"I got a spot over on the outside of Dock C, if that's all right."

"It'll do. There're clients who might want to pop into town, but that's fine. They'll have to figure their way back if they get drunk."

"Just have them pop in here. I'll get them back on board. I'll be here all night."

"Sounds good, Tom. Thanks."

Within three hours, just after 9:30 p.m., Mattituck was taking the lines from the Kimberly Marie and securing her to Dock C, where Graffinino had indicated.

The clients included a honeymooning actor couple from Hollywood who went ashore looking for pubs and clubs to have fun in, but the remaining clients, two additional couples, were hunkered down in their cabins.

"I'm in the crew quarters aft," Earl said, referring to the small berthing area aft of the engine room. "You can join me there."

The crew quarters had two single bunks, a small kitchenette, and a head. It was designed to house a captain and a deck hand for owners of the boat that might want to hire a crew rather than run the big yacht themselves. Jim Milner had always given up his cabin for clients, opting to sleep in the crew quarters, and Earl and Mattituck had adopted the same practice.

"Well, despite your snoring," Mattituck said with a grin, "I guess I'll have to."

"I don't snore!" Earl said, only slightly pained.

Mattituck clapped the man on the back as he stepped aboard.

"Let's have a beer or two on the aft deck," he said.

"Hell yeah!" Earl blurted happily, turning toward the galley.

Mattituck took his backpack to the crew's quarters, then met Earl at the chairs on the aft deck. Earl was already seated, smiling contentedly at the mountains behind the town of Cordova.

"Did you give the honeymooners a curfew?" he asked Earl, taking a seat across from him.

Earl opened a Guinness for him and slid it across the table to him. There was another Guinness on the table, and an additional Alaskan Amber, presumably for himself.

"You're prepared," Mattituck smiled.

"Always," Earl returned. "I told them we were casting off at 9:00 a.m. They said they'd be back after the last bar closes."

They chuckled together and let several minutes pass as they sipped their beers. Mattituck looked at Earl as the man continued gazing happily at the mountains.

"I love the golden sun as it hits the mountain tops," the former town drunk said.

Mattituck followed his stare to where the sunlight still shone on the upper quarter of the mountains. The town below was not yet in what one would call shadows, but it was dark enough to make the gold-yellow light seem brighter than it actually was. His partner's enthusiasm was contagious, and it helped put Mattituck into a better frame of mind. For a moment, Monica slid across his consciousness like the sunlight on the mountains before him. The peaks were warm and bright, but the relative shadows below always left one yearning for the golden warmth out of reach above.

The next morning was met with more golden sunshine, this time spilling through the valleys and onto the town with promises of beautiful days ahead. Mattituck was up to see it, and was on his second cup of coffee when Earl emerged from their shared quarters to begin preparations for breakfast for the guests. Mattituck took on the role of captain, checking the log for where Earl had taken the clients already, and planning the remaining three days on the voyage. Hank Porter was working his days off, taking the DeeVee8 clients out while not missing any additional charters on the Knot Skunked.

In short, Mattituck had four days before he would need to be back on task with Sound Experience Charters.

And at this point, with no word from Monica, he allowed himself to begin the painful process of assuming he and Monica were finished.

With no idea of when Todd might need him next, and with nothing better to do for the next few days, Mattituck took on the role of captain. He checked the weather buoy reports for Seal Rocks, south of the Entrance to the Sound, and decided he and Earl could take their clients for one of the greatest thrills for visitors to Alaska: humpback whales. There had been reports of a pod of the magnificent creatures near Hinchinbrook Entrance, so he set a plan to seek sightings, and announced his plans to Earl Darick.

"You got it!" the man declared in response. "I'll let the guests know after I rouse them all for breakfast."

"Great," Mattituck said. "Let's get them all fed, then we can get underway." Then his thoughts turned more gloomy and he added, "Lots of departures in the past day or so. I'm glad to be part of this one."

Earl took the remark in, but sensed the cryptic comment had nothing to do with him or their guests.

"Glad to have you aboard, Frank," he said, smiling genuinely. "Gives me a break."

Usually, they had a cook on board who also served as a deckhand when needed, such as for line handling. But Reynaldo, their cook, had had a family wedding to attend, leaving Earl to do everything himself. The line handling wasn't an issue, as most harbors had hands available to assist. But the cooking was too much for one person to handle while being the sole captain, purser, and deckhand.

Nonetheless, Earl sensed there was more to Mattituck's comments than what appeared on the surface.

"Well," he ventured. "Departures are never all there is. Eventually, we have to come to port."

# Chapter Fifteen

## Telling Discoveries

Todd had arrived in Anchorage without incident, off-loading the evidence directly into a cruiser that had met him on the tarmac. They had then driven straight to the headquarters office in midtown Anchorage, which housed the forensics unit as well as the primary evidence room. He worked alongside a young officer recently graduated from the academy in Sitka, carefully checking in each item and carefully cataloging it, then placing it on the shelving in the secure evidence room.

They worked in silence, Todd deep in his thoughts and the young officer attuned to the fact that the field veteran didn't want to talk.

Todd's thoughts were focused mainly on the case, but they drifted toward Keri more often than he would want to admit. He still hadn't heard anything from her since they'd had their fight the night he'd slept at the fire station in Valdez. Of course, he hadn't tried to contact her, either, he had to admit. But it was she who had said she wanted a divorce, so wouldn't she be the one who should--? No, he realized, that didn't make any sense. She said she wanted a divorce. That was a pretty final declaration. Why the hell would she call?

And for his part, why should he try calling her when she'd just dished out the ultimate rejection?

He turned to the rookie to get his mind on a different track.

"How long have you been out of the academy?"

"Just over four months, sir."

"And what are you hoping to do? Inventory?"

The young man looked slightly sheepish.

"Yeah," he said. "I know it's not that exciting, like what you do, but it's kind of my personality, I guess. I like cataloging and working with evidence. It's interesting in a way, you know?"

Todd smiled at the young man.

"Look, you do what you enjoy. Don't let anybody tell you it isn't exciting."

The young officer took a deep breath, feeling affirmed, and turned back to the label he was making.

"You got this now?" Todd asked. "I'd like to take this hard drive over to the computer folks and see what they come up with."

"Yeah, sure," the man said, not looking up. "And thanks. Not many say something like that."

"What's your name?"

"Vincent Marrazo. My friends call me Vinnie."

"Okay if I count myself among those to call you Vinnie?"

Vinnie grinned.

"Yes, sir!" he replied a little too enthusiastically.

Todd chuckled. "Don't call me sir. I'm Todd. Todd Benson. I'm the Fish and Game guy for Prince William Sound. Like you, I just do my job."

"Okay. Oh, say," Vinnie said, suddenly excited. "You were the one on that crazy drug guy's case. And that poacher fisherman!"

"Yeah, that was me."

"That was awesome work, Mr. Benson!"

"Todd. Call me Todd."

"Okay, Mr. Todd, will do!"

Todd shook his head, grinning. Something about the kid's enthusiasm restored his spirits. He tucked the computer CPU under his arm and headed down the hall to the computer forensics lab.

One of the many things about the Kimberly Marie that impressed Mattituck was how well she handled the seas. Even the large swell with cross-breezed choppy white caps didn't do much to upset the smooth ride the large boat provided. It had to do with the way her hull was designed, with the deep-vee at the bow tapering back nicely with the unusual addition of stabilizer fins along the midship-to-stern edges. But it was also the way she carried her superstructure, balancing height with a low center-of-gravity that kept her from rolling too much in rougher seas.

All of this was proved again when he and Earl took their clients out past Seal Rocks, well south of Hinchinbrook Entrance. Just as the reports had said, a large pod of Humpbacks were quickly spotted as three or four of the huge creatures catapulted themselves into magnificent breaches. Mattituck had managed to pilot the boat to within 100 meters, and their city-dwelling Lower 48 passengers had been nearly struck silent by the raw beauty of nature's gentle giants. Indeed, it took Mattituck's own breath away every time he saw the whales.

Now they were well within Prince William Sound again, northbound for Valdez where they would moor up for the clients' last night aboard. The next morning, they would ferry all eight passengers to the airport in the company van Jim Milner had purchased less than a year before his death.

Mattituck was steering just to the east of the shipping channel used by the cruise ships and oil tankers. His intent was to take them alongside Bligh Reef, where the infamous Exxon Valdez had gone aground and triggered one of the nation's worst oil disasters. To this day, traces of the spill were still being dug up and studied, and some fish species still hadn't recovered.

Earl appeared from the galley, a cup of coffee for his partner in hand.

"Thanks," Mattituck smiled. "Just the thing."

Earl grinned back.

"Always sad," the older man said, "the end of these trips. I love the solitude between charters, but then I miss all the people when they leave."

Mattituck nodded. "Yeah. I can see how that would be."

"You don't feel that way after your trips?"

"I only have people out for 12 hours, remember. You have them for 3-5 days. Sometimes longer. Easy to get a bit more attached."

"True that," Earl said. Then randomly added, "That one couple in the VIP cabin, they're on their honeymoon. Ever' time I see them, I think of you and Monica."

Mattituck swallowed down his irritation. He could have gone all day without hearing something like that. It was bad enough she still hadn't tried to contact him. Now he had to deal with an image of being with her. He peered into the radar screen, pretending to check a contact that was blipping with the radar arm.

"I'm going to get my head more in the game," he said without looking at Earl. "Realized earlier that I haven't been tracking our bookings very well lately. Sorry if I've been a bit checked out."

Earl scowled.

"The hell you talkin' about? You ain't been checked out. Hell, you're the most EN-gaged guy I know."

"Just not as on top of—"

"Cut that out," Earl said, almost too strongly. "I don't know what bullcrap's gotten into your head, but you put it away. You're the best business partner a guy could hope for."

Mattituck looked up then, and Earl was taken back by the pained look on the man's face.

"Thanks, Earl," was all he said.

They reached port five hours later, well after the dinner hour. Nonetheless, all except the couple from the VIP cabin headed into town as soon as the Kimberly Marie was safely moored and her engines shut down.

"You look like a truck's run over you," Earl said. "Howzabout I buy you a Guinness?"

Mattituck smiled. "Sounds great, actually."

Earl went to the parlor to post a note with his cell number for the clients, then came back topside to join Mattituck in securing the last of the unused fenders.

The two started up the dock toward shore, both glancing back one last time to make sure all looked right with the Kimberly Marie. They acted like proud parents worried about their toddler, despite her being perfectly safe in her crib.

"Crow's Nest?" Earl asked.

"Where else? We haven't seen Seamus for a while," Mattituck returned, referring to the now-famous and respected bartender Pappy Amatucci had hired the previous summer. The no-nonsense Irishman had broken up a fight Mattituck and Earl had been part of soon after the man started, and now he'd risen to the title of Manager under Pappy's keen business eye. Pappy had always been quick to identify people he could depend on.

This brought Mattituck's thoughts back to Pappy's niece, Izzy Giovanni. Whatever the hell had gotten into that woman's mind about him, he had no idea. He just knew it would be a while before he'd feel okay going back to Bella Luna alone.

Before they reached the steep ramp up to shore, they saw Hank Porter, coming from the opposite line of docks where the Knot Skunked was moored. The man looked the part of a salty captain, with a close-trimmed black beard and chiseled Icelandic features. He had, in fact, been born and raised in Iceland and immigrated all the way to Alaska with his parents while a teen. He grew up a fisherman, and had never sought a different lifestyle.

"Ho!" he hollered as he looked up and caught sight of them. "How do, boss?" he said to Mattituck as he approached.

"Max out today?" Mattituck replied to the skipper of his original charter boat, the Knot Skunked.

"When does it be otherwise?" Hank countered with his accent. Though he'd moved to the States during high school, probably some thirty years prior, he had never lost his accent.

"Never," Mattituck said. "In fact, Earl here's buying up at the Crow's Nest if you want to come along."

"Mighty temptin'," Hank said, rubbing his chin through his beard. "I should be gettin' to the family. . . but maybe a cup of grog wouldn't hurt."

Earl beamed. "Right on!"

Mattituck grinned inwardly at these two interacting—the only two full-time employees of Sound Experience Charters besides Mattituck. In addition to the three of them, there were 5 crew who served as deckhands off-and-on, and one bookkeeper who helped Mattituck with the accounting for the company. Soon, however, he would have to think of hiring somebody to handle the booking and logistical planning. Especially if Mattituck were to keep working with Todd Benson as much as he had been.

The three of them arrived at the Crow's Nest with a festive spirit and loud voices. Mattituck was glad to see Seamus O'Brien behind the bar, and led his group to sit at the bar instead of a table so that they could interact with the Irishman. As they crossed through the tables, Mattituck took stock of who was there, and saw several familiar faces. Among them were Rick Gardiner, a commercial fisherman, and—much to Mattituck's dismay—Izzy Giovanni. Apparently Pappy had her working The Crow's Nest instead of Bella Luna.

Her eyes met his, and she ventured a brief but seductive smile. Mattituck was glad he'd opted for the bar rather than a table, where they would have been served by Izzy. She was exactly the kind of woman he did not care for, although twenty years prior she was precisely the kind of woman he *did* care for. This forced his thoughts back to Monica. What had turned her so cold, and so quickly? He thought what they shared was far more than could turn her away from him so easily—or at all.

He caught himself and turned his thoughts back to his friends.

"Drinks on me, boys," he said.

Hank turned a grizzled face toward him. "Yeah? Well, maybe I texts the wife and let her know I be late tonight," he said with a broad grin.

"How ye' doin' this evening, lads?" Seamus asked as they each climbed aboard a stool.

"Good, good," Mattituck said. "You know mine. Earl? Hank? What are you drinking?"

"And eating," Earl added. "I'm hungry!"

"And eating," Mattituck added.

Seamus glanced at Mattituck long enough to say, "Right-o. A Guinness and what else?"

"Tullamore Dew for me!" Hank blurted. "Double."

This brought a wide grin from Seamus.

"Now there's a good lad," the Irish bartender said with glee. "Among the top 'o the Irish whiskeys."

Seamus turned an expectant gaze on Earl.

"Um, yeah," Earl said. "I'll have what he's having."

"A regular Irish celebration underway," Mattituck quipped.

"A right good lot, you are," Seamus said, and turned to get their drinks.

The Crow's Nest was full of tourists, as it often was in the summer months. This was partly because it was attached to what was considered the nicest of hotels in town, and partly due to the huge bay windows behind the bar, affording a panoramic view of the small boat harbor below.

Mattituck turned on his stool to take in the crowd, and met Rick Gardiner's eyes. The big fisherman raised his beer in salute, and Mattituck returned the gesture with a real salute. Rick nodded and grinned, and turned back to his mates.

A soft warm hand on his forearm turned Mattituck to his right, where he was less than two feet from Izzy's warm eyes.

"Any change of heart?" her alto voice asked. "None of the other guys seem interesting."

The smile that had been lingering on Mattituck's face faded.

"Look," he said, "I don't want to be rude, especially to a relation of Pappy's, but I'm really not interested. Flattered, but not interested. No offense," he added.

The woman's features didn't change in the least.

"The more you say things like that, the more sure I am of what I want," she said, her voice lilting as she turned back to her tables.

"I'm tellin' you, you're a fool," Earl said. "But I get why. Monica is a prize worth tending to."

Mattituck faced him. "She is."

For a moment, he was tempted to confide in his partner. But he kept himself in check. He had never been in the habit of confiding in anybody, and he sure as hell didn't see any value in starting now.

As soon as Seamus had delivered their drinks, he reached under the bar. His hands re-emerged with his cricket bat poised, and he strode around the end of the bar, making fast time toward the far side of the dining area. Mattituck turned to watch him.

A man had a hand clamped around Izzy Giovanni's wrist as he apparently tried to pull her onto his lap. Seamus, completely in character with what Mattituck knew of him, was quickly approaching with the cricket bat rising above his head in a threatening gesture. Rick Gardiner, rising from a nearby table, took two steps toward the scene as well.

The sudden movements sent a vibe through the lounge like a disruption on a spider web, and all eyes turned toward the drunken tourist gripping Izzy's wrist.

Without any indication of what was about to happen, Izzy's free hand swung wide in a roundhouse and landed edge first on the man's exposed neck in an expert chop. The placement of the blow was perfect as the man's grip on her wrist weakened and his hand fell listlessly away from her wrist. Her opposite knee shot upward as she leaned in toward him, increasing the momentum of the knee as it caught the man dead center in the gut. He folded over, and she raised her freed hand and gripped him at a pressure point between his shoulder muscle and his neck. Instantly, the man slid from his chair and dropped to his knees, grimacing in pain.

Izzy held the muscle under her thumb, and Mattituck imagined the end of her thumb finding that place between muscle groups that was particularly sensitive in the nerve bundles. He knew it well, along with several others that could bring even the toughest to their knees.

"Okay, okay!" the man gulped as Rick Gardiner and Seamus O'Brien reached the scene.

There was a dead silence and Izzy stood straight and firmly poised. Everybody in the lounge was stunned.

Mattituck, however, had recognized the entire maneuver as a practiced set of moves, and was gazing at Izzy with a new perspective.

Todd Benson had spent the evening with two members of the computer forensics team. He had watched with fascination as the two software engineers had worked their way through Justin Harris' computer. First, they had quickly unlocked the ghost drive on the CPU and had begun the long, arduous task of tracking down the various activities the deceased hunter had undertaken prior to his death.

There was the usual web surfing of a single man, the most interesting of which was his fixation on eastern European dating sites, along with his interactions with several women that included exchanges of webcam pictures that few would be proud to know would be looked at by forensics teams. This had occupied the two forensics guys and their snide humor until they discovered a thread of emails to a woman who had been accessing the same Internet Service Provider—meaning somebody in the same town.

This piqued Todd's interest.

The Trooper had leaned in more closely to look at the exchanges between the two. After a quick scan to see if there were other such interactions, the team had determined this was the only local contact of such email exchanges.

Todd's thought immediately went to the Copper River Inn, and the escapades Justin Harris had had with an unidentified woman, on an ongoing basis.

He leaned in to watch over their shoulders, and what he read as they worked their way through the messages gave Todd a fairly clear idea of who the woman was. It would be hard to prove, if the team were not able to find more concrete references to places and situations, but for Todd, the exchanges could only have been with one woman.

*. . . we have to remain very discreet, my love . . .* the woman had written.

*. . . I can't wait to do you in your own house, when he's no longer in the picture . . .* Justin had written in a later exchange.

*. . . I have to make sure the store is mine before we do it . . .* the woman had written. The context here was unclear, and seemed to refer to doing something other than having sex. And while there were many stores in Cordova, there was little doubt in Todd's mind who

the mysterious lover of Justin Harris had been. But what was it she and Justin were going to do after she was sure the store was hers? It was possible that Tara was planning to divorce Wilson, but that didn't quite add up with arranging things so she would have the store. In a divorce, they would have to divvy it up.

Todd had long since become wary of jumping to conclusions, but given the recent events, he wondered if the lovers had been planning to do harm to Wilson Garrett. Had Justin's accidental shooting happened before they were able to carry out their plan? That would be a kind of poetic justice, Todd thought as his mind raced through possibilities.

Or had Wilson Garrett figured things out and developed his own plan? Such as getting his lifelong friend-turned-betrayer out on a hunting trip where he could get revenge. Maybe Wilson had even figured out what his wife and Justin had been planning, and beat them to the proverbial punch.

Inwardly, Todd grinned. This was what he loved about his job. So many possibilities of what had happened, and it was getting more and more interesting with each layer he dug into.

# Chapter Sixteen

## Turning Tides

Izzy had seen the look on Mattituck's face after she had dealt with the man in the bar. He had been the only one in the room that hadn't looked surprised or curious. It had been obvious that the room's response was a mix of surprise at her ability to handle a rugged Alaska man, and a drunken one at that. Some were taken back by the petite and beautiful Italian woman taking the burly lecherous ass down, and others had been more taken with the quickness and seemed to be trying to figure out what had happened.

Except Mattituck. The look on his face made it clear that Izzy had made a mistake. The second mistake, come to think of it. First by being too forward in her seduction attempt, and now by not being attentive to Mattituck's past. The Uhing had briefed her thoroughly on the background of the man they referred to as 'The Takistus,' meaning 'The Obstacle.'

She knew his military record, every detail of his training in Special Operations, and all about his role as an enforcement agent with the U.S. Park Service. The service with the Park Service had been especially interesting to Izzy, as she hadn't even known that the Park Rangers had such an elite arm to their law enforcement operations, although it made sense, given the kinds of things that went on in the back country of the national parks and wilderness areas. Things the general public had no idea of.

So her quick, expert action had risked giving herself away. And Mattituck's gaze had told her he knew that she was no ordinary niece of Pappy's brought in from the homeland as charity for the family.

Perhaps worse, it was time for her to check in and report to The Uhing. This was not the kind of thing she would want to report. Particularly to that assistant of Das Kaptan, Karl. The man was as cold and calculating as anybody Izzy had come across in this profession — and she had come across plenty.

She had driven, as instructed, to a short hiking trail that led to a flat point of land free of vegetation. In addition to having a clear connection for the encrypted satellite phone, it was a location where she could not be overheard and could easily see anybody who might wander near. The Uhing was careful about communications, and spared no expense and overlooked no details to ensure that nobody discovered their existence. Only a few operatives, like herself, knew as much as she did, and even that was relatively little.

She pulled out the phone and dialed Karl's number.

"How are things?" the man's voice asked, dispensing with any pretention of niceties.

"Fine," Izzy replied. "I'm settled in and have made contact with The Takistus."

"Good, good," Karl said, pleased. "And this 'contact,' as you put it . . . it is as we hoped?"

Izzy stiffened.

"No," she said. "Not yet. These things take time sometimes."

There was a measurable pause.

"Perhaps I have been mistaken," Karl replied. "I was under the impression you were the right one for this."

Izzy allowed her eyes to close to calm herself.

"As I said, doing things right takes time. And you said observation first, then further instructions."

"Indeed. I did say that. But you need to be inside with The Takistus to observe, yes?"

"No. I can see what he's doing from where I am."

There was a pause, and Izzy listened to the encryption as it warbled the silence, waiting.

"Let me be direct," Karl said finally. "Izzy, have you failed in connecting with The Takistus?"

She felt her stomach tighten.

"Fail wouldn't be the right word."

"But it is accurate, yes?"

"He doesn't seem interested. He is involved with a woman that he seems very happy with, and he's not the type to be . . ." she searched for the right words, " . . . easily distracted."

"Or perhaps your skills—"

"That's not the problem," she interrupted, taking a chance. One didn't interrupt Karl.

He was quiet a moment, and Izzy braced herself.

"Perhaps this other obstacle, the woman, needs to be removed to clear the way for you to get in close."

Izzy was shaking her head, though Karl couldn't see her.

"No, there's a better way."

"Which is?"

"Let me work with this and see if I can make it happen."

"You are a professional. So I leave it to you. But know that if not," Karl said, the ice returning to his tone, "we will dispense with the woman obstacle, and you will be there to comfort the Takistus. In this way, you will get in close to him."

"I think my way is more likely to work."

"Nonetheless, have I made myself clear?"

"Yes," Izzy returned, resigned. "Yes, you have."

"I want a report within two or three days. If no progress, then we do it my way."

"I'll do my best."

"No, you will do it. It is as simple as that. This way or that way is no matter. Trying is no matter. Succeeding discreetly is what matters."

Izzy was silent, her thoughts returning to the scene in the bar. *Succeeding discreetly is what matters* echoed in her head. The Takistus knew there was something about her . . . perhaps not what exactly, but something. And Izzy knew that would not meet Karl's definition of 'discreetly.'

"I will succeed," she said simply.

"Of course you will," he said, then ended the call without another word.

Izzy put the phone in her handbag and looked out over the water, in the general direction of the Gulf of

Alaska and the Pacific Ocean. So many mountains and islands between where she stood and the open freedom of the ocean. Always, she thought, there were obstacles. And always, she overcame them.

She would do the same this time as well.

With a crunching of the rough sand beneath her feet, she turned and started back up the trail.

Monica was looking back through the documents in the Garrett files while she waited for Tara Garrett to arrive. She had laying side by side on the desk blotter a document with both Tara and Wilson Garrett's signatures, and the one with supposedly Garrett's signature that ceased pursuit of a property for a new store in Seattle. The more she compared them, the more clear it was that the signature on the second was not Wilson's. That had been clear almost from the start. What was intriguing Monica now was the increasing surety that it was Tara's writing, forging her husband's signature. There was an angle and curve in that signature that matched Tara's.

So she had called Tara, asking her to stop by. Now Tara was more than 15 minutes late.

This was nothing new to Monica, confronting a client. She had done so more often than she would have ever guessed while in law school that she might. But how that might go always made her nervous. There were ethical standards with the bar that Monica simply could not—would not—mess with. A client committing fraud with an attorney's knowledge changed the client/attorney privilege clauses under the law, and Monica would be obligated to remove herself from representing the client. Depending on the situation, she might even be required to report it to the court.

The office door opened and Tara Garrett entered the office, dressed as she usually did, which was to say better than the average Alaskan in a rural coastal town, and with an air of superiority.

"Okay, I'm here. What's so important that you needed to see me right away? Is there a problem with filing the papers?"

Monica shook her head.

"No," she said. "Why don't you have a seat?"

Tara stepped to the desk and took one of the two leather chairs facing the desk that Monica's father had bought years before, wanting to spruce up the office and give it an ambiance of an attorney's office.

"Well," Monica corrected. "There may be an issue with filing, yes. But it's more along the lines of forgery that I'm concerned about."

"Forgery? What do you mean?"

Monica turned the documents upside down and slide them toward Tara so she could get a close look.

"Are you familiar with these?" she asked.

Tara examined the documents, reading through them quickly.

"Yes. I guess so. Why?"

"Tell me about the signatures."

Tara shifted visibly, and she leaned in to study the signatures on the two documents.

"This one has Garrett's and mine, and this one has only Garrett's."

She looked up at Monica quizzically.

"Is the Garrett's on the second one? The one closing talks of opening a store in Seattle?"

Tara examined the signature again.

"It looks like his. Why?"

"It's not his," Monica said, a complete lack of doubt evident in her voice.

"What do you mean? Who would have forged Garrett's signature? And why?"

Monica sat back in her chair, watching Tara.

"Tara, when I agreed to represent you, we discussed the need for you to be completely open and honest with me. Even if you share something with me that could incriminate you, you need to share it. That's the purpose of client privilege: I don't have to disclose sensitive information about you. But you need to understand that I can't protect you if you commit fraud, and I absolutely can not be a party to it."

Tara's blue eyes held steady on Monica's, her face not changing expression in the least.

"I know that," she said. "I'm not doing anything wrong. If that's a forged signature, I don't know who would have forged it. Unless it was Justin."

*Classic*, Monica thought. *The dead guy's an easy body to throw under the bus.*

She decided not to pursue it.

"All right, Tara. I just wanted to make sure things were clear on my ability to represent you."

Tara continued staring at her.

"Okay. But maybe we should hold off a little while longer on the divorce papers."

Monica looked up at her.

"All right, if you'd like. As I said before, it might not be bad to wait a little longer with everything that's happened."

"Yeah," Tara said. "No need to rush."

Todd arrived back in Valdez on the afternoon flight. He had arranged for Mattituck to pick him up at the airport, since he couldn't ask Keri to. He still hadn't had any contact with her, which left him uncertain of what would happen next. Would she decide that perhaps they could work things out, or would the next communication be someone serving him with divorce papers?

Under different circumstances, Mattituck would have driven him home, but with Todd's apparent separation, Mattituck had invited Todd to stay with him at his house in the Robe River subdivision. This would make it easier to get back down to Cordova anyhow. The information that had turned up on Justin Harris' computer left Todd with a number of questions that he suspected had answers on the Wilson and Tara Garrett's computers, and possibly Wilson's computer in his office. First, however, Todd needed to get a warrant from the judge in Valdez who had jurisdiction over the Prince William Sound region and who carried the court cases in both towns. Right now, Judge Samson was in Valdez, so Todd would need to get the warrant at the Valdez Courthouse, then go to Cordova to exercise the warrant.

But that would have to be first thing in the morning. Tonight, Todd would be Mattituck's house guest . . . but not until he'd had something to eat. And he wouldn't mind seeing that niece of Pappy's again.

The plane landed safely after its usual bumping around in the turbulent air that was common in the Valdez bowl. After he gathered his gear from baggage claim, he and Mattituck carried it out to Mattituck's truck.

"Mind dropping me off at my office?" he asked as Mattituck started the engine.

"Sure," his friend replied. "Do you need me to wait for you?"

"No. I have a few things to do there, then I'll probably grab something to eat after I try to get hold of Judge Samson."

"Judge Samson?"

"Yeah. I need a warrant for the Garrett's computers."

Mattituck pulled his eyes from the road to glance at him.

"Their computers? You found something on Justin Harris' computer?"

Todd nodded. "Emails that are going to lead us in a whole new direction on this thing."

Mattituck shot him another glance. "Sounds exciting."

Todd was gazing at the road ahead.

"Which is why I need you," he said. "If you can spare the time, that is."

"Sure. Good timing. I have the next three days clear. Monica and I were going to take a little time together."

"Oh, well don't let this get in the way of that," Todd said with a grin.

Mattituck was silent.

"I don't think it's happening," he said evenly.

Todd looked him.

"Something come up?"

"Yeah. You could say that."

"Everything okay?"

Mattituck didn't look at him. "Yeah. I'm fine."

"That's not what I was asking," Todd clarified.

"I know," was all Mattituck said in return.

Mattituck shifted in his seat and leaned on the driver's door armrest as he turned right and accelerated onto the main highway. Todd watched his face for several moments, but Mattituck said nothing more, and his manner revealed nothing.

Todd fought mixed feelings as he stowed supplies from the Anchorage headquarters into the cabinets in his office. He hadn't allowed himself to be attracted to another woman since he and Keri had met, and the feelings he now harbored for Izzy instilled no small amount of guilt into the Trooper's conscience. He was very sure things with Keri were over; they had been teetering toward divorce for a long time now, and whatever smattering of affection they had shared over the last year or more had faded into the superficial.

If it was over, then why the guilt?

He resolved to grab something to eat someplace other than Bella Luna, where he was likely to see Izzy. Best to avoid her. For now at least. But as he finished stocking his supplies and turned to replenishing the used materials from his investigation kit which he would need in Cordova, his thoughts kept drifting back to Izzy. She was probably the most attractive women he'd seen in Valdez . . . or most anywhere, come to think of it. And she was visiting Pappy Amatucci—for how long, Todd wondered. Not that it mattered. It was the short term he was interested in at the moment.

But would she be interested in him?

The question gave him pause. He knew he was a good looking guy. He'd had many opportunities in his role to hook up with women who had made it clear they were attracted to him. But did Izzy find him attractive? She seemed receptive when he had been at the Bella Luna with Mattituck.

Keri's face came to mind, and the guilt returned. What exactly had happened to them? They had been so in love early on, then something happened that changed all that. There had been rumors that she had been involved with an intern doctor at the hospital the previous summer, and that coincided with things turning sour between them, but he never saw or heard anything that made him think there was substance to it. Nothing that would make him want to ask her about it. If he had, it would surely have caused a major fight, and one that they wouldn't have recovered from. For his part, he never had been a guy with a wandering eye.

Until now.

Izzy's shape imposed itself on his thoughts, and he felt a stir deep within, as if it emanated from the marrow of his bones. He really did want to see her.

And if things really were over with Keri, he'd hate to miss an opportunity with Izzy. A woman like her gets hit on all the time, and it would only be a matter of time before she was taken.

Everything was so fresh with Keri, though. Wasn't it too soon to be thinking about a new relationship—even if a short one?

He pulled his cell phone out and looked at the menu of recent text messages. He had to scroll to the third page before Keri's name appeared, a testament to how much they had drifted. It carried the sense of finality about it. Her name would continue to slide further and further down the pages of recent texts, until some weeks or months down the road he would clean out the contacts and her name would be gone permanently.

Try as he might, he just couldn't shake off the guilt, so he opened a text window to Keri. One last try, maybe.

*Are you still set on your decision? Or do we have a chance?*

He hit 'send' and waited, staring at the screen. 'Delivered' appeared beneath the message, then a moment later changed to 'read.'

He drew a breath and watched to see if it would show her typing a response. It did. Whatever she was now typing took no effort to decide.

*We're finished, Todd. Done. Papers will be on their way. Goodbye.*

"Wow," he whispered. "Wow . . ."

He'd more expected rejection than a note of reconciliation, but he hadn't expected it to be that harsh. He sat down on the corner of his desk, staring at the screen. Then he closed the window and slid the phone into his pocket. Words like that didn't deserve a response. Let her think what she wanted.

Still uncertain of whether he should pursue Izzy, Todd decided to grab something to eat at the Crow's Nest instead of Bella Luna. This way, he'd be putting off any complications with Izzy. Besides, he would likely run into somebody he knew at the Crow's Nest to help distract his thoughts. Even if he didn't, the noise and energy of the popular bar would be good for him.

Sure enough, as he entered crowded room, he spotted Earl Darick atop a stool at the bar, talking to Seamus O'Brien as the bartender poured a set of pints from the tap. Todd made his way through the room, making his way to them. He loved not being in uniform at times like this. It felt like traveling incognito, and he got to be a regular person— something he didn't get to be nearly enough.

He slid onto the stool next to Earl without a word and signaled to Seamus.

"Hey, there!" Seamus shouted with Irish glee. "What'll you have, lad?"

Todd was grateful the man made not reference to his being a Trooper. It always garnered attention.

"Do you have Pacifico, by chance?"

"Absolutely! A little early to be dreamin' o' Mexico, ain't it?"

"Never too early for that!" Earl blurted as he turned to greet Todd. He clapped Todd lightly on the back.

"How're things? Haven't seen you much lately," Earl asked.

"Busy busy."

"I guess so. Dragging Mattituck all over the place, from what I hear."

"Something like that."

Seamus appeared with a bottle of Pacifico, setting it on a square napkin in front of Todd.

"Busy with that case in Cordova, I'm guessing," he said as he wiped the condensation from the bottle on his apron.

"Yep."

"But you can't talk about it, I'd further guess."

"Yep," Todd said with a smile.

"Bet he tells Mattituck, though," Earl chimed in.

"What he needs to know, he knows. And he's a sworn officer, so don't go trying to pry anything out of him, either." Todd's tone was light and the beer was already putting him at ease. He breathed deeply, allowing a warmth to permeate his core.

"Hello," came a soft voice at his free ear.

Todd turned to find himself mere inches from Izzy's smiling eyes and partly opened lips. He had an urge to lean forward and kiss them, to feel their fullness against his own.

"Hi," he said, the surprise showing. "I thought you—" then he stopped himself. He'd forgotten that Pappy owned the Crow's Nest as well as Bella Luna. She was probably working here tonight.

*As fate would have it . . .* he thought, then smiled.

"Shall I keep an eye out for a table for you to sit at?"

"Ummm..."

"So that I can serve you . . . ?"

Todd felt his heart swell. *Those eyes . . . and her voice . . .*

"Yeah, sure . . . or," he turned to Earl, "want a table, Earl?"

"Naw, I'm good riiight here," he said, looking from Todd to Izzy, then back again.

Todd looked at Izzy.

"I tell you what," she said lightly. "There's a two-seat table that's more private. I am due a break. When those people leave, I will hold it and take my break, and you can join me."

Todd couldn't believe his luck. She was actually coming on to him. Maybe it was fate after all.

"Sounds great," he said.

Her head tilted forward seductively as she smiled, lifted on the ball of her foot and turned back to her tables.

"Well, Casanova," Earl teased. "Looks to me like she kinda likes you."

"Now here's your Sherlock," Seamus laughed, gesturing at Earl. "You could deputize him and solve all your crimes."

Todd chuckled.

"Well, I feel like maybe I should explain, since you guys know Keri. She's filing for divorce, so I figure I'm a free man."

The surprise he expected this to evoke didn't come.

"Yeah, well, sorry to hear that," Earl said, "but I gotta say I saw it comin'."

Todd looked at Seamus, who was nodding agreement. He felt stupid under their gazes.

"Really, guys?" The surprise was in his own voice. "Did everybody see it coming except me?"

Earl's eyes revealed a depth of compassion.

"C'mon now," he said. "You saw it pro'ly before any of us did."

"Okay," Todd said, side-stepping. "Since we're talking openly, was there anything to that rumor last summer?"

Earl didn't miss a beat. "The intern?"

Todd nodded.

"Do you really want to know?"

Todd nodded again, more slowly with a sense of dread creeping in.

"All right. We all pick our own poison, I reckon." Then Earl continued. "I didn't see anything directly, but I got a friend works at the hospital, and she says it was true."

He paused, reading Todd's face.

"You sure you want to know?"

Todd's eyes met Earl's, and Earl could see Todd's resolve and readiness.

"Yeah. I really do."

"My friend walked in on them in an empty hospital room. She wouldn't lie about this kind of thing. And I want you to know, Todd—because you're my friend. I haven't breathed a word of that to nobody until just now."

Todd tried a smile that came out a frown.

"I jus' want you to know I didn't contribute nothin' to the rumors. Ain't my way."

"I know that, Earl. Thanks."

Todd stared out the window at the boats in the marina as he tried to absorb the truth of his failed marriage. It was interesting, he thought, that with this news all emotion seemed to drain away, like the soap suds in Seamus' sink where he was washing glasses between customer orders.

Nothing had told him it was truly over like what he'd just heard. Before that moment, Keri had been done with him. Now he was done with her.

Todd sat at the two-seat table where Izzy had led him. For all their being forward with each other before, they now sat like a couple of shy teens. Maybe it was because of what he'd just heard, or maybe it was the finality of what he'd realized about his being finished with Keri, but he could tell he was off inside. Something felt very different about himself, as though he had been temporarily placed in someone else's body and didn't quite feel comfortable in it.

He looked up at Izzy. She was perched on the chair across from him, the corners of her mouth in a stale smile. She seemed to sense that he wasn't himself, and was giving him space.

"If it's better for me to go—"

"No, no," he interrupted. "I'm sorry—I just got some news that kind of surprised me."

A look of concern came into her eyes, then, "Is there anything I can do?"

"Oh no, I don't think . . ." his voice trailed off. "Maybe there is, actually." He sat up straighter and let his face brighten.

The real smile returned at the corners of her mouth.

"Anything," she said, the seductive tone returning.

"That's exactly what I was hoping," he said.

After Izzy's break was over, Todd returned to the bar and took the stool next to Earl.

"Happier now?" the former town drunk asked.

"I think so," Todd said.

Seamus winked at Earl. "Rhetorical question. Answer's written all over your face." He paused a moment. "That and you were walkin' kinda funny back this way."

That forced a laugh out of both Todd and Earl.

"Well, gentlemen, I have a couple of hours to kill before my date. Wouldn't mind killing it with you two, if you don't mind."

"I'm kinda working 'til closing." Seamus' sardonic edge must be the Irish blood, Todd thought.

"Hell," Earl shot in, "This here's my post most every night 'til round about 10 or 11. I'm good." He looked at Seamus. "And hungry. Damn hungry, in fact."

To which Seamus placed menus in front of each of them.

# Chapter Seventeen

## New Directions

Todd and Mattituck cast off the DeeVee8 just before 9:00 a.m., with the needed warrant in hand. It was a crisp morning, with the kind of white puffy clouds Todd remembered from his childhood days on the reservation . . . and in Idaho with his dad. He wasn't sure if it was the rarity of this type of cloud that brought the powerful feeling of joy, or the memory of his night with Izzy. All he knew was that he hadn't felt like this in a long time.

"You don't answer to me, of course," Mattituck said once he got the DeeVee8 up to speed, "but if you're staying at my place and decide to cancel, I'd appreciate a text or something so I can lock the door and sleep better."

Todd grinned at him.

"Aw, shucks, Frank," he said with sarcasm, ". . . were you a worried parent?"

Mattituck shrugged.

"Just sayin'."

"Yeah, you're right. Sorry. I didn't plan on not coming out, and when it was clear I wasn't it was too late to text you."

Mattituck gave him a quizzical glance.

Todd answered with a "None of your business," and turned to watch the water as the boat sped over.

"Fair enough," Mattituck said. "But if it's anything to do with that vixen niece of Pappy's . . ."

Todd watched a dead head with a pair of sea otters floating nearby as they swerved in a wide angle around them. Mattituck's jealousy, clear from the night Izzy had shown interest in Todd at Bella Luna, was beginning to annoy him.

". . . I'm not sure she's what she pretends to be."

Mattituck waited several minutes before saying any more.

"Some guy tried to latch onto her wrist at the Crow's Nest the other night. Seamus came after the guy with his cricket bat, but Izzy had the guy on the ground before he was halfway there."

Todd peeled his eyes off the water to look at him.

"What do you mean, had him on the ground?"

"Just that. She made damned quick work of the guy, and he wasn't a squirrel, either. A chop to the neck and a grip on a key pressure point, right back here," he reached over his shoulder and pointed. "She knew exactly what she was doing." He ended with penetrating eyes boring into Todd's.

"Martial arts?"

"Yeah, but a particular brand of martial arts. The kind you learn in Special Ops, or the FBI or Intelligence. Nothing like you learn from the local sensei who coaches Little League on the side, that's for sure."

Todd listened in silence, then said, "I'm sure there's some explanation." Then a thought came to him. "Say . . . what do you know about that kind of training?"

Mattituck kept his eyes ahead, looking for dead heads and wildlife as the bow ate up the sea at 35 knots.

"Look," Todd said. "We've been partners for a while now. Isn't it time you clued me in more on your previous life?"

"What previous life?"

"No more shittin' me, Mattituck. Come clean. You've dropped little references here and there, anyway. Were you in Special Ops?"

Mattituck turned the helm to the left, more to stall than to avoid anything in the water. Todd could see the muscles in the man's jaw working. Whatever this touched on, it seemed to run deep.

"Yeah," Mattituck finally said. "I was."

Todd waited for more, but Mattituck had fallen silent. Apparently, that was all Todd would get for the moment. Todd had known Mattituck had been in Special Operations from when he'd run some background checks poking around his past before he had deputized him, as well as that he'd been with a special unit in the U.S. Park Service. For whatever reason, though, Mattituck seemed to want to keep these parts of his life private. Todd understood this, and knew that Mattituck would tell him in his own time. Or not. And if that proved to be the case, Todd would be fine with it. He knew to respect whatever the man may have been through, and it seemed likely that he'd been through something pretty horrific.

The next hour passed with the drone of the DeeVee8's twin Volvo-Pentas as the only sound paired with the occasional salt water spray on the windshield. Todd filled Mattituck in on what he'd found on Justin Harris' computer, along with the various possibilities that came with it.

"It seems more likely that what they'd planned was divorce, but I can't eliminate the possibility that they had something more sinister afoot."

"Back to our musings on Justin's death not being an accident, then?" Mattituck pressed.

Todd nodded. "The divorce theory just doesn't add up. Unless Wilson Garrett just signed the company over to Tara, there's no way she'd have the store in her sole ownership after a divorce. They'd have to split it, or one of them would have to buy out the other one."

"That doesn't seem likely," Mattituck agreed. "No way Wilson would just give it up. From what I hear, he built that company up on his own know-how."

"All on Tara's family's money," Todd added, "and her own little stockpile of cash her parents had given her over the years."

"What I don't get, though," Mattituck started, "is how Justin ends up dead, if he and Tara were thinking of knocking Wilson off."

"Yeah, that's what I've been mulling over, too. I'm hoping we'll find something on the Garretts' computers that will give us something to go on."

"Such as?"

"Such as something more concrete than cryptic hints in emails. Maybe some documents Tara's been drafting, or a Quit Claim Deed, or something."

"Okay," Mattituck's tone took on a curious tone. "So if you're looking for something Tara's been working on, that explains looking at her computers. But why Wilson's?"

"Ah," Todd said with a grin. "That's the more intriguing possibility for what we're trying to run down. What if Wilson found out about the affair?"

Mattituck turned and met Todd's look.

"He might get insanely jealous and want revenge."

"Exactly. And what if he found something that tipped him off that Justin and Tara were going to kill him?"

Mattituck stared at his friend.

"Wow. You really are one hell of a mother-fucking good cop, you know that?"

Todd grinned in response.

"I know a thing or two because I've seen a thing or two," he said.

"So just to spell it out," Mattituck went on, "you're thinking that if Tara was working a plan that Wilson stumbled on, it might be on one of their computers."

"Something like that."

"I could see a guy who came across something like that taking his buddy out for a little walk in the woods."

"Hunting accidents happen all the time," Todd finished.

It was coming up on noon when they turned south into the channel leading to Cordova. Mattituck had been keeping thoughts of Monica at bay for most of the trip, but now found himself unable to do so. What aggravated him most was not knowing why. Whatever the reason Monica had turned, he could accept. He knew he could. He'd been through tough times many times, and his ability to get through difficulty and pain was one of the few things he was sure of. But not knowing why . . .

Not that it mattered. The way things were looking, he would never have the opportunity to work things through with her. That *was* new to him. The pain that came with knowing he could have worked it through with Monica was what set this situation apart from all the others he could remember. Before, he hadn't really cared that much. With the onset of the previous times had come an immediate distancing that allowed him to protect himself. This time, with Monica, he didn't want to protect himself. He wanted them to turn to each other and grow closer. That was impossible, however, if she didn't open up about whatever was bothering her.

"And it takes two to tango," he muttered.

Todd looked up, and Mattituck realized he'd said that out loud.

"What's that?" Todd asked.

"Nothing. Just muttering shit."

Todd gave a nod.

"I know you're going to want to see Monica while we're here," he said, "which works out well for the first part of being here. I can get Howie Long to give me a couple of guys to help with the warrant. Might be cleaner to do this with all uniformed officers anyway. So you'll have at least the afternoon with Monica, and we'll probably stay overnight."

"I'm good with helping you today," Mattituck said.

"I was about to say we need to head out early for Hinchinbrook again early in the morning . . ."

"But? . . ."

"Everything okay with you and Monica?"

"Why would it not be?" Mattituck kept his eyes on the boat traffic ahead.

"When have we come down here and you not been fighting for time with her?"

Mattituck's jaw muscles were at work again.

"You are one zipped up dude, you know that?" Todd said irritably. "Are you two on the outs?"

Still, Mattituck said nothing.

"Geezus, Frank. I've laid out my whole fucking marriage bullshit in front of you, I know how it feels to be vulnerable. But we all need someone to talk to, so if you think I can be a good ear, I'm here for you. Okay?"

Still, the jaw muscles. Todd slid off the passenger seat to step out to the fish deck. Too much tension to bear at the moment, he thought. Before he had taken two steps, however, Mattituck spoke.

"I don't know what's going on," he said. "I went to see her that last time we were here, and she didn't want to see me. No explanation, no nothing. Just said to go away."

Todd turned and stepped back forward, looking at the back of his friend's head.

"I have no fucking clue what I did, but it must have been pretty fucking bad." He turned to Todd as Todd took the passenger seat again. "How the hell does a guy do something that bad without knowing he did anything?"

"That's one of the great male-female mysteries, isn't it? We guys piss off the women and never know what it was we did."

Mattituck looked at him, then chuckled.

Todd laughed, knowing it was comic relief rather than anything truly funny.

"Fuck, Todd, I'm so sorry. Here I am sulking like toddler, and you're facing a divorce. Whatever it is with Monica, it's either her shit or mine, and she'll either open up about it or she won't. As it is, though, there's nothing I can do, so there's no sense in fretting about it." He looked at his Trooper friend. "But what you're going through . . . damn, I can't even imagine."

Todd was deep in thought.

"It's not much different, actually, when you think about it. Only with me and Keri, it's both her shit and mine, and we're neither one of us willing to open up about it anymore. It is what it is." He was quiet a moment. "I'll be fine."

Mattituck held out his fist for a bump. Todd clenched his fist and knuckled him.

"We'll both be fine," Mattituck said.

It wasn't hard to find something for Mattituck to do while Todd and his troop of officers from the Cordova Police executed the search and confiscation warrant. Todd pulled up a picture of Tara Garrett and sent Mattituck out to the Copper River Inn with it. Mattituck took the Alaska State Trooper vehicle while Todd rode with Chief Long and his crew to Justin Harris' place.

On the drive out to see Eddie Etano, Mattituck continued to fight back thoughts of Monica. It was beyond him how she could just close up like she did. What could possibly have happened that would turn her so absolutely against him? . . . Against *them*, for he realized that he had begun to think of Monica and himself as a couple. He hadn't had that with anybody since Janelle, and in retrospect he wasn't at all sure that he'd fully thought of Janelle and himself that way, even though they had been engaged. No, there was something very different about Monica and the way they were together that had worked its way into how he thought of himself. He had been thinking of himself as part a part of Monica and her life, and she a part of him and his.

He picked up his phone from the seat beside him and looked at the screen, shifting his eyes from the road to the screen. Then he thought better of it, and started to set the phone on the seat. Instead, though, he pulled off onto to a turnout and looked at the phone screen again. He pulled up the text thread with Monica and quickly scrolled up past that terrible exchange from the other day, and focused on their interactions prior to whatever had happened.

Within minutes, he found himself smiling and recalling the feeling he had when he was with her, how she made him feel connected . . . like he mattered.

His anger faded. The way she felt about him was all too evident in every exchange, and with that realization he knew that whatever had happened, whatever made her close up, was from a deep and powerful pain. She wasn't a bitch, and she wasn't mean spirited. In fact, she was an amazing, compassion, and caring woman. There was simply no way this could come from anything other than hurt.

That was something Mattituck could very much relate to. His empathy for Monica grew as his love for her returned. He opened a text window and began to type.

*Monica . . . I know you're hurting. And I know something happened to cause this, and it must have been something I did. I'm sorry, whatever it was. I want you to know that nothing can stop me loving you, and that if we open up to each other, nothing can come between us. Please give us a chance. Please open up so we can deal with whatever happened.*

He read back through the message while the cursor blinked at the end. In the past, he never would have written something like this. He would have dismissed it as silly . . . maybe even pathetic. He would have calloused himself and written Monica off as having some kind of emotional problems or something, but he sure as hell would never do what he was doing now. For a moment, he considered deleting it.

He sat for several minutes, gazing at the mountains across Eyak Lake.

Yeah, he thought, it'd be better to at least wait a few minutes. Let the feeling pass. Then see what he thought and either send it or delete it. He hit the power button and the screen went dark on the message. It must have been how her feelings for him had been when she decided to close him out: Hitting a button and letting the screen go dark on them as a couple, on her feelings for him.

The anger returned as he wondered how she could just close down without even talking to him about whatever it was that had set her off. It must be, he thought, that she really didn't love him. Maybe she had been looking for a reason to end it, and found something to use as an excuse. In any case, it was fine. She'd made her decision.

He would delete the message. What the hell had he been thinking? She didn't want him. She'd made that perfectly clear.

He hit the power button and the screen came on, its wallpaper photo shining into his eyes as if he'd never seen it before. It was him and Monica sitting on a beach, turned back toward the camera in a well-posed selfie. Their smiles were genuine, filled with contentment and comfort with each other. He looked into Monica's eyes, and the plethora of text messages from the previous months came flooding back through his thoughts. The memory of her affectionate words coupled with the image of her face, her eyes smiling with her mouth, washed away the words of her dismissive texts from the other day.

With absolute certainty, he knew the 'go away' texts were not the real Monica. That was an old Monica, much like the anger Mattituck had just been feeling was the old him.

He opened the text again, where it sat waiting, hesitated again for a moment, then determined that if they were going to work things out, one of them would have to reach out. He couldn't think of any reason why it shouldn't be him.

With a chest-expanding breath, he watched his finger hit 'send.'

He read the message again as 'delivered' appeared beneath it, and he wondered if she was reading it. He decided to give her some privacy to absorb and think.

It might take minutes, it might take days. All he knew was that she was worth the wait. He just hoped it would be sooner so he could draw her into his arms and comfort her, reassure her.

The vibration of the engine, still running, pulled him back to the assigned task at hand. He put the cruiser in gear and pulled back onto the highway toward the Copper River Inn.

He was pulling into the gravel parking lot in less than five minutes. He stopped in front of the door with the 'Office' sign above it and cut the motor, then took the picture of Tara Garrett and entered the office.

Todd had been right: the interior had undergone a complete transformation. The counter had even been redesigned, and tables and soft furniture added. Together with the fresh paint and new carpeting, the place didn't look anything like Mattituck had last seen it, when Norman Peck had come in with his gun blazing.

Eddie Etano sat behind the counter, only his head visible, looking down at something at his lap. Probably playing a game on his phone, Mattituck thought.

"Hey, Eddie."

Eddie's head jerked up. Apparently he hadn't heard the *bing* of the door alert. His face slacked when he saw Mattituck.

"Oh, man," he complained. "Not you guys again."

"Great to see you, too, Eddie. How've you been?"

"Whadda yuh want? Your partner was just here a coupla days ago."

Mattituck placed the picture of Tara on the counter and slid it toward him. Eddie lifted his substantial frame and stepped to the counter. He studied the picture, then looked up.

"Okay," he said. "What about it?"

"Is that the woman who was in here regularly with Justin Harris?"

Eddie looked at it again.

"Pretty sure, yeah."

"Okay, thanks."

"That's it?"

"Yep. Thanks again. Have a great day, Eddie."

"Yeah, man, you too."

Mattituck paused before he got to the door, a thought coming to him. He turned back and Eddie moaned.

"There is one more thing you might help with."

"Oh, maaan . . . What?"

"You know, Eddie," Mattituck said with a teasing tone, "you really need to work on your attitude. We're nothing but nice to you, and look how you act."

Eddie stared at him, unmoving.

"Okay, Eddie, we can play hard ball, if you prefer."

Eddie shifted his eyes uncomfortably, looking past Mattituck at the flat screen TV mounted high in the corner of the lobby.

Mattituck nodded and started to turn.

"Trooper Benson and I observed a business transaction of some type last evening. Would that have been one of your, uhh, side-business transactions?"

Eddie continued looking at the screen.

"You got nothing on me, man," he said.

"Just pictures. A lot of them. Basically just showing that you had something besides hotel business going on here. With the other evidence we have—"

"What evidence?"

Mattituck merely shrugged and continued for the door.

"Have it your way, Eddie. We can get our info elsewhere."

"Wait a sec," Eddie blurted, nerves sounding frayed.

Mattituck turned.

"Whadda yuh need to know?"

Mattituck turned and walked dramatically toward the counter.

"With this Justin Harris, I'm just wondering if there was anything else that seemed unusual."

Eddie gave a quizzical expression. "Like how?"

"Anything with Justin Harris besides the woman in the picture. Anything at all."

"Man, you just fishin', dude." He shook his wide flat face. "Bullshit, man. That's bullshit. You're just seeing what I'll say."

"Yeah, that's right," Mattituck returned. "I'm fishing. I'm fishing for whatever a cop might be interested in knowing, and I'm expecting you'll tell me because I know there is something."

Eddie stared blankly, indecisive.

"Let's just say Trooper Benson and I are testing your . . . usefulness. The most useful informants know what a cop wants to know."

"What about those who aren't so useful?" Eddie ventured.

"We stop using them."

"And what happens then?"

"The arrangement is gone. Meaning the less-than-useful informant's side businesses trip him up."

"Trip him up how?"

Mattituck's face hardened.

"Talk about bullshit," he said coldly. "You're playing games, Eddie. And I'm done."

He turned for the door.

"No wait. Maybe there is something."

Mattituck stopped, not turning this time.

"The owner of that outdoor gear store came in asking questions about Justin and that woman."

Mattituck was stunned. He figured some info would come out of his bluff, but this was far more than he'd expected. He turned and faced Eddie Etano.

"Wilson Garrett?"

"Yeah," Eddie nodded vigorously. "That's the guy. Wilson Garrett. The AK Outfitters."

"What would he want to know about Justin Harris and this woman?"

"He showed me a picture of the same woman you just showed me. He give me 500 bucks for the info. He showed me the picture and asked if I'd ever seen her, and I said yeah, I'd seen her."

"Before or after he knew it was Justin Harris."

"Before," Eddie said. "He came in with the picture and asked if I'd ever seen her in here."

"When was this?"

"Few days ago. A week maybe. No wait, it was a little more than a week, pro'ly two weeks."

"Okay, Eddie. Good work. You're back on the useful list."

Eddie smiled nervously.

Mattituck stepped closer to the counter and placed a hundred dollar bill in front of the Samoan hotel manager.

"I'm not rich like Wilson Garrett, but thanks."

"I thought cops couldn't pay for this shit."

"I'm not a cop," Mattituck said turning, then stepped out the door.

Mattituck and Todd met up for dinner at the Fisherman's Warped, a little hole-in-the-wall restaurant specializing in seafood and burgers that overlooked the marina on the south side. Half of the restaurant was on pilings over a shallow portion of the harbor, adding to the atmosphere of being a "fresh off the boats" cuisine—if you could call that brand of food cuisine. The décor consisted of old fishing nets, buoys, and boat cleats with distressed wood walls.

The collection of the computers had gone very quickly, with Tara Garrett putting up a vehement but short-lived resistance. Wilson Garrett was out of town, and Tara had been unable to account for his whereabouts.

"Which only raises my suspicion," Todd said. "Something's not right here."

"Are you thinking something's afoot with husband and wife here? Because what I got at the Copper River Inn affirms it."

"Eddie recognized her?"

"Yeah, but something more. On a hunch, I asked Eddie if there were anything else a cop might be interested in. He said that Wilson Garrett had come in with a picture of Tara as well, asking if she had been there with Justin."

Todd straightened in his seat.

"And before you ask, I checked on the timing. Wilson came in with the picture and asked before anything else. So, no way could Eddie have connected it by being led."

"You're getting really good at this work," Todd said. "You should consider a career in law enforcement."

Mattituck gave him a sidelong look, then went on. "He said he told him she'd been there, and Wilson asked if she had been with Justin. So totally unprompted by Eddie, Wilson knew what he was looking for."

Todd absorbed this. "So he knew."

Mattituck nodded. "Seems so."

They were both quiet as the server set two orders of beer-batter halibut and fries in front of them, along with two bottles of Alaskan Amber.

"And Wilson's out of town," Todd mused. "I wonder where he is."

"Want me to share my hunch?"

Todd looked up quickly. He was growing to trust Matttiuck's instincts.

"Yeah, what are you thinking?"

"I'm thinking Wilson is the one who shoved that orange hunting vest into the bushes."

"You think he might be out there trying to get it back?"

Mattituck nodded. "And covering up whatever other traces he left."

"We sifted the area pretty good," Todd returned.

"Maybe so. But that doesn't mean there isn't more out there somewhere."

"True," Todd acknowledged. "How do you feel about heading out there in the morning?"

"I feel like we have at least three hours of light left tonight," Mattituck said, "and nothing else to hold us to town."

The reference to Mattituck having no Monica to keep him in town pained Todd momentarily.

"Let's down this and get going," Todd said.

# Chapter Eighteen

## Hunter and Hunted

Monica sat in her office, staring blankly at the folders in front of her, illuminated by her computer screen. It wasn't dark outside yet, but it was getting there, and she hadn't changed the dark wood, old style library look her father had decorated the office in three decades prior. The décor always made the room seem dark early.

She had been fighting a listless feeling since she had told Mattituck to leave. The last text he'd sent had sent doubts reverberating through her resolve to end their relationship, although she wasn't sure she ever really had a permanent resolve. Sure, they had drifted apart before in their nearly three year on-again-off-again relationship, but this last time they had stayed together well over a year, and she had been sure in her sense of commitment—not just her toward Mattituck, but him toward her. There had been no doubt.

The picture Betty Ingram had shared, however, punched a huge hole in her confidence in them. As stunned as the pictures had left her feeling, driving her into that familiar dark place within, as well as to her bed for a long undisturbed sleep, she had doubted the story the photos had told even when she saw them. It simply didn't fit the sure image she had of Frank. Try as she might to convince herself otherwise, deep down inside, she just didn't believe he was involved with anybody else.

The woman's beauty struck a jealous chord in her, though, and that was enough to give a foothold to her desire to run away—as far away from Mattituck as possible, along with the trust that was necessary in any relationship in order for it to be successful. The hurt alone—whether based on fact or not—was enough to make her want to call it quits.

But still . . . she couldn't see this being the end.

She stood up and walked to the two lamps on either side of the office, turning the plastic switches under the lampshades so that the room was cast with a yellow light along with the dusk light from outside.

Where was Frank now? she wondered. Was he hurting? Or was he maybe hardening himself against her?

*No*, she thought, *that last text came a couple of days after I told him to piss off, and basically said he wanted to talk.* Her thoughts drifted to his gentleness. Despite his gruffness and reputation for being sometimes more than a bit surly, he was good and kind, and certainly affectionate and warm. Something was amiss about those pictures, she was sure, and it seemed likely that Frank would be able to explain.

But the pain. It was just too intense, and Monica didn't know how to stow that away. It ate at her, in spite of her rational thoughts.

She turned and looked at the desk and the blue light still visible from the computer screen. The Garrett files spread out on her desk, and the State Economic Board database on the computer screen. She had been trying to get more data on the AK Outfitters, hoping it would shed some light on her nagging feeling that Tara was up to something no good.

She pushed her hair back, along with her thoughts of Mattituck, and stepped around the desk to peer down at the papers.

It was going to be a long night. She dialed for Chinese food to be delivered and walked to the house for a bottle of merlot and a wine glass. When she returned, she turned on the stereo. The CD exchanger was old, and she'd been meaning to upgrade the receiver/amp to one that could pull in the Internet, but for now this was what she had. There were five soft jazz discs loaded, which suited her mood just fine. She stopped at the window on her way back to the desk, gazing down at the marina from her high vantage, and caught a glimpse of an aluminum hull boat with yellow paint down the sides and on the superstructure.

The DeeVee8. Frank.

She watched as the boat cleared the jetty, outgoing, and picked up speed as it turned north toward the main channel into Prince William Sound. Her stomach contracted. She wished she were aboard, that she'd never seen those pictures.

Where was he headed? Why had he been in town? Were he and Todd working the Garrett case?

She turned and looked at the desk after the DeeVee8 disappeared behind a stand of trees along the shore.

The Garrett case.

With the sommelier's corkscrew, she worked the cork out of the merlot bottle and poured a glass, then sat behind the desk and went to work.

A half hour earlier, Todd and Mattituck's digestive systems had hardly a chance to kick in on their dinner before they were aboard the DeeVee8, readying to get underway. They had split on the way to the harbor, with Mattituck stopping for food provisions while Todd checked in at the Cordova Police station and called his State Trooper reporting point in Glennallen. As they readied the boat, a gruff voice hollered a greeting from the dock.

Mattituck and Todd looked up in unison to see Harbormaster Tom Graffinino's rugged face beaming at them.

"Ho, Tom!" Todd bellowed back. "How goes it?"

"Leaving early I see," the tall Alaska sourdough replied. "Everybody's leaving all of a sudden!"

Todd and Mattituck exchanged glances.

"Who else?" Mattituck asked as Graffinino stepped to the boat and leaned on her gunwale.

"Well, the reg'lar gillnetter boys, of course, but they all got a midnight opener coming. That what you getting underway for?" he asked Todd.

"Nope," Todd shook his head. "Too busy on this hunter accident case."

"Ah, the Garrett thing?"

"That's right," Todd said.

"Inneresting you say that, 'cause the wife just got underway an hour or so ago."

Again, an exchanged glance between Todd and Mattituck.

"Tara Garrett?" Mattituck asked, unfurling the bowline from the cleat.

"Yeah, that's right," Tom said. "I'm covering the hourly watch, which is why I'm here now. She said she was heading up to Valdez for an errand for the store." A thoughtful expression crossed his face. "I guess it was two rounds ago I saw her. So probably a little more than two hours ago she headed out."

Todd stopped adjusting the fenders to look at the harbormaster.

"I've known you a long time, Tom. What's up? You sound like something doesn't seem right."

The tall man raised a hand and rubbed his forehead.

"Ain't. Leastways, to my thinkin' anyhow. She had a 30.06, a slug-bearin' shotgun, and a .44 on her hip."

"Damn," Mattituck chimed in. "That's quite an arsenal for a town-to-town errand."

"Right?" Graffinino said. "Seems overkill. I had the feelin' she warn't headin' to Valdez at all."

"Sounds right," Todd said. "Any idea where she was headed?"

Graffinino looked around the harbor and then up the channel. "Well, she did head up north, not that

that says anything. But she didn't fuel up before heading out, s'though she was in a bit of hurry."

"How much fuel does her boat hold?" Mattituck asked.

"Not sure, but it's one of those smaller Hewes Craft with a cabin. She's got the twin 125's on her, so she burns more fuel. Those boats tend to have only a 70 or so gallon tank."

"So the range would be less than a run to Valdez if not full up," Mattituck said.

Graffinino nodded.

"Does she tend to fuel up when coming in?" Mattituck asked, since a lot of folks topped their fuel tanks coming into port.

"Nope. Not usually. The lazy boater type, y'know?"

Mattituck nodded.

"So your best guess?" Todd asked.

"Not Valdez, for sure."

Todd shot a look at Mattituck, then turned back to Graffinino.

"I was going to ask," he said, "if maybe Wilson Garrett had gone out, but if Tara took the boat . . ."

"Oh, they've got two boats," Graffinino said quickly. "He headed out late yesterday."

"Can we get a description of both boats?" Todd asked, his gaze full of meaning as he caught Mattituck's eye.

"Sure thing," Tom said. "Follow me up to the office."

Twenty minutes later, Mattituck was pushing the DeeVee8 near her top speed as soon as they'd gotten the speedy charter boat up on step. He knew these waters so well there had been no need to plot courses on the GPS, and now they were barreling north, weaving slowly through the vessel traffic of the channel, as they headed for their landing cove on Hinchinbrook Island. There hadn't even been a discussion of where they were headed—both Todd and Mattituck were guessing where Tara had been headed; but they were very sure of where Wilson Garrett had gone.

As Tom Graffinino had said, there were a lot of gillnetters headed for the midnight fish opening, wherever that was scheduled, so Mattituck had to pick his way through the boat traffic while Todd spent most of the time on his satellite phone with his superiors at the State Trooper post in Glennallen, reporting in and making sure his plans for proceeding were approved. Most of the time, Todd worked at his own will and reported only when needed, but Mattituck noted that this time for whatever reason Todd felt he needed to be in closer contact with the rest of the AST network.

As he listened to Todd reporting what he'd found on Justin Harris' computers—which apparently had been the easiest to search and find information pertinent to the case—Mattituck thought about the implications of the separate boat trips by Wilson and Tara Garrett. From Mattituck's perspective, it seemed very likely that Wilson had figured out the affair between his wife and Justin, had gathered evidence for his own assurance, and then had planned, and then executed, vengeance against his old friend by plotting an accidental hunting death for him. He had shot and killed Justin, then run to the Coast Guard lighthouse and reported it. A simple enough scheme.

But something clearly had complicated the case he and Todd were working. First, there was the third set of footprints that Mattituck and Todd had noticed on their first investigative trek on Hinchinbrook. Then there had been the discovery of the affair between Tara and Justin, and this was where the supposed tidiness fell apart, leaving an array of possible stories lying parallel to each other. It seemed there were several alternate explanations lying side-by-side, awaiting the next concrete clue before he could speculate on what had happened. But for Mattituck's non-cop mind, and his acute intuition, things seemed more clear.

He mulled the possibilities, forcing himself to give each equal air. But still he settled on his gut instinct, which was that Tara was the third set of boot prints he and Todd had seen on Hinchinbrook, and that she was now in pursuit of her husband . . . with every intent to kill him.

Further, Mattituck felt that she had originally been on Hinchinbrook as part of a plan she and Justin had, in which she and Justin were to 'accidentally' shoot Wilson, rather than the other way around. Mattituck could imagine the surprise when the plan was turned against them.

He could imagine Tara following the pair of hunting buddies, awaiting the right moment, only to suddenly hear the crack of a gunshot that left Justin lying on the ground. Had Tara seen it? Or had she come on the scene after Wilson's grisly deed?

In any case, Mattituck agreed with Todd's assessment that Justin had been shot the first time from a distance—supposedly in a hunting accident—then when Wilson found that his first shot had not killed Justin, he walked down to his old friend lying on the ground, seriously wounded, and shot him point-blank in the chest.

Had Tara seen this?

There was no way of knowing at this point. But from what Mattituck and Todd had pieced together on the scene, Wilson had removed his friend's hunting vest and stowed it in the brush as a means of explaining how he'd accidentally shot the man. It was borrowing from a scenario that played out nearly a hundred times each year nationally—a hunter shed his orange safety vest for a variety of reasons, only to be mistaken for a deer by his own friends.

And now Wilson Garrett was likely headed out to the scene, most likely to retrieve the ditched hunting vest that Todd and Mattituck had already recovered, and Tara was in pursuit to try to kill him off as originally planned by Justin and her.

Mattituck checked the radar as they approached the sharp left turn around the point into Orca Bay. There were fewer contacts here, and he decided there was no need to slow his approach to their turn. They needed to move as quickly as possible. He checked their speed on the GPS, which read 37 knots, and he knew they were making the best speed they could. If Tara were about two hours ahead of them, there wasn't much chance of overtaking her. They needed to make sure they were close enough to catch up and observe—on land, not on the sea where they could be easily seen.

Ideally, they would get close enough to Tara's boat to track her on radar and see where she put the boat ashore. Mattituck wasn't holding out much hope for that, however. Most likely they would have to duck into a few coves to check, although it seemed likely it would be the same one Todd and he had been using.

Todd was off the phone, tucking it away into his pack.

"That was a lot of info to pass on," Mattituck said.

Todd nodded. "There's been a lot going on."

"Sounds like there was plenty on Justin's computer to seal the theory he and Tara were having an affair."

Todd nodded. "Corroborated by Eddie Etano recognizing Tara's picture. What I really like," he added, giving Mattituck a sidelong glance, "is that cool little sleuthing bit you did with Eddie Etano, getting out of him that Wilson had also been in there asking questions."

"Pretty good, eh?" Mattituck grinned.

"Damned good." Todd peered at the radar, then took the binoculars and peered out windshield ahead. "It gets the brain working. I've been thinking it through various possibilities, and the strongest possibility is looking like Wilson did murder Justin Harris."

"Glad to see you've come around."

Todd's smile broadened. "Well, the autopsy analysis came back this afternoon. We know the entry and exit wounds on Justin Harris tell us that he was first shot in the back at a distance of about a hundred yards. The shot that killed him, though, was fired no more than 20 feet away, and from a low angle. Meaning that Justin was probably on his back on the ground, his feet toward Wilson as he approached. It looks like Wilson shot him in cold blood, likely with Justin conscious and pleading."

Mattituck shook his head at the sobering image.

"What about Tara?" he asked, looking over at him.

"She's got to be one of these contacts up here," Todd replied, pointing at three different contacts that appeared to be moving in the same direction as them toward the center of Prince William Sound.

"No," Mattituck said. "I mean what about Tara in the scenario you just gave."

Todd's head jerked in surprise.

"Oh," he said with a chuckle. "I thought you were asking me to check on the boats ahead."

"We'll know which one she is in a few minutes," Mattituck returned. "Nobody will be headed to Hinchinbrook Entrance this time of day except her. The others will veer more north."

With that, Todd stopped peering at the radar and focused on the water ahead.

"So Tara," he said reflectively. "I'm pretty sure it was her boot prints we saw out there. So my best guess is that she and Justin were planning something to kill Wilson, but he beat them to the punch."

"And now?"

"She's headed out to finish the job."

Mattituck thought about this. It really did make the most sense.

"So what's our plan?" he asked, his eyes on Todd's profile.

"I figure we let her get ashore. She's going to head up the ravine to try to track Wilson down. Or she may lay low and wait for him to come back down."

Mattituck waited for him to go on.

"I feel like I could use some coffee. How 'bout you?" Todd asked.

"Sounds good."

Todd made his way to the small galley in the aft port area of the cabin and rummaged for the makings, lighting the propane stove as he did.

"I'm thinking we do our best to come in unseen. Even if she spots the boat, she probably doesn't know it, right?"

"Not that I know of," Mattituck said. "DeeVee8's a pretty standard looking charter boat."

Todd feigned a hurt look, clutching at his heart.

"What?! Your beautiful, sleek—"

"Shut the fuck up," Mattituck shot with humor.

Todd went on. "I figure if we put ashore someplace near where she does, we can move her direction and get a feel for what she's doing."

"With luck, we'll see her moving up the ravine before we're off the water."

Todd paused. "You think we could?"

"Very sure of it, if she heads up after Wilson. That first mile or more is all low scrub brush and muskeg. From where we were hiking, it felt pretty covered, but from out on the water, we should be able to spot her."

"Nice," Todd mused. "But if we don't see her . . ."

"We won't really have any way of knowing if she's already up the ravine, or if she's lying low near Wilson's boat waiting for him."

Todd shook his head. "Shit . . . not a good set of options there."

"No," Mattituck agreed. "It's not."

Monica had been at work for more than two hours, and was feeling the effects of the wine. The Chinese food had helped absorb the alcohol, but Monica rarely drank more than a glass of wine at a time, and she had just polished off the bottom of the bottle.

It had been a productive evening, however, and now Monica had a dilemma. Her poking around State databases had helped her piece together enough to tell her that Tara had been anything but forthright with her. In addition to what Monica was now sure had been a forged letter ending the expansion of the store into Seattle, she had found a business license had been purchased by Tara for a hunting guide business, something she nor Wilson had any experience with, but that Justin Harris had been working in for more than five years. The company name declared on the license was T & J Hunting Guides.

She had also discovered by searching the Fish and Wildlife database that Justin Harris had applied to have his hunting guide license expanded to include the business name T & J Hunting Guides.

There was no doubt Tara and Justin were preparing to start a business together. Where, then, did that leave Wilson Garrett? It was certainly possible that this was part of Tara's plans following the divorce, but Monica couldn't shake the feeling that there was more to it. Perhaps it was the general distrust she felt about Tara Garrett, but this new information about her and Justin going into business together smacked of much more. It just wouldn't work without complications with Wilson, even after a divorce.

Unless Tara and Justin had planned to make sure Wilson wasn't a complication.

Monica had no choice but to confront Tara about all this, and make it clear that if she were not disclosing everything that Monica might have to remove herself from representing her. A major piece of this, of course, was the fraudulent action of forging business documents in Wilson's name, but the rest of what Monica was discovering carried implications that went well beyond the professional and legal boundaries of the attorney/client relationship.

She picked up the phone and dialed Tara Garrett's number. With no answer, she dialed the store.

"AK Outfitters," answered a voice.

"Yes, I'm looking for Tara Garrett."

"I'm sorry, she's not here. Can I take a message?"

"No," Monica said, then out of curiosity added, "What about Wilson Garrett?"

"Oh, he's out on Hinchinbrook Island. Went hunting earlier today. He should be back in a couple of days."

"Okay," Monica said, her voice vague with her thoughts. "Thank you."

She set the phone back on its cradle.

Wilson on Hinchinbrook. Why? He shouldn't be returning to anyplace near the scene of Justin's death. Again following her instincts, Monica opened the file that listed the property and holdings of the Garrett's. She quickly located the two boats, one in Wilson's name and one in Tara's. She looked at the location listed for Tara's boat, then dialed the harbormaster's office. A gravely voice answered.

"Yes," Monica said, "I'm wondering if you can tell me whether the boat in slip B-17 is in port."

The voice chuckled.

"You mean Tara Garrett's?"

"Yes, that's the one."

"Hell, that's a popular one today," the man said. "she left several hours ago. Following her husband, is my guess."

"You said that's a popular one. What do you mean? The slip?"

"No," the deep voice replied. "Tara Garrett. Coupla other guys were asking about it. Something going on?" Tom Graffinino asked.

"Not that I know of. Just trying to find my friend. Who were the guys? Any chance it was a State Trooper and another guy? A guy with a close-cut beard?"

Again, the man laughed.

"You must mean Todd Benson and Frank Mattituck. Yep. That's them. Why?"

"Just wondering. Thanks."

"Can I ask who's calling?"

Monica decided it was best not to answer and hung up. If the man really wanted to know, her landline number was listed under the law firm's name. He could see who she was by looking at caller ID.

Monica sat staring toward the window. *So Frank and Todd are following behind Tara, who is probably following Wilson.* She mulled this over, trying to come up with more comforting possibilities. She could think of none. The only thing that made sense put Todd and Frank in danger.

Monica picked up her cell, sure now that Mattituck and the DeeVee8 were setting out for Hinchinbrook, and likely with no idea of Tara Garrett's intentions. She dialed Frank. This might put her in some jeopardy in terms of breaching confidentiality with her client, but she would sort through the details of the bar's ethical guidelines later. Right now, she was far more concerned that Todd and Frank might walk into a crossfire between Wilson and Tara Garrett.

There was no answer on Mattituck's phone, and it went to voice mail. She opted for a text message instead, even though it would leave a traceable record that could put her professionally at risk.

*Not ready to talk about us, but know where u r headed. U may be in danger. Call me.*

She read the message before hitting send, wondering if she should say something more about them. A part of her wanted to reassure him, to reach out like he had reached out to her. But she didn't feel ready, and the danger they might be in was a perfect cover anyhow. And really, when it came down to it, that danger was the only reason she had wanted to text him.

She read the message once more, then hit 'send.'

She waited to see if 'delivered' would appear below her message, but it didn't. She waited several moments, but it never appeared.

Clearly Frank and Todd were out of cell range.

The sun was low to the north-northwest as Mattituck and Todd motored through Port Etches, the large inlet of Hinchinbrook Island that provided access to the ravine leading to the scene of Justin Harris' murder. As they moved up the inlet, the tall spine of a mountain ridge that bordered this side of the ravine dropped sharply, and they soon had the view up the ravine that Mattituck had noted on their previous trips.

"I'll be damned," Todd said. "I hadn't noticed that, but you are spot on about that view up the ravine."

He grabbed the binoculars and trained them as low down the ravine as he could. They were not yet to a point where they could see inside the lagoon, where Tara's boat—perhaps Wilson's as well—were likely beached, so Todd began scanning upward along the expansive U-shaped ravine.

"I'll be damned twice over," he said under the binoculars.

"What? You see her?"

"Yep. She's either made great time, or she wasn't the contact we thought she was."

"Or there's another."

Todd pulled his head back from the lenses and looked at Mattituck.

"What do you mean?"

"Again, I don't know why anybody would be headed this way this late in the day."

"Unless there's a third party . . . ?"

Mattituck shook his head. "What would be the odds of that?"

"Pretty slim. The bigger question to me would be who?"

They were both silent as they each processed possibilities.

"We'd better be very fucking careful," Mattituck said.

"Agreed."

They were now coming around to the opening to the lagoon, and both watched eagerly as they swung around to afford a full view inside. On the other side of the lagoon was Tara's HewesCraft with the twin 125's. The boat was well up the beach, landed almost too high considering that the tide was outgoing. She would have to wait for the next high tide to launch, as the boat was far too heavy for her to drag back down to the receded water line.

But what had Mattituck's attention was the second boat, nearby.

"Didn't Graffinino say Wilson's boat was also a HewesCraft, but with a cuddy cab on it?"

Todd only nodded, looking at what held Mattituck's attention. The boat, a cuddy cab HewesCraft, was at least 15 feet lower on the beach. Since it was now an outgoing tide, it was clear the boat had been beached after Tara's boat.

Todd spoke first.

"Correct me if I'm wrong," he said. "But doesn't that look like Wilson came in after Tara?"

"No question about it," was all Mattituck said.

# Chapter Nineteen

## The Turn of the Hunt

Mattituck and Todd agreed that they were best off finding another place to land the DeeVee8 than next to Wilson's and Tara's boats in the lagoon they had used before.

"That ridge comes right down to that lagoon," Mattituck said, "so I think we're best off trying down that way a little farther."

"There's another inlet just ahead," Todd said, studying the chart on the chart table.

Mattituck peered at the GPS screen.

"Shit. I hadn't noticed that before."

"You're slipping, old man," Todd quipped.

"Uh-ha-ha," Mattituck returned in a flat voice.

He steered the DeeVee8 closer to shore, preparing to turn into the inlet.

"Hopefully," he said, "it's not rocky and has a place where we can land. Any rocks on the chart?"

Todd was leaning over the paper chart. He shook his head.

"No. Looks like it might be sandy, in fact."

Todd left the chart and picked up the binoculars again, pointing them up the ravine.

"There he is."

Mattituck turned to look, and Todd handed him the binoculars. Just emerging onto the moraine at the foot of the upward sloping ravine was a figure, too far to identify, but clearly moving into the ravine. Mattituck scanned up the ravine to see if he could spot Tara again.

"She disappeared behind some trees," Todd said, knowing what Mattituck was looking for.

"Well, I guess this tells us it's safe to boldly chase them up the ravine."

"We'll still need to be cautious and out of view," Todd disagreed. "We don't know that either of them is alone."

Mattituck thought about this as he steered the DeeVee8 around the point and into the next inlet down from Tara's and Wilson's boats. He scanned the shoreline as it came into view. There were a lot more trees down this way than around the lagoon, which might make it more difficult to hike up toward the ravine, but the beach looked free of rocks and offered a smooth sandy landing. The tall grass right in front of the line of trees reminded Mattituck of the wolverine that attacked him.

"Hey," he said suddenly. "Did you ever ask around about that wolverine?"

Todd pulled his eyes from the binoculars to look at him.

"I talked to a vet at the lab. She said it couldn't be rabies. There are some nasty viruses that can affect them like that, but nothing that would harm a human."

"Viruses, eh? Is that enough to make it go nuts like that?"

Todd looked at him again, then said, "You don't have much experience with wolverines, do you?"

"Not that close."

"Well, they're all pretty surly creatures, even without something driving them crazy. Doesn't take much to get them to come after you."

"But that ferocious?" Mattituck asked with a bewildered tone.

"Again, you don't have much experience with them, do you?"

Mattituck shook his head.

"The lab vet said those viruses are increasing with the change in average temperature in the region."

"Really," Mattituck said, no surprise in his tone. "We should alert the media."

Todd laughed, offering his agreement with, "Add it to the long list along with melting glaciers and volatile storms on the Sound and Gulf."

Mattituck nosed the DeeVee8's aluminum hull to the sandy shore, then powered up the twin Volvo Pentas, giving her a strong boost up. He was careful to disengage the props before they came close to hitting bottom. He shut the diesels down and systematically turned off the GPS, radar, and VHF radio. He had just recently installed HF, High Frequency, radio, but he only fired that up when he was on the Gulf. The VHF coverage was excellent in the Sound.

Todd was already on the bow retrieving the anchor. He carefully lowered it to the sandy beach and hopped down after it. He hauled it with both hands at least thirty feet up the beach, listening to the winch pay out line in its free-wheeling mode. He dropped the anchor into the sand with the point of the steel down, then pounded it in deep with his boot so it would hold should the tide come in before they got back.

Mattituck had a habit of doubling this up by securing a spare mooring line to the anchor and tying the other end off to a tree or other stationary object, just to be sure. He'd been stranded for a few hours once when the Knot Skunked had gone adrift while he was helping hunting clients set up their camp. He had no interest in repeating that unsettling feeling of losing his lifeline to civilization.

After they had the DeeVee8 fastened to shore, they gathered their gear without a word, Todd passing it down to Mattituck on the beach. Todd hopped down to the sand, kicking sand against Mattituck's boots and their equipment, producing a momentary pounding-surf sound as the sand splayed against the various materials. It was in the moment that Mattituck realized how quiet it was.

Mattituck held up his hand as Todd straightened, brushing off his pants legs. He froze, watching Mattituck intently as he shot glances to the brush at the edge of the beach.

"It's so quiet," was all Mattituck said.

"Geezuss!" Todd blurted. "I thought you heard something."

"Like what?"

"I don't know. Like somebody Wilson had left behind to keep watch or something."

"Or a crazy wolverine?" Mattituck smirked.

"You have a warped sense of humor."

"You first," Mattituck jibed, gesturing ahead. "See how it feels."

Todd hadn't been joking about being cautious, and it was clear he had intended to lead the way anyhow, Mattituck noted. Maybe it was because he thought he was better trained, or maybe it was because he felt that as the real cop he should take the bulk of responsibility. Although Mattituck had been in the wilderness in dangerous situations many times, he was in no mood to share all that with Todd right now, although he knew Todd knew about some of his background. Instead, he shifted the center-of-gravity of the pack on his back and kept an eye out past his friend's shoulders, his Ruger .375 rifle at the ready.

Todd paused and glanced back at Mattituck, then looked at the big bear rifle in his friend's hands.

"I'll be glad you have that thing if a bear comes along, but you're really weighed down with that deer rifle over your shoulder."

Mattituck shrugged. "It's not all that heavy."

It made sense to Todd, since the Ruger was a shorter range, heavy slug rifle and the Winchester 30 a sharper, longer-range rifle. Odds were on that if they needed to use their weapons out here, it wouldn't be a handgun.

Todd turned and continued to the tall grass.

"Besides," Mattituck said with an edge of humor. "I'm afraid of wolverines at short range."

"I don't blame you," Todd said over his shoulder. "I think we need to get through these spruce before we can size up the situation around the lagoon."

"We could just skirt wide around that lagoon," Mattituck suggested. The prime objective, to his thinking, was to get up the ravine and see what Tara was up to. And Wilson.

"What do you make of that, anyway?" he asked Todd's back.

"Make of what?"

"Tara heading up to the site, and Wilson behind her."

Todd thought for several moments.

"Not sure, to tell the truth. I had been thinking Tara was hunting Wilson down, and I still think she thinks she is. But here comes Wilson, up *behind* her instead of in front of her." He paused and turned to look at Mattituck. "Seems the hunter became the hunted."

"It does. But what doesn't make sense to me is where she thought his boat would be. I mean, she obviously didn't see it here, and I doubt she'd think he'd tie it up to that old lighthouse dock."

"I think you're overthinking it," Todd said.

"How do you mean?"

"I don't think she was thinking about where his boat might be. There are a lot of places a guy could put his boat to shore, right?"

"Not all that many on this island," Mattituck returned. "Big island with only a few access points. That entire south side is inaccessible because of the Gulf seas and high cliffs. And all along the western end, it's super shallow water and difficult navigation.

It's really just Port Etches to access the island. These little inlets are where hunters are almost always put ashore. Here or up around Point Johnstone."

"That's where Wilson and Justin Harris landed the boat on their trip," Todd offered.

"No shit? Damn . . . that's a long-ass hike down to here."

"It was planned as an eight-day hunting trip. They'd been out for four days."

"Wow. Die-hard. That is a seriously long way on foot."

Todd nodded agreement as he stepped into the line of spruce trees, picking a path through the underbrush.

"I don't buy it, though," Mattituck said suddenly. "I don't think Tara would know about this place and not be thinking about where Wilson's boat was."

Todd was picking his way through the densely wooded band of trees, not bothering to step over the undergrowth, but pushing his way through instead. Mattituck noted the snapping and crunching of brush twigs and branches as he pushed behind Todd.

"I think she knew where Wilson and Justin had put ashore," Todd answered, "and I think she knew where they were hiking and I think she knew precisely where they were at any given time."

Mattituck was genuinely perplexed.

"Are you thinking she and Justin were in contact? As in cell or radio? The signals suck back in here. There's no way—"

"No," Todd interrupted. "Radio and cell signals are bad. You're right. But GPS is solid."

Mattituck hadn't thought of this.

248

"Holy shit. You're absolutely right. Damn . . . that's a game changer, isn't it?"

"Yeah," Todd said. "Isn't it."

Monica stood on one of the docks in the marina at Cordova, watching the sun's rays project upward like a golden, pink-tinged halo around the two thousand foot mountains to the northwest. It was nothing more than a whim that had driven her to get in the car and drive down the hill to the harbor, then a vague urge that had called her to walk among the boats, with no other intention than to let her thoughts wander along with her physical presence among the sailboats and fishing seiners.

Mattituck had still not responded to her text, leaving her worried whether he and Todd would see her warning before they stumbled into a potentially lethal situation. Someplace over that mountain, she was sure, they were furthering their investigation or chasing who they already knew to be a possible killer. But she wasn't privy to knowing, because of her and Frank's falling out. A part of her cursed herself, while another part knew rationally that these things were not related.

Or were they?

She hunched her shoulders and pulled her crossed forearms up under her breasts. She drew a slow, deep breath as she watched a bald eagle swoop low over the water then catch an updraft. She told herself that she was only concerned about Frank because it was the natural reaction of any compassionate person when another person was in danger. But she knew better. The depth of her concern was far deeper than a mere acquaintance—or even a friend—would feel.

But he had been with that woman, the woman in Betty Ingrahm's pictures. What was the story behind that, she wondered. With a little distance, she was not as emotional in her thoughts. Only a couple of days before, a jealousy that bordered on rage had filled her when she thought of those photos.

No, she thought, that's not just jealousy. It's knowing how anybody in a relationship like that should be treated, and no matter what explanation Frank thought he could offer, there was no denying the woman's hands in his, her backside against his crotch, the way she looked at him.

But that look wasn't on his face, she thought suddenly. In fact, she couldn't remember what his face had looked like. She had been so focused on the woman and where hands and bodies were that she couldn't remember what expression might be on Frank's face. She wished she could see the pictures again so she could look, although she couldn't explain why.

Was it possible that deep inside, she knew that he wasn't a party to whatever that woman had been up to?

Still, he might be involved with her. Might be.

Monica shivered and shook off these thoughts. Irritated with herself, she turned and strode briskly back toward shore and her car.

She had work to do. This had been a nice break, in the cool evening air among the boats, but she had five active cases and a living will to draft. Time to get back to the office.

No doubt, a glass of merlot would help.

Having cleared the lagoon area without a trace of another human being, Todd and Mattituck continued up the ravine in pursuit of Wilson Garrett, and a mile or two ahead of him, Tara Garrett. The only common goal between all four individuals was the site of what now was clearly a crime scene.

Todd stopped a hundred feet before the ravine began to slope upward and peered upward. He pulled the binoculars from their case hanging from his neck and checked the terrain ahead. Mattituck came up beside him and stopped, waiting.

"I don't like it," Todd announced.

"Neither do I," Mattituck responded. "Too open?"

"Yeah. If they stopped to look back, they'd pick us up too easily." He lowered the binoculars and looked to both sides of the ravine. "Not many options, though."

Mattituck was already surveying both sides, but focused more on the south side of the ravine.

"It'd be slower going," he said, "but it looks like we could pick our way along that south edge. That line of spruce just in front of the ridge on that side would give us pretty good cover."

"But what we lose in speed could put us too far behind them," Todd said, squinting at the southern ridge. "What about up there?"

Mattituck followed his eyes upward, along the south ridge.

"It's pretty open up there, too," he said thoughtfully. "But if either of them were watching their back trail, they probably wouldn't think to look up there. Is that what you're thinking?"

Todd smiled. "That's precisely what I'm thinking."

"I wonder why Wilson wasn't concerned about Tara checking her back trail."

Again, Todd nodded agreement. "I was wondering the same thing. Two things: One is that he doesn't care. He's hunting her down, so who cares if she sees him? The other is that maybe he knows his wife, and knows she wouldn't check behind her."

Mattituck thought about these possibilities. "Well, I'm going to guess we'll never know which one. What we do know is that the ridge might be our best bet."

"Agreed," Todd shot back quickly. "Want to lead, or are you still shivering over wolverines?"

With a grin, Mattituck started for the south ridge.

It took them less than fifteen minutes to reach the rocky slope upward, most of which was picking their way through the thick band of spruce at the base. Todd stopped them to take some water and consult with the topographical map.

"It's getting dark, so I wonder if maybe we should take a rest before trying this slope."

Mattituck shook his head. He'd traversed such ridges many times before in the near-dark, and the 'dark' of SouthCentral Alaska this time of year wasn't nearly as foreboding as what he'd been through before.

"I think we'll be fine," he proffered. "I've done this before."

Todd watched him for a moment.

"All right," he said, deciding against probing his friend. "You lead."

Mattituck set out for the slowly increasing slope. Todd followed behind, thinking about his friend and his mysterious background. He knew that Frank Mattituck had a military background in special operations, and that he'd served in some kind of back country law enforcement branch of the U.S. Park Service, but little else. Both records were beyond even Trooper Benson's investigative abilities without his asking for assistance from those agencies. What he did know was that he trusted his friend and citizen deputy, and that it was best to let details of the man's past emerge on Mattituck's own time frame.

They quickly reached a steep slope, the last hundred yards or so before the ascent would become something close to rock-climbing. Mattituck pressed on, feeling his breath become labored as his boots slipped on the looser earth and spots of shale.

"Fuck!" Todd blurted behind him.

Mattituck turned to see Todd stabilize himself from a downward slide that made him look like a backward skier.

"Watch the footing," he proffered down to the Trooper. "Ground's getting a bit shaky."

"No shit," came the irked response.

After a half dozen more slips and slides, they reached the northern face of the ridge. Mattituck sat down, opting they should have a break before climbing up the hundred foot cliff.

He pulled his water bottle out of its pocket on his pack as Todd sat loudly next to him. They both faced the ravine below, Todd's eyes scanning the distance toward the crime scene.

"I'm not so sure this ridge hike was all that great an idea," he said, his binoculars now in hand.

"Yeah, pretty tough going for sure. But I still maintain it's the best way."

"I'm nervous about this cliff climbing bit."

Mattituck looked up at the sharp upward ascent.

"It's not all that bad," he said. "Not really a cliff."

"Close enough for government work," Todd said wryly.

"We'll be fine."

He pulled his cell out and checked the screen.

"Wow, a text from Monica."

"Really? What's it say?"

Mattituck scanned it first to make sure there was nothing too revealing, then read it aloud.

*Not ready to talk about us, but know where you're headed. You may be in danger. Call me.*

"Better give her a call," Todd said.

"I doubt its anything more than what we already know."

"Maybe," Todd said. "But she's carrying a case that might give her information we don't have."

"That's true."

A tightness gripped his mid-section as he thought about calling her. What would she say? She said she wasn't ready to talk about them, but what would he hear in her voice, in her tone? He didn't relish the thought of hearing the woman he loved in flat tones.

# Chapter Twenty

## Traversing the Darkness

"If you're going to call her, you should probably do it pretty quick," Todd said. "There's no sign of them up ahead. We need to get up on the ridge and hoof it to get sight of them before something happens."

Todd was right, Mattituck knew. He continued to stare at the screen.

"You want me to call her?" Todd offered.

Mattituck shook his head and dialed.

"It's about time," Monica's voice said without greeting.

"Hello to you, too," he said.

"Well, it's been almost three hours."

"We've been out of cell range," he said, ire rising.

"I'm sorry," Monica said, hearing the turn in his voice. "I was just worried is all."

"That's a good sign," he said, his voice softening. When she didn't say anything, he went on. "What's going on?"

"You're on Hinchinbrook?"

"Yeah, making our way to the scene."

"So's she. Tara. And Frank, I'm taking a risk telling you this because she's my client, but I'm going to take myself off her case. I'm going to drop her."

"You can do that?"

"Yes, when a client puts you in a position of violating bar ethics."

Mattituck absorbed this. Whatever she knew must be pretty serious.

"Okay," he said. "Got it. Listen. I don't want you to put your professional career at risk, okay? We know quite a bit, and will be very careful. We're behind both Tara and Wilson. We're not sure what they're up to, but it doesn't look right. Point being, we're being very cautious."

He sensed her relief.

"Good," she said. "Frank, I'm sorry. I'm just trying to process something that I'm not sure what to make of."

Mattituck's mind raced and settled on the only thing he'd kept from telling her.

"Is it about my past? I want to tell you about it, but there's . . ."

His voice trailed off. Monica waited.

"There's just a lot of stuff from that part of my life that I'm trying to sort out. Especially lately, since you've come along. It's just hard for me to even think about. Spent a long time not needing to. Or at least I thought I didn't." He was quiet a moment. "Monica, some of the shit I've seen . . . gone through. I'm not even sure I'm in touch with it all."

There was only a brief pause.

"You mean the Army and the Park Service?"

This took him by surprise. He'd hinted at the military to her in the past, but not the Park Service. How did she know about that?

"Yeah," he managed. "It's just—"

"I know. Don't worry about it. No, it's something else. Some pictures."

This took him by surprise.

"Pictures?"

"I'm sorry, Frank. I shouldn't have said that. I just need to sort through some things."

"You're sorting through pictures? Monica, listen, if there's something in your past," he said, thinking she had come across pictures from her own past . . . he couldn't imagine what in her past might have been so bad. "If there's something in your past, it doesn't matter to me."

"No," she said. "It's not that." There was a long pause. "I just need some time."

"Okay," he said. "I'll be here."

"I hope so," she said, thinking he was referring to the danger he and Todd were in.

He smiled into the phone.

"Good. That gives me hope."

Not knowing how to respond, she merely said, "I'll talk to you when you get back, Frank."

"Okay."

He slid the phone back into his pack, ignoring Todd's stare. Mattituck expected Todd to ask whether something was wrong between him and Monica, but he didn't.

"Anything we don't know already?"

Mattituck shook his head. "Not really." He turned his attention to the near-cliff ahead. The sun had dipped below the horizon over the Sound, which spread out to the west and north, well within view from this height.

"I don't want to get caught on this cliff when it's darker," he said to Todd.

"I thought you said it wasn't a cliff," Todd teased.

"It's not," Mattituck shot back with a grin.

Less than a half hour later, they made the top of the ridge and stood to stretch.

"You looked like you'd been up this way before," Todd said with admiration.

"That was a hell of a lot faster than I expected," Mattituck said, equally impressed at their luck. "We must have happened onto the only gully on the face of the cliff."

He caught Todd's quick turn toward him.

"I thought you said it wasn't—" Todd started.

"It's not," Mattituck said quickly, the grin returning. "Cliffs are more than 300 feet. This is only a hundred or so."

"Ah," Todd said, feigning the educated. "I wasn't aware. That's the only difference, eh?"

Mattituck quickly collected a set of larger stones and arranged them in a semi-circle with the open end at the point they'd crested the ridge. He placed two rows of stones atop each other across the narrow, flat top of the ridge from the semi-circle to the other side.

He looked at Todd's quizzical expression.

"In case we have to come back this way. Be nice to use that same route back down."

Todd nodded agreement, then turned and started up the ridge toward the crime scene. Mattituck quickly fell in behind him.

In the Alaska midsummer nights, it never really got dark, except in the southernmost parts of the state—Kodiak and Ketchikan, for example. In this part, and even more so farther north, the light remained through even the dark-ish part of the night. In South central Alaska, there was almost an hour when a person was tempted to break out the flashlight, but it wasn't entirely necessary. On a tall ridge with unsure footing, however, it was even more tempting to pull out a flashlight, but Todd and Mattituck didn't dare. Such a move would certainly draw attention from below.

So along they plodded, slowed by the need to be sure of their steps. To the right was the cliff they'd just come up, on the left was an unevenly steep slope that reached toward the Gulf of Alaska like a geologic plea. Still, they made good time. It was now far too dark to see down into the ravine. They could only imagine where Tara might be, and how much her husband had closed in behind her, if at all.

"Getting pretty dark," Todd said. "Watch your step."

Mattituck glanced up from the ground ahead at Todd's back.

"Oh," he said, "I guess I'll switch from being reckless and inattentive."

He heard Todd chuckle as the Trooper stopped and scanned the ravine below with his binoculars.

"How can you see anything down there?"

"Looking for fires."

"What kind of fool would have a fire with someone on their tail?"

"Just making sure," was all Todd said.

That's what made the man such a good Trooper, Mattituck mused. He was thorough, and kept assumptions to a minimum.

They continued along the ridge, the sun well below the horizon now. All they could see on the ground ahead was dark and light. It was difficult to discern the uneven ground, and both men began scuffing the soles of their boots on the rocky protrusions.

"Shit," Todd said with a sudden stop.

"What?"

"Take a look."

Mattituck stepped up next to Todd on the narrow ridge. In front of Todd was a sheer drop-off of at least thirty feet, as best he could see in the near-darkness.

"Fuck."

Todd looked around them. The ridge they were on was no wider than eight feet, but the cliff was more gently sloping on both sides, offering a possible way around the drop-off.

"Down here," Mattituck said, seeing the same thing.

He took the lead, stepping carefully downward as he leaned back into the mountain, his left hand out behind him to break his fall should he slip. He picked his way down. Todd's boots scraped and slipped on the loose earth behind Mattituck's ears. He imagined Todd losing his footing and sliding down under Mattituck and the two of them tumbling uncontrollably down the steep slope.

"Maybe you shouldn't be directly above me," he said back over his shoulder.

"Right," Todd said. "I hadn't thought of that. Be pretty shitty if we both took a fall."

Mattituck continued down as Todd moved to his left, still well above him but in a position where he would slide down past Mattituck if he lost his grip and fell. Both men, now spread out, moved diagonally downward, struggling to keep their balance as well as their boots gripped.

Todd was now moving at a faster pace, confident he had a good read on the terrain.

"Might slow it down a little," Mattituck warned.

"We need to move along a little faster or we'll never catch up to them."

Mattituck felt the same drive. If Wilson caught up to Tara before they did, there was sure to be another murder on their hands. He too picked up his pace, but Todd was still moving faster.

Todd moved over a rock outcrop that lifted brusquely toward the deep dark grey sky, then dropped out of sight. Mattituck cut down to the bottom of the outcrop, opting for the easier route.

He'd expected to see Todd's blackened body moving on the other side, but he didn't.

He scanned the area, but saw no trace of him.

"Todd?"

He wanted to holler louder, but dared not. Sound could carry down into the ravine too easily.

"Todd!?" he tried a little louder.

He stopped and straightened.

He was just about to panic when Todd finally answered.

"Over here."

Mattituck scrambled back toward the outcrop, then up. As he came abreast of it, he stopped short of a ten foot drop. He flailed his arms momentarily to regain his balance from the sudden stop.

At the bottom of the drop, Todd sat on a rock. Or lay. In the darkness he couldn't tell. What was clear was that his friend had fallen off the short cliff.

"Are you okay?"

Todd looked back up at him.

"Yeah, why?"

Mattituck was confused.

"Did you fall?"

There was only a slight pause.

"Hell no," came the annoyed reply.

Mattituck chuckled at his assumption.

"I thought you'd fallen. You just disappeared."

"I jumped down. It's flat dirt down here."

"How could you see?" Mattituck couldn't see anything clearly.

"I can see okay. Jump on down," Todd coaxed.

"No way. I am not blindly jumping down into a dark ravine."

"You need to. This is a nice runoff right down past the crest of the ravine. It looks like it'll lead us right to where we found Justin Harris' body."

"I'm still not jumping," Mattituck growled. "I'll hike down around." To his thinking, there was no way Todd could see well enough to make that jump.

"We don't have the time," Todd insisted. "It's flat down here, and—" he cut off and rummaged in his pack. He pulled out a flashlight. He turned so his back was to the ravine, then turned the flashlight on close to his chest, careful to minimize any light being visible down below.

"Great idea," Mattituck grumbled with sarcasm.

He crouched at the edge of the drop, then sprang forward and dropped and rolled on the ground below.

"Not bad," Todd said, impressed. "That looks like paratrooper training."

He could see Mattituck's eyes turn on him, but he didn't respond.

"Let's get going," he said and led the way down.

Todd was right, this cut in the ridge had all the signs of being a runoff, but from what? There wasn't enough land above to generate the water flow that would be required to cut this large and smooth of a runoff. It had to be one of those anomalies of the land, the erosion occurring in such a way that looser ground cleared away faster than the rock on either side. Maybe it had been volcanic lava flow on either side, with the earth in between. Over millennia, the earth slid away, but the hardened lava flow remained behind.

Without another word, the two struck a fast pace over the smoother ground toward where they hoped they would catch up to Wilson and Tara Garrett before they killed each other.

A shot rang out and echoed off both sides of the ravine. It was quickly followed by a terrifying curdling sound below them, only a slight angle from directly below. It continued unevenly, punctuated by growls and yelping sounds.

"What the—"

"Shh!" Todd silenced him.

The Trooper held perfectly still, silently listening with his ear cocked toward the noise.

"Animal," he said, keeping to minimal words so he could continue listening.

Mattituck could just make out the sound well enough to recognize that Todd was right. It was some kind of animal in distress. Or attack.

"Wolverine," Todd said.

Mattituck looked at him. He wanted to ask how he knew, but didn't want to interrupt his listening. Todd was an amazing tracker, having learned the skill from his hunting guide father, although his half-Hopi background added an element of the romantic mystique to his abilities.

Mattituck waited.

Another shot rang out, but the wolverine growling and yelping continued.

There was the sound of metallic clattering, and Mattituck felt he could almost pin-point where the sound was coming from. To their left, a good five hundred yards down the slope and up the ravine, the woods began again. Mattituck knew from their own hiking that route that it was a deep woods for a half mile before the crest of the ravine opened out onto a high meadow carpeted with muskeg. From there, it was another half mile or so to the next ravine, this one dropping westward toward Hinchinbrook Entrance and the lighthouse. At the foot of that next ravine was the site of Justin Harris' death.

Now there were additional grunts, and it became clear that the wolverine was at some prey. Given the shots and the metallic clatter, it seemed to Mattituck that the wolverine was at a human. Maybe it was the same one that had come after him. In any case, somebody who had tried to shoot the animal, but had now dropped their rifle and were now trying to fight off the vicious mammal.

Todd and Mattituck stood transfixed, as if the screen had gone blank on the movie they were watching at a crucial moment, and they were listening in desperation for any indication of what might be happening.

The noises continued, only to give way to a screeching yelp. Then silence.

"Guess we'd better go see what that was all about," Todd said, breaking the silence.

He looked at Mattituck.

Mattituck was looking to the north-northwest, where the sun was making its way back into the sky.

The midnight sun.

# Chapter Twenty-one

## Death of the Wolverine

Several hours before, Monica had been restless following the conversation with Mattituck on the phone. It was clear to her that Mattituck had misunderstood her when she'd said she'd hoped he would be there. She had meant that he and Todd would remain out of danger, but since they'd ended the call she had become more sure that Mattituck took it to mean she hoped he would be there waiting for her after she sorted through her thoughts.

It had been nearly 9:30 p.m., and her thoughts had continually drifted toward the pictures Betty Ingram had shown her. It wasn't so much the images that haunted her, but the succession of them. That and the fact that she had not even looked at Mattituck's face in the images, nor scrutinized his posture. She had been so focused on the woman and her own hurt that she hadn't given more than a fleeting glance at Frank's image.

Had he looked like he was into her? She hated to even think about seeing such a look on his face, but she also couldn't shake the feeling that she'd missed something by not paying attention. Frank did not seem like the type to cheat, and she knew he'd been deeply hurt by a past girlfriend who had cheated on him.

It just didn't seem to add up somehow. Something was missing. Deep down inside, she felt like Frank would never treat her that way. And certainly, she knew how much he loved her.

But what about the pictures?

She went to the kitchen and opened a bottle of red wine. It was a bottle of Shiraz she had been saving for Mattituck's next visit. She poured the wine into a stemless glass and walked to the window, gazing down at the harbor. Her eyes held onto the light to the west, bright gold over the horizon where the sun was setting, then looked down at the dark red in the glass. She swished it around, watching the fluid climb one side of the glass then cascade down the other. She held the glass up to the window, the sunlight behind the glass. The color was a deep violet, with a hint of ruby in the background. It was a quality shiraz . . . almost a pity to drink alone.

Under that same light that spilled through the window, a dozen or so miles to the west Frank and Todd were hiking in pursuit of at least one killer. A pang of concern gripped her belly, and in response she downed what was in the glass, then returned to the kitchen to refill the glass.

Ten minutes later, she remained in front of the same window, gazing to the west as though watching for a change in the light—a shifting from day to night. Or maybe night to day. Realizing on this last refill that she had finished the bottle, she sipped slowly, her mind meandering among the hills and valleys under the diminishing golden sunlight.

Todd and Mattituck were no more than halfway down to the bottom of the ravine when a shot pierced the crisp morning air. It was followed by three more in quick succession. They reverberated off the two sides of the ravine, diminishing with each return until they settled into silence. They paused only long enough to take the sound in.

"What's that about?" Mattituck ventured.

"No good, whatever it is."

They were nearly running down the slope until they came to the gradual leveling of the runoff. Here, the solid earth gave way to loose shale, and the pair worked their way to the left side until they gained more solid ground and could pick up speed once again. They nearly ran to the edge of the spruce tree woods, then became more cautious. From here, they were unclear on how far it might be to where the shots had been fired.

And they certainly didn't want to surprise Wilson or Tara, if that's who it was.

"Seems more likely to be Wilson than Tara," Todd said, as though continuing a conversation.

"Given he was tailing her," he agreed, "I'd think so."

"Let's spread out," Todd said, taking command. "You go to the other side of the ravine and work your way up." He pulled the hand held radios from his backpack and handed one to Mattituck. "Here. Channel 6."

He looked across the ravine, then where the rough trail headed up toward the spine at the top.

"I'd guess the scene is a couple of hundred yards up," he said, nodding upward, "along that trail."

Mattituck nodded and started down the remainder of the slope, then crossed over the rough trail and disappeared into the spruce on the other side.

Todd started forward along the spruce on this side, the AR-15 at the ready. He had his finger on the safety for a quick release.

He did his best to keep silent, but the dried twigs and branches on the floor of the woods made it impossible. He could only hope the sound didn't carry. Ducking and crouching in places, he made his way forward, hoping he wasn't lagging too far behind Mattituck on the other side of the ravine. It all depended on how rough going the woods were on that side, although it had looked thinner than this side.

Looking ahead, he saw that the woods were fairly thick for the rest of the distance he needed to cover, so he decided that any sound he'd make probably wouldn't carry through to where Wilson—or Tara—was up ahead. He picked up the pace, but was quickly slowed by unsure footing. Every few steps, his boot came down on a stone or fallen branch beneath the undergrowth that threatened to twist his ankle. But he didn't dare slow up too much and risk not being there if Mattituck came up either of the suspects.

He stepped over a fallen tree, only to find the ground on the other side gone. He had expected firm ground at an even level with this side of the log, but instead his boot found nothing until it had dropped a full two feet below the expected stopping point. The imbalance threw him forward and he lurched over the log uncontrollably, the AR-15 ahead and hitting the ground first. In the back of his mind, he was glad he'd kept the safety on.

He hit the undergrowth with a surprisingly hard thud, considering the illusion of the soft ground covering. Everything spun as his body turned in the fall. He closed his eyes to stop the effect just as he realized he'd already fallen. Time seemed to have wrinkled in its continuum, and he had a nagging feeling that more time had lapsed than he realized.

As he opened his eyes, he also realized that the spinning sensation hadn't been him turning during the fall; it was only now subsiding. He blinked and stared at a cloud passing between the tops of the spruce well above him.

*I'm on my back.* He closed his eyes tightly as the hand held radio crackled to life on his chest.

"Todd . . . do you pick me up?"

Mattituck.

Todd started to sit up, but a white blaring in his skull forced his arms to give way and he fell back to the ground.

"Todd . . . Todd . . . can you hear me?"

He pulled the radio from its Velcro and keyed the button for the mic.

"Yeah . . ." he said, unable to quell the groaning edge to his voice. "I'm here. What's up?"

"I've been trying to call you for . . . I don't know, several minutes. You okay?"

"Yeah," Todd returned. "Just took a spill is all."

"Well, I'm where all the noise came from. Where are you?"

"Any sign of either of them?" he asked, ignoring Mattituck's question.

"No. But there's a wolverine here with a—what do they call those? an Italian necktie?"

"A slit throat? Are you kidding?"

"Nope. Wide open. Somebody sliced its throat like it were a human."

Todd shook his head, forcing himself to think past the throbbing in his head. He looked at the undergrowth where his body had pressed the foliage to the ground. A large stone lay where his head had been. Apparently, he'd hit his head when he fell and blacked out.

"Okay," he said into the radio. "Making my way to you now."

Mattituck was sitting on a large rock outcrop, his binoculars trained up the ravine, when Todd broke out of the spruce wood.

"Ho!" he hollered.

Mattituck lowered the binoculars and turned, his hand raised.

He must be watching something—or somebody—up the ravine and was warning Todd to be quiet. It didn't make any sense, though. Why would he want Todd to keep quiet when he himself was sitting in the middle of a clearing, easily visible from up the hill?

He waited until he was close before asking, however.

"What are you talking about?" Mattituck replied irritably when Todd did ask. "I'm just scanning up there to see if I can pick up any sign of them."

"You raised your hand to keep quiet," Todd said, his ire rising.

"I raised my hand to greet you. It's a custom in this country," he added with sarcasm.

"Very funny."

"You okay?" Mattituck asked, peering into his face as Todd looked up the ravine.

"Yeah. I'm fine."

"You haven't even looked at the dispatched critter," Mattituck said, gesturing toward the dead wolverine a half dozen meters in front of them.

Todd blinked. He'd completely forgotten about the wolverine. He shook his head slowly, then stepped up to the still corpse. It lay on its left side, a large pool of fresh blood under his front half. Just as Mattituck had said, his throat had been sliced wide open.

"Wow," he said, crouching for a closer look. "Ugly."

"Isn't it." Mattituck said, his eyes peering upward through the binoculars again.

"What I don't get," Todd said absently, "is why anybody would kill a wolverine. And with a knife."

He looked at Mattituck. His friend was watching him, the binoculars poised half way down from his eyes.

"Are you sure you're okay?"

"Yeah, why?"

"You don't remember all that screeching and growling?"

Todd thought about this, closing his eyes as if it would help.

"It's what brought us down that ridge so damned fast."

Todd shook his head.

"Not so sure I'm okay after all," he said, his voice trailing off.

"What happened?" Mattituck asked.

"Took a fall on uneven ground when I stepped over a log, and hit the ground hard. I think my head might have clapped a rock."

Mattituck was on his feet, cupping Todd's head between his palms. He turned the Trooper's face up toward him, like he was about to kiss him. Todd felt momentarily uncertain and very uncomfortable, until he realized Mattituck was checking his pupils.

"They look normal," Mattituck announced, releasing Todd's head. "But we'll want to watch for signs of concussion. Any unusual thinking?"

"Like how do you mean?"

"You know, confused or disjointed thought, lapses in memory, anything."

"Yeah," Todd said, resignedly. "Both. The only lapse in memory was right after the fall."

"When you might have hit your head on a rock?"

Todd nodded.

"What about the confused thought?"

"I forgot about the wolverine, and there's been a few times that I didn't connect things."

Mattituck nodded. "All right," he said. "Let me know if it gets worse, and I'll be alert to how you seem."

He was still watching Todd closely.

"You okay to keep going?"

"Yes, of course. We need to."

"Need to doesn't matter if you're not okay," Mattituck returned without hesitation. "Let those fuckers shoot each other to death. We can't risk you being injured."

"I'll be all right," Todd said.

He looked down at the wolverine, as Mattituck crouched again to study it more closely. He felt like his thoughts were floating in a mist. Maybe the jarring of the head.

"This thing's been shot," Mattituck said with surprise. "Like several times in the head and chest."

Todd was leaned in next to him. It was getting light now, and he could see better than he had the first time he examined the dead animal.

"I hadn't noticed that." He leaned in. "Fuck. That's quite a bit of overkill, eh?"

"I'd say," Mattituck agreed. He stood up, still looking down at the furry mess. "From the noises we heard, I'm going to guess this thing attacked one of our people ahead, and they had to cut it in the struggle."

Todd watched, feeling a step behind.

"It's either that," Mattituck continued, "or some sick satanic ritual."

Todd had to look at him to make sure he was joking.

"Not all that funny," he said.

Mattituck turned a quick, sheepish expression. Then tried redeeming himself.

"What about the shots?" he asked.

"These shots," he continued. "I'm thinking it's adrenaline. People get weird when they're attacked. Especially by something as vicious as a wolverine. I'm thinking they cut its throat and broke away, then pumped it full of bullets out of anger. Adrenaline."

Todd nodded, squinting away the sweat seeping into his eyes.

"Makes sense," was all he said.

Todd rubbed his eyes. He was feeling tired, not just physically but . . . internally. It was the difference between being tired and being fatigued. Drained.

"You okay?" Mattituck asked.

Todd looked at him.

"Yeah. Fine. Let's go."

They started up the ravine, with Todd taking the lead. This time they followed the rough hunting trail instead of picking their way through the spruce. They quickly fell into a fast pace, and Mattituck wondered why Todd was barreling toward a potential dangerous situation at this speed. But he didn't say anything. Todd was keeping his head up, watching ahead attentively.

Mattituck's own gaze dropped to the trail, since he couldn't see past Todd very well anyhow. He watched as his partner's boot heels worked the trail, kicking back toward him with each step.

A dark patch appeared under Todd's heel, forcing Mattituck from his boot-watching trance. He stopped and stared at it, then looked to the sides of the trail. Five feet to the left was a log laying parallel to the trail with a larger patch. He knelt down and examined it.

Blood.

He walked over to the log to examine that patch.

Again, blood.

"Hey," he hollered to Todd, surprised the Trooper hadn't noticed him stopping.

Todd continued up the trail.

"Hey!" Mattituck tried a little louder, wary of going any louder for fear he might alert anybody ahead of their presence.

Todd stopped and turned, looking at him but not coming back down. He held his hands out palms up, as if to ask what was up.

"Blood," was all he said in a low voice only loud enough to carry to where Todd was standing.

With that, Todd came down fast.

"Where?"

Mattituck pointed, watching Todd's face.

"That's quite a pool," Todd said. Then looked up at Mattituck. "Funny there isn't any on the trail."

Mattituck pointed at the patch on the trail.

Todd looked at him, then stepped over to examine it.

"How'd I miss this?" There was an edge of bewilderment in his tone.

He looked back up at Mattituck, expecting the charter captain to answer, but he only held Todd with a steady stare.

Crouching for a closer look at the patch, he ignored Mattituck. He pulled a latex glove from his pocket and pulled it on, then poked at the darkened earth. He lifted his finger, the remnant of wet blood on the tip.

"Still wet," he said.

He pulled a Ziploc from his pocket and gathered a large pinch of the dirt, then dropped it into the baggie and sealed it. He dropped his backpack and stowed the sample in a compartmented tray. He donned the pack again and stood.

"We're losing daylight," he said, and started up the trail again.

Mattituck watched him for a moment before replying.

"Sun's on the way up, Todd."

Todd shot a quick glance back.

"What're you talking about?"

"Sun went down while we were on the ridge, remember? It's back up and climbing."

Todd looked to the north-northeast toward the slowly climbing sun. He rubbed his forehead and turned back to the ravine. Without another word, he was back at the quickened clip along the trail.

# Chapter Twenty-two

## Cat and Mouse

Mattituck had thought Todd would slow his pace as they potentially closed in on where they expected to find Wilson and Tara Garrett, but he hadn't. Even when they passed through a band of more spruce, which would normally warrant increased caution, Todd had barreled through, slowing only long enough at the far side to scan the clearing ahead.

"Todd."

The Trooper continued, ignoring him. It was as though Todd had slipped into a trance.

"Todd."

Still, his friend persisted forward.

"Todd, stop."

Finally, he stopped and turned.

"What?"

"Look at me," Mattituck said, stepping close and leaning in toward Todd's eyes.

Todd waved him away. "I said I'm fine."

"But you're not. And if you keep this up, you'll get us both killed."

Todd only looked at him, forcing back a twinge of anger.

"Look at you, you never get mad. Especially if somebody's cautioning for safety. Fuck, you're Mister Safety-first. 'Don't become another rescue effort,' you always say."

Todd didn't move for several seconds. Then, abruptly, his shoulders dropped.

"You're right," he said. "Been bugging me that I missed that blood back there."

"Exactly," Mattituck said. "You're a master tracker. You wouldn't normally miss something like that. And then barreling wild hog speed up this trail like you want to get your head blown off . . . it's not like you."

He paused to let it sink in.

"That hit on the head jarred you."

Todd pulled out his water bottle and downed a respectable amount of the coolness, feeling it coat his esophagus. Even that sensation seemed exaggerated, as if his senses were heightened.

"You'd better take the lead," he said to Mattituck.

"All right."

They started up the ravine again, this time with Todd keeping a closer eye on the ground. They had covered fifty yards or so when he blinked down hard and wiped the sweat from his eyes. Then he looked back down at the trail several feet behind Mattituck's feet.

"That blood is still spotting along here," he said.

Mattituck turned his head slightly so he could hear behind him.

"The pattern is about every ten feet or so, with some of the spots having a little pool."

"What do you make of that?" Mattituck asked.

"Whoever it is, they're stopping quite a bit. I can't make much of a boot print out, so we can't get help there, but I'd wager it's not keeping a straight line."

"You think that wolverine got it?"

"Let's just say that wasn't only its own blood around its mouth and throat," Todd said.

Mattituck grimaced at the memory of the wolverine attack on his Carhartt vest, his mind conjuring images of the wolverine tearing at a person's skin.

"Do you think it might have been the same wolverine?" he asked.

"That attacked you? Good chance of it, I think."

Mattituck looked back down the trail. The wolverine carcass had fallen out of sight long ago.

"RIP, you son of a bitch," he muttered toward it. He glanced at Todd while he was turned. The Trooper's head was down and he was rubbing his eyes.

"You okay?"

Todd looked, his eyes reddened from the rubbing.

"Yeah, why?"

Mattituck shook his head.

"I don't think you are," he said after a moment.

"Let's go. I'm going to guess that wolverine did a serious number on whoever it attacked. Either they'll need our help or—"

His voice stopped. He was looking over Mattituck's shoulder. Mattituck turned to see what he was looking at. Several hundred yards ahead, a figure was moving slowing up the ravine. They moved sluggishly, veering right and left as they made their slovenly way up the trail. Apparently, they had not picked up on Mattituck and Todd catching up.

"I don't know how we missed that," Todd said.

"We didn't," Mattituck responded. "They must have been off the trail or something."

"Sitting on a rock, maybe. That would explain the pools we've been seeing every ten feet or so."

"They must be losing a lot of blood."

The thought prodded them, and both men started up the trail, moving at a near gallop.

The figure continued along, despite their noise. It seemed to Mattituck it was careening more and more off the trail, and they observed it stop several times, never once looking back at them.

"Ho!" Mattituck hollered as they closed in. "Hello!"

The person continued, clearly oblivious to their approach.

Mattituck and Todd spread out as they came within fifty feet. Both men had their weapons trained on the figure. It was not a woman's clothing, so it was likely Wilson Garrett, but it was hard to tell from behind.

"Hello!" Todd tried. "Wilson? Wilson Garrett?"

The figure turned. It looked like it was probably Wilson Garrett, but his face was covered in blood, and appeared to have deep gashes on the left cheek and forehead. He had stopped, but now began wavering back and forth as though he were about to fall. He raised his right hand toward them, like a drowning man seeking to clasp a rescuing hand. But then he leaned forward at a ridiculously impossible angle, then followed through with a hard thud on the ground in front of them.

"Are you all right?" Todd asked loudly enough to make sure he was heard.

They reached the face down man in seconds, and after he wouldn't respond to attempts to rouse him, Todd went to work assessing his wounds. Mattituck knelt on the opposite side of Wilson, ready to help however Todd wanted.

Wilson's right hand was severely torn and slashed, with two particularly deep cuts running between the finger bones in the back of his hand.

"Geezus," Mattituck muttered. "He's in rough shape."

"I—I'm . . ." Wilson said feebly. "I need to sit up."

Mattituck and Todd looked at each other. Wilson had rolled to his back and was reaching up. Todd and Mattituck each gripped a forearm and pulled Wilson upright. The injured man sat for several moments, breathing deeply. Mattituck was aware of the breeze coming down the ravine with a cool edge of relief.

"What happened?" Todd asked him.

Wilson lifted a bloodied hand and ran it through his thick hair.

"Fucking wolverine."

"Yeah," Mattituck said. "We found him. But what happened? How'd it attack?"

"Damned thing came outta nowhere," he said. "Fucking jumped right out from the junipers or whatever the fuck they are. Those low bushes. Hit me like a Rottweiler and knocked me back on my ass. Then the little fucker went after my throat and started digging at my chest like a rabid cat."

He paused, looking from Todd to Mattituck.

"Wait a minute," he said. "You called me by name."

"Yeah," Todd said.

"Who are you?"

"Why are you up here, Wilson? Why'd you come back?"

"You're that Trooper," Wilson said to Todd.

"That's right," Todd replied. "And I need to know why you came back out here."

The man hesitated. Suddenly his shirt jumped from his chest and he slumped forward. Then, a full second later, the crack of a rifle shot came and echoed down the ravine.

There was a moment of awkward silence before both men sprang to action. They each hooked an arm under Wilson's armpit and started for cover. This took them straight down the trail to a heap of rocks splaying out from the side of the ravine. An old landslide that promised cover.

An ugly cracking sound emitted from Wilson, and Mattituck looked down to check on the wounded man. Instead of a face, a grisly tangle of muscle and tendons were separated by a gaping eye from the frontal lobe of Wilson's brain. At the back of his head the hair was messily parted by a clean bullet hole.

Whoever was firing at them was one hell of a shot.

They rounded the bottom of the rock slide and dropped Wilson's body, then fell low behind the rocks.

"What the hell?" Mattituck started.

"Sniper. And not bad at that."

"Tara?"

"Has to be. Who else is out here?"

"Fuck, that's gutsy as hell, picking him off right in front of us."

"She must have seen he was talking."

Mattituck looked at Todd attentively.

"She knew he was going to say something about her, I'd guess," Todd continued. "Maybe she knew he was coming up behind her . . . and why."

He paused to chance a peek over the rocks. With no shots coming, he remained there studying the terrain and the two sides of the ridge. Mattituck stared at Wilson's corpse, thinking about how many different ways a guy can die. Animal attack, or a bullet through the skull. He'd seen that kind of wound before, a couple too many times. And worse. But before his thoughts could wander any further down that path, he thought about Tara Wilson out there somewhere, possibly taking a bead on them.

"She's no novice," he said.

"That's for sure," Todd returned, still studying the terrain. "The way I figure, she's up on that ridge up that way. The same one we were on." He stopped to close his eyes hard, then rubbed them. "The only way she could have hit him in the head like that was from someplace straight up along a trajectory that puts her either at the top of the ravine, but to the left of the trail, or up on the ridge."

"My money's on the ravine," Mattituck said, poking his head up to see what Todd was seeing.

"How do you figure?" Todd asked. "Much easier shot from up there."

"Yes, you're right. It would be. But that doesn't mean that's where the shot was from." He was looking at Todd, who was rubbing his eyes again. "I think we need to get you to a doctor."

"I'm fine. Go on about the ridge."

"There's no way she would have had time to get up there. Besides, I was keeping a pretty good eye all the way up there while we were hiking up that last bit. There's not enough cover up that slope to keep her out of my sight."

Todd thought about this as he scanned the ridge, then looked at the spot at the top of the ravine.

"I suppose you're right."

Mattituck's eyes were on the area at the top of the ravine. The sun was still rising as it slide to the east-northeast, just far enough along to provide shadows close to the opposite ridge. To the left of the spot at the top of the ravine was a line of low scrub brush . . . with a narrow dark spot in the middle. It was too far to make out well, particularly with the shade cast over it. He held his eyes there for several minutes, hoping the light would shift enough to give him a view of what might be there.

"Well," Todd said, starting to stand, "Wherever she was, I think she's moved on to—"

Mattituck, eyes still on the dark hollow in the scrub, saw a pin-prick of a flash. Instinctively, he reached up and pulled Todd down. Just then, the rock several feet to the right splintered and flew behind them. Then the sound of a rifle crack echoed around them.

"Fuck!" Todd blurted as he landed cross-legged next to Wilson.

"I'm thinking you're wrong about Tara moving. She's in the scrub brush to the right of where the trail crests the ravine."

"She's got us pinned," Todd said, regaining his crouch and joining Mattituck in a low peek. "That's got to be 700 yards."

"She's a good shot," Mattituck said. "But not good enough."

"What makes you think that? She hit Wilson in the head from nearly that distance, and while he was a moving target."

"She hit Wilson when we were dragging him in a straight line down from her. He might as well have been lying and waiting for it."

Todd nodded. "True." He was quiet a minute. "Okay." His voice had an undertone of resignation. "I'm not thinking clearly. I think we need to follow your lead for now."

Mattituck looked at him.

"With my approval, of course," Todd added with a grin.

Mattituck nodded, then looked around behind them. The ridge on this side was too steep to climb, so there was no way to get up there without being an easy target in an arcade. He looked straight across the ravine trail to the other side, but that route would be just as easy.

"Down there," Todd offered, following along Mattituck's vision and thoughts.

Mattituck looked down the ravine through the low grasses. There was a line of scrub that looked high enough to move behind at a crouching run. The trick would be the thirty feet down to the scrub, and then clambering over the bottom of the cliff to the other side of the brush.

"I'll go," he said immediately.

"We'll both go," Todd said. "I'm in no condition to be left alone, remember." He was grinning at Mattituck.

"Yeah, yeah. What about him?" he asked, nodding toward Wilson Garrett.

"I think he'll sit tight 'til we get back."

Mattituck chuckled and hoisted his pack. He checked the Ruger .375, then slung it over his shoulder, opting for the Winchester 30 deer rifle instead.

"Better range," he said as Todd watched him, his own AR-15 at ready.

"And accuracy," Todd added.

With that, the two lurched into a sprint for the scrub brush down the ravine, quickly covering the thirty feet. At first, Mattituck thought that they were getting off scot-free, until he saw dirt and gravel kick up fifteen feet in front of him. He started slaloming to add difficulty to tracking them, sure to deviate the arches outward so that he didn't set a predictable pattern.

Gravel and dirt kicked up loudly 20 feet up the ridge, followed a second later by another kick 40 feet further down the ravine.

He had been right. She was a good shot if nothing was moving. A target range marksman, nothing more. Problem was, even a weekend target practice enthusiast could put a bullet through you.

They were half way along the bottom of the ridge, skirting along the edge of the scrub brush now . . . half way there. Gravel kicked up ten feet ahead, at about head level from Tara's angle.

*That's getting too close*, Mattituck thought.

He heard Todd stumble behind him, then a moment later an *ooff!* as he hit the ground. Mattituck spun as he continued running to see Todd rolling down the last of the ridge behind the edge of the brush.

Was he hit?

Mattituck paused for a brief moment, then dove for the brush. Either Todd had been hit, or he had realized they could duck below the edge of the brush and crawl the rest of the way. To Mattituck's thinking, Todd was either hit and needed his help, or was smart taking cover and Mattituck should as well. Either way, this was the move to make.

He hit the gravely dirt and rolled down to the brush, then spun around on his belly so his head was nearest where Todd had ducked under.

"Todd!"

"Yeah!?"

"You hit?"

"No. Just figured she was getting too close."

"Good thinking. I don't think she has much practice with moving targets." Todd was approaching him, crawling on his belly as Mattituck spoke. "Probably not a hunter, so she's used to shooting at cut-out targets at the range."

"Exactly," Todd agreed. "That'll work to our advantage. But by now she's realizing her shortcoming."

Mattituck turned and belly-crawled along the edge of the scrub, making his way down to the bottom of the line that would lead them across the ravine to Tara's side. From there, he was thinking, they could make their way up to her and hopefully surprise her.

They could no longer hear well enough to hear gunshots, with all the noise their bodies were making on the gravel, but Mattituck figured it didn't much matter. There was no way she could see them nor hit them where they were, and there was no way they could assess whether she was staying put or moving to a new position.

The only thing that was sure at this moment was that they had entered a game of cat-and-mouse with a calculating killer.

# Chapter Twenty-three

## Predators at Large

Izzy Giovanni had worked several days straight now at the Crow's Nest, and she was tired. Pappy Amatucci was a good employer, but that was likely due to the arrangement with The Ühing. Although he didn't treat her all that much differently than he did the other employees at the Bella Luna or the Crow's Nest, her cover as Pappy's niece was widely known now, and any preferential treatment was naturally ascribed to that.

She had grown to enjoy her hikes around the Valdez area during her time off from work. Her job, of course, was to get in as close to Frank Mattituck, the Takistus, as she could. That didn't mean she couldn't enjoy the time she didn't have to put into her real job, and she'd taken to regular excursions, increasing the distance into the wilderness as she became more comfortable. She never thought, as a person who'd lived nearly her entire life in large cities, that she would enjoy the outdoors so much. Valdez had awakened a part of her she hadn't known existed.

This evening, with the Alaskan summer evening that never really got dark, she had opted for the Shoup Bay trail, and was now traversing the long slow ascent that would take her to one of her favorite views. She had set out with water bottle and bear spray at the ready.

It was therapeutic, and Izzy had found that the long hikes and fresh air helped her clear her mind. And she had much to clear in her thoughts. There were no distractions out here, and the exercise was invigorating. It reset her focus and gave her time to think about how to carry out her duties. She never forgot the task she'd been sent for. Since getting in close to the Takistus himself hadn't panned out very well, she'd refocused on Todd Benson, the State Trooper who was close to the Frank Mattituck. There, she had found success. So far anyhow. The night she'd had with him had been good, and there was no doubt he was hooked. The biggest question she had was what information on the Takistus she could get through the State Trooper rather than from the Takistus himself.

She came to one of her least favorite sections of this trail: A long and deep mud hole that she'd come to think of as The Bog. A month earlier, one could pick a more or less dry route in the grass around it, but so many had hiked through here that even those areas were muddy and deep. Somebody had tried to lay a makeshift boardwalk with broken 2-by-4's and large branches laid along the firmer grassy edges, but most of these had sunk into the mud.

Izzy picked her best guess for the firmest route among a sloshy set of choices and ran through, hoping the speed would keep her from sinking too deep. She failed, and the mud covered her new boots by the time she reached the far side.

Continuing on the dry trail, her thoughts returned to her real work.

She had decided that the arrangement with the Todd Benson might even be better than sleeping with Mattituck directly. She had learned already that Todd Benson had deputized him. That alone was interesting. She hadn't known that kind of thing happened anymore, but apparently it could. And she'd found that Todd was willing to talk about his work.

And that meant an open door to the Takistus.

Her plan, then, was to build her relationship with Todd Benson. He was separated from his wife, the cheating nurse, and chances of reconciliation between them seemed remote at best. The road to information on the Takistus through the State Trooper was clear, to her thinking.

She crested a highpoint in the trail, where a cleared area beside the trail provided a 900-foot high view of the Port of Valdez and the small city tucked to the left against the mountains on this side of the water. She smiled until a thought forced the corners of her mouth downward again.

Did she expect Karl, the cold lizard-like assistant to Das Kaptan, to agree with this plan? No way. Not right away, anyhow. But with a little more information on the Takistus from Todd Benson, she knew she could convince him to her way of thinking.

Through Todd Benson, she had a much better avenue for keeping tabs on the Takistus. Everything Frank Mattituck did that was of concern to The Ühing, after all, was activity that involved him acting as a deputy. And that was a capacity he could only serve under Trooper Todd Benson.

Izzy stood for some time, she didn't know how long, gazing down at the beauty before her. Across the bay, she could see the oil terminus sprawled where it fed two large tankers that would be bound for the refineries of San Francisco after being filled. She looked to the right to the far end of the Port, toward the waterfalls spilling off the glaciated mountains high above.

She smiled and closed her eyes, breathing in the crisp cleanness, and let herself drift into the only sure place she knew—her own inner sanctum. Nobody had ever gotten in there, nor would they. Ever.

Todd's head was pounding. As he followed Mattituck, the two of them crawling on their bellies behind the scrub brush, he had to pause and close his eyes. If he were back home in Valdez, he'd be calling it a day and going to bed in a darkened room. A very dark room.

He was aware that he was falling behind Mattituck, but he didn't want to slow down. He had no choice but to pause periodically and let his head rest for a moment. He closed his eyes shut tightly, then opened them. He wondered if they had a radio signal yet.

He pulled out the hand held VHF and checked the signal strength. He dialed it to Channel 21, the Coast Guard channel.

"Coast Guard Anchorage, Coast Guard Anchorage, this is AST 32067."

He waited a moment, then tried again. No reply. They were still blocked from the line-of-sight signal capabilities of the VHF antennas.

Mattituck had stopped to wait for him.

"Sorry," Todd said as he approached on his belly.

"No worries," Mattituck said with a smile.

But Todd could see Mattituck was studying him closely.

"How do I look?"

"Not so good, my friend . . . not so good. You sure you're up for this?"

Todd gave him an irritable glance.

"Yeah," Mattituck concluded. "I thought that might be your response."

Mattituck turned and started crawling again. They were within 20 yards of the other side of the ravine. He moved quickly and efficiently, reminding Todd of the man's background.

"I'm thinking the quicker we can get you into a standing position, the better."

"Yep . . . sounds great," Todd returned.

They reached the edge of the ravine a few minutes later, leaving no place to go except up the ridge. Mattituck took several gulps off his water bottle, then rose to a crouch. He squinted up the ravine toward where Tara Garrett had been taking shots at them. He scanned the crest, looking for signs of her, but he couldn't even see the line of scrub brush where she'd been hiding. The entire area looked different from this side of the ravine, in fact, causing him to doubt whether he was looking in the right area.

"Well," he said to Todd, who was seated near his feet sipping his water and closing his eyes. "I'd bet my next paycheck she's not even in the same area."

"You're the boss of your company. You don't get a paycheck."

Mattituck ignored him, except for a subtle grin.

"I don't think we're going to have any clue where she is until we tempt her into shooting at us."

Todd drew a deep breath, then rose next to him, studying the terrain above.

"She'll be up and over the ravine," he said.

Mattituck looked at him.

"How do you figure? Why not find a better vantage and try to pick us off?"

"She's going to be on the run. She'll stop to fire at us if she has to, but she's going to be trying to get away from us."

Mattituck shook his head.

"I disagree. I think she knows her best chance for the future is to take us out as well."

"That'd be stupid," Todd said definitively.

Again, Mattituck shook his head.

"She has to know we've seen her boat. Even if she circled around—which I doubt would be an easy task with these ridges—she knows we came in by her boat. She's gonna know we've seen it." He looked at Todd. "She has to kill us, or she has no hope."

A grim expression eased onto Todd's face. He nodded.

"I have to trust your judgment right now. Honestly, Frank, I'm not sure how good I'm doing."

It almost felt good, a relief, to say it out loud.

"I know," Mattituck said with empathy. "I got this, man. Just follow my lead."

Todd nodded as they started along the edge of the brush at the bottom of the ridge, picking their way carefully and trying to hold as close to the brush as they could.

Mattituck was thinking both about the situation at hand and the well-being of his friend. It was clear now that Todd had taken a fairly serious blow to the head when he'd fallen on that rock. There was no cut and no swelling, but the effects were clear enough. And now even Todd was acknowledging the extent of the injury. No doubt he could still depend on Todd and his expertise, but only in a limited capacity.

In all the cases he'd worked with Todd, the Trooper had always been in charge. And in his own past experience as a law enforcement officer, Mattituck had always worked alone. Being in charge of somebody else presented a kind of burden he wasn't accustomed to, and a sense of responsibility that felt very much like a laden pack holding him back.

As they made their way between the rocky, shaled bottom of the ridge and the low brush, Mattituck kept a close eye on the top of the ravine. He saw no flashes and no movement, and there were no tell-tale signs of bullets hitting the earth around them.

"So far, so good," he said over his shoulder.

Todd grunted in reply. Mattituck's concern ratcheted up a notch. Todd never simply grunted.

"You doing okay?"

Another grunt, then, "Yeah, I'm fine."

The slides from the ridge were more recent on this side, and the sliding ground from the ridge had not fully solidified. The dirt and shale slipped and shifted under their boots as they half climbed, half scrambled up the ravine. With each gain of ten or twenty feet, Mattituck's surety that Tara was holed up and waiting for them waned, and he found himself starting to believe Todd's view that she was on the run. Still, he knew, caution was the best way for moving forward. And for staying alive.

By the time they'd reached the upper side of the brush, Mattituck's confidence that Tara was no longer waiting for them grew. There was a hundred yards or so of mostly open terrain sloping gradually up the ravine before the next stand of brush, and he was tempted to simply walk it. There was little doubt walking would be far better for Todd than running, especially with their heavy packs and weapons. But in the end, erring on the side of safety won out, and Mattituck decided on running the distance to cover.

"Can you run?" he asked Todd.

There was enough of a pause to firm Mattituck's concern.

"Yeah," came the reply. "Yeah, sure. I can do it."

Mattituck looked back at his friend. He looked worn, like he wanted to just lie down and go to sleep.

"You sure? You can stay here," he started to say, knowing there was no way Todd would ever go for that option. "Or we can call this off. We're pretty sure who killed Wilson. Ballistics will probably pin the bullet on her rifle."

"True," Todd said. "But are we sure it's Tara? If the ballistics come back negative on her gun, then where are we?"

Mattituck immediately saw the logic of this. He hoisted the Winchester to the ready and started at a run across the open tundra, zig-zagging enough to throw off what he already knew was a shooter who struggled with anything other than a stationary target. As he gained the cover of the next clump of brush, he dropped to his knees and looked back to see Todd sprinting twenty feet behind him, slaloming upward just as Mattituck had done.

Mattituck peered over the brush. They were now much closer to the crest of the ravine, and he could see the next line of brush where Tara—or whoever—had been holed up taking shots at them. Better yet, he could see pretty well into the dark hollow where the rifle shots had come from. There didn't appear to be anybody there.

"Wait here," he said impulsively, then dropped his pack and pushed through a narrow passage through the brush to the open clearing on the other side. He sprinted up the hill to the line of brush where Tara had been, then crouched in front of them facing the hollow. The Winchester was poised, and he switched the safety off. As quietly as he could, he stepped slowly toward the hollow, stopping every few seconds to listen.

There was no sound other than the whisper of the high breeze singing through the conifer leaves.

He was only a few feet away now. He placed his boot slowly with each step, futilely trying to be silent. With each step, though, there was a muffled crunch that he hoped was lost in the sound of the breeze and blocked by the brush. He held close to its low green line, close enough to smell the sage scent it emitted.

Every few seconds, he straightened and glanced over the top, hoping to see Tara's form moving farther up and over the ravine.

Did she know her husband was dead? What could be in a person's head that they would do such a thing?

With those thoughts, his mind began to drift into the past, the desert, the operations. He stopped it, pausing in his forward movement as if it would help push the memories back. He had to clear his mind. One quick way to die was to entertain a drifting mind.

He looked over the sage green. Three feet to his left, the top of the brush jumped violently, the end of a small branch flipping up and dropping to the ground next to him.

Then he heard the crack of a rifle.

Instinctively, he ducked. He looked back down the hill in time to see a pinpoint flash amid the black opening at the bottom of the clump of brush Todd was hiding behind.

Mattituck was momentarily confused. Was Tara behind him? Moving in on Todd, but took a shot at Mattituck instead?

No, that didn't make sense.

He heard another crack, then the echo as it reverberated down the ravine.

Nope. She was up ahead someplace. He turned to scan the ridges and ravine up ahead. He heard the rifle report behind him again, and he imagined Todd lying on his belly in the dark hollow under the brush. He should have known the man wouldn't sit still. He smiled to himself as he sighed a breath of relief. Tara was up the ravine someplace, and likely up on one of the ridges. This meant no poking a head into a dark hollow with a gun barrel waiting inside.

But it also meant the chase was on. If Tara was up the ravine, and especially if she was climbing a ridge, then she was moving away from them. It was clear she had never thought she would be followed out to Hinchinbrook while she was hunting Wilson down, so perhaps she was on the run now. If so, she'd probably want to circle back around to her boat for an escape.

Mattituck straightened again as he stepped in front of the hollow where Tara had been hiding, scanning the ridge to the left for any sign of her. In his peripheral vision, he caught motion about a quarter of the way up, about 500 yards up the ravine from where he was. He looked directly where the movement had been, but it was gone. If it had been Tara, she sure as hell had moved quickly.

For a fleeting moment, it occurred to him that maybe Tara wasn't the only one up ahead.

If that were true, then he had just had a potentially fatal lapse in judgment, stepping into the hollow with the assumption Tara wasn't there.

*Well, I'm still standing*, he thought, and continued walking through the hollow. He glanced behind him to see Todd jogging up the clearing toward him, binoculars in hand. Mattituck waited for him.

"She's headed up that ridge," Todd said as he approached.

"You sure it's her? She got up there awfully quick."

Todd nodded. "I thought of that, too, which is why I pulled the binoculars. I could see her pretty well in my scope, but these zoom in a bit closer. It was her all right."

Mattituck looked back up the ridge. There was still no sight of her. She must have dropped behind rocks or into a crevice.

"We'd better be careful," Mattituck said, thinking of his lapse of judgment. "Can't be sure she's going up."

They both took in water, then Mattituck turned to lead the way up.

"What are you thinking?" Todd asked.

"I was thinking a little while ago that she's trying to go over that ridge and circle back behind us—get back to her boat and make an escape."

"But?"

"But she accomplishes nothing with that." He stepped out from the other side of the brush onto the clearing.

From here, the mostly bare ground sloped to the crest of the ravine, then leveled out before dropping down into a large meadow framed in by the ridges on either side. The ridge on the left then cut back to the south to join the mountains that ran along the south edge of Hinchinbrook Island. The ridge on the right sloped down to join the high bluff that dropped into Orca Bay to the north.

"She has to kill us," Mattituck continued. "It's her only real hope."

Todd picked up right away.

"If she bolts, she knows we've seen her boat, and might have a good bead on a visual of her. She probably had no idea we were coming up behind until after we found Wilson's body. Or about that time."

Mattituck gave him a quizzical look.

Todd explained. "I doubt she was going to leave the body there for critters."

Mattituck nodded understanding.

"I see. We scared her off."

"Something like that," Todd affirmed.

"Then I'm right. She's not running."

"Nope," Todd said, looking through the binoculars up the ridge. "She's drawing us out so she can take us out. She'll return home, then, to await the horrible news of her missing husband's death. And my, my, there's a couple of troopers out there, too."

Mattituck finished the reasoning. "She'll set it all up to look like Wilson took us out, then the wolverine got him."

"They're married," Todd added, "so she can swap rifles with Wilson's body. Clean as can be, Wilson shot us."

"What about the bullets in Wilson's body?" Mattituck asked, enjoying Todd's forensics knowledge.

"The only one that would have killed him for sure is right about where some nasty gashes are, from the wolverine. It's a gruesome thought, but trust me, I've seen some nasty shit. The wolverine is a short way down the trail. She can carry her back up, cut Wilson up some more and dig out the bullet, and that's it."

"Couldn't the coroner figure all that out?"

"Could. But just easily might not." Todd looked at Mattituck. "This isn't Perry Mason."

Todd was looking up the ridge again.

"No sign of her. I think she dropped into a crevice and dropped back down."

Mattituck nodded. "So she'd be thinking we think she's heading up the ridge, but she'll be waiting to bushwhack us down there," he said, nodding up over the ridge, to the meadow down the other side.

"That's about right."

"You seem to be thinking straighter," Mattituck said to him.

"Not really," Todd said honestly. "That's all pretty routine. My head's still hurting in that weird sort of way, and my eyes won't stop with the dryness."

"Are those symptoms of concussion?"

"I don't know. I don't think so. But something's not right, is all I'm saying. I'd just assume we follow your judgment."

"All right," Mattituck said, and led them to the left.

His plan was to get in close to the ridge and follow the foot of it up and over. With luck, they might come up on Tara and surprise her.

# Chapter Twenty-four

## From Predator to Prey

It was mid-morning when they approached the general area beneath where Tara had disappeared. Mattituck slowed their pace and became visibly more alert. He had the Winchester poised in front of him, and began his scanning motion as he walked ahead in a partial crouch. Behind him, Todd followed suit, although he held the AR-15 pointed to the left so it never pointed at Mattituck, yet was at the ready should Tara suddenly appear on the ridge above them.

Neither man spoke. They moved as a unit, as though they had trained together, each keeping an eye in a different place as they advanced, and both ready to spring to action.

Mattituck paused, holding the palm of his hand backward toward Todd. Todd stopped behind him, silent. At this point, both seemed to know that talking needed to be kept to a minimum if not eliminated altogether. But Todd sensed that Mattituck had paused for a reason. He held perfectly still, trying to attune his ears to whatever Mattituck may have heard.

Then he heard it. The sound of shale sliding over other earth and rocks.

Mattituck looked back at him, and Todd nodded at him. The sound seemed to be coming from directly in front of them, sliding down the last several feet of the steep incline up the ridge. Todd's eyes appraised the incline. There was very little chance of somebody coming down at that point. Almost impossible, in fact. It seemed far more likely that the shale sliding was a mini-landslide.

Still, Mattituck didn't move. He seemed to be waiting for something.

Todd's impatience grew, but he suppressed it. His head was still hurting, and he could tell he wasn't thinking as clearly as usual. He knew he needed to trust whatever Mattituck was doing. As unnerving as it was for an experienced Trooper, he also knew that Mattituck had significant experience in the field — whatever precisely that experience was, Todd had seen enough of Mattituck's field work — and he'd dug up enough of the man's background — to know Mattituck was combat-tested and back-country savvy, to say nothing of some kind of law enforcement ability.

Then he saw her. A person had caused the mini-landslide after all. Tara Garrett emerged from behind a rock, obviously looking for them after coming off the ridge. She was looking far to their right, toward the middle of the meadow where the trail came down the middle from the ravine.

Mattituck crouched farther down, making the most of the rock pile in front of them for cover.

Tara gained her footing on the firm meadow after sliding down the unsteady ground of the ridge. She kept low, her rifle with scope in both hands, ready, as she made her way toward an escarpment that afforded a protected view of the meadow. When she reached it, she lowered herself and pulled a water bottle from her day pack to re-hydrate, keeping a wary eye on the terrain ahead of her.

It seemed to never occur to her that they might be behind her.

"She never planned to be here overnight," Todd whispered.

Mattituck shot a glance at him. "How do you know?"

"Day pack."

Mattituck looked to where Tara lay in wait for them. He nodded.

"She thought she'd come in, knock him off, then be back in Cordova in a few hours," Mattituck said.

"Funny how things don't always go as planned," Todd said sardonically.

Mattituck was still watching her. She hadn't moved, and appeared settled in.

"She's patient," he said. "I don't think she's going to move until we come up that trail."

Todd watched Tara thoughtfully.

"So what's the plan?" Mattituck asked. "I mean, what would normal protocol be in this kind of situation?"

Todd still had a dull ache in his head, and his eyes kept watering.

"Protocol," he repeated. "Arrest her." He rubbed his eyes.

Mattituck held him in a tight gaze. "Okay," he said. "How?"

Todd's eyes were bloodshot, and Mattituck's concern grew. The pupils still looked fine, but it was clear that Todd wasn't himself. He rested his forearm across a large round boulder and let his forehead drop onto it.

"Todd . . . you okay?"

Todd's head lifted.

"Huh?"

Mattituck could see Todd's eyes were glazing.

"We need to get you out of here," he said.

Todd closed his eyes briefly, then opened them.

"Fat chance. She's in our way."

It was true. Even if they considered aborting an arrest of Tara Garrett, there was no way they could get back to the boat without going around Tara. She hadn't moved, patiently lying in wait like a jaguar waiting for its prey to get close.

"How much do you think you can do?" Mattituck asked.

"Whatever I'm going to have to do."

"No. No you don't. Look, Todd, the last thing I need is for us to be in a tandem approach and you drop off or something."

Todd pressed his eyelids together tightly. He didn't want to admit it.

"I'll be all right," he said finally.

Mattituck was watching him, only looking away in glances to check on Tara's position.

"I said I'll be all right," Todd snapped.

"Okay, that's a clear—"

"Cut the shit," Todd interrupted. "I'll be fine."

"You don't look it, Todd. You always say Rule 1 is to make sure you don't become another rescue operation."

Todd was silent a moment, then blinked hard and peered over at Tara.

"You're right, but I don't think we have any choice."

"There's always a choice," Mattituck said. "But we'd better make it before she starts getting antsy."

Todd watched a bald eagle glide over the opposite ridge, head moving right to left in search of prey. It dropped a dozen meters, then swung to the left and caught an updraft, never once stroking its wings.

His eyes fell back to Tara, although he couldn't remember why he was looking there. She lay on her belly, looking toward the ravine. They need to arrest her. He knew that. But what had he been thinking a moment ago?

He looked at Mattituck, who was watching Tara as well, then started to rise. Mattituck turned.

"What're you doing?" Mattituck asked him.

"We need to arrest her."

"Yeah, but don't we need a plan?"

Todd paused, crouching back down. He surveyed the terrain between them and Tara, some 200 meters away.

"There's some muskeg on the ground on both sides," he said finally. "That'll keep our footsteps quiet as we approach."

Mattituck was shaking his head. "We can't cover that distance without her discovering us." He looked at Todd, his face softening. "Look, Todd. You're not doing well . . . that's obvious. Do you think you can keep alert and cover for me?"

"What are you thinking?"

"I think I can follow this low gulley here around to those shrubs over there." He indicated an area to the left, less than half the distance to Tara's position. "We'll have her in a crossfire then. She'll have to give herself up."

"Who's the lead in calling her to arrest?"

"If you're up to it, probably you. You're the Trooper, and that way we don't give away where I am if she tries to resist."

"You're deputized, so you're a Trooper as well. But yeah, you're right about the crossfire. I'll holler that there are three of us and have her covered."

"When I'm in place, I'll raise my hand so you know I'm ready."

Todd nodded, then pulled the AR-15 up and rested it on the boulder. He took off the safety and leaned in, placing Tara in his sights. He heard Mattituck step back behind the rocks and down into the low gulley that led away to the left.

He squeezed his eyes tight, then rubbed them with his support hand. The dull ache was increasing. *Probably the spike in adrenaline and blood pressure*, he thought to himself. He blinked again, fighting back the ache.

Mattituck's steps had faded quickly, so Todd glanced to see where he was. He had just gained the musket coming out of the gully and was approaching the scrub cover near his chosen position.

Dancing spots began.

"Shit," Todd whispered. He knew this sensation.

But before he could think any more about it, he dropped forward against the boulder and slid down to the ground, unconscious.

Mattituck stepped as softly as he could on the gravely dirt leading out of the low gully. Only a few steps more on the crunchy ground, and he would reach the muskeg and more silent steps. There would be about ten feet where he was completely exposed to Tara Garrett's position, but if anything went amiss he knew Todd had him covered.

He covered the muskeg section quickly, confident in his silence. He slowed back to a near crawl when he reach the rough dirt again, doing his best to raise no noise. When he finally reached the designated spot, he quickly spotted Tara still lying on the ground, awaiting her prey. He raised the Winchester and checked his sights. It was a clear shot to Tara.

He raised his right hand to signal to Todd, then readied himself. He had the cross hairs on her mid-back, finger on the trigger and safety off.

Nothing happened.

Maybe Todd hadn't seen him.

He raised his hand again.

Nothing.

Keeping a wary watch on Tara, he glanced back to the big round boulder where Todd was.

Or should have been. There was nothing but the big round boulder.

A momentary panic gripped him as he looked back to Tara Garrett. She hadn't moved. He swung around to look at the path he'd just followed, half considering backtracking to check on Todd. There was little doubt in Mattituck's mind what had happened. All the signs had been there, but neither of them had wanted to acknowledge it.

Mattituck had no choice. He would have to backtrack.

With no further hesitation, he started to step toward the gully, then stopped. He had a ten foot section where he was completely vulnerable to Tara should she turn and see him. He decided to keep the safety off and walk—as best he could—sideways across that section so that he could fire back toward Tara if she spotted him. He was trying particularly hard not to trip, despite a sense of urgency to check on Todd.

Todd must have passed out, Mattituck decided. The combination of exhaustion and even a mild concussion was a dangerous mix that could—though unlikely—kill Todd or put him into a coma. He had to get to his friend and wake him up.

He should have paid closer attention to how close he was to the muskeg, as he almost tripped on the spongy ground covering. Fortunately, he recovered his balanced with his right foot shooting into a wider stance. He looked up to Tara's position to make sure she hadn't heard him.

She had.

Her body was still in the forward-facing position on her belly, but her head had craned around to check on the sound.

There was a moment of absolute pause while their eyes met.

"Hold up!" Mattituck shouted. "State Troopers! You're under arrest!"

Her head moved slowly from side to side in response. Then they both burst into action. The lack of fire from the big boulder told Mattituck for sure that Todd was down. He ran hard across the soft vegetation, gaining the gully before Tara could sit up and spin her rifle around at him. He dove headfirst, not wanting to chance even a millisecond. While Tara didn't seem to be the best shot, particularly with moving targets, Mattituck didn't want to take a chance in testing this out at closer range.

He hit the graveled ground hard on his forearms and elbows, but his arms were too outstretched to properly break the fall with a tuck and roll. Instead, his chest and belly pounded into the ground, followed by his thighs and knees.

He didn't bother to curse, though he wanted to. Instead, he swung his body around under cover of the edge of the gully. He poked his head up for only a quick check on Tara. She was on her feet and running the opposite direction toward the ravine. Most likely, she was heading back down to her boat. Everything in him wanted to chase her down, but the question of Todd's condition pulled at him, and he hesitated. Tara cut down to the other side of a rock outcrop and ducked. A moment later, her head came up, followed by the barrel of her rifle.

Mattituck dropped into the gully, turned, and ran at a crouch back toward Todd. He heard no rifle shots, telling him he was low enough to keep well covered.

He scurried quickly over the loose gravel and patches of muskeg, slowed only slightly by his running in a crouch.

The situation took him back to a previous life, working alone in the back country. The tension and adrenaline were the same, but back then he was alone and didn't have to worry about a partner who was downed. He wished for a moment that he were working alone, although he immediately thought of the times he and Todd had worked together, complementing each other's talents and skills. No, partnership with a guy like Todd was better by far.

Besides, all this was technically not his gig. It was Todd's, and Mattituck was his citizen deputy.

Most compelling was that his friend was down, potentially suffering a serious concussion, and they had no radio contact. He needed to tend to him, even if it meant letting Tara escape.

As he came around the pile of rocks where Todd was, he thought about Tara stopping, taking cover, and turning to take aim back at him. She wasn't running at all, he realized. She had been merely taking cover. Moreover, she had gone straight to the best cover in her vicinity. It was as if she'd cased the area prior to taking shelter. In fact, the more Mattituck thought about it, the more sure he was that's precisely what she had done.

Best not to underestimate her. She was in a predator mode, and she was circling back on them like an eagle ready to dive in for the kill.

Todd was slumped over forward against the big round boulder, his face nearly touching the earth at its base. Mattituck looked him over quickly to make sure nothing else had happened—such as a shot from Tara that he hadn't heard. He was clear. It had to be the head injury. All morning, Todd had been disoriented so it was clear the fall on the rock had done something more serious than a bruise.

Mattituck peered over the boulder to check on Tara. He knew it would be naïve to think she was sitting behind the same rock. If he was right about her predatory role, then she was working her way to gain an advantage on them. The question was what that would be.

And whether he and Todd could anticipate it. Well . . . at the moment, whether *he* could anticipate it. More accurately, Mattituck was thinking how he could keep her at bay while getting Todd to medical help.

Satisfied Tara was not a threat at the moment, he inspected Todd's head. There was a nasty bump above the right ear that had to be where he had hit his head on the rock. He felt it through Todd's hair with his fingertips, trying to get a feel for how large it was and how it might be raised under the skin. Not that Mattituck had much medical training—just what had come with field medical for his special operations unit, Sierra Delta, the acronym for "Sweep Detail." His unit had been the team called in when other special operations units were at risk of failing . . . or had already. They were the team that swept up the mess, hence the "Sweep Detail," or Sierra Delta.

That was years ago, and before his time in law enforcement with the Park Service. All things he had hoped to leave behind when moving to Alaska.

But as they say, you can't teach an old dog new tricks.

# Chapter Twenty-five

## Dog Tricks

Monica hadn't slept well. By 5:00 a.m., she had convinced herself she wasn't going to get back to sleep and had risen to start a pot of coffee. At worst, she'd need to take a nap at midday. One more of the many advantages of being self-employed, she thought.

She had spent at least three hours on the Garrett files, although she hadn't been sure why. It seemed at this point that things had taken a turn that made it clear something was amiss not only with her client, Tara Garrett, but with her husband. Wilson had seemed to be savvy to what his wife was up to. The letter ceasing expansion into Seattle had always nagged at Monica, not only because the signature was forged, but because it seemed to her that at some point it would have had to have crossed Wilson Garrett's desk. He had to have known.

And as she thought about it now, sitting at her desk with the file's documents spread out in front of her, the import of that fact pressed in on her like an elephant pressing its trunk against a wall. She sat staring at the array of business memos, company statements, and emails. For several long moments, she thought of the divorce and the affair Tara had been having, and her stomach distended with a sense of urgency.

She had to do something. But what?

Her anger with Frank had faded, and the lawyer's skepticism about facts disappeared. That was a part of her that had its place, but there was another part of her that mattered just as much. And for one of the only times she could remember, she was acting on that side of herself.

The only boat that might be available, and that had any speed capabilities, was the harbormaster's rigid hull vessel. It was almost identical to Todd Benson's State Trooper boat, the smaller one, and was capable of high speeds and enough distance for Monica's purposes.

But could she get Tom Graffinino to buy into this?

She hardly knew the guy, but she knew he had worked with both Todd Benson and Frank Mattituck. Maybe if she were able to convince him of the danger.
. . .

She looked up the Harbormaster's number on the Internet and dialed the main office number.

"Harbormaster," said an annoyed, deep gruff voice.

It had to be the surly old harbormaster himself.

"Tom? Tom Graffinino?"

"Who wants to know?"

She smiled to herself. Bingo.

"This is Monica Castle. I worked with Todd Benson and Frank Mattituck."

His voice lightened with this.

"Yeah? They're stand-up guys. What's up?"

"I think they're in danger, and I think we can help."

"We?"

"I need you and your boat. They're chasing down a couple of very dangerous people, and—"

"You mean Tara Garrett?" Graffinino interrupted.

Monica stopped abruptly stopped speaking.

"Well . . . yeah, as a matter of fact," she said, the bewilderment in her tone.

"They were down here poking around, and we ended up talking about her. She'd taken her boat out a couple of hours before they were here."

"Last night? Was this last night?"

"Yeah," Tom said, his deep voice graveling across the line. "It was. They took off in a hurry after her." There was only a moment's pause. "What's going on? They're in danger, you say?"

"Yes," Monica said emphatically. "They are. With their lives. You're my only—"

"How soon can you get here?" he interrupted.

"Fifteen minutes, maybe."

"I'll have the boat fueled up. Grab some light grubs for us and meet me at the fuel dock."

Monica caught herself nodding excitedly at the phone.

"Yes, yes . . . I'll be there right away."

Mattituck had dug out the basic First Aid kit from Todd's pack, although there was little he could do that would amount to anything. He dressed Todd's bump, knowing that it didn't do any good. There was no cut, and he had no ice pack to administer cold to the injury. Nonetheless, it made him feel like he was doing something. If Todd were awake, he could at least give him something for the fever that seemed to have risen, and treat the pain Todd would no doubt feel as soon as he came to.

Throughout treating Todd, Mattituck had raised his head to see if he could spot Tara. He had not been able to do so, which presented an entirely new set of concerns. Where was she? What was she planning? Where was she moving to, and most importantly, did that location give her a shot at them?

He scanned the other side of the ravine first, paying particular attention to the cover of the rock outcroppings and scrub brush.

Nothing.

Mattituck couldn't decide which he would prefer: not seeing her at all, giving him the impression she might have left, or catching sign of her at a vantage and taking aim at them. At least with the latter, he would know where she was and what she was up to. What drove Mattituck most nuts—and always had— was not knowing what the enemy was up to, and having no clues whatsoever.

A movement across the ravine at the base of the sharp rise up the ridge, directly opposite him, caught his attention. It was a human form, scaling up the loose shale at the bottom of the landslide buildup.

Tara.

She was a considerable distance from them now, or he might have been tempted to take a shot at her. God knew it would be the easy way out. Maybe there would be a lot of trials and justifying involved, but at least he and Todd would be alive.

He watched as she climbed up part way, then scaled to the left, up and over a rock outcropping, then slid her way back down into the ravine.

She was clearly not trying to get back to her boat.

Todd stirred, groaning. He shifted on the ground, his back to the big round boulder, and then straightened his back, something he could only be doing in response to a conscious discomfort—as opposed to a muscular/skeletal shifting in a dead sleep.

"Todd," Mattituck said firmly. "Todd!"

His friend's eyelids fluttered open. His eyes fell on Mattituck's, trying to focus. He came into consciousness quickly.

"What?" the Trooper said dispassionately.

"You passed out," Mattituck said.

Todd's brows raised as he tried to force himself into full consciousness.

"Okay, so what's your point?"

Mattituck chuckled.

"Well, at least you haven't lost your sense of humor."

Todd shifted forward, attempting to gain his feet— or at least his knees.

"What's the situation?" he asked, seemingly not having missed a beat.

"Tara's on the other side of the ravine, moving left."

Todd surveyed the ravine in front of them. To the left, it dropped down at an even slope toward the area where Justin Harris had lost his life.

"One of two things she's possibly doing," Todd said. "Hoofing it down there because there's something she needs to take care of at the scene."

Mattituck waited.

"Okay," he said, finishing Todd's thought. "Meaning that she might have been in cahoots with Wilson on knocking Justin off. I don't buy it, though, just for the record."

"Neither do I," Todd said.

"So, the second possibility?" Mattituck prodded.

Todd looked at him.

"Number two is that she's after us, and is baiting us down that way."

Mattituck had considered that Tara was hunting them, of course, but that she might be baiting them specifically down that way had not occurred to him. If that's what she was up to, then she must be confident of having the upper hand.

Mattituck was well aware that a lot of men would underestimate a woman in the outdoors, but he was not falling prey to that mentality. Never had, actually. Not only had he seen plenty of women who were just as capable of firing a weapon and getting around in the outdoors as any man, but he'd seen enough hints of Tara Garrett's capabilities to show her abilities. Already, he knew she was a marksman with the rifle, albeit with a weakness for moving targets. She was also married to an avid outdoorsman, and had been the lover of a man who was also a die-hard outdoorsman. There was no doubt such a woman was versed enough in all things outdoors to attract the kinds of men who considered life in Alaska a ticket into paradise.

For Mattituck, this translated into a glaring cautionary sign to assume outdoorsman competence in Tara rather than an assumption that she was the stereotypical woman.

"Okay," he said to Todd. "Let's assume she's like the best of any sportsmen. What's your take?"

Todd thought a moment, pointing over the rock to indicate that Mattituck should check on Tara.

Mattituck complied, but saw no sign of their adversary.

"I think," Todd said, "that she's drawing us down into that valley where Justin was killed because there's a good chance there's no radio or cell signal."

"Little does she know we haven't had one for the last twelve hours . . . at least."

"Right," Todd said. "So from her view, there's no way for us to call for help. Her goal is to dispose of us. And by that, I mean not only kill us, but dispose of any evidence of us."

Mattituck thought about this.

"You seem to be more clear-minded," he said.

Todd smiled. "I think so. Feeling pretty good, actually," he said as he touched his fingers to the bump on his head.

"We'd better get going," he added, swinging around to his knees and reaching for the AR-15.

Mattituck watched him, surprised.

"You up to this?"

Todd fixed an even gaze on him.

"I'm good, Frank. We have a job to do."

Mattituck smiled inwardly.

"Yes, yes we do at that," he said in return.

After Monica and Tom Graffinino had cast off in the 26-foot Harbormaster rigid hull, Graffinino had turned to Monica with a stern look.

"Okay, so what's this all about?"

"I can't share everything," Monica ventured.

Graffinino had never served in the military, but he was an avid fan of espionage novels and had a deep appreciation for the 'need-to-know' culture. He nodded.

"Fair enough," he said. "Just tell me what I need to know."

"As I said, Trooper Benson and Frank Mattituck are in danger," she started. "There's a case going related to the Justin Harris death. You know about that, right?"

Graffinino looked offended.

"Are you kiddin' me?"

"Okay, sorry. Of course you do. So this is all related to that. While I can't disclose much," she said to Graffinino's accommodating nod, "what I can say is that I have reason to believe that a party or parties might pose a threat to Trooper Benson and—"

"Yeah, yeah," Graffinino interrupted. "Look, Ms. Castle. I know you need to speak the legalese shit and all, but I'm just an ex-logger turned harbormaster. And I happen to like those two guys. I just want to help out, okay?"

Monica drew a breath.

"Yes," she said. "Of course. Thank you. Here's the gist. I'm very sure Todd and Frank are in danger. Somebody out there wants to kill them. I'm not sure where exactly they went, but we were all at the lighthouse when it all started, including the guy who shot Justin Harris. So I have this feeling we need to get there."

"To the lighthouse? Hinchinbrook Lighthouse?"

"Yes," she said. "I know, I know . . . I have no solid reason for—"

"Don't matter. Sounds like it's our best hunch," the gruff harbormaster said. "So that's where we go. There's an old service dock on the outside of Hinchinbrook Entrance. That's the best access to the lighthouse."

Monica smiled inwardly. That was exactly what she had been hoping—to get to the service dock and then check out the Lighthouse. She had a strong premonition that's where Todd and Mattituck would end up.

They had lost sight of Tara, but knew she was headed west, to the left of them, and toward the place where Justin Harris had been shot and killed. The last they had seen her, she had been moving along the ridge, where she had an advantage for firing at them any time they were within sight. Mattituck was thinking of Tara's poor shooting at distances, and especially her difficulty with moving targets.

"I say we just move fast straight down that trail," he said to Todd.

Todd was moving swiftly ahead of him.

"Are you crazy? That's about as in the open as we can get."

"Which puts us in little danger if the shooter can't hit us."

Todd's head swiveled and his eyes met Mattituck's. "Meaning?"

"Meaning that if we want to head her off, we'd best get our asses moving."

"I think caution is the better—"

"Not this time," Mattituck said, and started at a slow jog for the trail at middle of the valley.

Todd was about to follow when movement a quarter way up the opposite ridge caught his attention. Tara Garrett. She was crouching behind a large boulder about four hundred meters away, her rifle coming level on Mattituck. Todd swung the AR-15 around and poised for a shot. He leveled the weapon as he took aim on her and released the safety. He wanted to get a shot in before she could fire at Mattituck.

*Pop! Pop!*

He liked the feel of the AR-15. As rifles went, this was a smooth one that had little kick. He saw granite powder flip up from the boulder three feet in front of Tara, then watched as she ducked behind the boulder.

Mission accomplished, Todd thought as he set the safety and swung the AR-15 back over his shoulder. He rose and began a near-sprint to catch up with Mattituck. They gained the middle trail quickly and turned to follow it to the left. They made a good pace, no doubt driven by the threat of Tara's rifle. As they made their way down the trail toward the scene of

Justin's death, Todd shot furtive glances back up the hill on the opposite side, but he saw no sign of Tara. After the third time checking and seeing no response, Todd slowed and called Mattituck to do the same.

Mattituck ignored him, and instead picked up his pace to a full sprint for several dozen meters, then cut to the right of the valley, to the same side that Tara was on. He paused under cover of a spruce tree and turned to face Todd. He raised a hand to signal him.

Todd stopped, confused and watching him. Mattituck shook his head vigorously, waving for him to continue down the trail. Immediately, Todd understood and continued at a fast jog down behind him.

Mattituck turned his attention to where Tara had last been. There was nobody behind the boulder she'd been using for cover, and Mattituck's thinking was that she would want to stay high so she was at an advantage for any shots she might have. He scanned the mountainside with his binoculars, but there was no sign of her.

Satisfied that she was on the move, probably trying to head them off, Mattituck packed his gear and slung the Winchester over his shoulder. He started down the slope toward Justin Harris' place of death. He had no doubt that Tara Garrett was headed to the same place.

# Chapter Twenty-six

## Closing In

Mattituck and Todd were at a full-speed sprint down the sloping trail, no more than a quarter mile from the scene of the crime. They still hadn't been shot at, leaving Mattituck wondering whether he'd been wrong about Tara's intentions. He fought back the fear that she might have cut back the other way, toward the boats and what would by now be a sure escape. They'd come too far this direction to be able to catch up with her now.

They couldn't keep on at this pace, Mattituck knew, especially with Todd's head injury.

A hundred or so meters ahead was a wooded area that the trail cut through. He'd been alert as they approached for any sign that Tara might be lying in wait there, but he was becoming more and more sure that she was either moving as fast as she could to the scene or was halfway to the boats in the opposite direction. Either way, they were safe in their approach to the woods.

As they came within 50 meters of the edge of the woods, dirt on the game trail ahead of Mattituck kicked up, followed by another to his left. He shot a quick glance up the slope on the right, but the jarring from his running was too violent for any details to stand out.

The ground kicked up in front of him again, then behind. This time he noticed the rifle reports. She was a distance away as there was a full second between the bullets hitting and the sound of the rifle.

"She's firing at us," he yelled over his shoulder.

"No shit!" came Todd's sarcastic reply.

Todd was slaloming in an attempt to be evasive.

"Won't do . . . any good," Mattituck panted as he ran. "She's a . . . crappy shot . . . chances just as good . . . either way."

"She sniped her husband back there!" Todd snapped.

That was true, Mattituck thought, but she'd been missing most of her shots by a wide margin. Maybe that one shot was a lucky one.

"Lucky shot, maybe, but more likely she sucks with fast-moving targets. Go straight and fast!"

Todd straightened his path and picked up speed.

The shots kept coming. For a few seconds, they were farther and farther off. Then, as they closed in on the woods, they came in tighter. They didn't need to reach the edge, though, Mattituck thought. Just close enough that her angle was lost over the tops of the trees.

He was right. Within a few seconds, the shots stopped.

"That settles any . . . thinking that she . . . might be heading back down . . . to the boats," Mattituck said, coming to a walk. No need to run if she couldn't even see them.

"Who was thinking she was?" Todd was out of breath as well.

"Me. I kept thinking maybe . . . she was headed back the other way."

Todd shook his head.

"No way. For the reasons we said earlier. She's committed now. It's put up or shut up. She has to kill us."

"Well, aren't we Mr. Positive Thinking."

Todd chuckled. "I have to admit, though," he said. "That hard running has my head fucking pounding."

They reached the woods and passed into secure cover. From what Mattituck could tell, Tara was part way up the ridge on the right side, a fair distance west of them. If his observation had been right, she would be forced back down very quickly as the side of the ridge became sheer cliff for a distance before sloping sharply back down to their level.

With a start, he realized they had an opportunity.

"Shit!" he blurted. "We don't have much time!" He began to bolt through the woods along the narrow game trail.

"We need water!" Todd called after him, bringing him to a stop.

Mattituck was nodding as he turned back.

"Quickly," he said as they both pulled their water bottles and drank deeply.

"What's the rush?" Todd asked.

"She's going to have to come back down from the side of the ridge before it turns to cliff."

Todd nodded. "And if we can—"

"Exactly," Mattituck cut him off as he tucked the water bottle away and began to jog.

"I may need to lag back," Todd said.

Mattituck stopped.

"That won't do," he said. "Is it bad?"

"Yeah," Todd said with his hand to his forehead. "I was starting to see spots back there."

Mattituck was shaking his head.

"Okay. We'll walk then. We'll just have to chase her down at a slower pace."

"No," Todd said emphatically. "It'd be better to cut her off on the slope."

Again, Mattituck was shaking his head.

"Honestly, Todd, how do you think this is going to end? Do you think she's going to give up when we shout—again—'you're under arrest!'?"

"Point well taken," Todd said.

They both knew the outcome was either Tara getting away, or Tara dead. And she had no intention of leaving without taking them out.

"We're in a true death match, aren't we?" Mattituck observed what they both had been thinking.

"All or nothing, apparently," Todd replied. "Most killers try to think up some defense argument to try to get off. I'm thinking she knows there's something out there that incriminates her no matter what."

Mattituck thought a moment as they started walking down the trail.

"So, wait a minute. Even if she killed us off and got away, she'd eventually be found out, wouldn't she?"

Todd shook his head. "Not necessarily. If she gets back clean and not observed, there's nothing to pin our deaths on her."

"What about her rifle?"

"I'd bet my next paycheck she's using Wilson's rifle. And she's got gloves on. After she killed us, she'd take it back to Wilson and leave it nearby. It'd look like he killed us, then while he was headed back to his boat, the wolverine got him."

"Fuck," Mattituck said with admiration. "That's iron clad."

"Yeah, isn't it?"

"So what's our best plan?" Mattituck was hoping the experienced Trooper was clear enough through his injury to guide them.

"Wing it. There's no other way. We wing it and hope for the best."

Mattituck stared at him for a moment. He had far too much history himself to doubt his friend for a moment. He turned and continued through the woods at an even walking pace. He completely abandoned his thoughts of heading her off and trying to capture her. And with that, there was no sense rushing now that they knew she was ahead of them. Whatever she was trying to lure them into—and it was clear that luring was precisely what she was doing—they had no choice but to follow and keep alert.

Izzy was halfway through her 12-hour shift at Pappy's establishments. She had started at 11:00 a.m.

for the lunch rush at Bella Luna, and the plan was that they would shift over to The Crow's Nest sometime after the initial dinner peak had hit Bella Luna. Pappy, she had found, was a driven man. It was no wonder The Ühing had maintained a long-term arrangement with him. In fact, that arrangement had started in the mid-1970s with the end of the Vietnam war.

This assignment had seemed at first to be a quick and easy assessment, then on to other things. It had turned out to be anything but that. First of all, she didn't understand the Ühing's obsession with Frank Mattituck. Perhaps it would have helped had they explained what he had done to them that made them . . . she hesitated a moment, then decided it was the right words: fear him. The Ühing actually feared this Frank Mattituck. From what Izzy saw, there couldn't be much to fear. Unless there was something they knew that she couldn't see.

Her mind went back to The Crow's Nest incident, when she'd decided to end the scuffle with the ugly lusty man. She'd made short work of him, then when he had been neutralized, she had straightened and looked up. Mattituck's gaze had been on her, and it carried the look of knowing. Had he recognized her training? He'd been looking at her with the knowledge of another who had been through that kind of training.

And it had unnerved her. It was a stupid lapse in judgment, assuming nobody would recognize those moves. But how could he?

How couldn't he?, she answered herself. Especially considering The Ühing wanted so desperately to know what he might be working on up here. And then there was that cryptic name. The Takistus. The obstacle. . . .

All afternoon, these thoughts haunted her. She couldn't put her finger on it, but she knew that The Takistus had seen something in her that it would have been better for him not to have seen.

She should know better, she scolded herself. She was young yet, she knew. But there were some things with no leeway for mistakes.

After reaching the scene where Justin Harris had been shot, Mattituck and Todd did a quick scan of the area. Nothing seemed changed, so they continued on their way.

"She doesn't seem interested in the scene," Mattituck observed as they resumed their fast pace down the trail.

"She's focused on us," Todd said, now leading.

"How's your head?"

"Better. Good enough, anyway."

And that was all they said for the next hour. Another quarter mile beyond the murder scene, Todd had picked up a fresh set of boot prints on the soggy soil of the trail.

"It's her," Todd said, crouched and examining the prints. He looked back up at Mattituck. "These match those boot prints we saw the other day. The ones that were tailing Wilson and Justin."

Mattituck nodded, then looked ahead.

"She's a dangerous woman," Todd said.

"I wonder where she's headed."

Todd stood and peered down the trail.

"Only thing down there is the lighthouse."

"Unless she's got a spot she's thinking for ambush," Mattituck said.

"That's the reason she's headed to the lighthouse," Todd replied. "It'll give her good cover and a clear shot at us as we approach."

That was true.

"We'd best be careful, then," was all Mattituck said as he took the lead.

Monica was studying the navigation chart while Tom Graffinino guided the Harbormaster vessel over the rising swells coming through Hinchinbrook Entrance. In a half hour or less, they would be at the lighthouse, and Monica wanted to be able to help Tom navigate in to the little supply dock.

She had never really known Tom Graffinino, but she was finding that he was at least a stand-up guy in an emergency situation. He had the reputation of being an extremely gruff and surly "sourdough Alaskan," a term used for those who had moved to the state and lived decades committed to The Last Frontier. Tom certainly fit that nomenclature. His reputation was of one who was harsh and difficult to work with, but he'd been anything but that in Monica's short experience with him. Maybe it was the thrill of the situation, maybe he was one of the machismo-filled guys who was soft with 'the women folk,' but whatever he normally was, he was extremely helpful and engaged now.

"You said you've run a boat?" he asked suddenly.

"Yeah, many times. Including Frank's boat, but—"

"No buts. I need to get our weapons together," he said firmly. He looked sternly at her. "You have fired weapons before, haven't you?"

Monica's shoulders shifted and her gaze penetrated his.

"I grew up in Alaska, Tom."

Graffinino gave a quick upward nod.

"Okay," he said, "just checking. If this situation is what you said it might be, we're going to need to go in armed and ready."

He was right. She had known this, of course, but the reality hit her with his words. Although she'd been to the firing range many times and had even gone hunting a few times, she'd never been in a gunfight situation before.

"Okay," she said. "What do you need me to do?"

"For now, just take over the helm. Keep us on course for that dock. As we get closer, I'll take over, but just keep us on course for now."

"All right," she said, stepping aside so he could slide off the captain's seat.

She took hold of the helm as he slid past and stepped aft, then she slid onto the seat and quickly acclimated herself to the boat's gauges and screens. The radar was on, set to 6 miles range. The GPS was in a good place for keeping the eyes to the seas ahead while tracking the course. All was well. Within moments, she was settled and comfortably steering the vessel toward the Gulf of Alaska.

Behind her, Tom was at work at the locked weapons cabinet secured to the aft bulkhead.

# Chapter Twenty-seven

## High Noon on Hinchinbrook

The lighthouse peeked through the foliage long before Mattituck and Todd could assess an approach, or whether Tara Garrett was even there. Every indication said she was there, however, as Todd had been picking up her boot trail the entire way. She was either sloppy about leaving a trail, or she wanted them to know where she was headed.

"When we're a few hundred feet from the edge of the trees, we'll survey the area around the lighthouse and figure out our plan," Todd said.

"Head doing better?"

Todd was annoyed for a brief moment, but then had to acknowledge it was right of Mattituck to ask this.

"Yeah . . . I think I'm good now. Hurts, but I'm thinking clearly now at least."

Mattituck nodded. He'd seen no signs of disorientation or confusion for well over two hours.

"Okay," he said.

They continued along the wooded trail, much more moist on this end of the island. The trees were taller and thicker, leaving tough going for anybody who ventured through the foliage rather than the trail. The wet from frequent rains kept the ground soggy and the leaves dew-kissed in the filtered light. Todd kept his eyes on the trail, making sure Tara's boots were still leading them to the lighthouse. When they came within a hundred feet of the clearing that was maintained around the lighthouse, he paused.

Mattituck came alongside of him and paused, squinting for a better look at the lighthouse.

Todd was also looking over the scene. There was no sign of Tara Garrett, but they knew she was there. Somewhere.

Mattituck waited, letting his friend plan out their approach.

"Okay," Todd finally said. "I think our best bet is to have you hang back and cover me."

"Are you up to that?"

"Yeah. And I need to be the front runner on this. If something were to happen—"

"It's not," Mattituck said.

"Sure, but—"

"It's not," Mattituck repeated.

"Point being," Todd side-stepped, "the state employee needs to be the one to take the hit."

Mattituck didn't immediately respond.

"So I cover," he said. "You're not going straight in, are you? From the trail?"

"No. See over there?" Todd pointed to the right, beyond the trees, to a line of excess equipment and containers that began near the trees and provided some cover to the lighthouse.

"Yeah," Mattituck said. "Looks like a good approach."

Todd nodded at Mattituck's experience. He had a military eye for this.

They moved down the trail toward the lighthouse, Todd in the lead, both with their rifles at ready and fingers on the safety. Mattituck was aware of his boots on the soft wet trail, a slight sucking sound as he lifted the soles out of the muddy spots, muffled by the thick trees and foliage around them. It was a stark contrast from his Special Ops days, where it was sand instead of mud, and bright barren sun-soaked expanse instead of closed-in rainforest.

Todd stopped thirty feet from the edge of the trees and held his hand out for Mattituck to stop. Mattituck obeyed, holding still and ready. Todd surveyed the scene silently, and Mattituck followed Todd's actions. Both men scanned the clearing around the lighthouse first, noting the areas that offered cover should they need to move in under fire. Then both looked over the lighthouse itself, noting the dark windows and great white walls.

Right of the center was the only door on this side. Mattituck was sure it was locked, which left the question of how Tara would have entered the building.

Todd started to cut through the foliage to the right, toward the line of abandoned equipment and other junk. Mattituck grabbed his arm.

Todd paused, looking back at him.

"Something's not adding up here," Mattituck said.

"Okay. I'm listening."

"That door's got to be locked. And there are no open windows or easy access in."

Todd was looking at him.

"So," Mattituck continued, "it's very unlikely she's inside."

Todd crouched next to him.

"You're right." He rubbed his eyes. "Shit."

"Todd, I don't think you're okay. How about I take the lead here?"

Todd closed his eyes and dipped his head, thinking.

Mattituck waited.

"Yeah," Todd said finally. "Okay. What are you thinking?"

"She wants us to think she's inside."

"But she's not. Okay, so where is she?"

Mattituck looked around, then scanned back up the trail.

"You were tracking her boots down this way, right?"

Todd nodded.

"No breaks into the woods? You would have been watching for that, right? In case she back-tracked to throw us off and then cut into the woods?"

"You're thinking she's in the trees to the left or right, waiting for us to come out into the open? Yeah, I was watching. No sign of that."

"Can you see ahead for tracks? In the clearing ahead, I mean."

"I'd have to get closer," Todd said, resigned and rubbing his forehead.

"Then let's do that. We need to know if she cut across the clearing or not."

They moved together, Mattituck in the lead. As they approached the edge of the woods, they slowed, cautiously scanning the open terrain ahead as well as the lighthouse. Mattituck especially watched the sides of the building where Tara Garrett might be waiting. He also kept a close eye on the line of abandoned equipment and junk. Cover like that could be used on either side.

Mattituck stopped ten feet short of the edge to the clearing and let Todd step forward. The State Trooper looked closely at the trail ahead.

"We've given her too much credit," he pronounced. "Looks like she just marched right on across to the left of the building."

Mattituck wasn't taken in.

"You sure?"

"Yep," Todd said. "No doubt about it. And no other tracks."

Mattituck was shaking his head.

"I don't buy it. She's up to something."

Todd looked at him. "Or not. Look, Frank, not everybody's a trained professional like our friend Norm Peck. Most people make big mistakes and leave glaring evidence. Tara Garrett's no expert. And guaranteed she's not thinking of her trail."

Mattituck had to agree. For the last several hours, he'd seen plenty to tell him that Tara Garrett was a poor shot and was in a desperate game to try to kill them. Nothing he'd seen indicated she might know what she was doing, nor that she was planning anything more than the superficial idea of luring them into an unplanned trap, yet to be devised.

Todd started for the trail.

"I don't know," Mattituck said hesitantly. "Todd..."

But the trooper carried forward boldly.

"Todd!..."

Nothing happened. Todd was walking down the trail, following Tara's boot prints.

And still nothing happened.

Mattituck realized the Trooper might know a thing or two, so he started following him toward the lighthouse structure. The two approached a rusty Caterpillar bulldozer, the yellow paint fading and giving way to the reddened rust-splotches.

Suddenly, Todd dropped to the ground, followed by a rifle shot. Mattituck's Winchester came up instinctively as he flipped the safety, swung to the right and took aim at the line of debris to the right. He fired off three random shots to cover Todd as he side-stepped quickly to the cover of the Caterpillar.

Todd was crawling the remaining three feet to the cover of the bulldozer. He stopped and grinned at Mattituck.

"Kinda had a feeling that'd happen," he announced.

"The hell you say!" Mattituck blurted with admiration. "That was expert. You knew she was going to fire?"

"I had a feeling she was over there," Todd said. "Figured she went around to the left of the building to throw us off, then cut back around behind the building. I was kind of keeping an eye that way, so my peripheral vision caught the motion as she moved and took aim. That's when I dropped."

"Just in time, too. Damn, that was really good, Todd. I have a new respect."

"Been underestimating me, eh?"

Mattituck was poised behind the driver's platform on the tractor, his rifle aimed where he thought the last shot had come from. His index finger was pulled back with enough pressure to be ready. His right eye was aligned with the sights.

Todd was moving to the right, behind the rear of the massive bulldozer.

"Where you going?" Mattituck asked.

"Key to winning is to keep the enemy guessing."

That was true enough. Mattituck waited to see what Todd was thinking.

Three quick shots erupted from Tara's position, which Mattituck still hadn't pin-pointed. The bullets glanced off the steel of the rig.

"That's a bit close for a bad shot," Todd mused.

"Yeah," Mattituck said thoughtfully. "She's been toying with us."

This sank in on Mattituck. Tara Garrett wasn't a bad shot after all. Just those three shots at the Caterpillar made that clear. All those bad shots back down the ravine had been a ploy to gain their confidence. The entire time, she had planned to lure them here.

"Fuck," Mattituck said aloud.

"What?"

"She's been fucking with us. Setting us up this whole time."

Todd grimaced. "I'd have to agree with that."

"Fuck," Mattituck repeated.

Todd slipped back toward Mattituck, well protected by the hulking steel of the bulldozer. He pulled his radio out and turned it on, peering at the tiny reception and channel screen.

"Still no signal."

Mattituck looked at him.

"How can that be? We're right under the damn Coast Guard lighthouse."

Todd was still peering at the screen on the hand held radio.

"Maybe the VHF antennas aren't anywhere near here. And if they're on that tower, we'd be under them. VHF is a line-of-site radio signal, isn't it? So we'd be literally under it."

"I'm sure they have VHF antennas up there," Mattituck said, pointing. "And the signal would pick us up. Remember when we were here the other day? We had a signal then."

Todd looked at his radio. "Something must be wrong with this thing, then."

"Cell?"

Both men pulled out their cell phones to check the signal, in hopes that the demand for the many cruise ships coming into the Sound might mean a decent signal. But both phones showed no signals.

"Now the cell signals," Mattituck said. "That makes sense there wouldn't be any."

Todd nodded. "We're too far out."

They were on their own.

Mattituck ventured to the left of the Caterpillar, to the front and the cover of the bulldozing blade. He jumped from the cover of the body of the machine to the cover of the blade, and hunkered down. He scanned forward, measuring the distance from his position to the next cover. Unfortunately, the next cover consisted of the lighthouse building itself, a good 50 meters or more away.

He looked back over his shoulder. The woods were at least thirty meters away. And now that they knew that Tara Garrett was a better shot than she'd let on, there was too much risk in trying even that short distance.

Mattituck caught Todd's eye, and the looks they exchanged were not very hopeful.

Monica turned the helm back over to Tom Graffinino as they entered the mouth of the small cove to the lighthouse dock. Tom had studied the nautical chart Monica had marked up with notations to help them as they sought to navigate the narrow opening between rocks to gain access to the small cover with the Coast Guard Lighthouse dock.

She moved quickly forward to the bow to watch for rocks and any other hazards as the boat moved slowly up the cove toward the dock. She stood high in the bow and kept a close eye for rocks and debris in the water. Tom had the forward cabin door open as the boat moved slowly to the dock. Monica, already well versed in boat operations, uncoiled the forward mooring line and readied the boat as she kept watch.

Once they were secured to the dock, Tom cut the twin outboard engines and the two of them moored the boat to the old wooden dock. He cut the engines, then made one last visit to the weapons cabinet. He came forward with a belt and holster for a .44 magnum sidearm for Monica as he clipped his own into place.

"I don't need—" Monica started.

"You might. Don't argue."

Without another word, Monica donned the holster and checked her rifle. It was an AR-15, a semi-automatic and the rifle of choice for the Alaska State Troopers as well as just about every assault weapon enthusiast in the United States.

The only sound was the breeze and the saltwater lapping at the boat and the pilings of the dock. Monica followed Graffinino onto the dock and then up the wooden incline sloping up toward the lighthouse. Both Graffinino and Monica knew the potential danger they were in, so they continued up the lumber path as stealthily as their crouched and quiet steps allowed.

As they approached the lighthouse with its helicopter pad on the south side in front of them, Graffinino pulled out his hand held radio to check the signal.

"Fucking-A," he said. "I have no fucking signal at all."

Monica only looked at him, unsure of what this meant.

Graffinino looked up at the lighthouse tower.

"Well, I'll be a sheep's motherfucker," he said, keeping his voice low. "The antenna array's down."

Monica looked up. On top of the lighthouse tower was a mish-mash of lines and antennas, all dangling haphazardly on this side of the building, strewn downward from the short steel-rail structure they were supposed to be mounted on.

"Somebody did that," Graffinino said. "That's not storm damage."

Monica wasn't sure what this meant, but it didn't bode well. Graffinino's perplexed complexion only confirmed that.

"I have a really bad feeling about this," he said. "With what you've told me and seeing this, I'd wager this is part of some killer's plan."

Monica stared at the mess of antennas, wondering where Mattituck and Todd were. Were they okay? Had she and Tom arrived too late?

"You stay here," Graffinino said, starting back toward the docks. "I need to get a backup call in. And to do that, I need a VHF signal."

"Okay," Monica said.

She watched the big ex-logger walking back down the dock, then turned toward the lighthouse. She ignored Graffinino's direction to stay where she was, and started at a low run for the building.

Within a few minutes, she was between the helicopter pad and the building, making her way around the base of the building to the left. She came upon the main door from the helo pad to the main building, and tried it to see if it was unlocked. Although she hadn't expected it to be open, she had hoped, only now to be disappointed. Nonetheless, she plodded forward to the left of the building.

It was then she heard shots.

They took her completely off guard. While she had been preparing mentally for the worst, the reality of it came unexpectedly. Instinctively, she crouched close to the building. She held tight to the stucco, waiting to hear where the danger was. She heard two more shots on the other side of the building, then settled in. She herself was in no danger, but it was clear that somebody was.

And there was little doubt that somebody would be Todd Benson and Frank Mattituck.

# Chapter Twenty-eight

## End of the Road

"She's got us pinned," Todd said, his back against the steel tracks of the big Caterpillar bulldozer.

"We're going to have to try," Mattituck said.

"No way. Too risky."

"If you cover me, I'll have a good shot getting back in the woods. If I get there, I can take shots at her and keep you well covered so you can get to the building. If you come around the other side, we'll have her in a crossfire."

Todd shook his head. "I don't like it."

"Got a better plan? Besides some miracle rescue out of nowhere?"

Todd thought for several moments.

"No, I guess I don't. So where is she shooting from?"

"No idea," Mattituck said, peering cautiously over the top of the yellow bulldozer.

*Ping!*

"Damn. She was right on that," Todd said.

*Ping Ping!*

"She knows we're thinking about a run . . . she's trying to pin us down," Mattituck observed.

Todd rubbed his eyes. "It seems like she knows a lot more of what she's doing than we thought."

"Yep," Mattituck agreed. "Male arrogance."

"Arrogance or stupidity?" Todd's annoyance came through the edge in his voice.

"What's the difference? Either way, she's got us pinned," Mattituck pointed out as he tried again to see where Tara was holed up.

*Ping!* A moment, then *Ping!*

"She must not be resting her aim for even a second," Todd said.

"I'm going to try it," Mattituck said.

"Don't be stupid."

"Stupid or arrogant?" Mattituck quipped.

"What's the difference, either way—"

"Don't finish that." Mattituck checked the safety. "Cover me."

"Where the hell am I shooting?"

"I don't know, exactly. When I covered you I fired into the bushes and trees to the right there. Pretty sure she's in there somewhere."

"I would have guessed the lighthouse," Todd replied, rubbing his eyes.

"You okay?"

"I think so. Head's hurting again."

"Adreneline and stress. With luck, we'll be outta here soon." Then he added, "Lighthouse is locked, most likely."

"Oh . . . yeah," Todd said. "Hadn't thought of that."

"You sure you're up to this?"

"Yeah. I'll be fine."

Todd readied the AR-15, then nodded at his friend. With that, Mattituck bolted like a jackrabbit for the woods behind them. Todd swung up and leveled the AR-15 at the bushes to the right of the lighthouse and began popping shots off. Behind him, he heard Mattituck running for the woods. Tara returned fire, likely at Mattituck since Todd didn't hear any *pings* off the bulldozer.

What he did get, however, was her location. He saw two quick flashes between two tall spruce surrounded by high scrub bushes. He focused his aim there and fired 5 successive shots.

The flashes continued. Either she didn't know he was firing into her position, or she was better fortified than it appeared.

Two quick shots erupted from the bushes.

Todd heard a sickening grunt behind him, followed by the tell-tale *thud* of a body hitting the ground.

He shot a quick glance over his shoulder. Mattituck was down, just short of the edge of the woods.

He turned back to Tara's position and fired three shots. He could see the bark fly off one of the spruce.

That got her attention. He saw flashes, then heard the *ping* of shots nearby.

He returned fire, looking back at his friend as he fired the last two.

Mattituck was gone.

Monica peered around the corner of the building, listening as she located where the shots were coming from. There was a pause in the shots. She waited, attentively watching. She was pretty sure she didn't need to put much effort into hiding at the moment. If Tara or Wilson were shooting at Mattituck and Todd— or at each other—they were probably all focused on each other. They would never suspect there was a newcomer on scene.

A quick burst of shots came from somewhere to the right. Monica scanned the open area between the other side of the lighthouse and the woods, about a hundred or so meters wide. There was virtually nothing between them except some abandoned equipment and debris, the largest of which was a large rusting bulldozer.

Gun shots came from the trees or bushes to her left, and from the sound, it was coming from an area about 50 meters away.

She looked to her left, checking for a way to cross to the line of trees and shrubs. From where she was, she could stay low and run thirty feet to a point of the same line of foliage that the shooter was in. Just then, shots came in a near-barrage from the clearing to the right. Monica looked and saw a figure running from the bulldozer to the woods behind it. Somebody was firing from behind the bulldozer into the bushes where the shooter on the left was hunkered down.

The shooter fired twice, and Monica looked in time to see the man running from the bulldozer go down.

She wasted no time. She bolted to the bushes and quickly started picking her way through the foliage toward the shooter. The gunfire exchange provided plenty of noise to drown out whatever noise she made, so she dispensed with trying to be silent.

Many times she'd been hunting with her father—one of the side effects of growing up in a place like Cordova. Those experiences had instilled the kind of outdoors savvy that was paying off now. She trudged expertly through the brush, ducking and side-stepping her way closer and closer to the shooter in the woods.

As she made her way, she suppressed any detailed thinking about who had been downed by the shooter. She allowed herself to recognize that it had to be either Mattituck or Todd, since of the four candidates for being here, only Todd and Mattituck would be working together.

That meant that the shooter was either Wilson or Tara Garrett.

There was always the possibility that there was a three-way firefight happening, but something about the antenna mess Tom Graffinino had spotted told her that the scene unfolding in front of her had been carefully planned. And that meant that either Wilson or Tara were dead, and the survivor was now trying to take out Mattituck and Todd Benson.

She was glad Tom had gone back to the boat to radio for help.

The gunshots continued as she half-ran toward the shooter. Within seconds, she would be coming upon them, and it seemed likely that she would have to shoot him. And with that pronoun, 'him,' she realized that she fully expected to find Wilson Garrett shooting at Todd and Frank. The antennas down, the planning that seemed to have happened, made it obvious that Wilson had the upper hand the whole time Frank and

Todd had been out here. And Tara. She had probably walked right into Wilson's trap.

Monica was getting close. The gun shots were coming from a thicker clump of shrubs just ahead, tucked nicely between two tall spruce trees. She slowed down, careful to keep her approach as silent as possible.

The gunfire stopped momentarily, and Monica froze. Then it started again. The shooter must have swapped out clips of ammo. In the distance, she could hear the return fire coming from behind the bulldozer. Whoever it was there—Frank or Todd—they were pinned down by this shooter, by Wilson Garrett.

Wilson was sending heavy fire, so Monica pushed through the shrubs. As she reached a small clearing in the middle of a perfect circle of shrubs nicely framed by the two spruce, she saw the shooter. He had his back to her—

Wilson turned, and Monica brought the AR-15 up and released the safety. His face appeared, and Monica drew a sharp breath.

Tara Garrett.

It wasn't Wilson at all. It was Tara. Monica was stunned enough to immobilize her momentarily. Long enough for Tara to spin and bring her rifle around.

*Pop! Pop!*

Monica was almost surprised at the AR-15 jumping in her hands. Her reaction to Tara's aiming at her had been automatic, unthinking. The animal instinct of survival.

For a long moment, time stood still. Tara didn't move, her rifle firing a shot several feet above Monica's head. Their eyes were locked, Tara's eyes surprisingly calm at seeing her attorney standing over her with a semi-automatic rifle aimed at her chest. Tara lowered the rifle barrel at Monica, her brow furrowed with determination. Everything slowed, and Monica's thoughts seemed to outpace physical motion a hundredfold as she pulled the trigger and pumped two bullets into Tara's chest.

Still, her client's eyes remained locked on hers, not reacting to what had to have seemed to Tara a shocking turn of events.

Then Monica realized that the woman was dead. The unfocused eyes slid with her head to the side as her body slumped back into the bushes, her rifle's aim going skyward but remaining silent.

Monica stepped forward. She kept the AR-15 trained on Tara's body, and took each step slowly and carefully.

Tara didn't move.

Creepily, her eyes continued staring with dullness at the sky. They didn't blink.

The reality of the situation pressed in on Monica. She had just killed another human being. Not only was this the first person she had seen killed in violence, but it was the only person who had died in a manner Monica never thought possible: at her own hand.

Todd kept down as much as he could. Tara was giving him short bursts that were dangerously close. With each exchange, he was increasingly surprised that he was still alive. They should have known—he and Mattituck—that the wife of an avid hunter and co-owner of a sporting good store would likely be more of a skilled outdoorsperson than the average person, whether male or female.

She was certainly in control of this situation. And with Mattituck likely wounded, everything in Todd wanted to make a break toward the woods. But he knew such a move would be suicide. There was no way around it: Tara was too skilled to take the chance.

But he couldn't sit here forever, either. And if Mattituck was wounded . . .

Todd tried to think clearly. His head had been increasingly throbbing in a way that made him doubt his judgment. He looked back to the woods where he imagined Mattituck had crawled through to cover. He turned and rose again above the bulldozer and was about to fire into the dark space between the two spruce when he realized there had been no shots fired at him.

He waited.

Still no shots.

Was Tara Garrett trying to lure him again? Should he rise and see if he drew fire from her?

But his judgment. He rubbed his eyes, the throbbing between his temples increasing. The world seemed off kilter as he gazed into the trees. No shots answered him.

He saw faint spots floating in his vision and recognized he was about to pass out. He couldn't have this. He'd have to chance ducking back down.

He turned and sat on the ground, his back supported by the track housing on the bulldozer. He lowered his head between his knees, the rifle lying on the ground next to him, but with his hand at the ready on its trigger. He slowly closed his eyes and forced himself to breathe deeply and steadily. At the same time, he listened closely for the sound of shots.

None came.

He waited until he was sure the fainting spell passed. He rolled into a crouch and threw up violently on the dried grass.

This was not good.

He had little doubt now that he had a concussion, and probably a fairly serious one.

Several minutes passed. He wasn't sure how many. But he had heard no shots. He forced himself to rise up to the high crouch he'd maintained while firing at Tara Garrett. Still no shots. All was quiet.

He waited, sure that if he kept his head where it was, he'd draw fire. He watched the bushes. Nothing.

Then a figure stepped out and he raised the AR-15.

"Todd? Frank?"

Was that Tara? What kind of ploy was this?

He leveled the rifle at the figure emerging from between the two spruce, his finger tightening. He realized that Tara was walking with her weapon down, the barrel swinging downward above the ground.

"Frank? Where are you? Todd?" the figure shouted.

That didn't sound like Tara. It sounded like Monica Castle.

Now Todd knew he couldn't trust himself. It had to be Tara. How could Monica be out here? She was in Cordova.

He started to take aim.

"No!" the figure shouted. "It's me! Monica! Monica Castle!"

She dropped her rifle, and Todd stopped.

"Monica?" he hollered.

"Yes! It's me! Todd, is that you?"

"Yeah, yes, it's me. How the—"

She was running now.

"Where's Frank?"

Todd was standing fully upright now. He pointed back to the woods.

"Is he . . .? Is he okay?"

"Dunno," Todd said. The surprise of events still had him doubting himself. Blood must have been rushing to his head, he thought, as the spots returned. He turned to sit down again, then doubled over and threw up again, this time dry heaves.

Everything went dark, and his body fell to the dead grass at the foot of the Caterpillar.

# Chapter Twenty-nine

## Aftermath

Todd awoke to yet another unexpected face.

Tom Graffinino's burly face hovered over his, studying his head, then when he saw Todd's eyes open, he broke into a wide grin.

"There he is!" the gruff harbormaster blurted.

None of this made sense. First Monica, then the Cordova harbormaster . . . randomly appearing at the Hinchinbrook Lighthouse.

He closed his eyes tightly and drew a sharp, deep breath, then opened his eyes again.

Tom Graffinino was grinning down into his face.

"I must be dead," Todd said.

Graffinino let out a hearty laugh.

"That's right—in hell! Of the two places, that's where I'll be!" The big man laughed loudly. "Nah, you ain't dead. Took a pretty nasty wrap on the noggin," the ex-logger said, "but you sure as fuck ain't dead."

"What . . . ? How?"

Graffinino nodded, then slid an arm under Todd's upper back and lifted him up, holding a water bottle to his lips.

"Drink this first," he said.

Todd drank deeply, suddenly realizing his mouth was hot and dry. The cool water flowed into his mouth and down his esophagus. He felt the coolness and imagined it sloshing into his belly.

"Monica Castle had a hunch you two fucks were in trouble, and she convinced me." He looked off into the distance. "Or maybe it's just the effect a hot woman has on me," he reflected. "In any case, she got me to haul her out here to check in on you guys."

"How's Mattituck?"

"Got shot," Graffinino said. "It's pretty bad, too. Coast Guard is on their way. They're scrambling a helo out of the air station by the airport at Cordova. Should be here any time."

"How bad?" Todd asked.

"One in the leg, and one in the mid-section. I don't know how bad. Not the heart, though. Not too much blood lost, far as I can tell, unless it's internal. And he's breathing real good. So I figure he's got a chance. Monica's with him."

Todd nodded.

"What happened to you?" Graffinino asked.

"Fell on a rock," Todd said. "Way back down the ravine."

"You probably got a concussion. How've you been feeling?"

"Pretty shitty." He tried to think, feeling like his brain was hiking through a fog. "What about Tara?"

"Tara Garrett? She's over in the woods there, dead."

"How?"

"Monica came up on your gun battle and snuck around behind her."

"Monica killed Tara?"

"Yep."

Todd shook his head and got to his knees, then rose to his feet. Graffinino held his elbow to keep him steady. Together, they made their way to the woods behind the bulldozer, Todd's steps unsteady on the uneven ground.

Mattituck lay on a grassy section of the undergrowth about ten feet into the trees. Monica was crouched at his side, keeping a close eye on his wounds, which she and Graffinino had bandaged with torn shreds of Tom's shirt.

"How is he?" Graffinino asked.

Monica looked up. She shook her head doubtfully. She felt that if she spoke her voice would crack. Mattituck didn't move, except to breathe. His chest rose and fell with each slow, deep inhalation. Other than the bloodied wounds, he looked normal: full color in the face, no bruises or pallid edge to his complexion.

The sound of a helicopter's rotary blades eased into the eastern horizon.

"Any risk of back or neck injury?" Graffinino asked.

"You can never be sure of that," Todd offered.

Graffinino looked at him, his face expressionless.

"In the real world, Trooper Benson. You're speaking like a lawyer." He looked at Monica. "No offense."

Todd relented.

"You're right," he said. "Every second counts and it could save several minutes if we could stage him for a basket lift."

Todd knelt next to Mattituck. He looked him over, noting the wounds where the bullets had entered, and then looking for exit wounds. He checked the torso first, and easily found the entry point several inches below a left lateral muscle, just below the rib cage. He found an exit wound at the left of his abdomen. Judging from the line the bullet likely had traveled through, the only major organs that might be hit would be intestines. If those were hit, there could be internal damage, depending on whether a full perforation had occurred. He was reasonably sure the bullet had missed the kidney on that side.

The only other wound was in the left leg, again, with both entry and exit wounds. This one appeared to enter the outer hamstring in Mattituck's mid-thigh, and exit on the inside of the same muscle. Very likely, this bullet simply passed through the muscle and exited without doing much damage other than to tear through muscle tissue. There was no major hemorrhaging, so it was unlikely this bullet hit any major arteries or veins.

"I'm guessing he's not in too bad of shape. Not from this leg wound, anyhow. That mid-body shot might be another story, although all signs externally are that he may have lucked out."

"We can move him, you think?" Graffinino asked.

"Yeah," Todd said, nodding. "I think so."

The helicopter was closing in fast. If they wanted to have Mattituck ready for a quick lift, they needed to get him to the middle of the clearing or to the helo pad.

"Most likely they'll land on the helo pad on the other side of the lighthouse," Graffinino said, peering through the trees for a glimpse of the approaching helicopter.

Todd rubbed his forehead, then his eyes, mustering the strength to help carry Mattituck the hundred meters or so to the helo pad on the other side of the lighthouse structure.

"Not to worry, Benson," Graffinino said. "I got this."

With that, he leaned over and effortlessly lifted Mattituck's respectably sized frame and cradled him like a child in his arms. He turned and started for the helo pad, Monica and Todd following behind.

Tom Graffinino was a former logger, who'd spent years in the wilds of Alaska in hard labor. Now, a gruff and lean man in his upper 50's, he towered over most and packed toned muscles that made most young trouble-makers think twice before picking mischief around him. No doubt that had a lot to do with his popularity as Cordova's harbormaster, a job requiring a tough demeanor to deal with whatever riff-raff sauntered in from the commercial fishing boats, both local and from Washington and Oregon. Since he'd taken the job, the Cordova Police had less calls to the harbor.

The Coast Guard helicopter appeared over the mountains to the east and began its descent to the lighthouse. Nobody spoke a word until the helicopter had landed and taken Mattituck aboard.

"This one needs medical care, too," Graffinino told the Coast Guardsman who appeared in charge of loading the aircraft.

The man turned to Todd.

"How are you doing, sir? Any injuries?"

Todd nodded.

"Head injury. Fell and hit my head on a rock."

"Any fogginess or headaches?"

"Yeah, both."

"All right, sir," the Coast Guardsman said. "Climb in. We're taking both of you to the Valdez Medical Center."

Todd nodded, then turned to Monica and Tom Graffinino. He wasn't thinking clearly, he knew, and exhaustion threatened to consume him.

"Somebody needs to tend to this body in the woods," Tom said. "Plus I got the boat down at the dock there," he said, "and the harbor to get back to."

The Coast Guardsman was alerted.

"Body, sir?"

Todd informed him that he was a State Trooper, and filled him in on the bodies of Tara Garrett and Wilson Garrett in the ravine.

The Coastie quickly relayed this to the pilot. There was a delay as the pilot radioed this to Air Station Kodiak and awaited instructions. They came quickly.

"I'm ordered to remain here until we can get someone else out here," the Coast Guardsman said. "Did you say you were going to stay?"

"Yeah," Graffinino replied.

"Okay, that would be good, sir. You can stay with me just to keep an eye on this scene, at least. They're going to send the State Troopers unit out here to investigate the scenes."

Graffinino nodded. "No problem. I'll stay as long as you need me."

Todd looked at Monica.

"Coming?"

She shook her head. "I'll ride back to Cordova with Tom."

Todd watched her face.

"Don't you want to be there when he wakes up?"

She held his eyes for a moment.

"No. Probably better that I not be."

Their gazes remained locked. Todd decided not to press it, and instead grimaced and nodded.

"I'll keep you posted on how he's doing."

"Yes, please. That'd be great."

He turned to the helicopter and climbed in next to his unconscious deputized friend, watching Monica as the Coast Guardsman clamored in and slid the door shut. Todd shifted forward and continued watching Monica and Graffinino out the window. Tom Graffinino stood straight and rigid, his usual posture, with hands on hips. Monica stood with her shoulders hunched, her arms crossed tightly across her midsection. Todd couldn't tell from this distance, but he would swear he saw tears on her cheeks.

# Chapter Thirty

## Lucky Shots

Monica Castle stood at the forward windows of the Alaska State Ferry M/V Chenega, a fast ferry that moved at a remarkable 43 knots, making the trip from Cordova to Valdez a short 2-1/2 hour ride. The large vessel had slowed now as it approached the Valdez Ferry Terminal. Todd Benson had said he would meet her there and give her a ride to the hospital, the Valdez Medical Center, to see Mattituck.

Mattituck had spent more than a week unconscious in the hospital in a medically induced sleep to allow his wounds to heal without his moving around too much. The bullet that had passed through his mid-torso had indeed cut through several intestines, but the perforations had quickly re-closed and posed no threat as long as he didn't move around. And the best way to prevent that, the doctors had agreed, was to not medevac him to Anchorage and to keep him from awakening and moving around.

After 9 days had passed, however, the doctors had determined that the perforations in his intestines were safely closed, and they allowed him to wake up.

Todd had been at his side when they brought him out from unconsciousness. Todd had waited with him, just sitting and watching baseball games and soccer matches for more than half the day, until Mattituck began to speak more lucidly. It was then that Todd told Mattituck what had happened after he had been shot.

"Monica?" Mattituck had asked. "But how? Where the hell did she come from?"

"She rode out with Tom Graffinino."

"The harbormaster? From Cordova?"

"Yep."

"But why did he come out?"

"Because Monica talked him into it."

"Wait," Mattituck said, confused. "Talked him into what?"

"Coming out to Hinchinbrook to check on us. She said she'd had an awful feeling all day long that day. So she convinced Graffinino to take her out to the lighthouse."

"Why to the lighthouse?"

Todd shrugged. "She said it was what made the most sense."

Mattituck shook his head. "So she somehow figured out more than we did, and with less difficulty."

Todd chuckled. "Remember she was representing Tara Garrett. Maybe she knew something she couldn't tell us."

Mattituck was silent, thinking this over. With the client confidentiality privilege, that seemed like it could very well be. And it would explain her misgivings driving her to go out to Hinchinbrook.

"Want to see her?" Todd said suddenly.

"Who? Monica?" He shook his head. "She wouldn't want to see me."

"You don't know that."

"I'm pretty sure," Mattituck said. He shifted uncomfortably on the big hospital bed. "I hate these fucking things. You can never get comfortable on them."

Todd's thoughts shifted to Mattituck and his mysterious background.

"When were you in a hospital bed long enough to experience that?"

Mattituck's head snapped to him.

"What do you mean?"

Todd smiled at him.

"Don't worry, Frank. I know enough about your past to know you've probably got some experience with all this."

Mattituck ignored him. He reached for the blue plastic water pitcher. Shaking it when he lifted it, he found it empty.

"What the hell?" he complained.

Todd laughed.

"You're not the best patient, I'm thinking."

"Shut the hell up," Mattituck snapped, feigning more than feeling irritation.

"So how about it?"

"How about what?"

"Do you want to see her?"

"I told you, she wouldn't want to see me."

"She does," Todd said.

"She wasn't too keen on me last I tried to talk to her. Or text, is more like it."

"Almost two weeks have gone by since then."

Several minutes passed. Both men's gazes were on the Mariners game flashing silently on the TV.

"If she wants to see me," Mattituck finally said.

Two outs in the 6th inning passed before Mattituck spoke again.

"So closing things off on Hinchinbrook was a bit complicated, huh?"

Todd nodded. "Yeah. Tom Graffinino and a Coastie stood by watching over Tara's body until the forensics team got there. All said, they took over four hours to get there."

"How was Wilson's body?"

"Not much to do in that kind of situation. Some ravens and critters had gotten to him, but not enough to alter evidence of what happened. It was pretty much as we thought. The wolverine attack had been bad enough to cause severe bleeding. All Tara did was finish him off. It's not clear he would have survived long if she'd left him alone."

"So she might not have had a murder rap on her after all," Mattituck speculated.

"Only if she'd left him to die. But then she'd have to explain why she didn't help or call for help."

"Her plan was to go up there and kill Wilson, so I'm sure she had a plan for escape."

"We don't know why she went out there. Remember . . . Wilson came up behind her. His boat arrived after hers. Maybe they had agreed to meet there for whatever reason. Or maybe he lured her out there and was the one hunting her."

Mattituck mulled this over. When he took his own assumptions out of the equation, he had to admit the evidence was open to interpretation.

"Guess maybe we'll never know," he said.

"Exactly," Todd said. "Frustrating how often that's the case. More often than I care to think about."

"We've been assuming that Tara and Justin Harris had plotted to kill Wilson," Mattituck said. "But maybe that wasn't the case."

"No. It's pretty clear that Wilson killed Justin. If he hadn't, he wouldn't have come running to the lighthouse to report him wounded."

"Isn't it possible he really did only wound him?" Mattituck asked. "I mean, maybe the entire thing was just all twisted around the fact that Tara and Justin were having an affair."

It was Todd's turn to think. Finally, he nodded.

"Yeah, you're right. I was thinking about why Tara was out there that first time, trailing Justin and Wilson, but for all we know she was spying on them for some other reason. Or maybe she knew Wilson had found out about the affair and wanted to protect Justin."

Mattituck was shaking his head.

"What's wrong?"

"It doesn't add up. You just nailed it. Wilson knew about the affair. That's the glitch in our theory that everybody's innocent. He went out there intending to kill Justin, and did just that. Maybe there's no ironclad evidence that wraps him up neatly, but no other story makes as much sense."

"That's true," Todd said. "But with all the suspects dead, we'll never know for sure."

"Be honest. How often does it end up this way? Where you're not 100 percent sure of your conclusions."

Todd looked at him.

"Too often," he said. "There are a lot of times you just don't know for sure. Even when the suspects are all alive, it's that way. They sure as hell don't spill it all out like in those old-time mystery movies. All you can do is put things together as they make the most sense, and match up with what you know. That's about it."

Mattituck closed his eyes. Todd watched the 7th inning pass with only a single and a stolen base between both teams. Mattituck's breathing became deep, with a hint of snoring.

The next morning, Todd stood with Izzy at the ferry terminal, waiting for Monica's arrival on the fast ferry, the Chenega.

"Do you think she'll like me?" Izzy asked, in that sexy Italian accent that Todd had come to love.

"Why wouldn't she?"

Izzy shrugged, watching as the Chenega sliced across the water toward the terminal. "Lots of women don't like me."

Todd looked her up and down.

"That's because they're afraid you'll steal their men."

Izzy smiled deeply and tip-toed to kiss his neck.

"I only want this man," she said into his collarbone.

The big blue canoe, as Alaskans loved to call the ferries, was easing to the dock. Todd scanned what he could see of the decks for Monica, but she must have been inside. Few braved the chilly morning breeze on the exposed decks.

A few minutes later, after the ferry had been moored, he spotted her coming up the ramp, her stride long as she disembarked the Chenega. She zig-zagged the ramps up to the terminal while Todd and Izzy waited, arms around each other's waists.

Monica was anxious to see Mattituck, and quickened her pace in keeping with her anxiety about how he might receive her. Or might not. It was entirely possible he would reject her, turn her away in anger. And who could blame him? While she still wasn't sure what to make of the pictures Betty Ingrahm had shown her, she was fairly sure there was an explanation. And even if it was what it had looked like—

She stopped as she entered the terminal and found herself face-to-face with Todd and a woman, their arms around each other's waists. She felt her breath cut short and stop.

It was the woman in the pictures. She was standing now facing Monica, a warm smile as she met Monica's eyes. Monica reached for the rail next to her, momentarily light-headed. She bent over and pretended to check her shoe.

This woman was with Todd? What was she doing with him? Or if she was with Todd, why had she been that way with Frank in the pictures? She straightened, forcing herself to gain composure. She smiled at them as she quickly covered the last few meters to them.

"Todd! How are you?" she said as she hugged him lightly. Izzy stepped back to allow their greeting.

"So good to see you, Monica." He stepped back and turned toward Izzy. "Let me introduce you to my girlfriend, Izzy."

"Your. . . . ?"

Izzy was smiling. "I've heard so much about you, Monica—from Todd and Frank both," she said.

She was every bit as beautiful as she'd looked in the pictures. If anything, more beautiful. Monica's mind wandered as they made small talk, walking through the terminal toward the parking lot.

Izzy and Todd walked as if Velcro-secured at their hips. They were obviously very comfortable with each other, as though they had been spending a lot of time together. Monica thought of Keri and wondered how this could happen so quickly, but also knew just as quickly that when a marriage goes through a slow death, the finality of the breakup often leaves little or no grieving on either side. Only the silent relief of freedom.

It was clear now to Monica that the pictures had told a lie. Whatever the reason for Izzy's hands being in Frank's at the table of the Bella Luna, it wasn't what it had appeared. Perhaps, Monica thought, she had been reaching out to Frank for help with some issue involving Todd.

Slowly, as she let herself think this, relief flooded her and threatened to force tears.

"I'm so happy for you, Todd," she said, in part to give an excuse for the flooding emotions. "And you too, of course, Izzy. Todd is . . ."

Her voice trailed and she gave Izzy a teasing stern look.

"You'd better treat him right," she scolded. "He's Frank's and my close friend. If you—"

"I won't," Izzy said. "I promise. It's been a short time, but . . ." her voice trailed. "Well, I shouldn't say too much, should I?"

Her voice was lilting and smooth. It at once put one at ease with reassurance. This was the effect Monica felt now, only moments after uncertainty. And the disdain she'd felt toward this woman for days instantly faded.

"How is he?" Monica asked, turning to Todd.

"Fine. No damage, as you've already heard. Just recovery time now. He's going to be just fine. The bullets missed everything vital."

At the hospital, Monica felt her pulse quicken. She had barely had time to process what she'd learned: that the woman she'd thought Mattituck had been cheating on her with was actually Todd's girlfriend. Her reaction to the pictures, her closing completely to Mattituck without giving him a chance to set the record straight, had been rash and cold. She had reverted back to the old Monica—the Monica before Frank Mattituck had come into her life, who defended herself by not allowing anybody into her inner circle.

Inner circles were complicated, and they were almost always cold, dark, and empty spaces. She didn't want to go back there. She didn't want to be alone . . . simply living day-by-day in a foggy, indistinct existence.

She drew a breath as they approached Mattituck's room. Though her reaction to the pictures had been understandable—at least in her thinking at the time—there was no avoiding the fact that she had misread the situation completely. She only hoped that she and Frank could get back to what they had become.

She followed behind Todd and Izzy as they turned into Frank's room.

He lay on the bed, staring out the window. He turned his head when they came in, first looking at Todd and Izzy, then Monica. His eyes slid past Todd and Izzy and met Monica's.

"Hello," she said, smiling uncertainly.

"Hello," he said, then returned her smile.

She took heart.

"I'm so sorry, Frank."

"Far as I know, there's nothing to be sorry for."

She hesitated, then looked at Todd and Izzy.

"I'm thirsty," Izzy said to Todd. "Perhaps we should go to the cafeteria and get something to drink."

"Yeah, I'm a bit thirsty, too," he said lamely, following her out the door.

Monica waited until they had left, then stepped closer to the foot of the bed, resting her hands on the side rail.

"I suppose I should explain," she said.

"Might be good," he said, waiting.

There was no anger in his voice, only a trace of a question.

"It was something a busy-body in Cordova showed me," Monica started. "She—"

"Whatever it is, Monica, you don't have to share if you don't want to. All you need to explain to me is why you wouldn't talk to me." His head tilted in query. "As far as I'm concerned, we might have this or that set us off, or hurt us. All that kind of stuff can be fixed. What I don't understand is not talking to me. Not even letting me . . . I don't know. Something."

Monica nodded, her eyes locked on his. She felt an inexplicable relief, like standing on a warm beach after riding out a bad storm at sea.

"You're right," she said. "That is what matters."

He smiled and reached out with his left hand. She slipped her hand into his. It was warm and rough, like the soul that wore the body it belonged to.

"What I can say in my own defense," she started, "is that a misunderstanding caused me to be hurt. Very, very deeply hurt. Turns out it was all wrong, but at the time it was so real for me."

"About me?"

She nodded. "I was just so hurt, Frank."

"I would never do anything to hurt you. Certainly nothing so bad that it would cause you that kind of pain."

She smiled grimly and nodded.

"I think maybe I'm learning that," she said. "Anyway, it just hurt so much I wanted to disappear."

Mattituck's eyes remained on her face. His head began to move back and forth.

"Please don't ever do that."

"Close up on you?"

"Yeah," he nodded. "Or disappear."

She stepped closer to him, trying not to tangle his IV and monitor cords, and leaned down to his face and kissed him. He pulled her in and held her close to his chest.

After a moment, she drew back.

"This was too close, Frank," she said. "I almost lost you."

"The tizzy we just got through? Or what happened on Hinchinbrook?"

She laughed lightly.

"Both, I guess. How'd you walk away from that, anyway? You took two bullets."

Mattituck smiled broadly, his humor restored. The smile waned, and his eyes nearly glazed. Then he refocused on her.

"Lucky shots," he said, then closed his eyes.

She kept holding his hand until it slackened, and she realized he'd fallen asleep. Todd had warned her that he was still on heavy pain killers, inducing sleep. She was fine with the solitude. She continued holding his hand, watching his face, and feeling they were both a couple of lucky shots.

# Epilogue

## Navigating Dire Straits

Todd and Izzy took a rare day off together to hike around Thompson Pass, the saddle of the mountains leading north to the interior of Alaska. The area was above the tree line and was housed in with towering peaks in a 360-degree panorama of stunning jagged rock and glaciers. Izzy had never seen anything like it, and like the solo hikes she'd been taking more and more often, it pulled her into a deeper appreciation of the natural world. It induced a sharp awareness of life.

Todd led the way as they climbed a steep ascent along a ridge. The trail was mostly gravel, but everywhere to the sides there were rock outcroppings and slabs of granite, giving testimony to the sharp geologic stories of violent upthrusts taking centuries of motion to move the mountains a dozen feet higher.

To the left was an expansive view of the valley leading southwest into Keystone Canyon, a deep narrow gorge that was bottomed by the Lowe River, flowing alongside the only highway into Valdez. To the right was a deep ravine carved by centuries of glacial cutting. At the head of the ravine was what remained of the glacier that had carved it out of the rock, hanging its icy cap over the top of the ridge like an English touring cap.

"How you doing?" Todd asked, turning and offering a bottle of water.

"Great!" she said, her voice carrying the wonder and excitement that she felt inside.

He smiled at her. They had been seeing each other nearly every day for close to a month, and she'd taken to staying overnight with him in his newly acquired apartment overlooking the marina from atop a Kayak rental shop.

"Blows you away, huh?" he asked.

"Yes, this is an understatement, I think," she said. She stopped next to him and stared up at the massive sheet of ice at the head of the ravine.

"That's the snow fields up there," Todd said, pointing. "All these glaciers along here come from that same snow field."

"Snow field?"

"Yeah. It's like one huge glacier. If you think of glaciers as rivers of ice flowing down the mountainsides, then the snow field is like the lake that the rivers spill down from."

"Ah," she said, looking up and wondering what it looked like. "We are hiking up to see?"

"No. We can't get up that high."

"Oh." Her disappointment was obvious.

"If you want to see them, we can hire a helicopter to fly us up."

She smiled at him and kissed him. "That would be wonderful."

They continued up the ridge, taking breaks for water and pictures.

"You haven't told me about the job on the island, with you and Frank," she said. "There was much danger, yes? Frank being shot . . . you with the concussion. But you tell me nothing of it."

"Not much to tell. Just another case in the job."

"But you were working on something, yes? Can you not say what?"

"No, it's not that. It's just a case is all. A couple in a spat, the wife having an affair with her husband's best friend, and then the best friend ends up shot."

"Is he okay?"

"Not really," Todd said, chuckling. "He's dead."

"Oh, my! Who killed him?"

"The husband, most likely."

"You don't know?"

"We don't always know for sure," Todd said, picking carefully around a rock outcrop that forced the trail along a cliff edge.

"How is the wife?"

"Dead."

"Dead? How?"

"She was the one who shot Mattituck."

"Oh," Izzy said, making the connection. "So, I have been wondering. How is it that Frank Mattituck can go on these cases with you? He isn't a cop, is he?"

"No, he's not. Not technically, anyway. He's deputized, though."

"Deputized? You mean like in the old cowboy movies?"

Todd laughed. "Yeah, something like that. He's a civilian that is officially recognized by the State of Alaska to help me on cases. It's really useful, I have to say, since I'm the only Trooper in the region."

"I can imagine. But he doesn't work cases alone? Or do investigations?"

Todd paused and looked at her.

"Why all this interest in Frank?"

"It is curious, this deputized thing, and him working with you when he's not a Trooper."

He smiled and nodded. "I can see that. No, he can't really work as a deputy except under my direction. Or the direction of another State Trooper."

"I see," she said. She pulled her water bottle and drank deeply. "Does he have a special background that makes him qualified for this?"

"He happens to be pretty well prepared for this line of work, but no, there isn't any kind of training, if that's what you mean."

"What makes him well prepared?"

"He has a military background."

"Oh," she said.

Not wanting to raise suspicion, she decided not to press any further. Instead, she refocused herself on enjoying the day. She stepped up and turned Todd to face her. She lifted her face to him, and he bent and kissed her. They held each other with the glacier in the background, their mouths exploring each other's.

"Have you ever done it up here?" she asked.

"Done it? Up here?"

She laughed, pulling at his shirt. "Yes, up here. I want to do it up here."

He looked around, desire influencing him more and more by the second. He took her hand and led her to a flat area between rock outcrops, then laid his jacket on the gravely ground. Together, they lay down and continued exploring each other's passion.

One difficulty for Izzy had arisen from her staying overnight with Todd Benson, and with spending more time with him. When the Ühing called for updates, it was difficult to excuse herself to take the calls. So far she had been able to excuse the calls as being from family in Italy, but this was risky and increasingly difficult. If Todd ever saw the screen on her phone when the calls came, the area code and phone number would reveal the lie.

When Todd was working, it was easy. And that was the case when Karl called for the first update following Mattituck's hospitalization.

"It is reported that the Takistus is in the hospital," Karl said when she answered.

"Yes, he is."

"Is it serious?"

"Two gunshot wounds."

"Gunshot wounds? From what?"

"He works with Todd Benson—the State Trooper."

"Yes, yes, I know this," Karl said, his irritation clear. "What I am wondering is the specifics."

"It's unrelated. I probed Benson about it today," she said.

"Benson. The Trooper? I've been meaning to speak with you about this arrangement. I am not convinced being involved with this Trooper will help us achieve our goal."

Izzy was walking along the waterfront, headed east to the end of the marina, where the boat launch provided a large parking lot where she was less likely to be overheard.

"It's working well," she said. "Perhaps better than if I were directly connected to the Takistus."

"That is hard to imagine," Karl returned.

"It isn't if you try," she quipped thinking of the John Lennon song, then immediately regretted it.

"Do not be funny with me. And do not think I miss the reference. Are you thinking of peace, Ms. Giovanni?"

"I don't understand the question," she said, sitting on top of a guard rail post at the far end of the parking area. She faced the boat launch with nothing behind her except the road leading to the fish packing plants on the far side of the marina.

"Of course you understand the question. But I know you are wiser than to answer. Do not make a mistake, Ms. Giovanni. I would hate to think of this as your last assignment. And a failed one at that."

The threat was clear and chilling.

"It won't be," she said, her professional steely voice unyielding, despite the growing conflict inside. "You need to trust me on this, Karl. Any time the Takistus is working on something that might interfere with the operations of The Ühing, I will know it through Trooper Benson. The man is putty in my hands, as the Americans like to say."

"Every man is putty in your hands," Karl returned. "That is part of what makes you so effective. I do not want to think what might happen should you ever become ineffective."

"You have no need to worry about such things," Izzy said. "I believe my reputation is sufficient to give you assurance that I know what I am doing. And that I am unwavering in doing it."

There was a pause.

"Very well," Karl said. "Continue according to your judgment. Only do not fail to contact me. I understand and support your concern regarding this Benson seeing you take calls. Text me an hour or two before you intend to call, and I will make sure I am available."

Izzy smiled to herself. She didn't know how long she could maintain a double-agency, but she had long since grown weary of the life she'd been living. What she was experiencing in this unique place had caught her unprepared, and had introduced a sense of meaning, of life, that she had never before experienced.

"All right," she said to Karl. "That is the plan. I text you ahead of time. Then I remove myself in time to call you."

"See that you do," he said.

"I wish you would stop saying things like that," Izzy said, forcing down her annoyance.

"It is my job to make sure our operatives never lose sight of their roles."

Izzy closed her eyes tightly and held her eyelids in silent defiance.

"Of course. I will not fail you, Das Kaptan, or The Ühing."

"I know, Ms. Giovanni. I know you will comply. There is no other option."

Izzy ended the call, but remained sitting on the guardrail post. She watched as a man backed his pickup and empty boat trailer down the ramp toward his boat, waiting to be pulled from the water. On the bow of the boat were what appeared to be his wife, motioning with her hands and forearms which direction the trailer was backing down the ramp. At her feet were two toddlers, watching in fascination as their father adeptly backed the complicated truck-and-trailer array down the steep slope.

Behind them, the marina housed countless small boats, most of which sat idle in their slips. Others enjoyed small groups of people sitting on their aft decks, drinking beer and eating shrimp or hot dogs. She heard laughter from one of these parties, distant and faint, as though no matter her reach, she would never be able to grasp the companionship there.

She stood and stepped over the guard rail, and headed for Dock Point Trail across the street. While it might not be a long, satisfying trail away from town and people, it offered a sufficient buffer between this life and the one she longed for.

It would be enough. It had to be. As Karl had said, there simply was no other option.

*- finis -*

*You may be interested.....*

If you missed the other books in The Frank Mattituck Series, you can continue enjoying the ongoing adventures of Mattituck and Todd Benson by ordering your copy of Books 1 and 2 at:

pwesleylundburg.com/page/

Or start the hard-boiled private eye series, the Clayton Chronicles by picking up a copy of The Stateroom Tryst and watching for The Desert Throwdown, due in January 2017:

*Keep in Touch....*

Get regular updates on all of P. Wesley Lundburg's books and writing at his website:

pwesleylundburg.com

Go to the Contact page and sign up for the email list and keep up with the progress on the next book in the series, connect with other fans of the series, and get announcements on promotions and sales. Or just drop him a line and strike up a conversation about his books or the writing process.

Like Wes' Facebook page at The P. Wesley Lundburg Author Page

Email him at pwesleylundburg@gmail.com

Follow him on Twitter @pwesleylundburg

Made in the USA
Monee, IL
20 December 2022

22630692R00225